A MANOR OF LIFE & DEATH

A BEAUFORT SCALES MYSTERY - BOOK 3

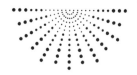

KIM M. WATT

For further information contact: www.kmwatt.com

Cover design: Monika McFarland, www.ampersandbookcovers.com

Editor: Lynda Dietz, www.easyreaderediting.com

Logo design by www.imaginarybeast.com

ISBN: 978-1-9160780-1-7

First Edition: March 2019

10 9 8 7 6 5 4 3 2 1

For everyone
who believes in dragons, friendship,
and the perfect magic of a good cup of tea.
I'm writing this for you.
Because the world needs more tea and friendship.

And dragons, obviously.

CONTENTS

1
DI ADAMS

D I Adams turned the car off but didn't move to get out. She just sat there in the slightly worn embrace of the seat, staring at the front of the house and considering just starting the engine, backing out of the parking space, and driving away again.

The house stared back. It was one of those big, rambling places that had probably started life as a Georgian estate, maybe the seat of some minor lord, then the Victorians had come along and added some spires and steeples and (almost certainly) a folly somewhere in the grounds. The gravel drive swept into a broad turning circle in front of the doors, a reluctant fountain as its focal point, and ivy roamed up the walls. Woods crowded the drive behind her, and, other than the crumbling outbuildings to the right of the manor, the only house she'd seen since leaving the main road had been a decrepit stone hut by the wooden bridge that crossed the river. It was the sort of place where, not a terribly long time ago, people with her skin colour would have been lucky to be allowed out of the servants' area to do the cleaning.

Which wasn't what bothered her. What bothered her was the sneaking suspicion that she'd come here for a weekend away with the very people who made her *need* a weekend away. She sighed, grabbed her bag off the passenger seat and climbed out, the slamming of the car door echoing against the front of the house and scaring a small, chubby bird out of the fountain. She refused to feel jealous of it as it fled into the trees.

"Oh, *well done*," someone said.

"Excuse me?" She stared as a man stood up from among the cars parked by the fountain.

"You scared it."

"The bird?"

"The bird." The man shook his head sorrowfully, and two more men unfolded themselves from the cover of the cars.

DI Adams stared at them, mystified. One had a notebook that he was scribbling in furiously, and another was staring after the bird and clutching a camera that looked both very expensive and very heavy, judging from the way the long lens dipped toward the ground every time his attention wandered. The man who had spoken to her was festooned with various bits of electronic equipment, and they were all wearing the sort of multipocketed camouflage gear that wildlife photographers and safari guides favoured.

She didn't know much about birds, but the one on the fountain had seemed a little dull and chubby. It hardly seemed to warrant much interest, unlike the peacock which was currently rushing toward them across the drive, doing his best to be noticed.

"*Bu-kurk?*" the bird said hopefully, displaying his tail feathers.

"Ugh," the one with the notebook said.

"I'm sure she'll come back," DI Adams said, feeling slightly guilty. Although a driveway was hardly the ideal place for bird-watching.

"He," the man with the camera said, boinking the lens off the bonnet of a car as he corrected her. "Male water rail. And they're pretty timid."

"Mind the camera, Keith," notebook man said. "Steph'll kill me if we damage that lens."

"It's *heavy*," Keith complained. "I can't believe you forgot the tripod."

"I didn't *forget* it. I told you, I had it in the room."

"Whatever."

"Well, he's gone anyway," electronics man said, and glared at DI Adams.

"Sorry," she said. "But you know there's a really nice peacock behind you, right?"

"*Bu-kurk!*"

"Peacocks are not the birds we're looking for," electronics man said. "Nothing but plump guinea fowl on steroids, them."

"*Buk?*"

"Is it afternoon tea yet?" notebook man asked.

"*Ooh*, afternoon tea," Keith said, and the trio gathered themselves up and crunched away across the gravel without another word to DI Adams. She watched them go, and after a moment the chubby bird flew back and started pecking its way around the fountain again.

"*Bu-kurk*," the peacock said to her.

"I know," she told it.

§

SHE STOMPED up the curving steps to the big main doors. They were coated in purple paint that was cracking to show the old green beneath, and the knocker was a frozen lump of purple-splattered rusted metal that might once have been a lion (although that was just an educated guess based on the fact that it seemed to have ears). There was a small and incongruously modern handle on one of the double doors, so she turned that and let herself in.

She'd expected to have to take a moment for her eyes to adjust to old-house dimness inside, but instead she stepped into an entry hall awash in light spilling from the tall windows to either side of the door, and pouring down from a domed skylight high above. The skylight had been painted in swirling purples and greens (along with oversized, panicked-looking goldfish), giving the hall aquarium-ish tones. She blinked at the fish, wondering if the same artist was responsible for the awful paint job on the doors, and pulled the door closed.

The house rested deep in silence around her, the tiles of the entry hall purple and white checks that gave to a sweeping staircase at the back of the hall. There was a single unmarked door directly ahead of her, and open arches to either side. The one to the left showed glimpses of the sort of deep, cracked leather sofas and dark red furnishings that made her think of old cigar smoke and crystal tumblers and casual prejudice, while the one to the right was a study in white and stainless steel and pale wood. It looked like a dining room in some minimalist eatery, and the cushions on the chairs were dark purple. She was starting to wonder if there had been a bulk deal on the colour somewhere.

"Hello?" she called. "Anyone about?"

There was movement in the lounge room, and she arranged a smile on her face. A moment later a walking carpet entered the hall, looked at her (she assumed, as its eyes were invisible under a mass of dirty dreadlocks), then wandered into the dining room and vanished. It left a scent of wet dog behind it so strong it made her eyes water.

She waited a little longer, but no one else appeared, and the only sounds were the old whispers of the house. She was just about to investigate the lounge when there was an explosion of shouting from the dining room. She turned, startled, and watched the carpet dog lope between the tables with an enormous joint of meat in its mouth, knocking a couple of the sleek dining chairs flying as it came. A man bounded after it, waving a rather large knife and screaming something unintelligible. He tripped over one of the fallen chairs, crashed to the floor, bounced off a table hard enough to knock over three glasses, and sat up just in time for one to roll off and hit him on the knee. He waved the knife after the dog, cursing inventively. The dog passed DI Adams and swerved up the stairs, and she could have sworn that it was emanating a smug sort of amusement along with the smell.

"Are you alright?" she asked the man on the floor.

"No," he snapped, rubbing his knee as he got up, then kicking the chair. It spun sideways, hit the table, and rebounded into his shin, making him yelp. "Does it look like I'm okay? That bloody dog just stole dinner!"

"Right. Unfortunate."

He glared at her. "Unfortunate? *Unfortunate?* That was hand-raised organic lamb, basted in a rosemary-caramelised-balsamic marinade and slow-cooked for 48 hours. And *the dog stole it.*"

"I see." DI Adams wondered what, exactly, the chef had been going to do if he caught the dog. It wasn't like he could still have served his organic, marinated, slow-cooked, dog-slobbered lamb. She hoped.

The chef waved his knife at her. "*You're* the ones who miss out! *You're* the ones who'll be asking, oh, where's my dinner, Mister Chef? Why's there no meat? Why's it just frozen bloody peas and brioche toast?" He turned and walked away, still muttering. "Where's my dessert? Where's my lamb? Where's my bloody *amuse-bouche*, they ask. But do they do anything about the damn wildlife? Do they heck."

DI Adams watched him go, wondering what the relevance of the brioche toast was. She shifted her grip on the bag, undecided as to where to go, then the door under the stairs popped open and a young man with thinning red hair stared at her as if astonished to find someone in the hall.

"Hello," he said in round, rich tones that suited the lounge room perfectly. "I thought I heard Keeley."

"The chef?" DI Adams asked.

"*Sous*-chef," he said, putting rather a lot of emphasis on the first part.

"Right. He was just here."

"Honestly, he's always making such a fuss about things. What was it this time?"

"The dog stole the lamb," DI Adams said. "Can I check in?"

"We don't *have* a dog," the red-haired man said, frowning at her as if he suspected her of sneaking the dog in herself. "My brother's scared of them."

DI Adams scowled back, and hers was rather more practised and effective. "I'd like to check in, please."

The man drew back as if he wanted to retreat behind the door. "Yes. Quite. I just— *Keeley!*" he bellowed, and DI Adams rubbed her forehead reflexively.

"Adams," she said. "I've got a reservation."

"Right, um— *Kee-LEY!*"

"Reid, honestly," a new voice said from behind the man. "What on earth are you *shouting* about?"

"This woman says a dog's stolen the lamb."

"The lamb?" A small woman shoved Reid out of the way and smiled at DI Adams uncertainly. Her hair was wisping in half a dozen different directions from at least as many hair clips. "Was it your lamb?"

"No, it was dinner, apparently."

"Oh." The woman patted her hair, managing to change the directions of the wisps but not to tidy it. "Was it your dog, then?"

"No—" DI Adams realised her hand was clenched tight enough on the handle of her bag for the fingers to start cramping, and willed them to relax. "I have no idea whose dog it was. I'm just here to check in. For the weekend." She swallowed. "With the Toot Hansell W.I."

"*Oh!* The detective inspector!" The woman lunged forward with her hand extended, and DI Adams just managed not to jump back. "Maddie Etherington-Smythe. Welcome to the manor. We're so excited you're joining us! I do hope your drive was alright."

DI Adams shook the woman's hand, the bones feeling fragile under her grip. "Thanks."

"*Kee—*" Reid began again, and Maddie swatted his arm.

"Stop screaming and go find him, Reid. It's not like he's actually going to come see you."

"He should," Reid grumbled, and slouched off with his shoulders hunched and his chin stuck out obstinately.

"Awfully sorry about that," Maddie said, and grabbed the inspector's bag before she could protest, heading for the stairs. "He's a good boy, really. Well, he can be. Anyhow. I've put you in a small room, so I do hope that's alright. We're quite full, what with all the W.I. and the other guests as well, and Ms Martin said you wouldn't want to share with anyone else. They're all doubled up, you see, but then they always do, because otherwise there just wouldn't be room, and they don't seem to mind. I mean quite a few of them are single, I guess. Are you single? Oh, sorry, that's a bit personal, isn't it?" Maddie trotted up the stairs rapidly, not waiting for DI Adams to respond. "So you're free to go wherever you want in the house and the grounds, except our personal rooms of course, which are in the very top floor, and the office and private rooms downstairs of course, but then that'd be like walking into someone's bedroom, which you wouldn't do, but I guess you're a police officer, so you have to sometimes, but you wouldn't have to now, of course, it's not like we've any crimes to investigate! It's afternoon tea soon, and the other ladies are just finishing up yoga on the terrace. You'll be able to see them from your room."

DI Adams trailed after Maddie, a small headache starting

behind one eye. The midpoint landing had a giant cracked vase in one corner and a tarnished mirror hanging over it, and the stairs ran on to a mezzanine-style balcony above. There were worn red runners underfoot, laid over older carpet that might once have been green. DI Adams was just glad nothing else was purple.

"Your room's just up here," Maddie said, "and the bathroom's in between your and Alice and Miriam's room. Breakfast—"

"Wait – it's a shared bathroom?"

"Oh, yes. I know that's awkward, but I'm sure you ladies can sort it out. Two of the rooms have en suites, and we do want to do the others, but it's money, you see." Maddie fluttered her fingers at the shadows of the hall, and DI Adams saw that some of the stair spindles didn't match and a lamp was missing its shade. "This year, though. I think this year will really turn things around for us."

"It's a beautiful house," DI Adams said.

"Thank you. Thank you, yes. It is. And my poor old husband had it in his family for *so* long, but you know how it is. It's expensive, these days. Maintenance, and insurance, and staff."

"I can imagine," the inspector said.

"Anyway. One does what one can. And the W.I. are always wonderful. They come every year, and it's such a boon to rely on them after being so quiet through the winter."

"I'm sure it is," DI Adams said, thinking of Miriam saying, *It's my sister's place, so it doesn't cost anything. Just come and enjoy yourself.* Bloody sneaky woman. She opened her mouth to ask how many guests were here in total, but before she could speak there was the crash of a door exploding open below, followed by a roar that threatened serious damage to vocal chords.

"Oh, *no*," Maddie wailed, and DI Adams turned to run back down the stairs just as Reid sprinted across the foyer with a look of utter panic on his face. The sous-chef – Keeley – followed him with another roar, moving with astonishing speed for someone who had to be over six foot and all muscle.

"*Stop!*" DI Adams bellowed after them, hitting the floor at a run and almost colliding with a woman in chef's whites carting an enormous pot of water. "You stay back," she snapped at the startled chef, and sprinted across the foyer into the lounge. Reid was scrambling across the room, trying to push the heavy leather armchairs into Keeley's path as he went but only succeeding in slowing himself down. He gave up and broke for a set of double doors at the back of the room with a wail of fright.

"*Stop!*" the inspector shouted again, but Keeley was roaring so loudly she doubted he heard her, and she didn't blame Reid for not stopping. She wouldn't have risked it either. Reid made it to the double doors and tried to slam them in Keeley's face, then shrieked when he saw how close his pursuer was. He bolted across the next room, dodging between cane chairs and glass-topped tables. DI Adams avoided a final coffee table and charged out of the lounge just behind the sous-chef.

She tried another "*Stop!*" but both men kept running. She hurdled two chairs that had tumbled in their wake, burst into some sort of conservatory with her hand inches from the back of Keeley's shirt, and tripped over an orchid that was sitting in a bucket in the middle of the floor for no good reason she could imagine. She swore, and scrambled up just in time to see Reid explode through a final set of doors and sprint across the terrace outside. For a moment it looked like he was going to make it to the corner of the house, then he went sprawling over a discarded yoga block and skidded to his knees, yelping. Keeley didn't even hesitate. He grabbed the back of Reid's shirt as the young man tried to scuttle away on all fours, and hefted him to his feet, then turned him around and screamed in his face like a big cat on a BBC documentary.

Reid made a horrified squawking sound that DI Adams thought she'd probably heard on the same BBC documentary, just not coming from the big cats. She sprinted across the terrace and arrived beside them, placing one arm across Reid's chest and raising her free hand just in Keeley's line of sight, in a *halt, who goes there* gesture. "Stop," she repeated, her voice calm.

The sous-chef glared down at her and took a deep breath, probably for another tooth-rattling scream.

"Police," she said. "Detective Insp—"

The water hit her just as the sous-chef started bellowing, and she took an involuntary whooping gasp that sent icy liquid rushing down her throat. She spluttered and started coughing, feeling Reid staggering away while Keeley spat and swore next to her.

"What the *hell?*" she demanded, spinning around to face the woman in chef's whites. "I told you to stay back!"

The woman shrugged, the empty pot hanging from one hand. "Only way to stop them. Like fighting dogs, y'know?"

DI Adams wiped water off her face and shook her head, although she couldn't actually disagree. The sous-chef was still swearing and stomping in an angry circle, but he hadn't actually attacked Reid again. Reid appeared to be trying to keep the inspector between him and Keeley.

"Anyone like to tell me what's going on, then?" she asked them, putting her hands on her hips and trying to sound authoritative, although her teeth were starting to chatter.

"The man's a psychopath and should not be working here," Reid said, then ducked and clutched DI Adam's arm when the sous-chef growled. She shook him off.

"I don't care about your opinion of him, just about what happened. You." She pointed at the woman. "Name?"

"Nita," she said. "I'm the chef here."

"Right. Detective Inspector Adams. You?" She pointed at the sous-chef, even though she already knew his name. It helped, sometimes, the simple act of naming. Of humanising.

"Keeley," the big man said. "Sous-chef." He pulled his buff off and squeezed the water out of it, then put it back on. "And he's a—"

"Facts," DI Adams said.

"I'm giving you facts," Keeley said, but his shoulders had dropped away from his ears, making him look less like a bull hunched up and ready to charge.

"Reid came into the kitchen, giving it some about the missing lamb. He accused Keeley of being unprofessional," Nita said.

"He accused me of stealing an entire shoulder of lamb," Keeley snapped. "That's more than just unprofessional."

"Well, where did it go?" Reid demanded, still huddled behind DI Adams. "Bloody expensive, that lamb!"

"The dog took it," DI Adams said, and Keeley threw his hands up.

"*Yes!* Thank you!"

"We don't *have* a dog," Reid said.

"I saw the dog," DI Adams reminded him.

"You *can't* have! Where would it have come from?"

"I don't know. But I saw it." She glared at Reid as he opened his mouth to argue, and he subsided.

"There," Keeley said, jabbing a finger at Reid. "Keep the hell out of our kitchen from now on, you get me?"

"*Your* kitchen? We *own* it!"

"Shut up," DI Adams said to Reid. She looked at Nita. "You need to get a better handle on your staff."

Both chefs scowled at the inspector, and she glared back at them.

"We work *together*," Keeley said, and Nita rolled her eyes but didn't say anything.

"Reid! Keeley! What on *earth* …" Maddie appeared in the door behind them, cradling the wounded orchid. "You're an embarrassment! Both of you!"

"Aw, Mum—"

"Maddie, I can only take being talked to like this for so long—"

"Being talked to like what?" Reid demanded. "You think I should bow to the mighty *sous*-chef?"

"Boys, please—" Maddie tried.

"Talked to like the bloody help, you—"

"Oi! Do I need to get the hose, here?" Nita snapped.

"I'm on a weekend off," DI Adams said. "But I find arresting people quite therapeutic."

"DI Adams, I'm sure—" Maddie started, her eyes wide.

"I'm joking," she said, not bothering to wonder if she sounded convincing or not. "You"—she pointed at the two chefs—"go back to work. You, Reid, go take a breather somewhere."

"Well—"

"*Now!*" Goddammit. She was very nearly shouting. She wasn't even in Toot Hansell. She was just in the *region* of Toot Hansell, for the grand total of maybe ten minutes, and here she was. Almost shouting. Also freezing, because her jumper and suit trousers were drenched and there was a smart little breeze out here.

"C'mon," Nita said to Keeley. "We need to make a plan for a lamb-less dinner."

"He probably sent the bloody dog," Keeley grumbled, but trailed after the chef as she led the way off the terrace and around the corner of the house.

DI Adams squeezed water out of the front of her jumper, and suddenly became aware that she had an audience. She looked around properly for the first time, pinched the bridge of her nose, closed her eyes for a moment, then opened them again, wanting to be sure of what she was seeing. Because sometimes, in the region of Toot Hansell, things weren't quite as you thought they were.

But, no. Things were exactly as she thought they were.

On the terrace, watching the altercation with expressions that ranged from amused to horrified, were the ladies of the Toot Hansell Women's Institute. They were decked out in an astonishing variety of shiny new Lycra and tracksuits that had been at their best a few decades earlier, wearing headbands and scarves and, in Rose's case, a woolly hat with an apple-sized pompom on it. They were standing on yoga mats laid out on the smooth stone flags of the terrace, and a young woman draped in scarves and flowing clothes was barefoot next to them, both hands pressed over her heart.

None of which was entirely unexpected. No, the unexpected bit was the two dragons standing on the grass next to the patio, holding front paws and using their tails for balance as they stood on one hind leg each. DI Adams resisted the urge to close her eyes again. The smaller dragon staggered and fell over sideways. The other, who was the size of a Newfoundland, raised a paw and gave her a toothy grin. She raised her own hand, mustering a faint smile from somewhere.

"Hello, DI Adams," the chairwoman of the Toot Hansell W.I. said, tucking fine white hair behind her ears. "Was your trip up alright?"

"Less eventful than my arrival," the inspector said. "Hello, Alice."

"I'm so sorry about this," Maddie said, a hitch in her voice. "They're impossible, both of them!"

DI Adams found a proper smile for her. "No need to be sorry. It's on them, not you." She plucked at her damp trousers. "I'd quite like to go get changed now, though."

🐉

HER ROOM HAD A CRACKED jug of daffodils on the dresser, and white and green curtains on the windows that overlooked the terrace. DI Adams changed into a grey hoody and walking trousers, then watched the W.I. and the dragons at their yoga practise. Dragons weren't invisible, but they were *faint,* and as very few people expected to see dragons, very few did. It still seemed needlessly risky for them to be wandering about joining in yoga classes, though.

She wondered again what she was doing here. This time last year she'd only just transferred up from London, and had no idea about such creatures as dragons and the Toot Hansell W.I. (although there had been the incident in London which had caused her transfer, but she tried not to think about that). It had been a rather blissful kind of ignorance, if she was going to be honest. Her fantasy of an easier life up north had come to a rather abrupt demise with the murder of a vicar, quickly followed by the discovery of Toot Hansell, the Women's Institute, and dragons in one fell swoop. After which came Christmas, and the revelation that dragons weren't the only magical Folk in the world.

It had not been the easiest year. A weekend in a spa hotel had sounded nice. It had sounded like the sort of thing that people did. It had sounded like the sort of thing that would not involve dragons, abductions, explosions, or goblins. And it hadn't cost her anything, and while she wasn't broke exactly, a free mini-break was nothing to be sniffed at.

She sighed. She had yet to have one encounter with the W.I. that didn't end in some narrowly averted disaster and her covering up the existence of dragons, because God forbid the wrong people got wind of that. Like the government. Or her boss. And now they were just out there doing yoga. She fished some paracetamol out of her bag. She didn't quite have a headache yet, but she had an idea she would before long.

"Well," she said to the room. "Nothing for it. There is no reason for anything to go wrong. This is all going to be absolutely fine."

She opened the door, and the dreadlocked dog that had been sitting patiently outside scrambled up, tail wagging eagerly. It shoved an enormous, well-slobbered bone at her and she jumped back with a yelp, but not before her trousers had been smeared from thigh to knees with, she assumed, rosemary-caramelised-balsamic-marinated, slow-roasted, organic lamb bone.

The dog dropped to its elbows and nosed the bone toward her, answering her yelp with one of its own that just about shook the windows.

"Well, bollocks," she said, and went to change into her yoga trousers, trying not to think that this was an inauspicious start.

2

MIRIAM

Miriam tried very hard to follow what Adele (who was both the yoga teacher and her niece) was saying, got her lefts and rights muddled, tried to reach for the sky and ground herself at the same time, then fell over sideways. She pitched into Teresa with a squeak, sending them both sprawling onto the cold stone of the terrace.

"I'm so sorry!" she gasped, disentangling herself from the older woman and helping her up. "Are you alright?"

"Of course," Teresa said cheerfully, brushing off her lime green leggings. Miriam thought they must be new. They had silver dragons on them, and were too short for Teresa's long legs. "One of the first things to learn is how to fall, Miriam."

"Oh," Miriam said, going back to her own mat and thinking that the first thing should be to avoid falling, if you could. She was more well-padded than Teresa, but that didn't make it pleasant. She'd knocked her knee fairly solidly on the hard stone of the terrace, and she gave it a comforting rub.

"Are you alright, Miriam?" Alice asked.

"I suppose so," she said, shooting Adele a dark look. The young woman had her arms entwined and her legs wrapped around each other, and was gazing dreamily over the heads of the staggering Women's Institute. "It's just a bit advanced for the first afternoon, isn't it?"

"Not really," Alice said. She hadn't tangled herself up quite as much as Adele, but she did have one leg crossed over the other and both arms reaching up to the sky. "You just have to focus."

"Should you even be doing this, with your hip?" Miriam pointed out, trying to balance on her left leg. Her toenail polish was already chipped, she noticed with some dismay. It had been expensive, too.

"It's good for my hip," Alice said, uncrossing her leg and exhaling as she straightened, white hair held back with a slim black headband. She shifted her weight to her right leg and inhaled, floating her left foot off the floor and tucking it behind her right calf. "The doctor said yoga was very good after hip ops."

"Falling over won't be very good for it," Miriam pointed out, although she had to admit that Alice looked in no danger of that. She swapped to her own right leg, hoping that one might be a little steadier. It wasn't.

"Unless you fall into me I'm unlikely to fall over," Alice said, shooting Miriam a warning look as the younger woman wobbled precariously.

"Ladies," Adele said, unwinding her arms and shaking them out. "You can ... take a break ... or you can ... keep going ... I'll ... walk around ..." She drifted off her mat in a swirl of multi-coloured scarves, her movement as slow as her words. Miriam thought the scarves were the loveliest part of the class, and she quite wanted to know where her niece had got them. Her attention wandered and she pitched forward with a squeak.

"Focus, Miriam," Alice said.

"Ugh, that's easy for you to say," she complained. "I don't think I'm built for yoga."

"It's not about being built for it," Alice said, doing something fancy with her left leg. "It's just practice."

Miriam scowled rather ferociously at her feet and tried lifting her left foot again, then stomped it back down hurriedly as Adele appeared in front of her, pale hands extended.

"I'll help you, Auntie Miriam," she said. "Just focus on your drishti point."

Miriam thought that she'd been focusing on drishti points when her niece wasn't even a point of conversation for her parents, but she took Adele's hands dutifully anyway. She didn't like to discourage her. Everyone always thought she should like yoga because she was Sensitive, and had a passion for tie-dyed skirts and herbal tinctures. But the *ohmm*-ing gave her the giggles and if she spent too long meditating she started feeling too *aware* of things. As if there were more hidden creatures in the world than even the ones she knew about (and she did know quite a few personally these days), and some of them didn't like to be seen. It made her uncomfortable, and unaccountably afraid. Besides, she'd never been able to touch her toes, even when she was a teenager. Some people just aren't built like that, no matter what Alice said.

Adele's hands were cold and smooth and steady, and after a few moments Miriam found she could stop gripping them quite so tightly and almost balance on her own.

"Excellent," Adele said, her words still slow and drawn out. "*Wonderful.*" She shook herself free and drifted off again, while Miriam concentrated on not falling over immediately. "Does anyone else need help?"

Miriam risked a peek around and felt slightly better when she saw that only Jasmine, Rose and Alice *didn't* seem to need help. Everyone else was either wobbling wildly, holding onto each other, or, in the case of Priya, had sat down with her face lifted happily up to the sky, eyes closed.

"How about – you," Adele said, waving vaguely off the terrace and making her bracelets clatter into each other. "Do you need help?"

Miriam promptly fell over, catching herself on her hands and scrambling to her feet. "Who?" she squeaked. "Does who need help?"

"The two – oh." Adele laughed, and shook her head. "I've had too much, um, too much tea. I thought there was someone there. But it's the topiary, isn't it?"

The ladies of the Women's Institute, who had given up any attempt at balance, agreed enthusiastically, and Adele wandered back to her mat, pausing to encourage her students to attempt the poses again. Behind her, Beaufort Scales, High Lord of the Cloverly dragons, stayed balancing on one foot, unmoving, his scales a deeper and darker green than usual. They were, in fact, the exact green of the topiary dotted around the terrace in tall cracked pots and sculpted into even more unusual shapes than dragons the size of large dogs. Mortimer, who had faded to an anxious grey that matched the stone of the terrace rather admirably, peered around a topiary pot.

"I thought this was meant to be relaxing," he hissed. "I thought this was going to *stop* me stress-shedding, not make it worse."

"Well, you're not concentrating, are you?" Beaufort said. "You're over there hiding behind a plant pot."

"It's very hard to concentrate when someone could see us *any minute,*" Mortimer pointed out, not moving, then waved at the peacock that had wandered up to investigate them. "Shoo!"

"*Bu-kurk,*" it said.

"Shh, both of you," Miriam whispered, flapping her hands at them.

"Miriam, do go back to your mat," Alice said. "You're not exactly helping."

"It's making me terribly nervous."

"No one here can see us, Miriam," Beaufort said, trying to move into a Warrior One. Miriam was pretty sure you couldn't do that with dragon feet, but the High Lord was certainly making a good attempt. "We checked with the gargoyles. They've been on this house since it was built, and no one has ever seen them. There's not a glimmer of sight in anyone here."

"Gargoyles?" Miriam said, and Alice shushed her.

"*She* thought she saw something," Mortimer muttered, trying to work his way into the pose without emerging from behind the pot.

The peacock opened his tail and shook it at him encouragingly. "*Bu-kurk!*"

"I really don't think yoga class is a place for dragons," Miriam said with a sigh, but went back to her mat and tried to get her feet to go one way and her legs another. She hoped the dragons were getting more out of the class than she was.

SOMEHOW THEY MADE it to the end of the session without anyone breaking anything (although, judging from the mutters, there were quite a few stubbed toes and shaking legs), and Miriam finally lay back on her mat in the gentle spring sun with a sigh, her eyes closed, listening to the soft breathing of the women around her and trying to not giggle every time Adele *ohmm*-ed. Someone was snoring, and from the raspiness she thought it was Beaufort.

He had been quite right, of course. Adele hadn't seen him. Not *quite*, anyway. That was what tended to happen – people thought they saw something, but when they looked again there would be nothing there, or it would make their eyes hurt, and they'd think they were getting a migraine. You had to be expecting dragons to see them. She still thought it was rather risky, though, as they didn't know who the other guests were yet. She did hope that this was going to be a relaxing weekend. She could really do with a relaxing weekend after the last year.

For a while there was silence, just the breathing of the women and the dragons, and birdsong in the trees beyond the terrace, where soft green grass rolled through more strangely shaped topiary and on to the untamed woods that circled the property, full of badgers and foxes and pheasants, and streams and rivers that would eventually lead to Toot Hansell. The sun was bright against her eyelids, blood vessels painting patterns on the insides, and she drifted, smelling cut grass and woodsmoke and the warm scent of stone in sunlight. Then a voice rang out around them.

"Ladies on the stone in the sun,

her lips spitting kisses like sunny secrets from the gods,

only to realise that none are there for him.

Oh! To be the lost man in such a place of beauty!"

There was a pause, and Miriam wondered if this was part of the class. She'd read that there were such things as beer yoga and dog yoga, so maybe this was poetry yoga?

Then Adele's voice rose, sounding rather less slow and smooth than it had a few minutes before. "Boyd! What are you *doing*? I told you, you have to stop this! You're ruining everything!"

"I'm not," Boyd said. "It adds an extra dimension to your classes. It makes them transcendent."

"My classes are already transcendent!"

Miriam thought that might be pushing things, but the poetry certainly hadn't added anything. She pushed herself up on one elbow and looked at her nephew.

"I raise you up through my words and create,

waking dreams through which rage-slash-love can play,

while buxom fancies fairly tintinnabulate,

and all too soon will be gone the way of spring."

"Buxom what?" Gert demanded, sitting up. "And tintinnabulate? That does not sound like something you should be doing on a yoga mat."

"*Umm*," Boyd said. He was a tall man with longish hair,

hovering at the edge of the terrace in a large white shirt and ripped jeans. "No?"

"No what?" Gert snapped. She was wearing a sleeveless floral top, and her biceps bulged rather alarmingly, making the mermaid tattoo on one arm dance. "Are you saying you want to tintinnabulate us buxom fancies on the yoga mats?"

"No!" he squawked. "I was just – I – poetry! Art, yes?"

"That is not art," Gert said, shaking a finger at him. "I think that was probably quite rude, to be honest. Is this what you do? Hang around your sister's yoga classes spouting bad poetry at people?"

Boyd spluttered. "It's good! It's *very* good! I've won prizes!"

"At *school*," Adele said. "And I'm pretty sure they only gave it to you to stop you submitting anything else."

"That's not true!"

"It so is."

"Now, kids," Priya raised her hands placatingly. "Aren't we all practising compassion and so on?"

"I'm practising lying down," Rose said, eyes still closed.

"It's called shavasana. Corpse pose," Jasmine told her.

Rose opened her eyes and sat up. "Well, I'm not so keen on practising *that*. Plenty of time for that later."

"It's just a name," Adele said, sounding slightly desperate. "Let's just go back to considering compassion—"

"*We all talk about compassion,*" Boyd proclaimed suddenly, and Gert made the sort of noise an angry llama might make. "*Till the furies comes, those wizened old crones—*"

"Those *what?*" Gert demanded, and Alice said, "*Really.*"

"Boyd!" Adele wailed.

"*Those – those angels of the Dales,*" Boyd managed, looking around wildly as if hoping someone would rescue him.

"Is he trying to poetry?" Beaufort asked, not bothering to keep his voice down. "Because he's really terrible at it. Doesn't he know that it's about creating beauty?"

"Well, I'm not sure modern poetry is exactly like that," Mortimer began, and Miriam waved at them wildly.

"*Shh!*" she whispered. "We don't know who might hear you!"

"Hear what?" Boyd asked.

"Nothing," Alice said.

"*Oh! 'Tis but the sound of the breezes!*
His heart grows faint, his hands begin to shake—"

"Terrible," Beaufort said, shaking his scaly head. "Once upon a time, someone that bad at poetry would have been burned at the stake."

"I don't disagree with the concept." Alice sat up and pulled her cardigan on. "He's quite ruined the mood."

"You see?" Adele said. Her arms were folded and she was glaring at her brother in what Miriam thought was a rather un-yogic sort of way. "You've ruined it. Happy now?"

"It was a very nice class until then," Priya said encouragingly.

"Well, not everyone can appreciate *art.*" Boyd tossed his hair. It would have looked more effective if it hadn't been so wispy, Miriam thought. Poor boy. It just sort of wafted around his face rather dismally.

"Oh, go do some of your crappy topiary," Adele snapped. "See if you can ruin the view as well as the mood."

"Well, that explains a lot," Carlotta said. "I did wonder why none of them actually look like anything."

"It's *art!*" Boyd insisted.

"It's rubbish," Rosemary said, and she and Carlotta exchanged short nods.

"It is *not,*" Boyd said indignantly. "Why should topiary always be animals? Why can't it be *abstract?*"

"And I thought we had problems with Gilbert and his abstract baubles," Mortimer mumbled to Beaufort.

"Oh, leave the poor man alone," Priya said. "They do get so

precious. And the class is over anyway." She got up and started rolling her mat up.

"Wait!" Adele pleaded. "We haven't done the breathing yet! Or the guided meditation!"

"Oh, no, I'm done," Rose said, getting up. "It must be gin and tonic time by now, isn't it?"

"But you can't finish now! You're not fully relaxed yet!"

"Teresa is," Pearl said, gesturing at the tall woman, still stretched out and snoring gently.

"*Boyyyyd!*" Adele wailed. "Why do you have to spoil *everything!*"

"*Your whining drains the peace from the day—*"

"Enough," Gert said. "I can't listen to either of you anymore. I've got plenty of kids and grandkids if I want to listen to squabbling." She scowled at Boyd, and he scuttled backward, trying to look dignified. He yelped as he ran into someone coming out the doors.

"Sorry! Sorry, sorry …" He shuffled sideways, looked at the W.I. and the newcomer, then gave up and headed across the terrace and into the garden at a pace that was uncomfortably close to a run.

"Oh, hello, DI Adams," Gert said. "You just missed the yoga."

DI Adams was staring at the front of her hoody, which was liberally splattered with the contents of her coffee cup. "I just put this on," she complained.

"Oh, we'll get that out," Rosemary said. "A little white vinegar and it'll be good as new."

"Glycerine," Carlotta said.

Rosemary frowned at her, agreement of a moment ago forgotten. "Oh? Just carrying that around with you, are you?"

"Any decent household will have some."

"Only if they're in the mining business."

DI Adams sighed, and finished the remains of her cup. "I was enjoying that coffee, too."

"Welcome to the manor house, detective inspector," Alice said. "I'm so glad you decided to join us."

"Yes," DI Adams said, rather unenthusiastically.

***

WITH ALL THE fuss over stolen lamb shoulders, afternoon tea appeared to have been forgotten, and they'd skipped straight to glasses of sparkling wine on the terrace, served with plates of mysterious pastries and bite-size pieces of fish and meat on mini-skewers. Miriam was trying not to eat too many of them in case dinner was just as good, but it was hard. DI Adams seemed to have resigned her hoody to whatever fate Rosemary and Carlotta had in store for it, and was ensconced in one of the deep chairs on the terrace with a blanket bundled around her as the sky turned pink and apricot and the shadows under the trees deepened. She had a glass of red wine in one hand, and was watching Beaufort sitting on a dangerously sagging sunlounger, drinking a pint of bitter with evident enjoyment.

"Is he sure about this?" the inspector asked. "I mean, he's very *obvious* out there."

"I can't even look," Mortimer said. He was curled up next to Miriam's chair, entirely hidden under a blanket from which his paw would appear at regular intervals to retrieve cheese pastries.

"I think it's giving me a headache," DI Adams said.

"Beaufort is completely confident that no one will see them," Miriam said, not feeling at all confident herself. She wanted to pat the inspector on the arm reassuringly, but wasn't quite sure if that was the sort of thing you did to police officers.

"*Hmm.*" DI Adams sipped her wine.

Alice settled a throw more comfortably around her shoulders and said, "It's very nice to see you off-duty, Inspector."

"It's nice to be off-duty," she said, not sounding entirely convincing.

"And what should we call you when you're off-duty?"

"DI Adams is just fine."

Miriam felt she'd made the right decision about the arm-patting.

Alice smiled and nodded at the three birdwatchers, who were waving various pieces of electronic equipment around the base of one of the topiary pots. Beaufort watched them with interest, interspersing sips of beer with generous helpings of sausage rolls, which he shared with the peacock who paced around him *bu-kurk-ing* in a friendly sort of way.

"They're an odd lot, aren't they?" Alice said. "Never seen bird-watchers with so much equipment before."

"It's for tracking night birds, apparently," Rose said. "I asked them about it, because in my day all we needed was a notepad and binoculars. And that was for work, not a hobby."

"It's not a *hobby*," the nearest man said, and frowned at them. "This is serious stuff, this is. We're hoping to identify a new species."

"Shh, Saul," one of the others said. "Don't give it all away."

Saul looked alarmed, and turned the collar of his coat up before he went to join the other two men fussing around the tree.

"Rubbish," Rose said rather loudly, and gave the men a sweet smile when they turned around. DI Adams made a sound that sounded quite a lot like a snort of laughter.

"So precious," Priya said, and clinked her glass off Rose's. The men looked like they were fairly sure they were being insulted, but couldn't quite understand how.

"Does anyone need any more drinks?" Maddie asked, appearing next to Miriam with her hair clipped into some semblance of order. "Appetisers?"

"Maddie, do relax," Alice said. "It's only us, and the boys over there chasing butterflies or what have you."

"New species," the tall one called back. "Just wait until we have a moth named after us."

"*Phsst*," Rose said, swinging her legs in her chair. "I've got two bacterium and an amoeba named after me."

The men stared at her uncertainly, then went back to what they were doing, talking a little more quietly.

Miriam reached out and tugged her sister's arm. "Mads, come sit down. Take a breather for a moment."

"Oh, no. I can't. I'm half-scared to leave the kitchen too long in case Reid makes a nuisance of himself again, and we've more guests arriving any minute."

"So what can we expect?" Gert asked. "Honeymooners? Ramblers?"

"Oh, no. Antique hunters, and a gentleman on his own. And a – a family."

Miriam wondered why the family required a hesitation, but she was much too comfortable in the early evening light, savouring the indulgent thrill of a glass of sparkling wine, to worry about it too much. Maddie collected a couple of empty glasses and hurried off again, and Mortimer poked his nose out from under the blanket.

"More guests?"

"Yes, dear," Miriam said, taking possession of a plate of salmon toasts and handing them to the dragon, who took six. "Try not to worry too much." Mortimer hadn't been any colour except anxious grey since he and Beaufort had arrived, padding down through the woodland trails and waiting expectantly for the Women's Institute to appear.

"How can I *not* worry?" he demanded now. "What if one of them spots us? I mean, Beaufort's just sitting out there in plain view!"

"Well, you did say he checked with ... some Folk?" She glanced at the roof line behind her, but couldn't see any lurking creatures.

"Oh, and they're so reliable," Mortimer muttered, taking four more toasts and retreating under the blanket again. She didn't blame him. She felt a bit the same around strangers at times.

DI Adams tucked her blanket a little more tightly around her. "So Maddie's your sister, Miriam?"

Miriam, who'd been concentrating on Mortimer, choked on a piece of toast, and Rose thumped her on the back a little too enthusiastically. She wheezed a couple of times, then nodded, wiping at her eyes.

"Miriam, do *try* to stop panicking every time the inspector talks to you," Alice said. "She hasn't arrested you once."

Miriam decided not to point out that the inspector *had* arrested Alice, and just said, "Yes. She married Denis Etherington-Smythe, who was the last of the Etheringtons, but he died in a horrible accident with a squirrel."

"A ... squirrel?" the inspector said carefully.

"Nasty little critters," Alice observed, and for a while no one said anything.

Then Rose said, "To be fair, it wasn't the *squirrel's* fault that he fell off the tractor."

"The squirrel bit him," Miriam said. "Though no one knows exactly *why* he was on a tractor with a shotgun chasing a squirrel at three in the morning."

"I imagine the whisky had something to do with that," Alice said.

"There's eccentric and there's just plain silly," Rose remarked.

Everyone was tactfully quiet for a moment, then the inspector cleared her throat. "Right. So, Maddie runs the whole place, does she?"

"She does," Miriam said. "All the kids help, though. Boyd takes care of the grounds, and Adele does the beauty treatments as well as the yoga, and—" she hesitated. "Well, Reid *used* to cook, but I think he does other stuff now." She waved vaguely.

"Thank God for that," Gert said, taking the last sausage roll. "Lucky we didn't all get food poisoning."

Miriam started to say, *that's not fair*, but stopped. It was fair, really. "Adele used to do foraging and plant identification, too, but there was a problem with some mushrooms a couple of years ago, so they don't offer it anymore."

"Problem?" DI Adams asked.

"Well, it depends on your point of view, I suppose. Some people rather hunt out that particular mushroom, I've heard."

DI Adams choked on her wine, and hurriedly brushed some drops off the blanket. "Right."

"They did have a lot of enquiries after the story was in the paper," Alice said, and for a moment Miriam thought the inspector was going to start laughing. In the end, though, she just raised her eyebrows slightly and made a noise that might have been acknowledgement or might have been disbelief.

"They work very hard," Miriam said. "Well, Maddie does. And this weekend's so important. They had a terrible year last year, and apparently she's got some guests staying who could really help out if everything goes well. If not, well, I don't know what she'll do. Have to sell, I suppose."

"That would be awful," Rose said. "Imagine if a developer bought it! They'd ruin everything."

Miriam sighed, and looked at the woods easing into darkness, vast and wild and fragile. "They would," she agreed.

3
ALICE

Alice's hip was stiff as she made her way from the chill of the terrace, through the plant-filled orangery with its deep cane chairs and sense that Victorian botanists were about to emerge from among the ferns, into the worn gentility of the breakfast room and through the next set of double doors into the warm, worn jumble of the lounge. It was packed with too many ancient leather sofas and heavy low tables, and taxidermied heads in various states of moth-eaten distress watched her as she headed into the foyer. She couldn't shake the feeling that no one had actually stopped to think about how the rooms would work when they'd decided to turn the place into a hotel, as there was no other way off the terrace.

The trek had warmed her up a little, but with no one around to see, she paused on the midpoint landing of the stairs to rub her hip. It really had healed remarkably well after the goblin attack last Christmas, but still – a hip replacement was a hip replacement. She shouldn't have sat out in the cold for so long.

She was about to start up again when she heard raised voices from the office below, and the door banged open.

"*This* is how you're going to save this place?" a man demanded. "Cheap weekends for locals and pandering to tourists? I had to drive them all the way to bloody Harrogate today!"

"Reid," Maddie said, the tone pleading. "What else can I do?"

"You *know* what you can do, Mum! Hunting weekends! Shoots! Bring some actual bloody money in here or just *sell* it before the place falls down around our ears!"

Alice looked at the stairs and wondered if she could sneak up without anyone hearing her. She didn't want to listen to Maddie being berated by her youngest son. It was quite awful of him to be doing it here, in the middle of the house, where anyone could hear.

"We're not selling. And you know how I feel about guns. Plus, I don't like those hunting types, shooting up the wood and being all loud."

"So put some *money* into the damn place, if you want it to work so much! Put the money in and get some corporate clients, like you wanted to before. They won't come here with shared bathrooms and all that rubbish."

"*What* money, Reid? Where do you expect me to get this magical money from?"

"Well, you can stop paying that awful sous-chef, for a start. And Adele. All she does is waft around teaching the odd yoga class, and you *pay* her!"

"I pay you, too," Maddie said, and Alice was pleased to hear a sharp edge in her voice. "And we need a decent kitchen team after the last couple of years. Don't you remember the reviews?"

"I still think you should get rid of him. He's claiming some dog stole the lamb for dinner, now. We don't even *have* a dog."

"Stop being such a child, Reid. I know why you don't want him here, and Nita won't have you in her kitchen. So forget it."

"Ugh. I'm *trying* to help, here, but I tell you – this can't go on. If you won't get some decent paying guests, we should just sell."

"We're not selling." There was a shake in Maddie's voice, but she sounded immovable.

"Then you *need* to do the shoots." The door slammed below Alice, and Reid strode across the foyer without looking back. Alice sighed, and wondered if she should go and knock on the office door. But either Maddie would be pretending nothing had happened, or she'd need a sympathetic ear. Either way, Alice couldn't be much help. Sympathy wasn't her area of expertise.

She rubbed her hip again and started climbing, her eyes on the worn carpet. Everything *was* looking tired, the boy was right about that. But wasn't that the charm of these old places? Wasn't it the fact that they were lived in that stopped them from being just a museum piece from a forgotten time?

She sighed, a little more deeply than she intended, and someone said, "Deep thoughts for a spring evening, eh?"

She looked up and found a young man with a lot of carefully cultivated stubble leaning against the wall at the top of the stairs. She was quite certain he'd listened to the little drama play out below them as well.

"It's always unpleasant to find oneself witness to such things," she said. "Don't you think?"

"Oh, maybe for some." He grinned. "It's rather my bread and butter."

"Is that so?"

"Yes. The study of people is fascinating, wouldn't you say?"

Alice stepped onto the balcony landing next to him and examined him for a long moment, watching his smile become a little fixed. "Study and spying are two different things," she said finally.

"Oh, come on—"

"Judging by how blurred that line is to you, I imagine you're a journalist."

His smile dropped, then reappeared, and he laughed. "You're very good."

"I am. And you, young man—" She didn't get to finish what she was saying, because at that moment a maelstrom of noise poured across the landing toward them, and she had to step away from the stairs to avoid getting caught up in it.

"Hey! Hello!" someone boomed, and Alice found her hand enveloped in an enormous fist. "You must be one of the ladies from the local village! Hun, look, it's a lady from the village!"

"Aw, Holt, let her go! She's obviously on her way to freshen up." Perfume assaulted Alice's nose, making her sneeze.

"Have you got a cold? Goddamn damp country – not surprising. Kids, did you take your vitamins? Have you?"

"Yes, Dad," chorused two children, standing behind their parents. They looked terribly fresh-faced and healthy. Tanned, perhaps. Or maybe it was the very white teeth, Alice wasn't sure. All she knew was that it all seemed very unnatural.

"Go on, kids, let the lady go wash up," the woman said, and beamed at Alice. "We'll see you at dinner, honey, yeah?"

"Yes, I imagine so," Alice said. She felt like she'd stepped onto the set of some sort of Americans abroad movie, and it was all very *loud*.

"Let's go, let's go," the man boomed. He slapped the journalist on the back and charged down the stairs. The journalist grabbed the banister to keep himself from tumbling down in their slipstream, then smiled at Alice.

"I imagine those would be the pandered tourists, then?"

She gave him her most severe look. "I don't make assumptions based on overheard conversations." She turned and strode down the hall to her own room, thinking that she couldn't imagine who else it would be.

IT DIDN'T TAKE her long to freshen up for dinner. There was a pair of damp walking trousers slung over the towel rail in the bathroom, smelling faintly of roast lamb for some reason, and she wondered if the detective inspector had been in the kitchen sorting out more disputes. She moved them to the shower so they wouldn't get toothpaste on them, and washed her face in the stained porcelain sink before padding quietly back to the room she was sharing with Miriam to get changed.

She was just brushing her hair out when Miriam came bustling into the room, her face pink with wine and excitement.

"Oh, Alice – you look lovely."

"Thank you, Miriam." Alice smoothed her cardigan down and smiled at the younger woman. "It's always pleasant coming back here, isn't it?"

"It is." Miriam sat down on her bed and kicked her flip-flops off, examining her chipped toenail polish critically. "But, I don't know. Maybe it's just me, but doesn't it feel a bit different this time?"

Alice didn't hold much with feelings of the sort that Miriam used in her business as a psychic and tarot reader, but she did believe in the sort of things that a Sensitive person picks up when they're around other people. "Different how, Miriam?"

"Oh, I don't know." Miriam got up and started digging through her bag, which she hadn't unpacked. Alice's clothes were all neatly folded in one drawer. Miriam seemed to have brought half her wardrobe, and it was mostly on the floor. "Less happy. More anxious." She paused, staring at a jumper as if it could answer the question for her. "Everyone feels on edge. Maddie's skinnier than she was last year, I'm sure of it. Adele is more odd than ever, and she got so *angry* with Boyd. It's like they're trying to hold up this theatre set, but it's curling at the edges, and you can start to see that it's all papier mâché and dust behind."

Alice said nothing, thinking of Maddie and Reid fighting in the hall, and after a moment Miriam shrugged, her face even pinker than it had been.

"I'm probably just being silly. Too much sparkling wine and worrying about the dragons and so on."

"You need to give yourself more credit, Miriam," Alice said, sitting down on her bed and crossing her feet neatly at the ankles. "You're not at all as silly as you make out you are."

Miriam went positively luminous, and busied herself with her toiletries. "Well, maybe. But it doesn't mean anything, right? It's probably just some family thing."

"Probably," Alice agreed, and watched Miriam scurry out the door to the bathroom.

ALICE WRAPPED a shawl around her shoulders and went back downstairs in search of the W.I. The foyer was still and abandoned, the tiles echoing under her feet and dim in the lamps on the sideboards, the skylight lost in shadows high above her. There was a most enticing scent of roasting garlic coming from the dining room, but it was quiet and empty inside. Across the foyer, light and warmth and noise spilled from the lounge, drawing her in.

The ladies of the W.I. had commandeered three large, cracked sofas in front of the fireplace, in which a small fire was smouldering rather unconvincingly, and had wedged themselves in with their elbows crammed together and glasses stacked up in front of them.

"I rather feel like I'm late to the party," Alice said, perching herself on the arm of a sofa next to Priya.

"No, no," Priya said. "Rose and Pearl haven't even gone to change yet."

"I don't see why I have to change," Rose said. "It's not like we've been on a cross-country run. I'm eighty-seven. I don't have to dress for dinner if I don't want to."

"Mightn't you get chilled, though?" Jasmine asked. "You don't want that."

Rose ran a hand back over her spiky grey hair. "I suppose that dining room does look rather cold."

"It does," Gert said. "Don't know what they were thinking with that."

"Modernisation," Rosemary said.

"I think they may have started in the wrong place for that," Teresa said. "If anyone turns on the bathroom light, the lights in our room go out. I'm more worried about the wiring than about being able to perform surgery in the dining room."

"There's a bird's nest in our lights," Carlotta said. "We haven't even turned them on yet. Don't want to disturb them."

Rose was just asking what sort of birds they were when DI Adams appeared among the chairs, trailing the journalist.

"Ooh," Jasmine said. "Did she bring a friend?"

"No," Alice replied. "He's press."

The W.I. quietened, and fixed the man with such a stern regard that both he and DI Adams stopped. It was one thing having civilians around the place, but journalists could be worryingly perceptive, which made a relaxing weekend for dragons somewhat more risky. Of course, the whole thing was risky, but Beaufort had read a yoga book of Miriam's and was now convinced it would fix Mortimer's shedding problem. Alice thought that, knowing Mortimer, it was likely to have the opposite effect.

"What's wrong?" DI Adams demanded. "This wasn't a 'dress for dinner' deal, was it? No one told me anything about it being dress for dinner." She was still wearing her yoga trousers, and had replaced her coffee-splattered hoody with a hiking fleece. She looked vaguely uncomfortable.

"No, no," Alice said. "You're absolutely fine."

"Well, if she's wearing workout gear, I'm wearing workout gear," Rose said.

"I always wear workout gear," Teresa said. "Everything else is so constrictive." She waved her arms about to illustrate, and clipped Rosemary around the ear.

"Ow," Rosemary said, without much conviction.

"Sorry."

"Do sit down, DI Adams," Carlotta said, and patted the arm of the sofa.

"Okay." The inspector looked unconvinced, but she perched herself carefully and gave the ladies a small smile.

"Room for one more?" the journalist asked, standing a little too close to DI Adams.

She glared at him. "Does it look like there's room?"

"Girl's night, got it." He scratched his head and smiled at them, revealing dimples. "I suppose I'll just go sit on my own, then."

Everyone returned the smile, waiting, and after a moment he wandered off with his hands in his pockets and his shoulders slumped.

"Honestly," Pearl said, "I thought he wasn't going to take the hint at all."

"I think journalists are trained not to take hints," DI Adams said. "Unless they can turn it into a story, of course."

IT WAS REALLY RATHER PLEASANT. The fire and the low lights, the big sofas forming a cosy little circle that encompassed just the W.I. and no one else. Miriam appeared, pink-faced and with her hair sticking out of some sort of gypsy scarf in an oddly endearing way, and Boyd brought more drinks. He tried a couple of lines about the sodden glory of grapes, then saw Gert's glare and scuttled away. Adele drifted past in a gauzy dress to remind everyone that the manor now offered Botox and bee venom therapy. Rose said that if she wanted bee venom she could stick her arm in the hive at the bottom of her garden, and Alice surprised herself by raising one smooth eyebrow and asking if being shot up with botulism was the thing to do these days. She wasn't normally so rude to anyone who didn't deserve it, and decided she'd probably had enough wine. Pearl patted the young woman's arm and said that massages and face masks were just what they needed, so not to worry about the fancy stuff.

It was only very reluctantly that they got up when Maddie came to tell them dinner was ready, and left their warm little oasis for the cool light of the dining room. The old wooden floors had been painted white, and looked almost as distressed as the tables. Modern chandeliers made of stainless steel and feathers hung low over one enormous long table formed from several smaller ones in the centre of the room, while the few individual tables left were pinned in place by spotlights in the ceiling. The chairs were very upright and made of the same pale wood as the tables, and Adele stood in the centre of the room waving a bundle of smoking sage around.

"Adele!" Maddie snapped. "Would you stop *doing* that?"

"I'm just trying to create some atmosphere, Mum. Good vibes, you know."

"Well, go and do it somewhere else. You know Nita doesn't like funny smells in the dining room. Ruins the meal, she says."

Adele rolled her eyes. "Whatever." She wandered off, still waving the sage about, and Alice wondered if Miriam was right to think that the place felt *off* somehow. Maybe Adele felt it too.

"Ladies! Hey there! We thought we'd all eat together, get to know each other, yeah?"

Alice raised her eyebrows as the ladies of the Toot Hansell Women's Institute – and DI Adams – exchanged glances. The American family were already seated at the big table, the father at the head. The birdwatchers were huddled together at the other end, staring at the electronic equipment they had scattered across the table and trying not to make eye contact with anyone.

"Well, it's not really the point of the weekend," Alice began, but Maddie turned to her with a tight smile on her face.

"Please?" she whispered. "They own a big travel company. If they like it here they might send so many people our way. So, just for tonight?"

Alice looked at the W.I., not willing to answer for them in this. There was a pause, then Priya stepped forward and pulled out the seat next to the American woman. "How long are you here for?" she asked.

There was a breath, then with the clatter of chairs scraping on wood and cutlery being shifted and rearranged, the Women's Institute descended like birds coming to rest. Alice found herself between DI Adams and Jasmine, with two spare chairs across the broad table. They frowned at them.

"Who's still to come?" Jasmine asked.

"None of us," Alice said.

"The antique hunters," the journalist said. He'd come in with them and managed to seat himself next to DI Adams. "They're not here yet."

Alice nodded. "What's your name, young man?"

"Ervin Giles," he said, giving her a broad smile.

"And what are you working on at the moment, Ervin?"

"A story about how stately homes are evolving to cope with the changing economic and social climate," the young man said, tapping his spoon on the tablecloth. "With varying degrees of success."

"I think they're doing a really good job here," Jasmine said. "We come here every year."

"Oh, it's wonderful," Ervin said. "If you like being in an IKEA catalogue one minute and a junk sale the next."

"That's very rude," Miriam said from opposite him.

"It's only true," he said, showing them the label on his napkin. "IKEA."

DI Adams made a strangled sound, and covered her mouth with one hand. "Sorry," she said, her cheeks twitching.

Ervin looked at her. "You're one of the detectives that busted that kidnapping ring at Christmas."

"And?" she said.

"And – well, what are you doing here?"

"Having a spa weekend. Because, you know, police are people, and do these things."

Ervin looked from her to Alice, then sighed and leaned back in his chair. "Journalists are people too. I'm not here to do a hack job."

Alice sniffed, and DI Adams looked unimpressed.

"Well, *hello,* dears!" someone exclaimed, and a woman who was as tall standing as Miriam was sitting appeared on the other side of the table, all soft curls and large glasses. "Are these chairs for us? Oh, I hope we haven't held things up. It was Edie. She takes simply *ages* in the shower."

"I don't at all," another woman said. She towered over the first, but Alice thought she was probably only average height. "It's really that Lottie couldn't decide what to wear, the silly thing."

Lottie giggled. "Well, one doesn't want to be overdressed *or* underdressed, does one? But really," she added, lowering her voice in a confidential manner, "I couldn't find my socks! No idea where they've gone."

"You can't have packed them, dear," Edie said.

"I'm quite sure I did."

DI Adams put her elbows on the table and cupped her chin in her hands, staring at the two women as if they were an entirely new and fascinating species. They were both wearing white ruffled blouses with cameo brooches, and jeans that had been ironed to permanent creases. Lottie wore pink cowboy boots that gave her an extra few inches in height, while Edie was wearing pink ballet flats. They both clutched little evening purses, and their hair was styled in waves that Alice rather associated with pin-up girls from the 40's.

"Let's sit down and stop holding everything up," Edie said, and pulled out a chair for Lottie, patting her fondly on the shoulder before sitting down herself.

"Are you the antique hunters?" Jasmine asked.

"Well, *yes*, dear," Lottie said. "And oh, we had such fun today! We'll tell you all about it!"

"Wine?" someone said by Alice's shoulder, and she leaned back as Boyd offered a bottle.

"Please." She had a feeling she might need it if they were going to be regaled with giggling tales of antiques.

"Red or white?"

"White, please."

"*White, like light, like the glossy skin of—*"

"Boyd."

"Sorry." He filled the glass dangerously high then moved on, proclaiming something about wine lighting the cerebral pathways of pleasure while Gert glared at him. Adele had reappeared with her sage and was dancing around the table in a swirl of scarves, Maddie following her and waving a tea towel enthusiastically. Alice was just wondering whether there were smoke alarms or if it would just go straight to sprinkler systems when the American's voice boomed across the table, cutting through the chatter and silencing even Lottie.

"Friends," he bellowed. "We are *so* happy to be here with y'all. Let's get to know each other, yeah? We can all go around the table and share a little. It'll be fun!"

"Oh, God, no," DI Adams said into the startled silence, and Jasmine gave a funny little squeak of alarm.

"I'll start," the American continued. "My name's Holt Miller, and this here is my wife Paula, my son Roper, and my daughter Dell-Marie. We come from America, and we're so happy to meet y'all."

"Odd accent," Ervin mumbled, and Alice agreed silently. She couldn't shake the feeling that these Americans were just *too* American. She'd known quite a few in her RAF days, some rather well indeed. And they'd never been so, well, *obvious*. Everyone stared at Holt, the dining room entirely silent but for the faint sound of Adele still chanting, and her bare feet on the floorboards.

"You next," Holt said, and nodded at Priya encouragingly.

"Um," Priya said, and everyone looked at her nervously. She twisted her napkin in her hands. "Er—"

"Starters are served," Maddie called brightly, and a sigh of relief washed down the table.

DI Adams took a gulp of wine. "Thank God for that."

"Why? Something to hide, Detective Inspector?" Ervin asked, grinning, and the inspector gave him such a ferocious look that Alice had to cover a smile with her napkin.

IT SEEMED that neither the thieving dog nor the small matter of a scrap with the owner's son had caused too many problems in the kitchen. The food was perfectly presented, the flavours of spring vegetables stark and crisp against tender meat, with none of the fussiness that so many restaurants seemed to tend toward these days. Even DI Adams seemed well-catered for, and was so busy eating that she didn't even notice Adele pat her approvingly on the shoulder and say, "Veggies united." Miriam was making small happy noises across the table as she cleaned her plate, and not even the Americans were talking. The birdwatchers had stopped messing around with their equipment and looking superior, and there were no giggly tales of antique hunting forthcoming. Alice took a sip of wine as she observed the table approvingly. All in all, it was a most satisfactory meal indeed.

Dessert was an astonishing mix of rhubarb jelly and crumble and panna cotta, served with a small scoop of apple sorbet that Alice doubted had seen the inside of a store-bought container.

"This is amazing," DI Adams said to no one in particular, poking the panna cotta. "Agar agar or something, I guess. I *never* get decent veggie meals."

"The standard has certainly gone up," Alice said.

"It couldn't exactly go down," Rose pointed out.

"Maddie put a lot of work into finding good chefs." Miriam said. She was scraping her plate carefully, looking as if she'd rather like to lick it clean.

"Thank God," Pearl said. "Reid's a nice boy, but I think he did some weekend cooking course and decided he was on *MasterChef*." She looked up from her plate, the tip of her small nose reddening. "I'm so sorry. That was really rude."

"Accurate, though," Rose said, cleaning her plate with one finger.

"Still, if you haven't got anything nice to say," Pearl mumbled, and took a sip of dessert wine.

Alice smiled, then looked up as Boyd cleared his throat at the corner of the table. Jasmine and Miriam looked at him expectantly, but conversation carried on everywhere else. Holt was telling Gert very loudly about his swimming pool, and she was leaning back in her chair with her arms crossed and a disapproving look on her face. Priya was nodding a lot at something Paula was saying, and looking increasingly uncomfortable. The birdwatchers had pushed their polished plates away and were assembling tripods and flashes on complicated-looking arms, and Carlotta appeared to be scolding them.

Boyd cleared his throat again, louder, and then a third time, loud enough that Alice thought he might damage something. But people were finally quieting and looking at him.

"Coffee and tea," he began, clasping his hands behind his back. *"The liquid of life, the dance of—"*

"Boyd," Adele warned him as she wandered past with a tray of *petits fours*, not looking like she was entirely sure where she was going with them.

He rolled his eyes. "Will be served in the lounge."

"And nightcaps?" Ervin asked, one arm slung over the back of his chair.

"Well, yes."

"I'm in." He pushed his chair back and stood up, ambling toward the mellow light of the lounge with his shirt sleeves pushed up and his sharp, dark eyes examining the hall like he was looking for something. Alice frowned after him, seeing DI Adams doing the same. He didn't *seem* to be the sort that would see dragons, but one never knew.

"We'll take the coffee in a thermos," one of the birdwatchers said. "We need to get to work."

"Er—" Boyd looked uncertain, and Maddie, sweeping out of the kitchen with a tray of cups, saved him.

"Of course, gentlemen. I'll have it ready for you by the time you have your boots on. Shall I add some milk and sugar?"

"That'll be fine," he said, starting to pack equipment into a backpack. One of the others strung an enormous camera around his neck, bouncing it off the table.

"Keith," the first birdwatcher said.

"Sorry." He patted the camera.

"Any chance of biscuits?" the skinniest of them asked hopefully.

"How can you possibly eat after all that?" Rosemary asked. "Where does it go?"

"I don't know." He shrugged. "But it's cold out there. Biscuits will help."

There was a general scraping of chairs as everyone started to move toward the lounge, and Alice stayed where she was for a moment, rubbing her hip to ease the stiffness. Holt stopped next to DI Adams, clapping her on the shoulder as she finished her wine. She stiffened, frowned at his hand, then turned the frown on him.

"I hear you're an officer of the law," he said, his face round and red-cheeked as he leaned over her. "We'll have to watch our step around you, huh?"

She raised an eyebrow. "Is that not something you usually do?"

"Well, no. I mean, yes. Um, tough job, huh?"

"Holt, come on," his wife said, catching his arm and smiling at DI Adams. Holt didn't move, just grinned at the inspector.

"I enjoy my job," DI Adams said. "But yes, it's not always easy."

"I bet! Especially being a woman, and, you know." He waved at her vaguely.

"What?" DI Adams said. "A bit short?"

"Um, no."

"I'm actually average height," she confided, and Alice's lips twitched. "It's just that half the blokes I work with are over six foot, so I *look* small."

"Um," Holt said, and his wife dragged him away, making little apologetic noises as she flushed redder and redder.

DI Adams looked at Alice, who was smiling properly now. "What?"

Alice patted her lips with her napkin. "You enjoyed that, didn't you?"

"Absolutely," the inspector said, and grinned.

"So did I," Alice said, and they clinked their empty glasses together, then got up to go through to the lounge.

4
MORTIMER

Mortimer was slightly astonished that Beaufort had been happy to leave the W.I. to themselves for the evening. The High Lord was far too intrigued by the concept of a spa weekend for Mortimer's comfort. "But why do you have to go away from home to be relaxed?" he kept asking. "Surely home is the most perfect place for relaxing and being comfortable?" Which the ladies had agreed with, but they did point out that caverns required rather less window-cleaning and vacuuming than did houses, and getting someone to pop over to the house to give you a massage or a private yoga lesson just wasn't the same as going somewhere you could get all the pampering you wanted in a weekend. Beaufort had been enormously impressed by the idea of massages and yoga, and absolutely insistent that Mortimer try both.

"Your stress levels are terribly high," he told the young dragon. "I've been reading about how bad that is for you. We need to do as much of this yoghurt as possible. It's going to be wonderfully good for you."

Mortimer supposed he should just be happy that the old

dragon hadn't tried to book him in for some sort of dragonish massage and mud bath treatment. He sighed, rather heavily.

"Are you alright there, Mortimer?" the dryad asked him, sitting down next to him cross-legged and patting his shoulder. "You just about scorched the moss."

"*No*," Mortimer said, looking around the little clearing on the edge of the stream. His breath painted magical creatures on the night. "He did yoga, you know. We both did yoga on the back terrace, in full view of the house."

"Oh, you're safe with yoga-girl," the gnome said, picking raw fish from his pointy teeth with a twig. "She's all airy-fairy floaty person, and she comes wandering through the trees collecting herbs and talking about communing with nature, but she never sees anything."

"You're mean to her," the dryad said. "You run around that terrace hiding all her blocks and belts and things, or putting them where people will fall over them, and she never knows where they go."

"Aw, lighten up, Mabel," a tiddy 'un said. He was leaning back in a puddle on the edge of the stream, a thimble of beer resting on his belly. "Like you don't go about hiding the garden shears and breaking the electric clippers."

"Well, that Boyd does awful things to trees," the dryad snapped, her weathered hands balled into fists. "Have you seen the topiary by the kitchen? One of them's shaped like a middle finger, and the other – well, it's anatomical, put it that way."

The gnome chuckled. "Yeah, he doesn't much like that big chef-type. Or likes him too much. I can never work it out with humans."

"They could be worse," the tiddy 'un said. "They leave my ponds alone, and that's all good. Don't rip up any of the old trees or anything. No infinity pools or hot tubs or any of that rubbish. Just a couple of nice ponds and a fountain, and I can keep on top of those easily. You hear about some of these places – you remember

Earl and Kathy, near Grasmere? *Two* hot tubs and an outdoor pool! They worked themselves ragged they did, and Earl had a breakdown. He sabotaged the whole lot, ripped all the pumps apart, and they ran away to some tarn up in the fells. You can't expect a couple of tiddy 'uns to take care of all that."

"It won't have been on purpose, Pat," the dryad said. "They don't know we exist, so it's not like they were deliberately making work for anyone."

Pat huffed. "So what do they think? Ponds just stay clean *all on their own?*"

Mortimer decided he was best staying out of the conversation. The magical Folk of the world had remained hidden for centuries, while the humans bred and spread and shaped the world in their own image. The Folk had become nothing more than legend, stories to tell children, shadows in the dark. But, rather recently, the dragons of the Cloverly clan had begun to edge out of hiding, and he knew a lot of it was due to the trade he'd set up with Miriam in dragon-scale baubles and barbecues. Although he had in no way imagined that was going to lead to spa weekends and dragon yoga, and if he had, he might never have created that first, magic-filled bauble to present to his human friend. He'd rather reckoned without the High Lord's enormous enthusiasm, and felt he spent far too much time trying to keep that in check when he could be designing more baubles.

And however it worked for the dragons (if *worked* was even the right word, as he felt sometimes that things were in a constant state of almost-not-working), he didn't feel at all qualified to pass advice or recommendations. Every kind had to figure out their own way to navigate this world. Cats, for instance, just never bothered changing. They still assumed the world was theirs to rule, just as it always had been. Considering the fact there were two cats in the human government, and that was common knowledge even among humans, they were probably right. Other Folk had to be rather more circumspect, as humans had a nasty habit of killing things they didn't understand, no matter how similar it was to them. Dryads with moss-encrusted skin, and tiddy 'uns with webbed feet and proboscis-type noses, and gnomes with stone teeth and frog-skin jackets would probably be a bit much for most of them.

Then again, he'd originally thought dragons would be too much for humans, even dragons as small as the Cloverlies. But when Miriam had caught him stealing both her barbecue gas bottle and a scone, she'd just offered him cream and pointed out that the bottle had been empty for three years, but she could get it filled for him if he liked. So you just never knew with humans.

"Have you seen Beaufort?" he asked Mabel. "He hasn't gone back to the house, has he?"

"No," she said. "He's chatting to Agatha. They were talking about improvements in the water table, last I heard."

That didn't sound exactly like Beaufort's area of enthusiasm, but he'd always had a soft spot for the river goddess. When Mortimer was small, a century or more ago, he remembered that she would spend time in the tarn beneath the dragons' mountain, sitting on the edge of the water looking like a great sleek silver dragon herself, talking to the High Lord and scaring the hatchlings by spitting steam at them. She could take on whatever form she wished, and people tended to see what they expected to see. He imagined the dryad saw someone similar to herself, liquid silver hair instead of leafy green, while the tiddy 'uns saw a creature with webbed feet and knobbly knees and lidless eyes. And if a human was Sensitive enough to glimpse her, she probably looked rather like them. And was also likely naked, as from what Mortimer had seen of Miriam's mythology books, humans seemed obsessed with depicting any nature spirit as naked. Well, all the female ones, anyway.

He trotted upstream, deeper into the woods and climbing

gently, weaving his way through low bushes and leaving clawed footprints in the soft earth. He wanted to go home. He still had a lot of dragon-scale boats and gliders to make for the summer fete, and he was really getting somewhere with the dandelion clocks. They only crumbled to dust at twelve instead of exploding now. Amelia and Gilbert were wonderful, of course, but it was his business. He couldn't just run off and ignore it like this. Beaufort had said three days would make no difference, but it was *three days*. A lot could happen in three days. And as for this idea that he should join a yoga class led by someone who didn't even know about dragons because it would help his stress – well, he was fairly sure he'd lost three scales during the class itself. And now they were waiting on a gargoyle to see if any of the other guests were likely to see them. Mortimer had a sneaking suspicion that gargoyles weren't the best litmus test, as if humans did see them, they assumed they were *meant* to be there. Dragons were hardly a common house ornament. He sighed again, setting some daffodils smouldering. Yes, he really did want to go home.

HE HEARD laughter before he saw them, the stony chuckle of the river goddess and the rasp of the High Lord.

"And then," the river goddess was saying, "and *then* one of the mermen jumped on the stern of the boat and shouted, 'Come get me, sailor!'"

"Oh, humans," Beaufort said, chuckling. "I'm still not sure how they got mermen and sirens mixed up."

"Wishful thinking," Agatha said, dabbling a paw in the stream where it ran into a deep, clear pool between the trees. "Oh, hello, Mortimer."

"Hello," he said. "Not interrupting, am I?"

"Of course not, lad," Beaufort said. He was sittting with his back against a tree, gazing across the pool with old gold eyes. "Catching up on old times, is all. How long since you've been up to the lake, Ags?"

"Oh, eighty, ninety years," she said, her paw turning to liquid in the water. "Since the farming got too intense. The water started tasting a bit off."

"You should come by again," Beaufort said. "It's got better, hasn't it, lad?"

"It has," Mortimer said. "The humans are learning about all that sort of thing."

"Takes them long enough," the goddess said. "You know, poison the water and the air, then a century or so later realise they should clean up the mess before it chokes them. Too late for everyone else, of course."

"It's because they don't live very long," Beaufort said. "They don't think in the right terms."

The goddess blew a divine raspberry. "You're so soft, B. How have you survived this long?"

He gave her a ragged, toothy smile. "Survival's not about being hard. It's about being adaptable. You know that."

"Ugh. Spare me the dragonish moralising." She slipped into the water, blending into the stream until only her snout showed. "You going to be around for a bit?"

"A few days."

"I'll catch up with you." Then she was gone, not even a ripple to mark where she'd been. Or she wasn't visible, anyway. Mortimer didn't think that river spirits were ever actually gone. That's what made it so hard, as their tributaries were dammed or dug up or dried out. They were still there, whether they wanted to be or not, feeling the pain of their missing streams like a phantom limb.

"You alright there, lad?" Beaufort asked. "Did you get bored of the pond and tree talk?"

"It wasn't too bad."

Beaufort rolled onto his feet. "Are you sure? Mabel told me three times about a new lichen she found on an oak tree and how she's worried it might be an invasive species, then spent half an hour talking about squirrels. Pat kept talking about it being tadpole season and the importance of allowing the birds their share while still protecting enough tadpoles to ensure the gene pool continues, and I'm not even going to mention Steve. I think he spends an awful lot of time in that wine cellar he was on about."

Mortimer snorted. "Well, true. It's not exactly afternoon tea with the W.I. And snails are not scones."

"Oh, I could just do with a scone," Beaufort said. "I wonder if they've gone to bed yet?"

"We can't go inside," Mortimer said. "There are all the new people about, and the whole place seems very crowded. I don't like it. And shouldn't we be going home, really? Making sure everything's alright?"

Beaufort gave him an amused, sideways glance, then headed off through the trees. "Are you really that worried about leaving Amelia and Gilbert unsupervised for three days?"

Mortimer hurried after him. "No! Of course not! But, you know, there is a *lot* to do—"

"Amelia will have it all in hand, lad. Relax. We'll do some more of the yoghurt thing tomorrow. I think it'll be very good for you if you'll just let yourself go."

Mortimer thought of Beaufort snoring flames over the topiary and wondered if letting oneself go was really such a good thing. "Aren't you worried about Lord Margery? I mean, she did try and take over the clan at Christmas. Should you have left her in charge?"

"Who else would I leave in charge?" Beaufort sounded honestly curious. "Lord Walter?"

Mortimer pictured the ancient dragon stomping about the caverns shouting at everyone and railing against the very existence of humanity. "Well, no. Definitely not." *He'd probably start the first dragon/human war,* he added to himself, but didn't say.

"There we go, then. Margery will look after things wonderfully, and Amelia will make sure Gilbert only makes appropriate baubles. Plus I quite like being away for a bit. It's nice to have a little change of scenery. Do you think we should take a holiday, Mortimer?"

"A *what?*" Mortimer tripped over a stick and bumped his chin. "Ow."

"A holiday. You know, go and see things somewhere else. And buy fridge magnets."

"Fridge magnets?"

"Yes. Maybe mugs. That is what people do on holiday, isn't it? Buy things and get sunburned?"

Mortimer was having visions of Beaufort wandering around some Mediterranean beach town with a straw donkey in one paw, a fruity cocktail in the other, and a sun hat on. The damp, cool air under the trees was unaccountably hard to breathe. "I – I guess it depends on the holiday?" he gasped.

"Very good point. Because you wouldn't get sunburned if you went to Iceland, say." Beaufort trotted on through the forest with his head high and his wings folded against his back. "But I think somewhere warm might be nice, don't you?"

Mortimer shook his head, wondering if Mabel's birch cordial had been mildly hallucinogenic. Hoping it was, to be honest. You never could tell with dryads, and it was a much better option than imagining Beaufort on holiday. "I've never heard of dragons going on holiday."

"High time we started, then, isn't it?"

Mortimer couldn't for the life of him come up with an argument that wasn't just, *No, Beaufort, that's a really bad idea,* which he knew from experience was pointless, so he just focused on his breathing and padded after the High Lord. Trees leaned over them in a friendly manner, and they left the path of the stream to pick up a trail that wound faintly through the heavy cover of the woods, heading toward the manor house. One thing at a time. He'd tackle the holiday problem after he'd figured out how to convince Beaufort that yoga and spa weekends weren't for dragons.

"SOMEONE'S OUT HERE," Beaufort said, coming to a stop and taking on the muted greys and browns of the deep shadows under the trees.

Mortimer froze, the colour running out of his scales. "Where?"

"*Shh.*"

They stayed where they were, the night whispering softly through the trees, a breeze rumpling the leaves above them and night birds calling to each other dubiously, less disturbed by the dragons than the other, unidentified intruders. They were too far from the house for any stray light to reach them, and the dark was deep under the cover of the trees. The dragons' prismed eyes collected the tiniest scraps of illumination, but even so, the shadows were dense.

Then the warm, familiar scent of coffee drifted to them over the rich damp smells of the woods, and a moment later came the flicker of a torch somewhere further down the trail.

"Keith, can we go yet?" someone asked.

"Quiet," another voice said. "You're going to draw attention to us."

"There's no one here."

"Well, there certainly won't be if you keep whingeing," a third voice said.

"I'm not whingeing, I'm just saying—"

"*Shh!* Did you hear that?"

Mortimer and Beaufort exchanged glances. They hadn't heard

anything, and Mortimer was certain their hearing was rather better than the birdwatchers'.

"Are they really out looking for birds at this time of night?" he whispered to the High Lord.

"Owls?" Beaufort suggested. "Although you did notice that they said no *one*, of course."

"Of course," Mortimer said, feeling his snout flushing an embarrassed lilac. There was a pause, then he added, "Which means they're expecting a person, rather than birds."

"Yes."

"Yes." Mortimer thought about if for a moment, then gave a strangled little gasp. "But they were on the terrace! What if they were just pretending they didn't see us? What if they're looking for us? What if—"

"Do you remember those monster hunters that came to the village, Mortimer?"

"What— Well, yes. But it was all for TV. They didn't even believe in it." The monster hunters had been investigating the rumours that the pond was bottomless, but had rather reckoned without an angry water sprite setting a horde of geese on them. The question of bottomlessness had remained unanswered, but the goose attack had made for exciting footage.

"Quite. *They* didn't believe in it, but I rather imagine a number of their viewers did."

"But they didn't get anything on camera."

"It's a curious thing I've noticed about humans, Mortimer. Sometimes they believe the most when there's no evidence. And these ones did seem to have rather a lot of electronic-y things for birdwatchers, didn't you think?"

Mortimer gave a little strangled noise that indicated agreement of a rather reluctant sort.

Beaufort gave a good-humoured huff. "Never mind, lad. Leave them to it. Even if they are looking for something other than birds, they won't find it – anyone with half an ear can hear them a mile off." The High Lord set off down the trail toward the voices, and after another turn or so they found the three men occupied with cable – tying cameras to branches and positioning furry microphones in the trees.

"One more here," the shortest one said. "Then we'll have the trails covered. I still think we should set something up nearer the stream, though. They love streams and stuff."

"How do you know, Saul?"

"Well, they've got to drink, right? Like in those wildlife shows – the animals always come back to the stream."

"You know how many waterways are in these woods?" a skinny man asked. "They've got plenty of choice."

"Yeah, well. Have to start somewhere, right?"

"It'd help if *someone* hadn't lost the other GoPro," the third man said.

"Dammit, Keith," the skinny man snapped. "I didn't *lose* the GoPro. Someone must have tidied it away. We'll ask in the morning."

Beaufort scratched his chin and looked at Mortimer, who was huddled on his belly among the tree trunks, wishing they could go. The High Lord blended nicely with the gravel and leaf litter on the trail, but to anyone expecting them, there was very obviously a dragon sitting next to one of the men's camouflage print backpacks.

"Would you like a biscuit?" the High Lord asked.

"*What?*" Mortimer hissed.

"There's half a pack of chocolate Hobnobs here."

"I'd really rather just go—"

"You're right." Beaufort plucked the biscuits out of the bag and set off down the path with the packet gripped in his teeth. "Let's go see if anyone's around. Maybe we can get a cuppa to go with these," he added, slightly muffled by the biscuits.

"Did you hear something?" the skinny man asked, turning to shine his headlamp toward the dragons and making Mortimer dive into the undergrowth.

"Chill out, Marv. It's just the wind."

"It kind of sounded like voices."

Mortimer stuck to the soft earth at the side of the trail and scampered after Beaufort, who was walking straight down the centre of the path, entirely unconcerned.

"Beaufort," the younger dragon began, but got no further, because at that moment a scream rose in the night, muffled by the house and the distance, but unmistakable anyway. The dragons looked at each other in horror, then the High Lord dropped the biscuits and broke into a thundering gallop, stones spinning away under his paws, the trees too tight on either side for him to take flight. Mortimer plunged after him, hearing the men behind them dropping their equipment with shouts of alarm and following. The night rose dark and suddenly unfriendly around them, and as he ran Mortimer hoped deep in his dragonish heart that it wasn't one of the W.I.

Please, no, he thought, the breath rasping in his throat as he ran, not even sure who he was asking. *Please, not them.*

5

DI ADAMS

The scream brought DI Adams out of sleep so fast she found herself gasping for air. She tried to sit up, disoriented and unsure of where she was, wondering why it was so dark when the streetlights usually bled orange luminescence into her apartment. The scream came again, clearer this time, full of panic and terror, and she tried to push herself up. The bedclothes were unaccountably heavy, and for one panicked moment she thought she'd been tied down. Then the bedding moved, she gave a yelp of fright that almost swallowed a third scream from downstairs, and she scrambled out of the bed and fumbled the lights on. The carpet dog sat in the middle of the bed, wagging his dreadlocked tail at her.

"What the *hell?*" she demanded, but before the dog could offer any sort of explanation for appearing in her locked room another shriek rose into the night. She kicked her feet into trainers, grabbed her walking jacket, and ran out into the hall, almost colliding with Miriam, who squeaked and waved a jug at her.

"Put that down," DI Adams said, pushing past her and spotting Alice and Gert already at the top of the stairs, armed with those

Nordic walking sticks people use when they get all overenthusiastic and start buying Lycra. "And you two can put those down, too."

Gert gave a reluctant grimace, and Alice just smiled. "If you say so, Inspector."

"I do." People were emerging from rooms and crowding around the mezzanine balcony, staring into the shadowy foyer.

"Hey," the journalist said, appearing at her elbow. "What's going on? Did you hear those screams?"

DI Adams scowled at him, and Alice said, "No, of course not. We're just having a little W.I. pyjama party on the stairs at"—she glanced at her watch—"quarter past midnight."

Ervin grinned as if Alice had shared a private joke with him, and DI Adams said, "Stay here, all of you." The screaming had stopped, and she liked the silence even less. She ran down the stairs, hearing the inevitable rush of slippers and bare feet behind her. Because of course they hadn't listened. They *never* listened. She wondered briefly if all ladies of a certain age were this bloody impossible, or just these ones, then found the lights on the wall and flooded the foyer with light.

THE ENTRANCE HALL WAS EMPTY, the doors still shut. DI Adams found the dining room lights, but it felt deserted even before she'd put them on, and it was the matter of a moment to check around the tables. She turned back into the foyer, and found the Women's Institute gathered at the foot of the stairs, looking on with interest. Ervin was trying the main door.

"Open," he announced, peering out into the night.

"Apparently," DI Adams said, and crossed to the lounge. There were a couple of dim, red-shaded lamps still on, and she was halfway through the thicket of low tables and fat chairs before she spotted Holt huddled in the depths of a sofa, clutching a glass to his chest and trying to look inconspicuous.

"What're you doing?" she demanded.

"Um." He raised the glass unsteadily.

Behind her, DI Adams heard a distinctly Alice huff of disapproval. "Go to bed, sir," she said.

"Yeah. Will do. Just …" he raised his glass again, showing them it wasn't empty, and the DI scowled at him, but couldn't waste any more time. She headed for the doors to the breakfast room, pushing through them into a deeper darkness, the clusters of chairs and tables grey shadows in the thin moonlight and the green glow of an emergency exit sign that was hanging askew.

"Police," she announced to the room. "Please stay where you are." She patted the wall as she waited for a response, found the switch and flooded the room with harsh light. It was empty, white tablecloths crowned with cutlery and glasses, waiting for diners.

"Hello?" she called. "Respond if you can."

Still nothing, and she crossed to the orangery door, checking the corners of the breakfast room and under the tables as she went. There was nothing, and she ducked into the orangery itself, finding only cushioned cane chairs and rambling plants, the night dark against the glass. She turned back and saw Alice and Gert standing in the lounge doors while the journalist peered over their shoulders. Neither woman seemed inclined to move.

There were two more doors out of the breakfast room, one marked *Private*, the other *Treatment Rooms*. *Private* probably gave onto a whole other area of the house. *Treatment Rooms* probably had no other exit. She glanced at Alice, and the older woman nodded slightly. She might not be very good at following orders, but she appeared to be quite efficient at holding journalists at bay.

Ervin caught the detective inspector's eye. "Let me through," he said. "I'll stay out of the way."

"No," Gert said, before DI Adams could reply.

"I'm the *press*."

"And I'm *unimpressed*," Gert said, looking inordinately pleased with herself. Ervin gaped at her.

DI Adams turned back to the treatment room door and opened it warily, letting out a draught of warm air scented heavily with essential oils. There were lights on inside, low and warm, and a lot of purple. Purple walls, purple cushions, purple flowers. And, in the corner, someone with soft white-blonde hair was curled into a ball, crying.

"Ma'am?" DI Adams said, crossing to her warily. The woman gave a shriek, scrabbling at the floor with one bare foot and one slippered one as she tried to push herself further into the wall. "Detective Inspector Adams, West Yorkshire Police. Are you hurt?"

The woman just cried harder, and the inspector crouched down a couple of metres away, examining her. There didn't seem to be any blood. "I'm here to help," she said. "What's your name?"

The woman risked a peek over her shoulder, just quickly, but it was enough for DI Adams to recognise the woman who had sat across the table at dinner. One of the antique dealers. "Lottie?"

Lottie took a whooping gasp of air, then wailed, "*He's dead!*"

"Who? Who's dead, Lottie?"

She just pointed to a curtain (purple, of course) hung over another doorway, then started crying again. Someone had started shouting for Lottie out in the breakfast room, but DI Adams ignored it and went to push the curtain aside. Beyond was a lounge area dotted with soft lavender chairs and lined with big windows overlooking the terrace. The smell of essential oils was stronger in here, and there were three more doors on the back wall. The first two said *Treatment Room 1*, and *Treatment Room 2*. She couldn't see what the third said, because it was open, and a body was sprawled face down on the floor in the doorway.

THE BODY WAS the white of cellar mushrooms, the back broad and muscular and somewhat hairy. DI Adams crouched next to it, tried to find a pulse, then rolled it over, not without some difficulty in the confines of the doorway. It was Keeley, his eyes wide open and staring in a perplexed way into the distance as if he wasn't quite sure how he had got there. He was wearing nothing but a towel that was a little too small for his frame, and DI Adams established an airway, then checked for breathing and pulse again. There was still nothing, and she hadn't expected there to be. She could see the first bruising of lividity on his chest and belly, which usually meant he'd been dead a couple of hours. But the heat still pumping out the open sauna door made the place all but tropical, so it could have been less.

She rocked back on her heels, hands loose between her knees as she examined the wood-lined room. There was a glass and a half-full bottle of bourbon sitting just outside the sauna itself, on the little shelves under the towel hooks, and the sous-chef's clothes were abandoned in the middle of the floor. Nothing knocked over, nothing broken. She got up, pulling her phone from her jacket and opening the camera as she peeked into the bin in the corner of the room. A wrapper from a chocolate bar, which seemed impractical eating in a sauna, and an essential oil box.

"Lottie!" someone screamed beyond the treatment rooms again, and this time Lottie gave a little wail in response. DI Adams gave an annoyed little growl and got up to deal with the living people, since it seemed they weren't dealing with themselves.

Lottie was still tucked into the corner of the room, her wide eyes on the door, and this time she didn't pull away when the inspector went to help her up.

"Are you hurt?" DI Adams asked her again, and she shook her head. "Did you see anyone else down here?"

Another shake of the head, and this time Lottie whispered, "I only wanted a cup of tea."

"In the treatment rooms?"

Lottie started crying again, and DI Adams managed not to grimace as she supported the tiny woman through the door into the breakfast room. This was the part of the job she always tried to avoid.

"*Lottie!*" Edie screamed, and somehow managed to shove both Gert and Alice out of the way as she flung herself toward the smaller woman, who'd let go of DI Adams and was tottering forward on her own. "Oh, Lottie, are you alright?"

Lottie burst into fresh tears, and DI Adams squeezed the bridge of her nose, eyeing the women in the doorway. Ervin had tried to take the opportunity to slip past the W.I. defences, but Gert had him wedged against the door frame. His face was an uncomfortable shade of red, and he waved at her rather desperately.

She ignored him and took her phone out again. "Has anyone got coverage?"

"The signal here can be a little iffy," Alice said.

"It's not iffy. It's non-existent."

Alice smiled. "Country living, Inspector."

"This is why I don't agree with it." She jammed the phone back into her pocket, scowling.

"We'll have to use the landline," Alice said.

DI Adams glanced around, then crossed to the door marked *Private* and pulled it open, barely containing a yelp as it revealed four forms crouching in a narrow hall. "What're you doing?" she asked.

Maddie looked at the poker she was brandishing, gave a little squeak, and lowered it hurriedly. "We didn't know if it was safe."

"What's happened?" Adele asked from behind her, not moving from an attack pose with an umbrella.

"I need to use a landline, and I need the keys to the treatment rooms," DI Adams said. "It's Keeley." She didn't take her gaze from

Reid – hovering behind his mother with a coal shovel – as she spoke.

"*Keeley?*" Maddie said. "Oh, *no!* Is he going to be alright?"

"Not so much."

Boyd made a small unhappy noise, looking for once as if he had no poetry left in him, and Reid said, "Well, I hope no one thinks *I* did anything. Be a bit bloody stupid, wouldn't it?"

DI Adams just watched him.

He shifted uncomfortably. "Well, it would!"

"No one ever said you were a brain surgeon," Adele said.

"*Hey—*" Reid began, and his mother talked over him.

"Stop it, both of you," she said. "Reid, go get the keys from the office."

"But—"

"Go get them."

Reid screwed up his face as if he was trying to think of a stinging response, then turned and stomped back down the hall.

"Is – is he *dead?*" Boyd asked, and Lottie, still wrapped in Edie's arms, gave a surprisingly powerful howl.

"I just wanted a cup of tea!" she wailed. "Just a tea!"

"Oh, well done," Edie said. "Just wonderful."

"I told you this house needed cleansing," Adele told Maddie, who scowled at her.

DI Adams winced as Lottie's crying threatened to shatter the glasses on the table, and Boyd said, "I was just *asking.*"

She started to tell everyone to go back to bed, but was cut off by a wall-shuddering crash from beyond the lounge.

"What was that?" Maddie asked, her eyes wide.

"No idea," the inspector said, although she had a nasty feeling it might be dragon-related. She headed for the door to the lounge, where Ervin had already vanished and Alice and Gert were peering toward the foyer. "No one goes in the treatment rooms, okay?" She was almost having to shout over the sirening Lottie.

Alice moved aside to let her through, snapping her fingers at Boyd. "Get her some whisky."

"Sorry?" he said, looking confused.

"You set her off, you get her some whisky. And a blanket. Hurry!"

He gave her an alarmed look and scampered back down the hall, and DI Adams headed into the warm low light of the lounge, stopping short as Miriam rushed in from the foyer. Her face was even pinker than usual and her hair was standing up at strange angles.

"It's all good!" she said, her voice a little too bright. "Under control! Absolutely!"

Given the choice between dealing with the Toot Hansell Women's Institute and securing a crime scene, DI Adams would choose the latter every time, but she had doubts that anything was under control. "Show me," she said with a sigh.

Miriam backed away with a squeak and hurried back to the foyer. DI Adams followed her, noticing that the American had vanished at some stage. She stopped in the archway, staring at the front doors that were hanging ajar with an unhappy, broken-hinged droop. The ladies of the W.I. were milling about in their dressing gowns and nighties, clutching torches and walking sticks, chattering loudly and doing quite a good job of hiding the two dragons that were huddled at the foot of the stairs. They were trying to blend into the chequered tiles, and doing a terrible job of it. Mortimer was cycling from blue to grey, never quite settling on a colour, and looked like he was going to throw up at any moment.

Ervin was standing in the middle of the floor staring at the door with his arms crossed over his chest. "Who did *that*?"

"I did," Rose said before the inspector could do more than glare at him. The tiny woman stood in the middle of the floor with her hands on her hips and her feet planted firmly apart, wearing walking boots and pyjamas.

"What?" the journalist said.

"Tai chi," Rose replied, and looked back at the door. "It was locked, and there was shouting outside, so I just channelled my energy. I may have channelled a little too much, though."

"Right," Ervin said. A careful sort of look had crept over his face, as if he thought he might be getting a little out of his depth. Then he swallowed and said, "So, who was shouting?"

"Mister," DI Adams began, then waved at him impatiently.

"Ervin," he said. "You haven't forgotten me already?"

"Ervin ...?"

"Yes?"

"*Your last name*," she said, trying not to shout and wondering if there was a good place for locking people up around here. The cellar, maybe.

"Giles."

"Mr Giles," she started again, but Rose talked over her.

"They were shouting," she said, and pointed at the three bird-watchers hovering just outside the door, clutching their cameras and looking as alarmed by the W.I. as they were by everything else. They were fully dressed in their camouflage gear and woolly hats, headlamps strapped to their foreheads and jeans tucked into their mud-encrusted walking boots. One of them was looking at the mud the dragons had tracked across the floor with an expression that said quite clearly he expected to get blamed for it.

"Right." DI Adams rubbed her face, took a deep breath, and tried to spot someone who would be listened to. "Miriam," she said, and the older woman squeaked again, which wasn't a good start. But she'd been very handy with a cricket bat when there were goblins to deal with. "Can you make sure everyone heads upstairs? Everything is under control," she added, a little more loudly. "You can all go get some rest."

"I can do that," Miriam said, and looked at the W.I. expectantly. There was a pause.

"Bed," Priya declared, and clapped her hands. There was a general movement toward the stairs, the dragons sneaking along with the women, and DI Adams looked at the journalist.

"That includes you, Mr Giles."

"I'm entirely within my rights to remain down here and observe."

DI Adams gave him a tight smile. "Of course you are," she said. "But you won't see much from in here."

"I can wait," he said.

"You can do whatever you want as long as you stay out of my way," the inspector said, and headed back into the lounge.

DI Adams sat down at the table across from Lottie and Edie, and tried her best to look friendly and approachable. Judging from the sudden renewed crying from Lottie and the way Edie glared at her, she'd achieved threatening instead. She gave up on the having a friendly chat idea and went back to businesslike. She'd always been most comfortable with that. The treatment rooms were locked, and she'd sent Alice and Gert away, not without some difficulty. Now she clasped her hands together on the table and leaned forward.

"Lottie," she said. "I know this must be such an awful shock, but can you try and answer a couple of questions for me?"

"I can't believe you're doing this right now," Edie snapped, rubbing the back of Lottie's head and pushing it more firmly against her bosom. She had quite a formidable bosom for someone so skinny, DI Adams thought.

"The sooner I can ask these questions, the sooner you can both go back to bed and try and get some sleep."

"Sleep *here?* We're not staying here! As soon as Lottie's feeling a little calmer we'll be packing up and going!"

"I can see how you'd prefer to do that," DI Adams said. "But it'd be really helpful if you didn't. There has been a death, and some questions have to be asked—"

"Are you *accusing* Lottie of something?" Edie was clutching the smaller woman so hard now that the inspector was actually having some concerns about whether she could breathe. That would put a new angle on the treatment of suspects in questioning. No over-comforting. She shook her head slightly. Apparently she was more tired than she thought. And it wasn't as though Lottie was a suspect, either. What possible motive would she have for killing the sous-chef, and how on earth would she even do it? He could have picked her up in one hand.

"No one's accusing anyone of anything," she said aloud. "It's routine questions." Routine. Ha. Nothing was ever routine where the Toot Hansell Women's Institute was concerned. She rolled her shoulders and tried for a smile again. "It's just much easier to get it out of the way here and now, rather than having to come into a police station at a later date, when you really just want to be forgetting about the whole thing."

"We'd like to forget the whole thing right now," Edie said.

Lottie pushed herself away from the taller woman, running shaking hands over her fine hair. "It's alright, Edie. It really is. I'll answer her questions."

"Lottie, I don't think—"

"It's alright," she repeated, using both hands to pick up the whisky glass Boyd had brought out. Her eyes and nose were red, and she spilt a little of the drink as she sipped it. She wiped her chin with one hand, a curiously indelicate gesture, and nodded at DI Adams. "Ask what you want."

"Thank you." DI Adams watched her for a moment longer. Her cheeks weren't wet, but she imagined Edie's substantial bosom had dried them quite well. Lottie looked small and scared and tired, just the way you'd expect someone to if they came across a body in the middle of the night. It made the inspector uneasy. She wasn't used to people reacting just the way you expected them to. In her experience, things rarely worked that way. She tapped her fingers on the table and said, "Why were you in the treatment rooms at quarter past midnight, Lottie?"

"I just wanted a cup of tea," she said, and her voice wobbled momentarily before she got herself under control again. "I couldn't sleep after all that rich food, and I thought a cup of tea might settle me."

"Don't you have a tea station in your room?"

"Yes, but then I would have woken Edie." She looked at the other women, who put a hand against her cheek gently.

"I wouldn't have cared."

"You always wake so early. I didn't want to wake you in the middle of the night too." Lottie turned a lopsided smile on DI Adams. "Edie's the early bird. I'm the night owl."

"I understand," the inspector said, making a quick note on the paper she'd taken from Maddie. She'd rather her notebook, but it was better than nothing. "So you wanted a cup of tea. But surely you saw everything was closed up for the night?"

"Well, yes. But Maddie's so nice, and she did say to make ourselves at home ..." Lottie trailed off, fixing DI Adams with wide, unhappy eyes. "I looked in the lounge first, and that American gentleman was still there – I think he was a little drunk, actually." She stared at DI Adams until the inspector made a little *keep going* gesture. Holt had looked more than a little drunk to her, but he hadn't been the one stumbling over bodies. He'd keep till later. "Well," Lottie continued, "there's this big coffee machine in there, but I wasn't going to turn *that* on. So I thought maybe there'd be a tea station in the treatment rooms. You know, for the clients, rather than the beauty therapist having to go find one."

The inspector nodded. "That makes sense. Did you find one?"

"Well, no. I mean, I walked in and the sauna room was open— he was— the door—" She choked to a stop, one hand flat against her chest, and Edie put her arms around the smaller woman, glaring at DI Adams. "I think that's enough. You can't make her relive it like this."

"I'm really very sorry. It must have been a huge shock, Lottie."

"It *was*," she whispered. "The poor, poor man. He must have been trying to unwind in there, and ... and I don't know. A heart attack, maybe?"

"I wouldn't like to guess," DI Adams said. "I'm sure the medical examiner will clear all that up."

"The medical examiner?"

"Well, he was a young man. They'll need to determine cause of death. You didn't touch him, did you, Lottie?"

"No! Oh, no." She shook her head firmly. "I— he was just lying there, and when he didn't move— well, I knew he was— he was *dead*, so I just— the shock, you know. I screamed. I'm sorry. I must have woken everyone, but I just couldn't—" She stopped again, sniffling, and took a large mouthful of whisky. "I suppose that was wrong, wasn't it? I should have checked to see if he was breathing."

"You did fine," DI Adams said, rolling the pen in her fingers. It all made perfect sense, didn't it? Which didn't sit right at all. She sighed. "I'd appreciate it if you'd stay here at least for tonight, so the local investigators can ask you any questions they need to tomorrow."

"We can stay," Lottie said.

"Really?" Edie asked her. "Will you sleep, knowing this happened?"

"Probably not," the smaller woman said, giving her an uneven smile. "But I want to help. And it must have been an accident. A horrible, horrible accident. They happen all the time. It was just my bad luck to stumble on it, is all."

"Well. If you're sure." Edie looked at the inspector. "If you're quite finished, then, I think I have some herbal tablets that might help Lottie sleep, if we're lucky."

"I'm finished," DI Adams said, and watched Edie help Lottie to her feet and lead her through the door into the lounge and away. She poked her signal-less phone with one finger and sighed. The techs would be here soon, breaking the scene down into photographs and fibres, and so would the DI in charge. The case would be out of her hands. If it even was a case. She tapped her fingertips on the table, picked up the cordless phone Maddie had handed her, and entered the number off her phone screen. It only rang twice.

"DI Collins," the voice on the other end said, made hollow by the Bluetooth in the car.

"Collins," she said.

"Adams! What do you have for me? Goblins? Dragons? Unicorns?"

"I'm pretty sure that last one is fictional."

"I'm not ruling anything out after last year," he said, and she touched the scar on her wrist, remnant of the Christmas goblin attack. Collins had escaped with just singed hair.

"Well, this isn't one of those cases."

"You know you could just pop in for a cuppa. You don't have to keep finding crimes to come visit."

"I'm starting to have doubts about your peaceful countryside."

"I think you bring it with you," he said, and she snorted. "So, foul play?"

"It looks like an accident."

"But?"

She hesitated. "But he's young. The odds of someone his age just up and having a heart attack in a sauna? I mean, sure, could be drugs, definitely alcohol involved. But still. Something feels off."

"Who've you talked to?"

"Just the woman who found the body. Might be another witness, but he's passed out."

"Reliable."

"Yep."

"And no one's left the house."

"No."

"Other impressions, Adams?"

She looked around the empty room and at the deep country night pressing against the windows, and wished he hadn't asked about *impressions*. *Impressions* are terribly subjective. She didn't like subjective. But then, she'd been the one that said something seemed off, hadn't she? She wondered if the W.I. were proving to be a bad influence on her. "Nothing I can put my finger on," she said finally.

"Well, then." She heard him yawn. "I'll be with you in forty minutes or so, then we can go look at a body."

"I get to do the most fun things with you."

"I knew that's why you were hanging around."

He was still chuckling when she hung up, staring at the finely carved moulding circling the ceiling. No, it didn't seem to be one of *those* cases. And maybe it really was an accident. But then again, maybe it wasn't.

She wondered if she'd be able to get a coffee. There were some little sachets of fake cappuccino in her room, which was even worse than the normal instant coffee she'd brought with her, and she didn't think she could cope with Collins without some proper caffeine. She got up and went to find some.

ALICE MET her in the lounge. She walked with perfectly trained RAF bearing, but the inspector had a feeling Alice had always walked like that. If she had ever been a little girl – and the DI harboured some doubts – she probably made her stuffed toys stand the same way.

"So?" Alice asked.

"The local police are on the way," DI Adams said. "You can go to bed, Alice."

"If you don't need anything else. Should we be worried?"

"No. It looks like an accident. A heart attack or a stroke, and he tried to get out of the sauna to get help and fell."

"The poor man."

There was a moment of silence, and DI Adams clasped her hands together and said, "Whether it's an accident or not, I don't want anyone poking around or asking questions, alright? Think of Maddie and the other guests."

Alice lifted her chin slightly. "We don't willingly get involved in murder investigations, DI Adams."

"Really? Because I can think of one murder and one kidnapping that you were very involved in."

"We were implicated in one, and the dragons in the other. This is nothing to do with us."

"Good. Well – keep it that way." She tried to sound stern, but was quite sure it was wasted on Alice.

"Well. I guess I shall get some sleep." Alice straightened the cuffs of her dressing gown. It was grey and tasteful and rather neatly tailored, although DI Adams could see some cat hair clinging to the collar. So Thompson, the Watch cat that had adopted Alice at Christmas, hadn't moved out. It was slightly reassuring to think that even Alice couldn't avoid stray cat hair. She smiled.

The chair of the W.I. smiled back. "Nice pyjamas."

DI Adams looked down at the cartoon hedgehogs dancing across the trousers and said, "Thanks." She just hoped Alice never saw the truly bad pun on the top, hidden under her jacket. She could stand many things, but Alice knowing she loved very bad puns was not one of them.

6

MIRIAM

When DI Adams returned to the crime scene, Miriam found herself left somewhat uncomfortably in charge of the last few members of the W.I and the journalist. He scowled at her as the others made their way upstairs. "I'm not one of your party, and I'm not going to be ordered away from a story," he said.

"No one's ordering you away from it," she said, as firmly as she could.

"You can't force me to go upstairs," he insisted.

"Of course we can't," Rose said, looking up at him with wide, bright eyes. He shuffled away from her, then jerked backward when she put her hand on his arm.

"*What?*"

"Do you want to see how I busted the door open?" she asked.

"How …? No. Look, there's a story here. Even if it's an accidental death one, it's my duty to report it."

"It absolutely is," Miriam said, crowding a little closer. "And it's very important, too."

Ervin looked at his feet as if they'd betrayed him by leading him to the first stair. "You can't hide things from the press, you know."

"No one's doing that," Miriam said. "We just don't want a panic. And we have children staying here, too. Think of them. Everyone needs to stay calm and out of the way."

"I don't see why I can't just shadow the inspector quietly," Ervin began, half turning as if he was going to push his way back to the lounge, and Miriam wondered if she should have brought a cricket bat. Not to *hurt* him. Just for emphasis. He stopped short as Gert and Alice appeared in the foyer, blocking his path. "I'm just doing my job!"

"That's what they all say," Gert said, and the journalist looked bewildered.

"Who?"

Gert waved. "All of them."

Ervin looked at Alice, who nodded. "They do."

In desperation, he tried making eye contact with the bird-watchers, but they were very studiously ignoring everyone, and he raised his hands in surrender. "Fine," he said. "I get it. I'll go."

He turned and headed up the stairs, still complaining about journalistic integrity, or rights, or something along those lines. Miriam mostly tuned him out as she followed. She was all for everyone's rights until it came to the point where they endangered dragons. And because dragons were *actually* endangered, never mind their rights, she felt their need to remain secret rather outweighed the need of a journalist to go poking around where some poor person had passed away. Besides, it felt icky and distasteful. Imagine being so excited because someone had *died!* Never mind the awful impact on the poor man's family and friends, as well as on Maddie's. It put a terribly nasty note to the weekend, as far as she was concerned, but young Ervin looked like he'd woken up to discover it was Christmas Eve. She frowned at him as he hesitated on the midpoint landing, peering down into the foyer. Alice and Gert were talking quietly below.

"There really is nothing to see," she told him. "DI Adams has everything under control, and she won't be letting you or anyone else near the, the …" What did you say in this situation? *Deceased* was terribly cold, and *body* made the skin at the back of her neck break out in goosebumps. "… treatment room," she finished triumphantly.

"Yes, but what's going on, really? People don't just drop dead for no reason, especially not someone as young as him."

"We don't know the whole situation," Miriam said, stepping onto the landing and making herself as, well, *solid* as she could. She was neither as tall nor as well-muscled as Gert, but she could definitely be *solid* when she fancied it. And right now she fancied it.

"Did she even try CPR? She was barely in there five minutes. She didn't have time. Why didn't she try?"

Miriam frowned at him. "I'm sure she had a reason." Although she didn't like to think about what that reason was. She hoped it hadn't been an unpleasant death. Was there such a thing as a pleasant death? She supposed there must be, but she doubted it happened in a manor house spa treatment room. And, either way, she was fairly sure that the deceased wouldn't have wanted some journalist pawing around them. She knew she wouldn't.

"Look, I know you're trying to help out the inspector and so on, but you can just say I got away from you. I'm not going to mess up a crime scene or anything—"

He stopped as Miriam put both hands on her hips, gathered all the dignity her multi-coloured polka-dot dressing gown could afford her, and hissed, "Go to bed!"

He stared at her with a look on his face that she rather thought his mother would have recognised – a mix of reluctance, stubbornness, and the distinct sense that he was looking for a way out – then Rose peered under Miriam's elbow from a step lower down.

"Are we stuck?" she asked. "Because I could clear the steps. You know, like the door."

Ervin scowled at her. "I don't believe even slightly that you broke the door."

"Are you sure?" Rose asked cheerfully. "Because I can demonstrate."

Miriam wondered what would happen if Ervin did tell her to demonstrate. She didn't think Rose could destroy any doors, but she wouldn't put it past her to try. And then they really would need an ambulance. Rose shifted her position on the step, centred her breath, and floated her hands out in front of her, palms toward Ervin and fingers curled in. "My favourite move is the dance of the dead pigeon," she said. "It's very elegant."

Ervin's frustrated little boy look vanished, and he just shook his head at them both. "I don't know what's wrong with you," he said. "But I think there is something, you know." Then he turned and trotted up the stairs, still grumbling.

Miriam and Rose looked at each other. "That was very rude of him," Miriam said.

"I know," Rose said. "Imagine not believing me like that!"

Miriam clasped her hands in front of her. "That wasn't what I meant. And, to be fair, you didn't really knock the door down."

"That's no excuse for not believing me," Rose said. "He had no reason not to believe me." She sniffed, and pattered up the stairs, small as a child in her giraffe pyjamas. Miriam sighed, and checked the hall below. Gert was coming up the stairs and Alice had vanished, presumably to check on the inspector. The rest of the W.I. had already gone back to their rooms. The birdwatchers were still huddled by the crooked door, whispering to each other and passing the coffee flask around, but Miriam thought she'd just leave them there. They seemed pretty harmless, if a little *overenthusiastic*. At dinner, one had told her about some owl they were hoping to see, and he'd been so excited he'd knocked his wine glass over. She supposed it was always good to have a passion.

She climbed the stairs and paused at the top, checking that the journalist had actually gone. She didn't know which room was his, but the only door open had Holt peering out of it with red-rimmed eyes. At some point in the midst of dragons crashing through doors and the W.I descending to create a diversion and Edie running about the place screaming for Lottie, the big American had dragged himself away from the bar and vanished. His family had never even come downstairs, just huddled at the balcony above looking panicked, then scuttled away again.

"Any news?" he asked her.

"About what?"

He waved impatiently. "About what's going on. Is it safe? I don't trust the locks on these rooms, you know. Pretty flimsy. And I think someone's been meddling in our stuff."

She sniffed. "I rather doubt that. And there's nothing to worry about," she added, which was true. Well, true-ish. She was sure if there was a murderer running about the place, DI Adams would have told them. Probably.

"This was not what we expected, you know. We came to the country for a nice getaway, see some of this English refinement, y'know? Like Downton Abbey."

"Well. I'm sure everything'll be back to normal in the morning." She tried to give him a reassuring smile, but it was a bit hard to make her expression cooperate. Someone had *died*, and they were worried about their holiday? Horrid people.

"I hope so. I don't see how we'll ever be able to recommend our clients visit a place like this, though. Things running about in the walls, and stuff being moved around, and now this."

Miriam gave up on the smile. "Accidents happen. I'm sure poor Keeley didn't time his death just to inconvenience you." She turned and walked back to her own bedroom, her back straight and her hands trembling. Awful, *awful* people! Poor Maddie, having to put up with this. She wondered if she should go back downstairs and see if her sister needed some help, but she didn't know if it'd be welcome. Maddie had her children with her, plus Alice and DI Adams were down there, probably investigating. Still ...

She hesitated, looking at the closed doors of the hall. She should go back to her own room and wait for Alice. She wasn't going to sleep, but she should stay out of the way. The last thing anyone needed in a crisis was another busybody poking around. She stayed where she was for a moment longer, tapping her fingers on her crossed arms, thinking of Maddie and the fragile balance of the house, and that undefined yet strong sense that all was not as it should be.

She took a deep breath and turned back to the stairs, padding down them in bare feet and hoping there would be no unexpected running called for. It happened more often than she was comfortable with.

THE BIRDWATCHERS WERE STILL CLUSTERED by the door, and they stopped talking when she came down the last few stairs, looking at her expectantly. She smiled at them, straightening her dressing gown self-consciously.

"Everything alright?" the small one, Saul, asked.

"Yes," she said, then amended, "Well, you know. As much as it can be. You don't have to stay down here."

"We're just deciding whether to go back out again," the one that had been so enthusiastic about the owl said. Keith, if she remembered right.

"Oh, right. Must be pretty chilly out there by now."

They mumbled agreement, then just looked at her. She looked back, then nodded slightly. "Right. Okay. Well – have a good night?"

"Night," Keith said, and the rest made agreeable sounds. Miriam wandered away, the tile smooth and cold under her feet, thinking that there was a fine line between being passionate about something and being fanatical about it, and she wasn't quite sure just where the birdwatchers were sitting. She didn't fancy heading out in the dark if there was a murderer about the place. She shivered, and padded to the door under the rise of the stairs. The room beyond had once been some sort of music room, but Maddie had made it into an office, closing off access to the unused rooms and staff areas beyond.

She knocked on the door lightly, and almost yelped in fright when it was jerked immediately open.

"What?" Reid demanded, then sighed. "Oh, hello, Auntie Miriam." He sounded less than enthusiastic.

She gave him a small frown, making allowances for the fact that someone *had* just died, after all. "Hello, Reid. Is your mum there?"

"Yes. Come in." He stepped back, letting her into the brightly lit office, the old wood walls lined with newer shelves crammed with files and books and an eclectic mix of ancient jugs and horseshoes and mysterious bits of broken machinery. A big old desk sat at one end of the room, crowned with an incongruously modern monitor, and there were a few deep soft chairs around a coffee table in the middle. Every piece of spare wall space had a cabinet of some sort pushed against it, stacked and overflowing with drifts of invoice books and old receipts and postcards, held in place by gardening tools and plastic ducks. Old photos and bad paintings in mis-matched frames hung above them, peering through a thick layer of dust at the room. Boyd was sunk into one of the chairs, scribbling in a notebook, his lips moving as he wrote, and he didn't look up as Miriam came in. Adele, swamped in a huge purple blanket, rushed to give Miriam a hug. The young woman looked pale, her eyes swollen.

"Are you alright?" Miriam asked her, patting her back gently.

"Sort of," Adele whispered. "Isn't it awful, though?"

"Absolutely." Miriam looked over her shoulder at Maddie getting up from behind the desk. "How are you doing?" she asked.

"Fine. Well, sort of." Maddie rubbed her hands over her face and gave Miriam an awkward smile. "You know, as well as I can be with a dead body in the treatment room and a journalist upstairs." She laughed, a short little bark. "God, that sounds awful. I'm sorry. I didn't mean it like that."

"Well. Yes." Miriam disentangled herself from Adele and went to her little sister. Maddie didn't come out from behind the desk, cupping her elbows in her hands, so Miriam just leaned over and touched her shoulder lightly. "Can I do anything? Can I help?"

"Not really." Maddie looked from Reid to Adele as she spoke, her face all tight lines, and Miriam had the impression that if her sister unwrapped her arms it'd unravel her entirely, spooling her helplessly onto the floor. "Everyone should probably just get some sleep."

"Well." Miriam dropped her hand and glanced around the room. "If you're sure. But do let me know if I can do something."

"I'm sure we'll be fine, Miriam. But it's very nice of you." Her voice was tight, lady-of-the-manor expressionless.

"It's not about being *nice*, Mads. We're family. You don't have to do this on your own."

Maddie nodded, and finally let go of one elbow, pressing a hand to the side of her face. "I know. I'm sorry. I'm just worried, and tired, and there's really nothing any of us can do right now. So just go back to bed, and I'm sure the police will sort everything out." That humourless bark again. "I hope."

Miriam sighed. "Alright." She gave Adele another hug, then turned to the door, and hesitated with her hand on the smooth metal of the handle, remembering the same sorry group gathered in the lounge fifteen years ago. "I'm just so glad it's not one of you."

Maddie laughed, a cracked little sound. "I sort of hope we couldn't be that unlucky twice, but you never know, do you?"

Miriam smiled, and spotted the empty whisky glass on the desk. Well, why not. If anyone needed it, she had a feeling her sister did right now. There hadn't been any more money when Denis was around, but at least he had been support of a vague, purple topcoat-wearing, bushy-haired sort. And that was better than nothing.

"Bloody Keeley," Reid said. "What a nightmare. If we'd fired him when I said—"

"You just didn't want him here because he was better than you," Adele spat. "And because Nita won't work with you."

"That's not it at all! He was a *nightmare!* You saw him last night! And he was always walking around like he owned the place, and all this ridiculous stuff about a *dog* stealing the dinner, when I tell you, *he* was stealing—"

"Oh, do shut up, you two," Maddie said wearily. "Reid, go make me some coffee. I'm not going to sleep again."

"Aw, Mum—"

"Reid, *please.*"

Boyd stood up suddenly, flailing out of the grip of the chair. *"Death comes as a guest but chooses the cook,"* he announced, flourishing one arm.

"No more salmon mousse! No spinach espuma!

Only the seasoning of—"

"Boyd, *shut up!*" his mother, brother and sister shouted, and Miriam only just managed to stop herself joining in.

He sniffed, and adjusted the cuffs of his pyjama shirt. He had some sort of velvet smoking jacket over it, and Miriam wondered if it had been Denis', or if he'd got it in a costume shop. She didn't think anyone actually wore such things anymore. "I'm commemorating Keeley's passing, and you heathens can't even appreciate it."

"That's not a commemoration, it's drivelling rubbish," Reid snapped.

"You two are completely *ruining* the house's need to grieve," Adele shouted at them.

"Well, it's going to take more than some essential bloody oils to fix this," Reid told her.

"The oil of death, floating like soap scum—"

Maddie sat back down behind her desk and pulled a bottle of whisky from the bottom drawer. "I've changed my mind," she said. "Miriam, do you want a glass?"

At that particular moment Miriam rather wished she drank spirits, but she wasn't about to repeat last year's mistake with the Metaxa. "I think I might go to bed after all," she said.

❦

MIRIAM LET herself back into the room she was sharing with Alice. The only light came rather reluctantly from a heavily shaded lamp next to Alice's bed, and after the brighter light in the foyer, the room was a mass of shadows. She supposed Alice must still be downstairs, helping the inspector. She pulled the door shut behind her and tottered toward her bed.

"Careful," a raspy voice advised her. "You're going to trip over your flip-flops."

She gave a little squeak of surprise, tripped over the flip-flops anyway, and steadied herself on the bed. "Beaufort?"

"And Mortimer's here too."

"Hi," someone whispered. Even the voice sounded like it was stress-shedding.

"What on earth are you doing in the dark?" she asked, turning on her own bedside lamp. It didn't exactly banish the shadows, but it did chase them up into the cobwebby reaches of the ceiling. The dragons' eyes glittered back at her, old gold and bright amber. Beaufort's scales had taken on his usual comforting deep greens and golds, but Mortimer was a rather anxious grey that was becoming more familiar than his natural blues and purples.

"We didn't want to start putting lights on in case someone came in," Beaufort said. "You know, snooping for clues. We may not be the only investigators."

"We're *not* investigators," Miriam said firmly.

"And those birdwatchers are still about," Mortimer said, apparently talking to the floor. "They could be watching the house. *Spying.*"

"Why would they be watching the house?" Miriam asked. "I think they're looking for some sort of owl that digs burrows, so they're not going to find that in the eaves. Besides, they can't see you. They were on the terrace this afternoon and they never even glanced at you."

"They might have been pretending," the young dragon said darkly, then gave a heavy sigh. "And we heard them talking about creatures in the woods."

"Miriam's quite right, lad," Beaufort said. "They haven't seen us, and they're looking for owls in holes. You really mustn't worry so much."

"How can I *not* worry? It's happening again! Murders, and investigations, and – and *stuff!*"

"Well, no. Not really," Miriam said, although she didn't even sound convincing to her own ears. She certainly didn't *feel* convincing. Or convinced. "Look, DI Adams has everything in hand, and it's not even a murder, and it's *definitely* nothing to do with us. At all. So it's not happening again. It can't be."

Mortimer sniffed. "It's already happened *twice*. I don't see how you can say it can't happen again."

"It— it just can't. It *can't*," Miriam repeated, and sat down rather more heavily on the bed than she intended to.

"What I find interesting," Beaufort began, his voice thoughtful, and both Miriam and Mortimer rounded on him.

"*No,*" they said together, and he blinked at them.

"No what?"

"Don't start," Mortimer said. "Please, please, Beaufort. Don't start investigating."

"I wasn't. I was just going to say that I found it interesting the antique lady was looking for a cup of tea in the middle of the night. That was what she was saying, wasn't it? We could hear her shouting about tea from the foyer."

"Well, yes. But why's that interesting?" Miriam asked, unable to help herself, and trying not to meet Mortimer's horrified gaze. "If she couldn't sleep, it makes sense."

"Because she could have made it in the room." The big dragon nodded at the little tea station set up on top of the dresser, his paws crossed neatly over each other and his wings folded gracefully against his back. He looked perfectly calm, but there was a gleam in his eye that Miriam didn't much like.

"Maybe she didn't want to wake her friend," she said.

Beaufort nodded. "Maybe. But does one really just wander about a hotel in the middle of the night and make oneself at home?"

Miriam got up and filled their own kettle from the sink in the corner of the room. "Some people have very little respect for private space," she said. "And that really is all there is to it."

"People can be very rude," Mortimer agreed, his voice strained.

Beaufort scratched his chin with one talon and didn't answer, and Miriam set the kettle to boiling, then unpacked two big soup mugs from her bag, plus a Tupperware full of teabags and another of sugar. The milk was outside on the windowsill, where it'd stay cool. It was all very well, these places with tea stations, but they barely gave you enough tea for two humans, let alone two thirsty dragons. And the silly little UHT milk packets were awful.

"Tea?" she said.

"Lovely," Beaufort replied, and eyed the cake tin she took out of her bag.

"Try not to set the napkins on fire," she said as she shared out slices of Bakewell tart. "I didn't want to bring plates."

"Napkins?" Mortimer asked, and she decided not to tell him he was eating it along with the tart. It didn't seem to be spoiling his enjoyment. She was never sure if the dragons' indiscriminate appreciation of everything, even Jasmine's hazardous baking, should be taken as a compliment or not. On balance, that was how she tended to take it. She tipped boiling water over the teabags and wondered just how strange it was for Lottie to be in the treatment room in the middle of the night. Personally, it wouldn't be the first place she'd go to look for a cup of tea. But maybe when Lottie hadn't been able to find one elsewhere she had just thought she might sit there watching the night from the treatment room lounge. Maybe.

There was a niggling little voice at the back of her mind suggesting that it seemed unlikely, and that Beaufort might be right.

She decided to see if the little voice could be silenced with a generous slice of Bakewell tart, even though she was fairly sure it was only a few hours since she'd sworn she'd never eat again. All that stress had obviously burned her dinner off.

7
MORTIMER

Mortimer supposed that transporting cream and jam for scones would have been a bit tricky, and he was willing to accept that Bakewell tart was a reasonable substitute. He was on his third slice, and was pleased to see Miriam appeared to have brought quite a few cake tins with her. He'd been a little worried that staying at a spa hotel might mean everyone eating nothing but kale or spirulina, whatever those might be. He'd seen that mentioned on Miriam's television, along with the looming spectres of cleanses and boot camps, which sounded less pleasant than one would hope for on a weekend away. But judging by last night's dinner (which the ladies of the Women's Institute had, on the pretext of numerous trips to the loo, smuggled substantial servings of to the two dragons on the terrace), there wasn't much to worry about on that front.

There were other things to worry about, though. Such as dead bodies and suspicious birdwatchers, whom he really felt should be taken rather more seriously than the High Lord seemed to be doing. He took a mouthful of tea and looked sideways at Beaufort. The old dragon definitely looked a little too *interested.* He rather wished they'd stayed up by Agatha's pool, and known nothing about the whole affair until it was all tidied up.

"I suppose we'll have to go home tomorrow," Miriam was saying. "Poor Maddie! She just doesn't need this sort of thing. I know she was really hoping to get a good write-up from that journalist, and maybe even a whole new market with the Americans. Reid's cooking and that mushroom incident made such a mess of things last year."

"What exactly happened with the mushrooms?" Beaufort asked.

"Well, Maddie did a whole promotion around identifying plants, finding your own wild food, then having it prepared and served by a chef. The idea was that Adele took everyone out foraging, they collected a load of mushrooms and leaves and so on, then Reid turned it into a meal."

Mortimer swallowed the last of his tart. "They had to collect their own food? That doesn't sound like a holiday." Between that and the boot camps, he was a little puzzled by humans' ideas about relaxation.

"It's very popular," Miriam said. "Or it was. I think it might have been one of those things that everyone got very enthusiastic about, then realised it wasn't actually as easy as they thought. Anyhow, they found all these mushrooms, and Reid made pasta. But it seems neither of them actually identified them properly, even though Adele's usually very good at that sort of thing." She hesitated. "I mean, they weren't *poisonous*, exactly, so it wasn't as bad as it could have been. One guest hated mushrooms, and he ended up the only one not affected. He videoed the whole thing – people dancing in the fountain and running naked through the rose garden."

"That sounds painful," Beaufort said.

"Well, it certainly got them some attention, but not the right sort. This was their relaunch, with the new chefs." Miriam looked at her hands as she spoke, twisting her fingers together. "Maddie's put so much work into trying to get it all right."

Beaufort scratched his chin, and Mortimer padded to the bed, sitting back on his hind legs so he could put a scaly paw on Miriam's hands. "I'm sure everything will be fine. DI Adams has it all in hand."

"But what if it *is* murder?" Miriam asked. "What then? Who wants to stay in a hotel where someone's been *murdered?*"

"Oh, lots of people," Beaufort said cheerfully. "Like that Monster Hunter lot on the television. They love that sort of thing."

Miriam stared at him as if she had lots of responses but couldn't find a suitable one, and Mortimer picked up the cake tin. "Bakewell?" he suggested.

"I'd rather some more wine," Miriam mumbled, but took a piece of Bakewell tart instead.

"It'll be alright, Miriam," Mortimer said. "It really will."

"We shall look into it," Beaufort said, with the air of one who has made a grave decision. "Your family is our family, Miriam."

She stopped with the Bakewell tart still in her mouth, apparently not sure whether to spit it out or take a bite, and Mortimer squeezed her hands a little harder than he intended to. "We'll what?" he said, as Miriam yelped around a mouthful of tart.

"We'll look into it," Beaufort said, his tone indicating that this should be obvious. "It should be very easy to determine if there's been any foul play."

"*Mnmmnnmnnm,*" Miriam said, and both dragons looked at her curiously. She chewed rapidly, shaking her head and sending curls bouncing across her face. "*Mmmnmmmn!*"

"We really can't just go poking around the house," Mortimer said. "I know no one's seen us yet, but—"

"*Mnmn!*" Miriam managed, pointing at Mortimer.

"We'll be terribly careful," Beaufort said. "We just need to wait until everyone's in bed, then we can go have a good look around."

"No," Miriam said breathlessly, wiping crumbs from her mouth. "No, Beaufort, you *can't.*"

"I don't see why not."

"Well, it's a *hotel!* With lots of people in it who don't know about dragons, but might be able to see you. It's just a really bad idea."

Beaufort sniffed. "Well, what on earth are we going to do, then? Just sit here?"

"Yes," Miriam said. "That's exactly what we're going to do. We're going to just sit here and let the police deal with all of it."

"I don't like it."

Mortimer did like it. He liked it very much, in fact. He patted Miriam's hands again and sat back down, examining his cup. "Is it too late for another cup of tea ...?"

Beaufort *hmph*-ed, but he didn't complain when Miriam picked up his mug.

ALICE LET herself into the room just as the kettle was boiling, and eased herself down on the bed with a sigh.

"Tea?" Miriam offered.

"Please." No one asked if Alice was alright, even though she was rubbing her hip gently. That was a sure way to a sore ear and a red face.

"What's happening down there?" Beaufort asked, his eyes bright. "Is DI Adams rounding up suspects and beginning interrogations?"

Alice smiled at him and settled herself back among the pillows more comfortably. "She thinks it's probably an accident."

"Oh." Beaufort's shoulders drooped slightly, then perked up again. "But she's not sure?"

"She doesn't want to speculate. The police are on the way to collect the body, but it looks like the poor man had a heart attack or something in the sauna."

"So there may still be an investigation."

"I'm sure there'll be some sort of investigation."

Mortimer groaned, and tried to turn it into a yawn, not very successfully judging from the amused look Alice gave him. "But we're not going to get involved, are we?"

"I don't see that we need to," Alice said.

Well, that was something. Beaufort would be – or *should* be – less keen without Alice behind the idea of an investigation as well.

Alice accepted her tea from Miriam. "Thank you, dear." She regarded the cup for a moment, then said, "I don't suppose you saw that American, Holt, when you came up?"

"I did," Miriam said, offering her the cake tin. Alice waved it away. "He was very rude."

"He was very drunk," Alice said thoughtfully. "Or he seemed to be."

Mortimer thought that if Alice wasn't going to have her share of the tart, he would. He was going to need it if people kept making what sounded very much like *investigative* remarks so casually.

❧

"MORTIMER? MORTIMER!"

Mortimer wondered if he could keep pretending to sleep on the big rug under the windows, or if Beaufort would know he was faking.

"Mortimer, come on, lad. We've work to do!"

Gods, his whispering was loud enough to wake the whole room, but Miriam was still snoring softly, and Alice's breathing was slow and even.

"What?" Mortimer mumbled. "What do we have to do?"

"Go and ask some questions, of course."

Mortimer opened one eye and stared at the High Lord. "Alice said we didn't need to get involved."

"We're not getting *involved*, lad. Just using local knowledge to help out the inspector. Talking to our contacts."

Mortimer closed his eye again and stifled a little whimper in the matted rug. There was no use refusing. Beaufort would just go on his own, and that was not an idea that he enjoyed contemplating. That sounded *messy*. He sat up.

"Good lad." Beaufort patted him on the shoulder, sending him nose-first into the mat again. "May as well make ourselves useful, hadn't we?"

May as well sleep, Mortimer thought. Not that dragons needed an awful lot of sleep, not after the first hundred years or so, but he was sure it hadn't been more than an hour since Alice had turned the light off. "What about the inspector?" he asked. "What if she sees us?"

"She's downstairs with that other detective chap, Colin Collins," Beaufort said. "She'll be busy for a while, but I'm sure she'd like our help. We could even go and say hello."

Wonderful. A possible murder, a hotel full of guests, an investigation that was nothing to do with them (presumably involving a whole lot of other, non-dragon-aware police), and the High Lord wanted to go and say hello. Mortimer was almost certain that the inspector would *not* want their help, and would *not* be pleased to see them. "I don't think that's a good idea."

"Well, then, we can check her room and make sure everything's in order. Those birdwatchers said they lost their Pro–thingy, and you heard that American in the hall talking about someone moving things about in their rooms. That definitely sounds like our area of expertise, and hers is the only room that'll be empty." Beaufort was standing by the door already, looking terribly *expectant*. Mortimer swallowed a sigh. How much trouble could they really get into, investigating an empty room? It'd be fine. It'd all be fine.

The hall was silent and empty, the old carpet muffling the pad of their paws as they pattered to DI Adams' door. There was no sound from downstairs, no voices drifting up from the foyer, just the soft light of the lamps on the sideboards and above the faded paintings. Mortimer hoped Beaufort was right, that the inspectors were still occupied with the investigation and they weren't about to walk in on DI Adams asleep in her bed. He had a sneaking suspicion that she probably slept very lightly, and with a large stick handy. Or maybe even a taser. He shuddered, and wished he'd never watched that particular show on Miriam's television. He kept having nightmares about it.

Beaufort eased the door to DI Adams' room open, then gave Mortimer a toothy smile. "See? Empty."

"Oh, good." Mortimer scuttled into the room after the High Lord and pushed the door closed, then sat with his back to it trying to come up with a good excuse for being here.

Beaufort was sniffing around the corners of the room, searching for traces of intruders or creatures. Dragons don't smell things the same way humans (or indeed anything else) do, but they can sense traces of people and creatures that have come and gone, emotional impressions left behind by incidents and thoughts. And Folk leave their very own trace behind, glittering at the edges with mercury and magic.

Mortimer had a half-hearted sniff of the room without moving from the door, but all he could really smell was the inspector. She was a tight, slightly perplexed blue, like the scent of strawberries in a thunderstorm. Plus she'd very much enjoyed a tuna sandwich at some point recently, which made his stomach growl.

"Notice anything, lad?" Beaufort asked.

"Nothing."

"And have you actually had a sniff, or have you just been sitting there looking like someone stole your scales?"

Mortimer hiccoughed. It was easy to forget sometimes that the High Lord had seen kingdoms rise and fall, that he'd fought for the survival of both himself and his clan, that he'd ridden the changes of a world that had run down so many others. That he was old and honed, not old and worn down. Until he poked you, and suddenly it was very obvious where his sharp edges were. *"Um."* He scratched his chin violently, dislodging a scale. "I – well, that is—"

"Never mind, lad. I know you're not a fan of investigating. But I do rely on you, you know. You see things these old eyes miss. And we don't want a nest of pixies in here making trouble or something."

Mortimer strongly doubted Beaufort missed anything, but his nose went a happy, flattered orange anyway. "I can't smell much except the inspector. And lots of other less recent people. But no pixies or anything else."

"No, no Folk." Beaufort sat back on his hind legs to pull the curtains open. There was the sound of heavy fabric tearing. "Oh. Bit soft, these," he observed.

Mortimer hurried over. "You've got to get the angle right, and not dig your claws in." He grabbed a pawful of cloth to demonstrate, and managed to get it halfway across the track before it started shredding against his scales. "Ooh. It *is* soft."

"I did say," Beaufort said, giving another tug on his side of the curtain that got it halfway open, but not without a chorus of tearing. "That'll do, anyway." He scrabbled with the sash window, the latches not being made for dragons, then eventually levered it open and stuck his head out. "Evening, Godfrey," he called.

Mortimer squeezed in beside him and came face to face with a grey, weathered visage. "Oh! Hello!"

"Evenin'," the newcomer said, scratching an ear and unleashing a shower of lichen. He was missing a forelimb from the elbow down and his nose was somewhat eroded on one side, but his chipped wings were broad and powerful. "Can't say as I've seen dragons in the rooms before."

"It's a whole new world," Beaufort said, sounding very satisfied with the prospect.

"I hear it's all tea parties and village fetes," Godfrey said, settling heavy claws into the brickwork around the window. "Can't see the point myself, but I guess for social Folk it must be quite pleasant."

"We do rather enjoy it," Beaufort said. "And we've even been doing yoghurt."

"Yoghurt? Isn't that some sort of fermented milk?" Godfrey asked, and peered at Mortimer. "You're looking a bit threadbare there."

Mortimer clutched his tail reflexively. "It's stress."

"That's the reason for the yoghurt," Beaufort said. "And the weekend off."

"It's really helping," Mortimer muttered.

"You were right," Beaufort said, ignoring Mortimer. "No one's noticed us. Must be rather comfortable for you all, not having to worry about it."

"Well, I'm the only one doing much prowling these days. Our Antigone lost a wing to a bloody roofer about eighty years ago, and she's been in a bit of a sulk ever since. Doesn't move more than once or twice a year."

"Ah, that's a shame," the High Lord said, sounding genuinely sad. "Is it just the two of you left?"

"Used to be six, but you know how it is with gargoyles. Weather gets the better of some if they get too lazy. Old Rufus got himself into a contemplation of romantic poetry and hasn't moved since 1793. I keep the swallows out of his ears, but I think he's too far gone now to come back. Gabrielle and Lucius got dislodged by winter storms. Patricia's still going strong, but she's studying the language patterns of the common pipistrelle bat and its relation to folklore traditions, so I don't even know what she's saying half the time."

Mortimer tried to imagine what it must be like, watching your friends and family fossilise around you, and found he didn't really want to try. It was like how some dragons withdrew into themselves and went into hibernation. Not Lord Walter's sort of hibernation, where you knew he was just resting up so he could wake again with enough energy to keep shouting at everybody. No, this was a different sort. There was a cavern in the Cloverly mount where such dragons slept, their scales the colour of the grey stone, cold to the touch despite the fire that was kept burning for them. They just ... stopped. Became overwhelmed with the hurtful confusion of a world where they weren't meant to exist and weren't believed in, where hiding was the only way to survive. Became lost to the dragons around them, and lost to themselves. So they slept, like scaled statues in a dragonish graveyard, their heartbeats as slow as the earth and their breath softer than a dusty whisper.

The younger dragons were tasked with bringing wood for the fire and keeping cobwebs off the still forms, and it had been the chore Mortimer dreaded the most. The frozen dragons filled his heart with a terrible foreboding, with the sense that such a thing was only a thought away for any of them, and he always rushed to finish as quickly as he could. But one day he'd stumbled upon Beaufort in the cavern, the High Lord's own scales grey and drained in sympathy. Beaufort hadn't seen him. He'd been preoccupied, laying his head next to the sleeping dragons', telling them in his old rumbling voice that he knew they were still there, and that was perfectly fine. That they could sleep as long as they wanted, and the fire would stay lit and their home caverns would wait empty for them. That when they were ready they could come back into the world, and that maybe it'd be easier this time. And if they didn't want to come back, that was perfectly fine too. They were cared for. They were loved. They were Cloverly dragons, always.

Mortimer had crept away with the wood still clutched to his chest, and not gone back until he was sure Beaufort had gone. Some things weren't for sharing. But somehow the cavern had stopped being so frightening after that, and he'd taken to speaking to the sleeping dragons whenever he was in there, rather than sneaking about as if he were in a museum or a morgue. He didn't know if it helped, but maybe it did. And sometimes maybe mattered.

Now he pulled his attention back to Godfrey as Beaufort said, "Have you seen any pixies around here? Anyone making mischief?"

"Nah," the gargoyle said. "Not tonight, anyway. Maybe before."

"Before tonight?"

"Probably."

"Yesterday?"

Godfrey snatched a moth out of the air and shoved it in his mouth, chewing happily. "I don't think yesterday. But it might have been. Or it might have been tomorrow. Outside now, time is all one."

Mortimer thought that was singularly unhelpful, and judging from Beaufort's expression the High Lord thought so too. "You can't be sure if you saw anyone today?"

"I can. Today is now, here, sundown to sunset. All other days are as one."

Beaufort glanced at Mortimer and muttered, "But 1793 he remembers. I'm sure Miss Marple never had to deal with this." But aloud he just said, "Well, that's most helpful, Godfrey. Thank you."

"I tell you what I did see," Godfrey said, and the dragons, who had started to pull back into the room, leaned out the window again. The gargoyle grinned at them.

"Yes?" Beaufort prompted.

"The smallish house human being thrown out of the kitchen by the very big human. The smallest house human shouting at the very big human. Humans sneaking and house humans creeping. The smallish house human arguing with the smallest house human. New humans shouting at each other about their things." He scratched an ear. "They're very excitable, humans, aren't they?"

Mortimer and Beaufort looked at each other. "They are," Beaufort agreed. "And you say some of the new ones were shouting about their things? What were they saying?"

"That the things were lost, or gone. They were very excited."

"And you definitely didn't see any pixies, or gnomes, anything like that?"

"Not tonight."

Mortimer swallowed a groan. This was entirely pointless.

"Oh, and some humans were talking about dragons," the gargoyle added, and both dragons stared at him.

"Which humans?" Beaufort asked.

The gargoyle shrugged. "Can't tell. They change skins all the time, and they all look the same otherwise."

Beaufort scratched his chin. "Which room were they in?"

"Downstairs. The lounge. They were by the window."

Mortimer found his voice. "How many were there?"

Godfrey yawned. "More than one."

For a moment Mortimer thought Beaufort might actually lose his patience, but instead the High Lord just said, "Well, that's very interesting, Godfrey. Can you tell us if you see any other Folk, or humans talking about Folk?"

"Sure," the gargoyle said, and nodded to them both. "I'd best go. I want to get an extra frog for Antigone before the sun comes up. Sometimes she eats them." He ambled away down the wall, walking on it upright as easily as if it were a floor, and the two dragons withdrew into the room.

Mortimer sat down heavily as the High Lord muscled the sash window down. "It has to be those birdwatchers. Has to be! I *knew* they were up to something, and now they're sitting around talking about us, and—"

"Or it could be the W.I.," Beaufort said, giving the curtains an experimental tug before giving up. "There's no need to panic."

"But what if it *is* them? What do we do?"

Beaufort just grinned, and Mortimer dropped his snout in his paws with a sigh.

"Investigate?"

"Quite right, lad. And now there are missing things to consider, too. We have an awful lot to look into." He trotted to the door with his snout high, and Mortimer wondered if he could will himself into hibernation. If he found a quiet spot he thought he might just try.

8

ALICE

Alice woke to the sound of whispers and dragonish rustling. She sat up and found two dragons sitting amid the scattered contents of Miriam's bag, looking at her with their snouts flushed embarrassed lilac.

"What *are* you up to?" she asked them.

"Miriam said something about egg sandwiches," Beaufort said.

"We've been up all night," Mortimer added. "And we've had no time to go rabbit-hunting or anything."

"Miriam brought egg sandwiches?" Well, that certainly explained the size of her bag. Everyone had brought a little something to keep the dragons going, but she rather thought Miriam might be the only one to have packed her entire pantry.

"What?" Miriam asked, pushing herself onto her elbows and regarding the room though a messy veil of hair. "Who's on their last legs?"

"The dragons are looking for egg sandwiches," Alice said.

"The witches are legless?"

Mortimer, who had been holding a Tupperware behind his

back, gave Miriam an alarmed look and put the container back in her bag.

"I think some tea is in order first," Alice said, pushing the covers back and swinging her legs off the bed. They were quite comfortable mattresses, but one never slept as well elsewhere as one did at home. Particularly not when there were dragons sneaking in and out of the door all night. There was going to have to be a discussion regarding the etiquette of sharing a room.

She filled the kettle from the washstand in the corner of the room, and said, "Well, if you've found the sandwiches you may as well have them. They'll be no good tomorrow." She heard a sudden scuffle as the Tupperware was retrieved from the bag again, and she doled tea and sugar into the mugs with a smile curving the corners of her mouth. It was strange, how easy it was to have dragons in your life. It had only been a couple of years since they'd turned up at the door – well, window – of the village hall in the middle of a W.I. meeting, and she couldn't imagine how she'd thought life had been interesting before. And not just because the arrival of dragons had somehow resulted in them being pitched into investigations and murders. After all, she'd already found herself in the middle of one of those when her husband had vanished. No, the dragons brought something else, something undefinable. Hope, she supposed. Hope that not all the magic in the world had been crushed and forgotten. Hope that friendship was a stronger bond than difference was a divider. And, of course, they also brought goblins and gargoyles. That certainly made things interesting.

She pulled the curtains open on a bright, early day, the tops of the trees stained with early sun and a quiet mist tangled around the trunks as the dew began to burn off.

"Tea?" Miriam mumbled. She sounded slightly more coherent and was still sitting up, but Alice wasn't at all convinced she was actually awake.

"Tea," Alice agreed, and was about to turn away from the window when movement caught her eye. "Hello. They're up early."

"Who?" Beaufort hurried to her on three legs, an egg sandwich in thick slabs of white bread held delicately in one front paw.

"The antique hunters. Edie and Lottie."

Beaufort peered over the windowsill. "They've got bags."

"I imagine they don't fancy staying after last night," Alice said. The room faced over the front of the house and the drive, and they had a perfect view of the two women putting their bags into the back of a rather immaculate old Morris Minor van. It was a very nice blue and had gold lettering on the side that read, *Two Lovely Ladies, Antique Experts. Evaluations, Removal, & Sales.* She wondered if the s had come off *removal* or if it was a typo.

"Should they be allowed to leave?" Miriam asked, her voice still fuzzy. "I mean, Lottie was the one who found the body."

"I'm sure DI Adams got all the information she needed last night." Alice wasn't sure at all, but if it was an accidental death then it didn't matter. *If.* She wondered if Beaufort's passion for Agatha Christie was starting to rub off on her.

"Do you think DI Adams knows they're leaving?" Miriam asked.

"She won't be awake yet," Beaufort said. "She was up terribly late with Detective Inspector Collins."

There was a pause, and Miriam tried to persuade her hair out of her face while Mortimer looked at his egg sandwich as if it was about to bite him.

"Someone's going to have to wake her, aren't they?" he said, apparently addressing the sandwich with a defeated slouch to his shoulders. Alice resisted the urge to tell him to smarten up.

"I rather think we should," Beaufort said.

"Oh, gods." Mortimer crammed the sandwich into his mouth. "If she tases me, I'm going to be having words." He didn't specify who he'd be having words with, just marched out the door, pulling it to behind him with a slam. The two women and the High Lord looked at each other.

"I didn't say he had to go," Beaufort said.

"You didn't," Alice agreed, and set the tea to brew. "We're going to need another mug."

⁊⦿

DI ADAMS TRAILED Mortimer through the door in the same hedgehog pyjamas she'd been wearing the night before, this time with her fleece over the top, her hair lassoed into something approximating order. She had the look of someone who was determined to appear as wide awake as possible, but was fighting a losing battle. She shoved a mug and a jar of instant espresso at Alice and said, "They're not suspects, you know. They can leave."

"It wasn't my choice," Mortimer said. "They were the ones who wanted to wake you up."

"Have some tea, Mortimer," Alice said. "And maybe some cake."

"There's cake?" He sat up a little straighter.

"It's"—DI Adams checked her watch—"not even 7 a.m. yet."

"They've been up all night," Miriam said with a yawn. "Investigating." She yawned again, then gave a squeak of alarm as she noticed the inspector glaring at her.

"*Who's* been investigating?" DI Adams demanded.

Mortimer backed under Miriam's bed until only his snout showed.

"We were just looking for evidence of house Folk," Beaufort said, giving what Alice assumed was meant to be a reassuring smile. It was quite alarming.

"House Folk? What, like house elves or something?"

"You're aware of house elves?" Beaufort asked. "How fascinating! I haven't heard of them being around for at least four or five centuries, yet the stories must have persisted. How wonderful! How did you learn about them?"

"Harry Potter," the inspector said faintly, staring at her mug.

"Is he a historian?" the High Lord asked, and Miriam snorted.

"It's a movie," she began, then stopped as Alice shook her head sharply. The last thing they needed was Beaufort watching Harry Potter. He'd already singed Miriam's TV during an episode of *Supernatural* involving werewolves. It appeared that the High Lord held strong views regarding the depiction of Folk.

"House Folk, then," Alice said, topping the mugs with boiling water. "Did you find any?"

"Not personally, no. But we've heard some of the guests saying things have gone missing—"

"They have," Miriam said. "I wanted my pink scarf with the elephants on it for yoga yesterday, and I couldn't find it anywhere."

Alice looked at Miriam's bag, open on the floor with clothes and cake tins spilling everywhere. "Are you sure it's not just misplaced?"

The younger woman flushed. "*Yes.* I wore it up here, then left it on the dresser when we all went for a cuppa. When I came back I couldn't find it."

"Worth stealing?" DI Adams asked, looking rather more awake now there was discussion of criminal doings.

"Not really. I bought it for seven pounds fifty at the market."

The inspector sighed, and accepted a mug of coffee from Alice. "That's a shame."

"It is. The elephants were lovely."

There was a moment of silence for the lost scarf, and Beaufort busied himself with the last egg sandwich. "Oh – would you like one?" he asked the inspector, holding the Tupperware out to her.

She made a face. "No, you go for it."

Alice topped the remaining mugs up with milk and handed

them out. "Well, we just thought you should know that the ladies were leaving. But it was definitely an accident, then?"

"We didn't find anything to indicate otherwise." The inspector tried to cover an enormous yawn with her sleeve. "The tech team turned up a sharps bin with some empty syringes in it, but they were just Botox – standard single-use things. So it looks like a pretty straightforward case of stroke or heart attack brought on by too long in the sauna. The autopsy will throw up anything out of the ordinary."

Alice pulled out the chair at the dressing table and regarded it dubiously. It had a terminal wobble to it that made her think it might be more for decoration than use, so she put it back gently and sat down on her bed instead, sipping her tea and watching the light strengthening outside, losing its golden tones as the sun rose higher.

"So, other than not finding any house Folk, what else were you up to last night?" she asked the dragons.

"And did you run across a dog?" DI Adams added. "About yay high, and a bit stinky." She waved her hand vaguely in the air, giving Alice the idea that the dog was as big as the dragons were.

"No, no dog," Beaufort said. "Not a whiff. Although we could have missed it," he added hurriedly, as the inspector scowled and started to say something. "You know, if there's been a lot of cleaning, or lots of people about, the scents can get muddled."

"I didn't imagine the dog. It was in my room."

"We didn't smell anything there at all."

"*You* were in my room?"

"Well, yes, we needed to check if there were any pixie nests—"

"*Pixie nests?*"

"The birdwatchers are looking for dragons," Mortimer blurted, and everyone stared at him.

"Now, lad, we don't know that," Beaufort said. "Godfrey wasn't certain."

"*I'm* certain," Mortimer insisted. He was a terrible grey, shot through with alarmed threads of pink. "I knew they were suspicious, with all their cameras and pros and things!"

"Oh, Mortimer," Miriam said, and scrambled out of bed to sit on the floor next to him. "If Beaufort says Geoffrey wasn't certain—"

"Godfrey," Beaufort said. "And he really wasn't. He just said *someone* was talking about dragons, not who it was. It could have been the W.I."

"And who's Godfrey?" DI Adams asked.

"Our source," Beaufort said, somewhat smugly.

"Your *source?* What, you have informants now?"

He took a sip of tea, his claws delicate on the mug. "From what I've been reading, it appears vital to cultivate an excellent network of contacts. Although I'm still not sure what a Rolodex is, exactly, or why one puts one's contacts in it. I'd have thought you'd want them out in the field, not all cooped up together."

DI Adams stared at him as if she wasn't sure if she was entirely awake, then nodded. "Right. So your informant—"

"Godfrey."

"Godfrey, yes. He said someone was talking about dragons? This seems serious."

"It *is*," Mortimer wailed. "And I know it's those birdwatchers, I just *know* it! They're poking around everywhere, pretending they're looking for … for blue tits or something, but really they're looking for *us!*"

"Now, lad, don't take on so—"

"Cake," Miriam said firmly. "Bakewell tart, how about that?"

"I finished it last night," Mortimer said, not meeting her eyes.

"Right. Okay. Spiced apple cake. There we go. I've got apple cake." She got up and started sifting through her clothes. "That's just what we need."

"Should we be worried?" Alice asked the High Lord.

"I don't think so," he said. "The birdwatchers gave no sign of seeing us yesterday. If they are looking for Folk, then I think they're rather like those monster hunters last summer. They don't actually know anything, just poke around being hopeful."

Alice thought that was how a lot of people went through life, poking around being hopeful. The problem was, sometimes it paid off.

"Did your informant at least know if they overheard male or female voices?" DI Adams asked. "That'd clear a lot up."

"Humans all look and sound the same to gargoyles," Beaufort said.

"*Gargoyles?*" DI Adams said, and Alice thought she really must need more sleep. It was hardly unexpected once one started talking about house elves and pixies, never mind dragons.

"Do you mean the ones on the roof?" Miriam asked. "The ones you asked if the family could see Folk?" She'd finally found the apple cake tin among half a dozen others, and Mortimer was munching disconsolately on a slice.

"One of them," Beaufort said. "The others aren't quite so active."

"Of course they're not," the inspector mumbled, staring at her coffee cup, and Alice got up to put the kettle on again. The younger woman looked like she was going to need quite a bit of coffee today.

§❧

ALICE LEANED against the window while Beaufort related everything else Godfrey had told him. None of it was very enlightening. They could guess that the "big human" had been the sous-chef, but they'd already seen that he had plenty of altercations with the family, if that was who the "house humans" were. The most worrying thing was the possibility that the birdwatchers were actually Folk-hunters, even if they didn't seem to be very perceptive ones. Just the fact that they were sniffing around seemed like a bad sign.

Movement outside caught her eye, and she turned to peer out the window. "Well," she said. "It looks like no one wants to hang around."

"Who is it now?" DI Adams asked, getting up. "Tell me it's that bloody journalist. Please, please tell me it's him."

"No such luck," Alice said. "It's the Americans."

Miriam made a small noise that suggested she felt this was a close second to getting rid of the journalist, and joined the other two women and the dragons at the window. They peered down at the driveway as the family piled themselves into a Nissan Micra, stacking bags in the tiny boot and between the two children in the back.

"Doesn't that seem odd?" Miriam said.

"What's that?" DI Adams asked.

"Such a small car. I thought all Americans drove Hummers or suchlike."

"I doubt the car hire company had Hummers," Alice pointed out, but she was thinking of the luggage. It was a very small amount of luggage for a family on an extended holiday, especially (in her experience) an American family.

"He's a big human," Mortimer said suddenly. "Maybe Godfrey was talking about him."

They considered this for a moment, then DI Adams said, "That's entirely unhelpful, Mortimer."

The smaller dragon's shoulders slumped, and he picked up the end of his tail, tugging at the scales. "Sorry. It was just an observation."

The inspector sighed, and patted him on the shoulder in the awkward way of someone who's not very good at offering sympathy. Alice was quite familiar with it herself. "I'm sorry. I shouldn't have said that. It was a perfectly reasonable observation."

"No, it just confuses things," Mortimer said, then looked alarmed when a scale came away in his paws.

"*Ooh,*" Miriam said, pulling their attention back to the window. "Oh, dear!"

Alice looked back in time to see the Nissan pulling out of the parking area, going too fast and sending a spray of gravel against the fountain. It fishtailed across the drive as the driver slammed the brakes on, just in time to avoid the Morris Minor van that had been coming up to the house at a rather more sedate pace. The van braked hard as well, its weight sending it into a lumbering slide, and for a single, flinching moment Alice was waiting for the painful crumple of metal against metal or stone. But the cars crunched to a stop less than a metre apart, and Edie got out of the van, shouting and waving her arms. The windows were too old to be double-glazed, but even so, from this distance Alice couldn't hear what was being said. Holt was leaning out the driver's window of the Nissan with a red face, seemingly shouting over the top of Edie.

"Is that a bit strange?" Beaufort asked. "Why did the ladies come back?"

"It does seem rather odd," Alice agreed. "And whatever they're telling Holt, he doesn't seem too happy about it." The American was jabbing his finger at the drive angrily, but Edie was shaking her head at him, hands on her hips. Holt pulled his head back in, and the Micra revved backward, weaving a little too close to a large topiary pot for Alice's comfort. Although, given that the shape of the topiary leaned toward the Picasso-esque, she supposed it wouldn't have been a great loss. The Micra stopped, then roared forward again. Edie jumped back in the van and slammed her door as the little car squeezed past at an imprudent pace and accelerated down the drive, raising cold dust in the early light.

"If I could be bothered, I'd go caution him for his driving," DI

Adams said, and yawned again. They waited, watching Edie get back in the car and park it beneath the fountain once more, then stand there with her arms crossed, staring down the drive. Alice was quite sure she was waiting for Holt to come back.

Sure enough, the Nissan Micra came skittering back less than ten minutes later, while Alice was making more tea. DI Adams had been waiting by the window, and as soon as the little car came racing into view through the trees she headed for the door, looking much more awake than the coffee accounted for. Alice looked at the full mugs rather regretfully, then followed the inspector, tightening her dressing gown as she went.

"Are we going outside?" Miriam called, scrambling to find her jacket. "What about the tea?"

"What about the *cake?*" Mortimer complained.

THE DRAGONS SLIPPED SILENTLY DOWN the stairs ahead of them. Their scales had taken on a mix of reds and browns that blended into the shadows, as well as (in Mortimer's case) a little anxious, blotchy grey.

Jasmine had been coming out of her room as they went past, and as she hurried down the stairs Alice could hear voices in the upstairs hall, doors opening and closing, and the scuff of slippered feet on the old carpet. She followed the inspector out the door and down the wide curve of the steps to the gravel drive as the ladies of the W.I. trailed after them.

"Edie?" the DI called. "Is everything alright?"

"They shouldn't let Americans drive over here, you know. He almost had my wing mirror off! And my van's a *classic.*"

"Well, yes—"

"And he didn't listen! Just rushed off to see for himself. Just like a man."

The DI give a strange little grimace that somehow indicated both disapproval and agreement.

"What's going on?" Holt bellowed, unfolding himself from the little Nissan Micra, which he'd pulled up right in front of the steps. Alice found it quite astonishing that he'd got his belly behind the wheel. "Who's blocked the bloody road?"

"The road's blocked?" DI Adams asked.

"Yes!" Edie said. "That's what I told him. But would he listen? No, of course not. Men." She shook her head and turned to Lottie, who was stood shivering next to her in an enormous puffy jacket printed with flowers. The jacket was so big and she was so small that Alice had the impression of a rose balancing on a short-cropped stem. "If we can't leave, we'd best get inside in the warm, then, Lots."

Lottie wiped her eyes and gave a wobbly smile. "I guess we have to, don't we? I really didn't want to have to go back in there, but …" She trailed off, then squared her shoulders and widened her smile. "Nothing for it."

Edie took her arm and glared at the DI as if it was her fault. "I hope we're able to get that road cleared before lunch."

DI Adams rubbed the back of her neck. "I imagine that depends on what the problem is, Edie."

"It's a *tree!* My God, doesn't anyone listen around here?" She hurried Lottie past Alice and into the foyer, leaving a whiff of rich, dark perfume in their wake.

"There's a *tree,*" Holt shouted, as if this was a revelation. "A *tree!*"

"Don't they have those in America?" Gert muttered, and Priya snorted.

"On the *road,*" he insisted, planting his hands on his hips and glaring at them all.

"So I hear," DI Adams said, her tone neutral. "You were leaving early."

"We don't want to stay in a house with a body in it."

"The body's gone."

"Well, a house where someone died."

"I imagine quite a few people have died in a house this old," Alice observed, tucking her hands into her pockets to protect them from the sneaky little wind.

"Yes, but someone died *now*," Holt said. "While we were in it!"

"Holt," his wife called, half out of the car. She still had one foot inside, as if expecting to have to jump back in at any moment. "Are we leaving?"

"Well, we can't, can we, Paula? There's a *tree* on the *road*." He sounded like he was speaking to a child, and Alice raised her eyebrows.

Sitting behind a potted topiary, Beaufort said rather piercingly, "I say. That tone's a bit off."

DI Adams glared at him as agreeing mutters passed through the Women's Institute, then looked at the ladies as if wondering where they'd come from. They looked back, Teresa in her Lycra and a workout jacket, Rose in the sort of clothes one imagined a nineteenth century explorer favouring, and everyone else in a haphazard collection of nighties and pyjamas and dressing gowns. Carlotta had her hair in curlers, and she was staring at Holt as if memorising his features to pick him out of a line-up.

"Ladies," DI Adams said. "Aren't you a bit cold?"

There was a general murmur which indicated that yes, they were, but it didn't mean they were going anywhere. The inspector pinched the bridge of her nose.

"Holt," she said, turning back to the suddenly uncomfortable-looking man, "I'd suggest you head back inside with your family and leave this with me. I'm sure everyone'll be able to leave by lunch."

"It's a *tree*," he said, his red face getting redder. "You'll need chainsaws, and bulldozers, and you should—"

"Thank you, Holt. I'm sure I'll be able to figure it out," the inspector said, as another wave of irritated muttering ran through the W.I.

"Well, I should go with you. You won't be able to do anything on your own."

"He just sounds rude rather than helpful," Beaufort announced, and Alice could see Mortimer shushing him wildly as Rosemary and Carlotta chuckled.

DI Adams fixed Holt with an admirably stern look. "I certainly have no intention of setting you loose with any sort of power tools. Go inside and have some of the lovely breakfast that I'm sure is waiting for you."

There was a long, expectant pause, then the young girl, who had climbed out of the car and stood shivering next to it in a skirt and stripy leggings, said in a small voice, "I don't like it in there. There are things in the walls. Mice, maybe."

Everyone looked at her.

"There's definitely something in the walls," Beaufort said cheerfully. "Probably not mice, though." Mortimer looked like he was about to faint.

"Not that I don't like mice," the girl added quickly. "But I'm not sure they should be in the walls."

"Shut up about the bloody mice, Dell-Marie," Holt said, and Alice saw his lip actually curl, as if he was disgusted by his own daughter. She frowned. "I've never known a kid to be so worried about mice."

"They were running around," Dell-Marie insisted. "And my blue socks are gone. I think they ate them." She sounded oddly *English*, and Alice wondered if she went to school over here, or was just one of those children who picked up accents very quickly.

"Oh, sure. The mice ate your socks." Holt sneered. "More like you *lost* them."

"But how would I lose socks?" Dell-Marie asked, sounding genuinely bewildered. "There isn't even a laundry in this place."

"Just shut up about the bloody mice and go inside," Holt said. "Let the policewoman here sort it all out."

"I don't like him," the High Lord announced, setting off a ripple of agreement in the W.I.

"Police *officer*," Jasmine said in a small but very firm voice, then looked suddenly worried. "Or is that insulting for a detective inspector?"

DI Adams folded her arms across her chest. "It's just fine, Jasmine. Why don't we all go in and warm up?"

The ranks of the W.I. did not move.

DI Adams glared at them.

They still didn't move.

Paula closed her car door and headed for the steps, Dell-Marie trailing behind until Miriam offered her an encouraging smile, which made her squeak and grab her mother's arm. Alice thought that probably had something to do with the fact that Miriam had yet to brush her hair.

The family were almost at the doors when there was the unmistakable click of a camera. Alice looked up to see the journalist leaning out of one of the upstairs windows.

"Morning!" he called cheerfully. "You ladies really do love your pyjama parties, don't you?"

"That is exceptionally rude, young man," Alice said, before DI Adams could say anything. "I would rather hope you're not going to use a photo like that in any of your stories."

He grinned at her. "All these lovely ladies of the Women's Institute, out in their dressing gowns of a morning? Excellent local colour."

"I'll show him local colour," Rosemary muttered.

"I could get the camera …?" Beaufort offered, and Jasmine shushed him. He looked like he was enjoying himself altogether too much.

"What's going on, anyway, Detective Inspector?" Ervin added. "A crime scene last night, and now a showdown in the car park?"

"Entirely unrelated," DI Adams said. "The road seems to be blocked, but I'm sure we'll have it all sorted by lunch." She was looking less and less sure of herself every time she said it.

"Curiouser and curiouser," Ervin said, and grinned.

DI Adams made a dismissive gesture and stomped up the steps, almost colliding with Adele as she rushed out.

"Morning!" she exclaimed, rather too brightly. "Is everyone ready for some yoga? I think we'll have class on the terrace, so wrap up warm!"

"Yoghurt!" Beaufort said as Adele rushed off again. "Come along, Mortimer. We're going to sort out this stress-shedding yet!" Mortimer groaned, and Alice decided it might be time to play the hip-op card. She had no intention of heading out in the cold to do yoga, not when she could be sitting in the warm with a plate of toast and tea.

ADELE, however, was so desperately determined that things should continue as normal that Alice found herself on the terrace twenty minutes later, holding a gentle lunge while wearing gloves, a scarf, a woolly hat, and her thermal walking gear. Miriam stood next to her complaining that she couldn't feel her toes, and even Teresa was looking unenthusiastic. The only one who had managed to escape was DI Adams, who had rounded up Boyd as the resident arborist and headed for the blocked drive.

Beaufort had tried to persuade Mortimer to stay while he followed the inspector down to the river. DI Adams had been very clear that she did not wish to be accompanied by dragons, no matter how sure they were that no one could see them, but that was not the sort of thing that could dissuade the High Lord entirely. Mortimer had insisted that the stress of wondering what was happening and not knowing if Adele was actually seeing him or not far outweighed the benefits of learning to do a perfect downward dog. Beaufort patted him on the shoulder and said, "You're even getting the terminology, lad! You're going to be wonderful at this yoghurt carry-on, I can just tell."

Mortimer sighed deeply and said, "Can we just go? Before Adele sees us?"

"She never really sees us," the High Lord replied. "She just thinks it's her tea." But he had led the way into the woods anyway, leaving dragon-sized footprints in the dew behind them as the Women's Institute rolled out their mats with much huffing and groaning. The peacock, who had hurried up to the terrace, watched the dragons go, shaking his tail out disconsolately.

"*Bu-kurk?*" he called after them, but the dragons didn't turn around. Alice thought she should mention to Maddie that it might do to get the peacock some companions.

Adele walked past her, bare feet apparently impervious to the cold stone of the terrace. "Breathe, ladies, breathe!" she commanded. "This will light your internal fires!"

There was more huffing and muttering, and Rosemary said very clearly, "My internal fire has been banked up nicely for at least twenty years. I'm quite happy with that, thank you very much."

"Can get you in a lot of trouble, over-stoking your internal fires," Pearl said, not quite grinning.

"Quite a bit of fun, though, too," Rose said, and laughed so hard she staggered sideways off the mat.

Adele gave her the same bemused look she'd given the dragons the day before and wafted off. Alice supposed that when you were in your twenties, the idea that ladies of a certain age might still have internal fires, stoked or not, was probably as unlikely as dragons in your yoga class.

9
DI ADAMS

DI Adams was somewhat concerned by the tree. It wasn't a big tree. It was, to be honest, quite weedy, but that probably accounted for what it was doing in the road. Someone had nailed a bunch of splintery planks up in the branches, like a My First Workshop attempt at a tree house. And that, specifically, was what was concerning the inspector. No one was in the tree house – or rather tree platform – now, as the rickety planks had either come loose or were in pieces, and the branches they'd been nailed to didn't look much better. The tree's roots were exposed rather sadly to the air on the riverbank, and its leafy head was buried in the undergrowth on the opposite side of the drive, tangled in what the inspector assumed were the telephone lines.

Which was not helping her mood, as she still had no mobile signal. Beyond the tree, the drive snaked up to the ancient wooden bridge and over it to the grey stone of the decrepit hut she'd passed yesterday. There had been an equally decrepit old man collecting 50p tolls and drinking tea from a *World's Greatest Lover* mug then, but there was no smoke coming from the chimney this morning.

The ancient toll collector was probably home having his breakfast, DI Adams thought, not without a little pang of jealousy.

Shouting from the other side of the tree brought her back to her contemplation of the blocked road.

"No hunting!" shouted a woman with a sleeping bag still zipped around her, stomping toward the inspector from the far side of the tree. Booted feet stuck out one end of the bag and very curly hair was trapped under a woolly yellow hat the other. "Down with the elite!"

"Ban the barbarians!" a man shouted. He was very round and dressed head to toe in camouflage gear, with an incongruously purple hat pulled down around his ears. "Save the country!"

"Nature first!" someone else shouted, and now DI Adams could see them scrambling out of a makeshift camp just off the drive, the smoke from their fire hanging low and still as mist around them.

"Save the trees!" a woman in a turquoise eighties ski suit yelled, and DI Adams blinked at the downed tree and its torn roots.

"*The protest rises – like a boiled egg—*"

"This really isn't the time for poetry," DI Adams said, and Boyd looked at her blankly.

"Life is poetry," he said, and tried to fling his cape around him. It tangled around a branch with a nasty tearing sound.

"Down with the elite!" a man in Speedos and a slightly too-small white tank top shrieked, brandishing a blue and white umbrella at them.

"Barry, put some clothes on," the woman in the sleeping bag said, not unkindly. "You'll catch your death." Then she looked back at the DI and Boyd and shouted, "This land is the land of the people! Capitalist scum like you stole it from us! Generations of elitist abuse!"

"Hi, Auntie Rainbow," Boyd said, and it was the inspector's turn to stare.

"Hello, Boyd, love. How's the poetry?"

"Good! I've submitted to a few magazines recently, but no luck."

"Ah, well. It's the System." The capitalisation was noticeable. "Rigged against the true artist and the true believer."

"Word," Boyd said, nodding solemnly.

They smiled at each other across the tree, and DI Adams scratched the back of her neck. "Um," she started, and Rainbow glared at her.

"Who're you?"

"Detective—"

"Tool of the System!" she shouted. "Collaborator!"

"Yeah," Boyd shouted. "Collaborator!"

"Oi," she said to him. "None of that."

"Sorry." He fiddled with the rip in his cloak, and DI Adams turned back to the protesters. There were six of them, all lined up on the other side of the tree, waving badly made placards and, in Barry's case, his umbrella. He'd put a jacket on but was still in his Speedos.

"So what's going on?" she asked Rainbow.

"They're *hunting* at the manor," Rainbow said.

DI Adams sighed as the protesters erupted into enraged squawks. "Down with the hunt!" a pretty girl with dreadlocks shrieked in the sort of tones a very posh person uses when they're trying not to sound posh.

"They're not hunting," the inspector said.

"*Are*," Rainbow insisted.

"Hunts are for—" camouflage man started, and DI Adams jabbed a finger at him.

"Stop right there, sir. Let's keep this civil."

"Down with the police!" shouted the woman in the ski suit.

"That's enough—"

"*Pigs!*" Barry shrieked. "Pigs! We've been infiltrated!" He started bounding back and forth across the drive like a startled, barelegged antelope, all knees and unappetising glimpses of white belly as his jacket rode up. *"Pigs!"*

Everyone was shouting at once, and DI Adams raised her voice over the babble. "Everyone *calm down*. Who's in charge here?"

"Don't talk to us, *pig!*" the young woman screamed, then looked horrified at her own words and ducked behind a young man with an aspiring beard. He shook a placard that said *Woods are for the Wild* at the DI, his eyes wide and his nose a rather uncomfortable shade of red.

"You shall not pass!" he shrieked, and DI Adams sighed again. She checked her phone, but no signal had miraculously appeared in the last five minutes.

"Have you got signal?" she asked Boyd.

"The phone like an umbilical ... biblical ..." He stopped, puzzled, and pulled a small dictionary out of his pocket. "Bilious?"

"Toff scum!" the young woman shouted, still trying far too hard not to sound like a toff herself.

"Hunts are for—" camouflage man tried again, and DI Adams fixed him with a warning glare. He gave her an uneasy look, and finished, "pretentious uncaring rich toffee-nosed, er, prats."

She didn't disagree, but it was rather beside the point. "Who's in charge here?" she asked again.

"I am," Rainbow said, planting her booted feet very solidly on the half-frozen ground and glaring at the detective inspector. "And we're not moving!"

DI Adams looked at Boyd. "Is this private land?"

"All land – belongs to the heart—"

"Boyd."

"Er. Yes."

"It's not," Rainbow said.

"Boyd?" DI Adams said again.

"It's, well—" he looked at his aunt nervously.

"It's a public right of way!"

DI Adams pulled out her phone again, intending to check on an ordnance survey map, and *tsk*-ed at the empty signal bar.

"Well, the *drive's* public," Boyd said. "Part of it, anyway."

"Public right of way, you toff!" camouflage man shouted.

"Toff!" the young woman echoed, pogo-ing up and down while the bearded man stared at her with the sort of besotted gaze that only comes from someone who's making no progress at all with the object of their affections.

"Pigs!" Barry added, and stopped bounding long enough to throw a handful of leaves at DI Adams. She scowled at him as the leaves fluttered to the ground before they even reached the tree, and he did a couple of nervous star jumps. She wrinkled her nose and was suddenly glad she hadn't had breakfast after all.

"DI Adams?" a familiar voice said. "Do you require assistance?"

She tried to look at Beaufort without actually looking at him. Mortimer was lying on his belly among some daffodils, staring fixedly at a flower and ignoring the High Lord. "What are you doing?" she asked, talking out of the corner of her mouth.

"We thought you might need some help moving the tree."

"I told him not to talk to you," Mortimer said to the daffodil. "I told him these are the sort of people who might see us."

"Well, sometimes risks have to be taken to help a friend," Beaufort said, giving the inspector a toothy smile. "So what can we do?"

"Get out of sight," she hissed at him. "There's no telling what this lot will see."

Beaufort examined the motley collection of protesters. Rainbow was making encouraging noises as Boyd struggled through some sort of free-form poetry regarding roads and eggs, posh girl and camouflage man were still shouting about public rights of way and toffs, Barry had apparently grown bored of the whole thing and was splashing in the edge of the river, and the young bearded man and the woman in the ski suit were chanting slogans and waving their signs. "Unlikely," the High Lord said. "They don't seem very perceptive to me."

"Except him," Mortimer said, nodding at Barry. He was still had his umbrella, and was currently using it in a tug of war with … Well, most of DI Adams' mind wanted to say it was nothing, but the bit that saw dragons, the bit that was old and smart and knew that sometimes you have to see what's there, no matter what the loud parts of your logical brain say about it … That bit said the creature was muscular and dragonish and pure, flowing liquid all at once.

"What the hell's that?" she mumbled.

"Knucker," Beaufort said cheerfully. "Type of water dragon. She's just playing, though. Can't be much more than a hatchling."

DI Adams stared, watching Barry thrashing about as the half-seen dragon surged and played around his legs, splashing his pale thighs and nipping at his ankles, making him yelp and prance among the stones. He was waving his umbrella wildly, which the knucker seemed to take as encouragement. She seized the umbrella delicately in her teeth and tugged it until he fell over with a shriek.

"*He'll* see us," Mortimer said.

"You need to go," the inspector said. "We can't take that risk."

The younger dragon looked like he wanted to hug her, and Beaufort looked disappointed, but it was camouflage man who replied.

"Hell no, we won't go!" he bellowed. He jumped onto the tree, wobbled for a moment on the damp trunk with his arms flailing for balance, then pitched off backward. He landed hard enough to make DI Adams wince, then bounced back up again, still shouting. He must be wearing a lot of layers under that camouflage. She gave the dragons a little, urgent wave – *get out of here, get away* – and turned to Rainbow.

"You're Boyd's aunt?" the inspector asked. "Maddie's sister?" And Miriam's. The hair was certainly the same.

"Rainbow Harmony," the woman said, raising her chin as if daring DI Adams to doubt her. "I changed it by deed poll, and I am no longer the sister of that sell-out, that traitor, that wh—"

"*No*," DI Adams said, and Rainbow Harmony stopped.

"Well. She is."

The other protesters were still shouting and trying to form some sort of circular march, but with only four of them it was fairly ineffective. Behind them, Barry fell face-first into the water as the knucker gave him a playful bump. Beaufort was in the river up to his ankles, remonstrating with the water dragon, and Mortimer was attempting to imitate a boulder on the shore. Barry looked both terrified and elated, and kept waving his umbrella at the High Lord. DI Adams dragged her attention back to the tree and said, "Ms Harmony—"

"Rainbow's fine, woman to woman."

"Rainbow. Okay. Can everyone just take a break for a moment while we discuss this?"

The older woman examined DI Adams as if looking for treachery, then nodded.

"No!" the young woman shouted. "Don't trade with the pigs!"

"Pigs," the young man agreed.

"Make us take a break," camouflage man said. "*Make* us!"

Rainbow looked at the woman in the ski suit, who shrugged and clapped her hands. "Breakfast," she announced. "Jemima, collect some more wood for the fire. Tom, get the kettle on. Ronnie," this last directed at the man in camouflage, who looked downcast, "Go get the porridge from the van."

He brightened at the mention of porridge, snapped her a salute and said, "Yes, Harriet, *ma'am*." He strode off like a rotund beefeater, his placard over his shoulder, and DI Adams wondered if anyone was going to help Barry. He was dripping wet and shivering on the riverbank, while an anxious grey Mortimer seemed to have become involved in a game of tag with the bouncing water dragon. He didn't look like he was enjoying it much, although Beaufort was perched on the bridge cheering him on. She rubbed her forehead and wondered why the residents of Toot Hansell, scaly or otherwise, never listened to her. She'd never had this problem in London. She didn't even have this problem in Leeds. And she was getting really very tired of having this problem here.

She dropped her hand and looked at Boyd. "Go back to the car, please."

"No. Why?" He sounded genuinely astonished.

"Because I would like to talk to Rainbow on my own." *Adults only*, she managed not to add. The boy had to be at least thirty.

"*I walk my land, a man of wet dreaming—*"

"Go back to the car *right now*," DI Adams snapped, aware that her voice was louder than she would have liked, and all the protesters turned to look at her, even Ronnie, who had started across the bridge. All except Barry, of course, who was still out there freezing in his Speedos.

Boyd gaped at her.

"Mr Etherington-Smythe, in the car, now. You are not helping this situation." Rainbow started to say something, and the inspector said, "*No.*"

There was a pause, and she was aware of her control of the situation hanging quietly and undramatically in the balance. Dragons or not, she was on her own here. But it wasn't about being in the majority, or even about being the biggest or the loudest. It was about knowing you had the situation in control, and convincing everyone else of that. Even if you actually didn't.

There was a loud splash from the river as the knucker breached like a small, winged whale, and Ronnie said, "Cor. Must be some big pike in this river."

Barry waved his hands and shouted, "Water spirit. It's a water spirit!"

"Course it is, mate," Ronnie said. "Best go and put some trousers on, though, eh? Don't want frostbite on the old fella."

Barry looked down as if just becoming aware of his bare legs, and said, "Oh. Right." He waded out of the river without a backward glance and sloshed toward the fire in his waterlogged wellies, while behind him Mortimer sat in the shallows making placating gestures at the knucker, who didn't seem to notice.

DI Adams looked at Boyd. "Well?"

"Okay," he said, and gave her a disturbingly big smile then went back to the car. He got in and started the engine to get the heater going. DI Adams felt momentarily jealous. She still couldn't quite get used to the hard, crisp cold of these northern mornings, and her yoga trousers didn't offer much in the way of insulation.

"Smash the patriarchy," Rainbow said, raising her fist to DI Adams. The inspector blinked at her for a moment, then realised it was probably a compliment.

"Every day," she said, putting her hands in the pockets of her fleece. She was losing feeling in her fingertips. "So, what's this all about then, Rainbow?"

"Shooting," she said, crossing her arms over her chest.

"There's no shoot here. It's not even the right time of year."

"They're planning it. I know. He's harmless," she said, nodding at Boyd, who was scribbling in his notebook. "His brother isn't, though. I've got inside info that he's planning a secret pheasant mini-shoot, out of season and all. And if that goes well, then there'll be more, and probably hunts as well. It's cruel, and unfair, and inhumane. We won't stand for it."

"We won't," the woman in the ski suit agreed. She'd dispatched everyone else but had stayed put herself, mirroring Rainbow's stance, a little skinnier and younger than the other woman.

"And you are?" DI Adams asked.

"Harriet Trott. I run the bookshop in Toot Hansell."

"Are you all from Toot Hansell?"

"From the area," Harriet said, and DI Adams' shoulders slumped. Of course they were. *Of course* they were.

"Right," she said. "Well, look. If they're planning an out of season shoot, there are channels to go through to deal with it legally, get the whole thing shut down for good. But you can't go blocking the road like this. What are you doing knocking trees down, anyway? I wouldn't have thought that was your thing."

The women exchanged glances. "That was kind of an accident," Rainbow admitted.

"An accident?"

"We were going to sleep in the tree, but I guess the roots weren't that firm."

"It was Ronnie," Harriet said. "That's not all layers, you know. He's ... solid."

"We did tell him to sleep on the ground, but he said it was better in the event of a surprise attack if we were all in the tree."

DI Adams scratched the back of her neck. "I see."

"We wouldn't deliberately cut a tree down," Harriet said. "That would be terrible."

"But now it *is* down," Rainbow said, "it's obvious that Mother Nature herself is supporting our protest."

"I'm sorry?"

"Well, the tree wouldn't have fallen if she didn't want it to."

"But you just said it fell down because the roots weren't strong enough and you had too many people in it."

"Oh, sure. Those are the *physical* reasons," Rainbow said, nodding. "But not the *real* reasons."

"Right." DI Adams put her hands back in her pockets. "So you won't move it, then?"

"Of course not!" Rainbow looked shocked. "We can't go against the will of the Earth Goddess herself!"

"Definitely not," Harriet agreed, and DI Adams sighed.

"Right," she said. "Well, I'm going to get the chainsaw out of the car, and chop the tree up. Because there are people at the house who need to leave." *Like me*, she added to herself. *I'd rather like to leave, and bollocks to a spa weekend. I'll get a face mask from the chemist.*

"I don't think you should do that," Rainbow said.

"And why not?"

"Because you seem rather nice, and you should understand that we're doing this in the name of feminine power and against centuries of male oppression. *White* male oppression."

"I'm doing it in the name of law and order, and wanting to get back to my own bed," DI Adams said, and trudged back to the Land Rover.

"I'm warning you!" Rainbow shouted.

"That better not be a threat against a police officer," DI Adams shouted back, opening the back door of the Land Rover and taking the chainsaw out.

"Let me do that for you," Boyd said, materialising close enough to her that she had to swallow a yelp.

"I need this done now, and quickly, Boyd. No poetry."

He took the chainsaw from her and looked at her with wide eyes. "No poetry."

"Alright." She peered around the Land Rover at the protesters, who had gone suspiciously quiet. Ronnie had come back off the bridge and they were all clustering by their little makeshift camp. She turned her attention back to Boyd, who was still staring at her. "What? Get it done!"

"I will," he said, nodding eagerly. "I will do this for you. Thank you. Thank you for seeing past the distance between us and recognising that I can do this for you, that I *will* do this for you—"

"Are you going to do it or not?"

"Yes. Yes, I will. I just wanted to say that I wouldn't do this for just anyone. The chainsaw is an art form in itself. But you— you *astound* me."

"This … place," she managed, and snatched the chainsaw off him. "Get in the damn car!"

"No! No, I want to help!"

"If you don't get in the car right now I will astound you with a set of handcuffs and a night's stay in a jail cell." She waved the chainsaw at him rather more threateningly than she intended to, which seemed to work. She was a bit worried that mentioning handcuffs may have had the opposite effect to the one she'd intended.

Once he was back in the car, face pressed to the window, she marched to the tree. The protesters had regrouped on the other side, holding buckets they must have fetched from their camp. On the one hand, she hoped they weren't going to do anything stupid. On the other, she was *dying* to arrest someone.

"I'm going to have to ask you to move back," she said, in a tone that said she wasn't actually asking.

"Don't do this," Rainbow said. "Don't support the white, elitist patriarchy."

"I'm not supporting anything. I'm making the only road out of this place passable again."

"Traitor!" Jemima shrieked.

DI Adams glared at her, and pulled safety goggles down over her eyes. "Please stand back. I don't want anyone getting hurt." The chainsaw screamed as she started it, an ugly sound, and the young woman reached into her bucket. DI Adams eyed her for a moment, then turned her attention back to the tree.

"You're just a pawn of The Man!" Rainbow shouted, but the inspector could barely hear her over the roar of the machine. She hadn't been able to find ear protectors, but hopefully this wouldn't take long.

She took a wide-legged stance in front of the tree, glimpsing

Boyd climbing out of the Land Rover and waving wildly as he shouted something. She ignored him and brought the chainsaw down on the trunk of the tree. The scream turned to a hungry grumble, the assault of the teeth on the wood jarring her whole body, and she caught a flash of movement out of the corner of her eye just before something hit her shoulder. She jumped, jerking away from the tree, and said something the W.I. would definitely not have approved of. The missile flopped to her feet, and she turned the chainsaw off as she looked down at it, globular on the gravel.

"A water balloon?" she said, her eyebrows raised. "You're throwing *water* balloons at me?"

"I told you they wouldn't break!" Ronnie said, hopping from one foot to the other. "I *told* you!"

Tom grabbed a balloon and hurled it, hard. DI Adams ducked. The balloon sailed harmlessly over her and hit Boyd's cheek with the wet whump of a dropped pumpkin, and lumpy red liquid exploded across his face. He yelped, and DI Adams spun toward Tom.

"Stop that!" she shouted, and a balloon caught her full in the face. This one did burst, and she said something unrepeatable as sweet, sticky red muck flooded down her neck and into her fleece. "Stop it, all of you!"

But the success of the first balloons seemed to have given the protesters confidence. They started shouting, bursting into chants of *Down with the Man* and *Save the Country*, with Ronnie throwing in his own, less PG-rated versions here and there, making Jemima shriek with delight. The air was full of sauce-packed missiles, exploding against the Land Rover and the tree, and DI Adams grabbed Boyd.

"Get in the car!" she shouted at him, as two more balloons hit her back. "*Would you bloody well stop that, you numpties?*"

"I will stand between you!" Boyd shouted. "I will suffer the stings and blows of—" He took a balloon to the face that set him spluttering, and DI Adams almost revised her opinion of the protesters.

"You're assaulting a police officer, you know!" she shouted at them, with slightly less heat than before. Then Jemima jumped onto the tree and started scooping handfuls of feathers out of her bucket, flinging them in the general direction of the inspector. Boyd had recovered from the direct strike and was shouting at his aunt that this sort of thing was a little much, really, while she took careful aim with another balloon. The feathers drifted in the eddying breeze like fairy clocks and stuck to the sauce, turning Boyd and the inspector into fluffy, misshapen monsters. DI Adams gave up shouting at the protesters, because not only was no one listening, the possibility of ending up with a mouthful of mysterious sauce seemed quite high, and turned her attention to Boyd. She wouldn't have objected to abandoning him, but it seemed a little unfair.

She grabbed his arm and snapped, "I'm leaving now. In the car now if you're coming."

He gave her a confused, almost hurt look, and said, "You'd leave me here? But we're a team!"

She let him go and stalked to the Land Rover, ignoring another direct hit to her back and the cheers of the protesters. She hauled the door open and got in, Boyd scampering after her with a final pleading look at his aunt. He scrambled into the passenger seat, shedding sauce and feathers everywhere as she put the car into reverse. She backed around, then headed up the drive toward the house. The protesters stayed on their side of the tree, cheering and shouting and hugging each other as if they'd just won a major victory. Feathers drifted in the air, and the plastic skins of balloons littered the ground.

"Would you have breakfast with me?" Boyd asked.

"No."

There was a pause, neither as long nor as calm as DI Adams would have liked. There was sauce dribbling down her neck, and she had just realised that these were her last clean clothes. Had been. Her walking trousers still smelt of slow-roasted lamb, her hoody was never going to be the same after Carlotta and Rosemary had attacked it, and now she was covered in roast dinner condiments. She sighed.

"*The feathers are as an angel's wings,*" Boyd began.

"Shut up before I shoot you in the leg." She spat a feather out.

"You don't have a gun."

"I'll find one."

He subsided, and they drove back to the house in silence, surrounded by drifting feathers and the sharp scent of cranberry sauce.

10
ALICE

lice was in the shared bathroom brushing her teeth when
DI Adams came in without knocking. Well, she assumed it
was DI Adams, as it had the wrong build for Miriam, and didn't
seem surprised to see her in there. Alice stood by the sink, electric
toothbrush still whirring, and examined the apparition, then
switched the brush off and rinsed it before turning back to say, "I
presume this means the road is still blocked?"

"Bloody protesters," DI Adams grumbled. She was dripping
crimson sauce on the carpet, and soft white feathers floated off her
every time she moved.

Alice nodded. "Protesting a shoot of some sort?"

"Yes. How did you know?"

"Feathers, plus those look terribly like cranberry and bread
sauces."

DI Adams looked down at herself. "What are they shooting,
turkeys?"

"Pheasants, but I suppose cranberry sauce has a certain visual
impact that mustard sauce lacks."

The inspector made a face. "It's certainly had an impact on my clothes. My pyjamas are the only clean things I have left now, unless my jumper's dried."

"I'll see what we can round up for you," Alice said. "Teresa always has about five sets of workout gear with her."

"Fantastic," the inspector said, scooping bread sauce out of the neck of her fleece and flicking it into the sink. "This was just the relaxing weekend I was looking for. Really. And having to wear a 72-year-old's Lycra running outfit really just caps it for me."

"73," Alice said. "She's had a birthday."

"Well happy bloody birthday," the younger woman said, and Alice let herself out into the hall before she could laugh. She was quite sure the inspector wouldn't appreciate being laughed at right now.

⁊₂

SHE ALMOST BUMPED into the journalist as she pulled the door to behind her.

"And what are you doing hanging around ladies' bathrooms, young man?" she asked him.

"Less ladies' bathrooms than the detective inspector's bathroom," he said, giving her that dimpled grin.

"She isn't giving me the sense that she's very interested in you hanging around her bathroom."

"But I'm very interested in why she's come in covered in feathers and"—he stooped to swipe a blob off the carpet and taste it—"cranberry sauce."

Alice gave him a disapproving look. "I doubt that carpet is any too clean."

"I think I've eaten at dirtier takeaways."

The bathroom door banged open, and DI Adams glared at Ervin, the effect spoilt somewhat by the beehive of feathers and sauce she was wearing. "Sod off, you annoying little newshound."

He tried the grin on her. "Oh, come on. This is *so* much more interesting than writing two thousand words on how the gardens are being shaped to modern aesthetics with middling results."

The inspector appeared to be immune to the grin, much to Alice's approval. "Why don't you go down the drive and find out yourself?"

His grin widened. "Pass. So, shooting protesters? Are they local? This could be an interesting angle. It's not pheasant season, so what's that all about? And what's the connection with the sous-chef? Was he anti-shoot and infiltrating from the inside, and got busted? Pro-shoot and a protester wanted to teach him a lesson?"

"He was pro-hors d'oeuvre, and pro-taking a sauna at silly hours of the night," DI Adams said. "Now go interview a squirrel or something." She slammed the door again, but not before Alice had seen a twitch in her expression that made her wonder just how comfortable the inspector was with the accident theory. But it wasn't the time for speculation.

She put her sternest look on and poked the young man in the arm. "You heard her. Off you go."

"Freedom of the press," he reminded her.

"Freedom of a woman to take a shower without being disturbed," Alice said. "I believe in it very much. Now I suggest you go down to breakfast, and don't bother anyone else."

He gave her a smile that was uncomfortably close to a smirk, and sauntered away. Alice found herself wishing he would go talk to the protesters. She rather fancied seeing him plastered with feathers and sauce.

❧

THE CANE CHAIRS and glass-topped tables in the breakfast room were of the sort that Alice remembered being popular when she was too young to be coming to fancy hotels. They hadn't aged particularly well, but they looked right in this room, with the leafy orangery leaning in on one side and the woods visible through the windows. A table in the centre of the room was crowded with jars of muesli and platters of fruit, bowls of dried apricots and prunes and nuts, a selection of mini-muffins and what looked like a very acceptable banana cake topped with walnuts, as well as a couple of boxes of brightly coloured cereal that no one had opened. She supposed they were for the American children, but they were polishing off big plates of sausages and eggs and bacon, a leaning tower of toast in the middle of their table. The birdwatchers were sitting at a corner table as far from the Americans as they could get, looking rather bleary and dishevelled, cradling cups of coffee and not talking to each other. The antique hunters were holding hands at another table, and all of them were sat as far from the treatment room door as it was possible to get, even though there was no crime scene tape on it or any other sign of what had happened. Alice didn't blame them.

The W.I. were slowly filling a collection of tables under the windows, and although Ervin followed Alice down the stairs he swerved toward Lottie and Edie once they got to the breakfast room. He dimpled at them, and Lottie smiled quite sweetly back, but Edie looked at him like something unidentified that she'd just found in the bottom of the veggie drawer in the fridge. By the time Alice had fetched herself some fruit and sat down next to Miriam, the antique hunters had excused themselves, and Ervin was looking around the room hopefully.

"He's such a nuisance, that man," Miriam said. "Tea? We've just got a fresh pot."

"Please." Alice watched Miriam fill her cup. "It seems the detective inspector had no luck clearing the road. Protesters."

"So we heard," Gert said from across the table. "Maddie's in a right state about it."

"Poor Maddie," Miriam said. "I mean, she hates guns. She'd never let any shoot happen, let alone an out of season one."

"*Hmm,*" Alice said, watching Reid pop out of the *Private* door, glance around the room, and hurry into the lounge with a worried look on his face.

"Do you think she might have to sell, Miriam?" Rosemary asked.

"I hope not," Miriam said. "She loves this place."

"Well, if this is her relaunch, it's not boding well," Rose said, dipping a toast soldier in her boiled egg. "She might have to cut her losses."

"Maybe it wouldn't be such a bad thing," Pearl said. "It must be such a stress for her. And I love this place too, but it's starting to get a bit beyond what a little DIY can handle. The shelf in our room all but fell on Teresa's head this morning, and we didn't even touch it."

Alice thought that Teresa's habit of starting the day with jumping jacks might have had something to do with it, but it was still no excuse for shelves falling down.

"And that young girl was right about the mice in the walls," Priya said. "I heard them all last night."

"This place is beautiful," Miriam said, setting the milk jug back down with a little more force than was entirely necessary. "Imagine if a developer bought it and turned it into – into a *golf course* or something!"

A general shudder went around the table as Alice mopped milk up with her napkin. "That would be quite dreadful. But an illegal shoot is no answer, if that's what certain family members are planning."

"No one's shooting here," Maddie said, and everyone fell silent. Pearl went a startling shade of pink, and Maddie placed two fresh pots of tea on the tables. "You know I don't agree with guns, not after Denis. And I am going to make this work." She looked at each of them, her hair pinned back with a ferocious amount of bobby pins but still escaping in curls around her face. "Somehow."

"It'll work," Miriam said. "It will." There were a lot of agreeable noises and compliments on the new food and the new decor offered up around the table, and Alice added her own, then sipped her tea thoughtfully. She wondered how far someone might go to make sure a hunt *did* happen, if they believed that would save the place. How much it would take to force someone to see that the choice was a hunt or a sale. They weren't nice things to be thinking about people she knew, but she'd learnt a long time ago that you couldn't always think well of people, not matter how much you wanted to. There was no point in fooling yourself. It might be more comfortable to start with, but not in the long term.

Adele appeared at her elbow, almost making her jump. "Breakfast?" the young woman offered.

"Just some toast, please," Alice said.

"Rye? Wholemeal? Gluten-free? I recommend the gluten-free, personally."

"Wholemeal will be lovely, thank you."

"Oh. Alright. Are you sure you wouldn't like to try …?"

"No, thank you." Alice inspected the teapot. It was astonishing how many cups ten ladies could get through. "And a little more tea, if we might."

"Green? White? Rooibos? Ginger and—"

"Just regular. Yorkshire if you've got it," Alice said, wondering when toast and tea had become so complicated.

"Okay. Would you like soy or nut milk? We have—"

"Adele, I'm far too old for such fancy things," Alice said. "I should like Yorkshire tea with regular cow's milk, and regular toast with plain butter and a little marmalade, if you would."

The young woman sighed, her very posture indicating that she thought Alice was destroying all the good work the yoga had done. "Well. Alright, then."

"Thank you very much." Alice turned back to Miriam, and found a cat in her chair instead. "Excuse me?"

The cat purred, and hooked a kipper off Miriam's plate.

"Stop that!" Alice said. "What've you done with Miriam?"

"I went to get more juice," Miriam said, arriving back at the table with a glass in each hand. "I was still eating that!"

The cat crunched on the kipper with every indication of enjoyment, his front paws braced on the table and the fish half on the tablecloth.

"Honestly, you're so uncouth," Alice said to him, and the cat stopped eating, giving her a narrow-eyed glare. "You know you won't eat it all, but Miriam can't eat it now. If you'd just asked, I'm sure she'd have cut a piece off for you."

The cat licked his lips. "Alice, that almost sounds as though you're accusing me of having germs." His voice had a smoker's rasp but the clear accent of a BBC presenter.

"You probably do. You clean … everything with your tongue."

The cat huffed. "So this is how it goes. I come to say hi, make sure you're okay, and this is the thanks I get."

Alice glared at him.

He huffed again, giving the impression that he'd roll his eyes if he could. "Fine. I was bored."

"Well, I was having a nice weekend away with my friends."

The cat sat back in the seat and examined a paw as Miriam sighed and pulled out a different chair, reaching over to take her cup of tea. "Hey," he objected. "I need something to wash this lot down."

"I don't think cats should have tea," Miriam said.

"Cats?" Adele asked brightly, putting a plate stacked with toast in the centre of the table. It was piled somewhat haphazardly, and looked like it might have had a bit of a fall on the way through all the doors from the kitchen. "Terrible luck are cats. And a bit creepy."

Someone said *pah* rather loudly, and Alice coughed to cover it up.

"Can I get you anything else?" Adele asked.

"No, that's wonderful," Alice said. "I don't imagine I'll need anything more." There were at least ten pieces of toast on the plate.

"I'll share it," Miriam said, as Adele left and the cat pushed his head out from under the tablecloth. "Since my kipper was stolen."

"It's pretty tasty, too," the cat said, taking another bite. "But yeah, sounds like a really peaceful weekend, Alice. Murder always is."

There was a sudden, frozen silence on the W.I.'s side of the room (which had been the only side with much conversation anyway), as the ladies stopped pretending they couldn't see the talking cat, and stared at him. One of the birdwatchers said, "*Yes!*", and the three of them huddled more tightly around a laptop, and Holt shouted at his son for taking the last piece of toast. The cat licked his lips.

"Oh," he said. "You didn't know that bit?"

Alice opened her mouth to say something, just as DI Adams leaned over the table and said in a low, sharp-edged voice, "Thompson? Seriously?"

"Hey," the cat said. "You fallen out with the big man, then? He not giving you all the details?"

The inspector picked the cat up by the scruff of the neck and headed into the orangery and toward the terrace, supporting his hindquarters with her other hand and not allowing him the slightest hope of escape. The ladies of the Toot Hansell Women's Institute got up with a scraping of chairs and clattering of silverware and followed.

Gert pointed at Ervin as he started to get up. "Stay there," she advised him. "This is W.I. business."

"That was a cat," he said.

"It was," Alice agreed.

"Why are you all rushing about with a cat?"

"You heard the girl earlier," Priya said as she walked past. "There are mice in the walls."

"What ...?" He stared at Alice and Gert, who smiled at him, then looked back at his plate. "My eggs are on the way," he told it. "Although I may need something stronger."

Alice followed Priya through the orangery.

IT WAS chilly on the terrace, the little wind that had been creeping around earlier building muscles as the day brightened. There was heavy cloud above the fells beyond the woodland, low and threateningly fat with rain, and Alice pulled her cardigan tightly around her as she crossed to where the inspector was setting Thompson down on one of the terrace tables.

"That was totally uncalled for and so undignified," the cat said, licking his coat urgently. "And I was in the middle of breakfast."

"Murder?" DI Adams said, and Alice glanced up at the windows. She didn't trust Ervin not to sneak up to one of the rooms to spy on them.

"Murder?" someone rumbled. "Is it not an accident now?" Beaufort padded up onto the terrace, followed by Mortimer, who seemed to have lost more scales since this morning. He was also steaming gently in the sunlight, and he sneezed twice then sat down heavily behind the women, looking rather less interested than the High Lord in what was happening. Alice wondered what they'd been up to.

"The echo out here is quite spectacular," Thompson said, and DI Adams tapped his nose lightly with one finger. "Hey!"

"Why did you say murder?" she asked him. "How do you even know about it?"

"Look, doesn't your big cop boyfriend keep you updated on this?"

She sighed. "He's not my boyfriend, and we've got no phone signal. Plus the landlines are down."

"Ah. That makes sense." The cat went back to his grooming, and the inspector tapped his nose again. "*What?*"

"So tell me."

"Well, it's not really my place to say, is it? And you're not really making me feel like sharing. Besides, I'm sure that as it's murder, our Detective Inspector Colin Collins will be here soon. He'll drive up when he can't raise anyone, right?"

DI Adams sighed. "The road's blocked."

"Oho," Thompson said. "The plot thickens." He found something between his toes that required urgent cleaning, and Beaufort growled slightly. The cat ignored him. Mortimer wheezed, then coughed a small fish onto the stone and stared at it in alarm.

The inspector looked at Alice. "Can you do anything with him?"

"Nothing but withhold salmon when we get home."

"Hey! Look, I came to check on you. *I* didn't know you weren't up to date." His tail twitched. "Nice trousers, by the way."

DI Adams looked down at the kitten-print leggings and pink workout jacket Alice had borrowed from Teresa and said, "I'm so glad you approve."

Beaufort put his chin on the table next to the cat and exhaled air hot enough to make Thompson's ears flatten against his skull. "You're not being very helpful."

"I'm a cat. It's not in the job description."

"I'll take you to the vet unless you tell us," DI Adams offered. "Get them to clean your teeth or something."

"You'd never get me there." Thompson started on another paw. "Look, I know when I'm not wanted. When I'm *meddling*."

"Stop being such an awful little brat," Alice said, and the cat eyed her, then sighed and sat up.

"Fine, fine. But some appreciation would be in order, you know. So I have a friend in the Leeds station. She was cruising the lab and heard the autopsy report. She knows I'm interested in anything Toot Hansell, so passed it on. I recognised the name of the manor and thought I'd come see what was happening."

"They let cats into the morgue?" Carlotta asked. "That doesn't seem very hygienic."

"They're dead, what do they care?" the cat said. "Anyway, it was in the lab, where they were doing the tests."

"Even less hygienic," Teresa said.

"Ugh, stop it with this cats are unhygienic thing. It's very insulting." He scratched an ear. "Anyhow, my friend heard them say it was poison."

"Oh, God. *Again?*" Rosemary said, and Alice had to agree. One poisoning was more than enough for one Women's Institute.

"What sort of poison?" DI Adams asked.

"Bollocks," the cat said, and the women and dragons stared at him. "What? It was! Or something similar."

"I've never heard of bollocks being poisonous," Jasmine said.

"Maybe it's a certain type," Rose said. "Like porcupine fish."

"I think I've quite gone off fish," Mortimer observed, and sneezed again. Beaufort patted his shoulder.

"Isn't it the liver that's poisonous?" Priya asked.

"Yes, but I mean, you can eat a lot of types of liver. You can't eat a porcupine fish liver."

"You can if it's prepared correctly," Carlotta said.

"Would you eat one?" Rosemary asked.

"I might," she said carefully.

"I've eaten bollocks," Rose said cheerfully.

"Ew," Jasmine said.

"They're not bad with a bit of nice tomato-y sauce and a whole lot of garlic."

"In the old country—" Carlotta began, and Rosemary made a rude noise.

"In Manchester? I guess you probably do eat anything around there."

Carlotta huffed. "I'm only first-generation Mancunian, you know. I'm proud of my roots!"

"I wouldn't be," Rosemary said. "They're coming through very grey these days."

"Botox," Miriam said, as Carlotta spluttered in fury.

"What?" DI Adams asked.

"Botox."

"That's the one," the cat said.

The silence that followed was long and thoughtful, and Alice could hear something calling in the woods. It sounded like crying.

MIRIAM SAT DOWN HEAVILY and stared in a perplexed way at a rose bush shaped like a duck wearing a top hat. "Murder by Botox?"

"That's what they said the poison was," Thompson said.

"But ... but Adele ..."

"No one's saying it was her," Alice said firmly. "Are we, Detective Inspector?"

"No," DI Adams said, not very convincingly, then when Alice glared at her, she said, "We can't discount anybody at this point."

"*Nobody?*" Jasmine asked, horrified.

Miriam burst into tears. "It's not Adele," she wailed. "It's *not!*"

DI Adams looked almost as horrified as Jasmine, and Priya shoved past her so she could put her arms around Miriam.

"Come on now. No one's accusing anyone of anything. *Of course* Adele had nothing to do with it."

Miriam snuffled, burying her head in Priya's shoulder. "She *wouldn't.*"

"Of course not." Priya helped her up. "Now let's get out of the cold before you freeze."

"Wait," DI Adams said, and Miriam lifted her head from Priya's shoulder, wiping her nose with the back of her hand. Alice handed her a tissue. "I'm not accusing anyone right now, but this can't go back inside. If the sous-chef really was murdered, the murderer's here. And we can't risk them making a run for it. So I'm trusting you to make sure nothing leaves this group." The inspector looked from the women, to the dragons, to the cat. "Am I understood?"

"Yeah, like I'm talking to anyone else," the cat said.

"I want to know more about this bull-tacks," Beaufort said. "Is it a common poison?"

"Botox," Alice said.

"It's a toxin derived from botulism that people use to paralyse small muscles and make themselves look younger," Jasmine said, then added hastily, "I mean, that's what I've read." She touched her forehead reflexively.

"Works bloody well, too," Gert said. "I've had it a few times."

"Really?" Carlotta said. "I was wondering about trying it myself."

"I imagine that's not the kind of thing they do in the old country," Rosemary said, but Carlotta ignored her.

"I only stopped because the beautician got it too close to my eye once and it went a bit droopy," Gert said. "That made me feel a bit weird about it all."

"You put a poison that paralyses you into your face?" Beaufort said, his voice tinged with wonder. "How fascinating."

"That's one term for it," the cat replied.

"Enough about Botox," Alice said. "Thompson, did your friend tell you anything more?"

"Just that there was Botox poison," the cat said.

"Maybe it stopped his heart," DI Adams said. "Or paralysed his lungs. A big dose, delivered straight into the chest, might do it."

"But who could have done it?" Pearl asked. "He was a big man to tackle."

"The American?" Rosemary suggested. "He's at least as big."

The inspector made a *hmm* sound. "Maybe. But just being obnoxious isn't actually a motive."

"Maybe it was more than one attacker," Rose said. "Maybe some hunters did it. Maybe he was a spy for the protesters, and they offed him before he could, um, pour porridge in their guns."

"That would have been pretty effective, if it was the same porridge as this morning," Rosemary said.

"That was chia porridge," Jasmine said. "It's always like that."

"Why?" Rosemary asked. "It was awful."

"Maybe it was Reid," Teresa said. "He used to hunt."

"*And* he used to be the chef," Priya said. "And they were fighting last night." Her eyes were bright, and although she still had an arm around Miriam she seemed to have rather forgotten she was there.

"Can't be Boyd. He'd have just killed him with bad poetry," Pearl said.

"Those are my nephews," Miriam pointed out.

"And this is just the worst sort of speculation," DI Adams said. "I shouldn't have even got you started on this."

"It was the cat," Miriam said, and they all looked at Thompson, who shrugged.

"Hey, don't shoot the messenger."

"It doesn't matter who started it," DI Adams said. "It stops now. No speculation. No discussion. No one can be tipped off about this. If this has become a murder investigation, the local police will be back here before lunch. You are *not* to discuss this with *anyone*, understand?" She pointed at the dragons. "No investigating."

Mortimer sneezed, then nodded enthusiastically, but Beaufort said, "Well—"

"No investigating."

Beaufort sighed, but nodded, and DI Adams turned to Miriam. "And Miriam? I know you'll be worried about your family, but you can't talk to them about this. You *can't*."

"I won't," she mumbled.

"Not even Maddie. I'm not saying any of them are suspects, but they may inadvertently tip off the murderer."

"I *won't*," she said, hugging her arms around herself. "Can we go back in now? It's freezing."

"It really is," Alice agreed, looking out over the trees. The clouds were building toward them and there was the smell of rain in the air as the day darkened rapidly. "Has anyone seen the weather forecast?"

"Feels like a storm," Beaufort said.

DI Adams sighed. "Let me guess. Big storms that'll probably wash out the road and stop the police getting here?"

"That's if they can get past the protesters," Mortimer said, then squeaked when she glared at him. "Sorry."

"I should go back to London," the inspector said, not addressing anyone in particular. "This was meant to be a low stress position."

"Well, you're not technically at work," Rose pointed out.

DI Adams covered her face with her hands as a rumble of thunder rolled around the horizon, faint but threatening as an unseen dog. "I need coffee. And breakfast."

"Let's go in," Alice said. "It's starting to rain."

11

MORTIMER

The dragons shadowed Alice and Miriam as they climbed the stairs to the bedrooms, keeping close to the walls, their feet quiet on the carpet. Mortimer thought he might sneeze again, and was trying to hold it in until they were in the room. That was the last thing they needed, him setting the hall on fire or something.

They were at the midpoint landing when a voice called from below them. "Should we be worrying about the impromptu meeting of the Women's Institute on the terrace?" Ervin asked. "Plus the detective inspector, of course?"

Mortimer pressed himself into the wood panelling and tried to be a tree.

Alice leaned on the banister. "You should worry about your own business, Mr Giles," she said. "Unless the matter of cats is of such concern to you."

"Oh? Was that what it was? It took all eleven of you rushing outside to deal with one cat?"

"You have evidently never dealt with a cat. Eleven people is barely enough."

Thompson purred as the journalist snorted and shook his head.

"I don't know what's going on here, but you can't keep sneaking around and expecting no one'll notice. Maybe the rest of them are slow, but I'm a journalist. I'm a trained observer, me."

"Trained tosser, more like," Thompson mumbled, and Alice's lips twitched into a smile. Ervin sighed, and for a moment he looked young and vulnerable. But he was still far too nosy for Mortimer to really feel sorry for him.

"Come on," he said. "I'm not here to do a hack job. I love these old houses. I'd like to see them succeed. But someone's died, and the way you're all carrying on makes me think there's more to it that just an accident in the sauna. I know the inspector won't help me, so just give me a break. I don't want to be writing lifestyle pieces my whole career."

Alice straightened up. "In that case, Mr Giles, I recommend you find a proper story, and stop sticking your nose into W.I. business. It's liable to get bitten." She started back up the stairs, catching Miriam's arm and urging her on, and Thompson lingered just long enough to spit at the confused journalist.

THE BEDROOM WAS WARM, and once the lamps were on it was bathed in a cosy light that pushed back the lowering sky outside. Rain was already starting to leave fingerprints on the windows, and the wind rattled the frames as if testing them out for a later assault. Thompson leaped onto Alice's bed and made himself comfortable, while Alice put the kettle on and Miriam pulled the cake tins out of her bag, much to Mortimer's relief.

"Any kippers?" the cat asked.

"*No*," Miriam snapped. "You stole my kipper."

"You bring cake for dragons. Why not fish for cats?"

"Because you are not an invited guest," Beaufort said.

"Harsh."

"But fair," Alice said, setting the mugs out.

"Hey, you wouldn't have even known you were hanging around with a murderer if it wasn't for me."

"We're so grateful," Miriam said. "Really. I feel so much better knowing that."

Alice patted her shoulder. "Why don't you go and get changed, dear?"

Miriam looked down at her tie-dyed purple and orange skirt and furry green jumper. "Why? This is very comfortable."

"Because sometimes it pays to have practical clothes on. Just in case."

Mortimer didn't like the sound of *just in case*. *Just in case* sounded like investigating. *Just in case* sounded like they were going to ignore the detective inspector's instructions. Evidently Miriam thought so too, because she stared at Alice for a long time before she fished her walking clothes out of her bag and went to the bathroom to change.

Alice rinsed the mugs in the wash basin and retrieved the milk from the window sill. "Mortimer, would you like a fat rascal?"

"Er," he said, not sure if that was something he should like or not, or even if he was possibly being a little insulted.

"It's a bit like a scone."

"Oh! Yes, please, then," he said. Murder or not, scone-like things should never be turned down.

"Where's the DI?" Beaufort asked.

"Having breakfast, I imagine," Alice said. "Why?"

"Well," the High Lord said thoughtfully, "we have a murderer running around here somewhere. So shouldn't we take a little look at the crime scene? We might be able sniff something out."

"No," Mortimer said, almost dropping the squat cake Alice had handed him. "No, Beaufort, she *specifically* said not to. What if she catches us?"

"What if we catch the murderer?"

Mortimer gave a disconsolate little huff and ate the fat rascal in one bite. "What if we just tip them off?" he asked, muffled by cake.

"Mortimer, dear, don't leave crumbs everywhere," Alice said. "I heard those mice while you were out last night, too. Sound more like rats to me, to be honest."

"Do they?" Beaufort asked. "Anything missing, by any chance?"

He and Alice looked at the scattered clothes and cake tins that had apparently exploded out of Miriam's bag, and Alice said, "Hard to say, really."

Mortimer took the opportunity to take another fat rascal, thinking it would be better with butter. It was still good, of course, but butter made everything better.

Miriam let herself back into the room, and looked from the worried Mortimer to Alice and Beaufort, who were both looking rather determined. "Oh, no," she said. "What're we doing now?"

"WHAT IF THE murderer sees us poking around?" Miriam asked, staring at her mug of tea.

"That's what I said," Mortimer told her.

"I don't think they will," Alice said. "There are enough of us to keep a good watch and to distract anyone who heads for the treatment rooms. No one should be in the orangery or on the terrace with this weather, and the inspector's the last at breakfast, so there's no reason for anyone to go past the lounge. I think it's a good idea."

"You would," Miriam mumbled, then went from pale to pink as Alice gave her a surprised look. "I just mean, why do we always have to get involved?"

"You think the dragons should do it on their own?"

Mortimer choked on a scrap of cake.

"No, of course not! But maybe we should at least ask DI Adams, and let her decide."

"Maybe," Alice said. "But she does have some control issues."

Miriam made a funny little snorting sound and covered it up by sipping her tea. "If she says she doesn't want help—"

"She fails to appreciate just how much we can help," Beaufort said. "She's all on her own with this, and we could sniff out the murderer straight away! If she realised, I'm sure she'd be very glad of our assistance."

Mortimer thought rather darkly that he doubted very much DI Adams would be happy in any way, and took another fat rascal.

"Then we should just tell her," Miriam said.

"Oh, she'd just say dragons get in the way," Beaufort said.

"And that we shouldn't meddle," Alice added.

"Then maybe we should listen," Mortimer said. "You know, to the person in charge?"

"Just because they're in charge doesn't make them right," Alice said.

Thompson got up and stretched. "I like your thinking. Someone needs to take some sort of action. I'll go keep an eye on the DI and let you know when she's out of the way."

"Right," Alice said. "We'll pass the word and meet in the lounge. Beaufort, you and Mortimer stay here, and come down when Thompson says it's safe."

"Wait for my signal," the cat said.

"Of course," Beaufort replied. "Hairballs at dawn?"

The cat gave him a disapproving look, then vanished the way cats do, leaving behind nothing but a few stray hairs and a vague sense of superiority.

"I wish he wouldn't do that," Alice said. "It's like the laws of physics don't even apply."

"He's a cat," Beaufort said. "They don't."

ALICE AND MIRIAM departed by rather more conventional means, and the dragons waited. It didn't take long, but Mortimer still managed to eat most of the fat rascals in the time they had.

"You'll ruin your lunch, lad," Beaufort said.

"I don't care. It gives me something else to think about," he said, pushing the nearly empty container away sadly. "And they're really good."

"Not quite as good as scones," Beaufort said. "Although I suppose it's not really scone weather."

The rain had grown heavy, drumming against the windows and turning the world outside faint and wobbly. The clouds were low and dark, the fells beyond the woods long vanished in the murk, and wind was raking heavy fingers through the trees. Mortimer didn't envy the protesters camping out in this weather. Not that he felt all that much better in here, with murderers running around and unauthorised investigations in the offing. He'd rather be home in his workshop, folding dragon scales into baubles while the fires warmed the corners of the cavern and the prisms above him collected and concentrated the warm red light. He wondered how Gilbert and Amelia were getting on. It was good thing Gilbert wasn't here, at least. He'd have been horrified by the idea of any sort of hunting for fun, and would probably have joined the protesters. Mortimer rested his chin on his paws, his eyes half-closed, and was drifting in warm thoughts of fire and fat rascals when the cat appeared in the middle of the room.

"Up and at 'em, scaly buddies," he said. "The DI's gone out to see about clearing the road and the ladies are keeping the crime scene clear."

Mortimer sat up. "Is this a good idea? Really?"

"You don't have to come, lad," Beaufort said. "But you do have a much better nose than mine."

Mortimer groaned. He was getting more and more sure that was just empty flattery, but he couldn't let Beaufort go off on his own. Who knew what he'd do?

"Really, lad. Just stay here. I'm sure we won't find anything anyway."

Mortimer wriggled, torn between the idea of staying curled up here in the warm, where there were still a couple of fat rascals, and venturing out where anyone could see them in order to sniff out a murderer. "Do *any* of us have to go?"

"Well, no. But the DI is on her own here, as Alice pointed out. That's hard."

Mortimer looked at his claws and made one more wish that he was back in his workshop. When he looked up, he was still in the room with the impatient-looking cat and the High Lord, so he got up with a sigh. "Fine. Let's go."

The cat led them to the stairs with his tail low and his feet soundless, glancing back at them occasionally to hiss, "Quiet!"

Mortimer was doing his absolute best to be quiet, but compared to the cat he felt like a rhinoceros in hobnail boots lumbering down the hall, the floorboards creaking under his feet and (much to his horror) his tail bouncing off the wall twice. The harder he tried to be quiet the noisier he was.

Thompson paused at the top of the stairs and peered between the banisters, then nodded. "We're clear." He ran down the stairs, Beaufort following him quiet and quick, and Mortimer came last, concentrating on not tangling his claws in the carpet and falling on his nose. Rosemary was sitting in a chair pulled up by the door to the lounge, knitting enthusiastically, and she nodded at them. They ran across the tiles, claws *tock-tock*-ing, and slipped into the lounge with the cat loping ahead of them. The lounge itself was empty, and the cat and the dragons scuttled between the old sofas and out into the breakfast room. Jasmine gave them a nervous little wave from the orangery doors, and Mortimer spotted Alice sat in a chair by the treatment room with her legs crossed at the ankles. She got up as the dragons bolted toward her, and opened the door. Mortimer's heart was pounding wildly, and he felt horribly dizzy. This was a crime scene! They were tampering with a crime scene! *Again!* Thunder rumbled rather ominously outside, which seemed appropriate.

Alice followed the dragons in and locked the door behind them. "Good thing they thought it was an accident," she told them. "The police must have left it unlocked after they were finished."

"Where is everyone?" Beaufort asked.

"Miriam's making sure Maddie doesn't come wandering around."

"And everyone else?" The fat rascals were suddenly feeling very heavy in Mortimer's stomach.

"Well." Alice smiled at him. "We can't have you dragons bearing all the responsibility of investigating, can we?"

Mortimer thought that sounded an awful lot like *you can't be having all the fun,* and found himself wanting to point out that he wasn't having much fun at all. Not even slightly, in fact.

"Do tell," Beaufort said, grinning hugely.

"Gert and Pearl have gone to have a little chat with the Americans. Hopefully they can get Paula away from that horrible man for a bit and see if he was up to something other than drinking last night. Priya and Carlotta are going to ask the chef all about her kitchen and generally try to make nuisances of themselves until she tells them more about Keeley, and Teresa and Rose are going to be sympathetic ears for the family. I don't like to think it was one of them, but we all saw that altercation with Reid."

"Most satisfactory," Beaufort said. "If we find a scent, then we'll know who to focus on, and if not we'll be ahead in the next stage of the investigation. What about the journalist and the bird-watchers?"

"We'll get to them," Alice said, sounding rather too comfortable with ignoring the inspector and running a rogue operation. "Eliminate the most likely suspects first."

Mortimer thought it was possible that he could actually feel his scales shedding as he stood here.

"I don't like the journalist," Thompson announced. "No consideration for the importance of cats."

"I'm not certain that makes him guilty of murder," Alice pointed out.

"Probably means he's capable of it, though."

"Be that as it may, I fail to see a motive, unless he really is trying to create a story." She paused, looking thoughtful. "Which isn't impossible."

"And the antique ladies?" Beaufort said. "One of them did find the body."

"Yes, but that seems just a little too obvious to me."

"Well, nice work," Thompson said. "I'm out of here. I'll go and keep an eye on the DI, make sure she doesn't come back unexpectedly and find you lot cluttering up her crime scene." Then he was gone, stepping sideways into nothing.

Mortimer wished he could do the same, and wondered why everyone was talking about nice work and things being satisfactory. He thought DI Adams would relish the opportunity to try arresting dragons. She was very enthusiastic about her work.

Beaufort gazed around the room. "It's very … purple."

Mortimer had been too distracted to notice until now, but Beaufort was right. It was very purple. Even though Mortimer's natural colours were purples and blues, he felt that he really wasn't purple enough to do the room justice. Admittedly, he was so terribly anxious that he had faded to a purple-tinted grey, but still. He padded over the purple rugs, wondering if the walls were actually mauve or if it was just the reflection of the rest of the room. There was even a dark purple phone.

"Well, I don't think the colour was the problem," Alice said, and pulled aside a purple curtain. It opened onto the treatment room lounge, which was lit by those sort of lights that imitate the sun, and was full of ferns and climbing plants living on shelves that lined the walls. There was a door marked *Private* at the end of the room, and two that said *Treatment Room*, with numbers. The third was marked *Sauna*, and this was the one the dragons approached, Mortimer lagging a little. The whole place smelt like the essential oils Miriam used sometimes, but stronger and more layered, drowning the fresh scents of the plants and the hint of cleaning products.

"I can't smell much," Mortimer said.

"Me neither, lad," Beaufort said. "Let's take a look, though."

They stopped in front of the door. It was just like the others, plain and white with a wooden plaque proclaiming its use. It didn't even *feel* wrong, not really. Or no more than the rest of the room, which had a vague sense of self-consciousness and uncertainty about it. Beaufort got up on his hind legs and opened the door, letting out a gust of eucalyptus-scented moist air that made Mortimer sneeze. The High Lord huffed a couple of times, and rested back on his haunches.

"Well, that's terribly strong."

Mortimer sneezed again, covering his snout with one paw. "'Scuse me."

Beaufort ventured a couple of steps into the room then retreated rapidly, shaking his head. "Oh, dear. No, that's no good at all."

"Nothing?" Alice asked.

Mortimer sneezed in reply, his eyes watering rather alarmingly. He supposed it would at least clean out the last of the river water from his encounter with the knucker. Beaufort gave a choked snort. "I don't know what they're using in here, but it's terribly strong."

"I guess they've already cleaned it," she said. "Can you get any sense of anyone at all?"

Beaufort tried peeking into the room again. Dragons pick up the traces of emotions the way dogs pick up scents, but just as a dog can be confused by competing scents, so too are emotional traces drowned under the passage of people and, apparently, by the use of an awful lot of essential oils.

"I'm sorry," the High Lord said. "We'll have to focus on the more human methods of investigation."

Mortimer rather thought that they didn't have to do any such thing, but he kept that to himself. There was no point trying to dissuade Alice and Beaufort.

Beaufort pulled the door shut, and as he did Thompson appeared in the middle of the floor, fur soaked and feet matted with mud. "You two," he snapped. "You need to get to the river *now*. DI Adams is in the water."

"*What?*" Mortimer demanded. Alice was already running for the door, waving the dragons to wait. "How's she in the water?"

"Knucker," the cat said, his voice tight. "Stupid bloody human playing with it. *Hurry!*"

Alice peered around the door, then jerked it open. "Clear," she said. "Jasmine, open the doors!"

The dragons exploded out of the treatment room and barrelled toward the orangery, Mortimer's tail catching a chair and sending it flying. Jasmine was already running ahead of them, leaving the doors to the orangery open in her wake and heading for the terrace. The dragons followed her, and she reached the terrace doors just ahead of them, flinging them wide and letting in a roar of rain-torn wind that made her stagger. Beaufort and Mortimer shot into the dim day without speaking or stopping and launched themselves off the stone steps, catching the air with the crack of heavy wings and swinging low over the trees, not caring who might be watching. There was no time for it. The rain exploded off their scales as they took flight toward the river, taking on the colours of the cloud and becoming living scraps of the storm.

⁎

BEAUFORT WAS FLYING HARD, his great wings carving the sky, his body buffeted by the gusts, but Mortimer was lighter and quicker. He arrowed past the High Lord, the old dragon shouting him on, riding the wind and curving his wings to catch every lift, his eyes narrowed against the whip of the rain. What had taken them half an hour on foot earlier that morning took less than five minutes in full flight, but he was still scared they were going to be too late. He heard the river before he saw it, turned into a flood by the rain on the high fells, rampaging through crumbling banks and sweeping branches and bushes and boulders before it. It was neither clear nor chuckling any more. It had been turned into a beast by the storm, and he hated to think what would happen to something as fragile as a human in its grip.

Something hit his shoulder and he yelped, rolling instinctively and dislodging whatever it was. An instant later he was hit again, and a sharp voice snarled, "For the gods' sakes stay still! It's hard enough to get hold of you once!"

"Thompson?"

"No, it's bloody well Little Red Riding Hood. He doesn't keep you around for your intellectual prowess, does he?"

Mortimer considered rolling again, but didn't. "Where is she?"

"Downstream. Go low. She's got the other silly human with her, and the knucker's trying to help, but honestly it's like the bull trying to fix up the china shop. She's pushing them under as much as she's helping them."

Mortimer tucked his wings in. "Hang on."

He dived, just enough of his wings out to steady him, feeling the cat scrabbling to keep a grip on his scales, a hiss of annoyance just audible over the roar of wind in his ears. They tore down-stream, the wind chasing them, Mortimer flying as fast as he dared while still having a hope of spotting the inspector. He kept over the centre of the river, pupils wide in the dark day, scanning desperately for movement that was more than just the tumble of debris in the water. And there was so much debris. Such a terrible amount, all being pounded and broken and tossed together, while the river thrashed itself against the boulders in its path, and the wind whipped it all to a frenzy.

"Can you see them?" he shouted to the cat.

"Not yet," Thompson bellowed back. "Go lower!"

He went lower, feet almost skimming the surface, dimly aware of the pound of Beaufort's wings behind him, hoping they were going to be in time.

12

DI ADAMS

A fter they left the terrace, DI Adams let the W.I. return to their breakfasts or wander off through the lounge, presumably back to their rooms (and hopefully not with any plans of investigating), then sat down alone at a table as far from everyone else as she could. The birdwatchers were arguing over the battery life of the current GoPro model, and the American family were sitting in silence, staring at their empty plates. She rubbed the side of her face. She was tired, and her hair still smelt of cranberry sauce. There was no proper shower in their bathroom, just one of those horribly ineffectual rubber hose set-ups that you pushed onto the bath taps to turn it into a low pressure dribble that might charitably be called a shower. She was going to be plucking cranberries out of her hair for the rest of the weekend.

"DI Adams," Adele began, approaching the table with her hands clasped.

"Coffee," the inspector said, before Adele even reached the table, then added, "please."

Adele stopped short, and said hesitantly, "Food?"

"Maybe. But coffee first. Please."

"Would you like French press, espresso, filter, latte?"

"Strong. Lots of it." Adele looked uncertain, and DI Adams sighed. "French press. With an extra scoop in it."

"Okay. Milk? We have soy, nut, coconut—"

"No. Just coffee. Lots of coffee. Lots of *strong* coffee."

"No problems. Are you sure I can't get you some toast or—"

"Coffee." Her foot was tapping nervous time under the table. "Just coffee. Strong coffee. Lots. Enough for two."

"Right. Well, there's fruit and—" Adele stopped and gave a nervous grin as DI Adams glared at her. "I'll get your coffee."

"Thank you." DI Adams looked at the bare plate in front of her and the cutlery stacked next to it, trying not to make eye contact with anyone. She needed coffee before she could deal with anything else.

"Did I hear you say enough for two?" Ervin asked, appearing next to her.

"Yes. But it doesn't mean I'm sharing."

"Oh, go on. I just saw two of your W.I. ladies heading upstairs looking very worried, and all the rest are whispering like they're planning a revolution."

She scowled at him. "You journalists have such suspicious little minds."

"Oh, come on. What was that little conference about outside? Don't tell me it was about the cat."

"What else would it be about?"

"Murder."

DI Adams raised her eyebrows slightly. "Really. Do you have a confession to make, Mr Giles?"

"No. But I bet someone does."

The inspector stared at him until he shifted in his seat uncomfortably. "I would imagine we all have confessions to make. It doesn't make it any of your business."

"Oh? So what's your confession, Detective Inspector?"

She smiled. "Sometimes I have terrible thoughts about the things that should happen to interfering journalists."

Ervin grinned. "You like me, really."

"Such *terrible* things."

"Come on. Tell me something. One little thing. It's not like I can tell anyone about it. Phone lines are down, and I've got no signal."

"The *worst* sort of things."

"You're not even in charge of this investigation. You're on a weekend off."

"Terrible, terrible things."

"Of course, it wouldn't be the first time you were involved in someone else's case. Or in a case involving the Toot Hansell W.I."

"It's hard to imagine just how terrible." She was still smiling, and was pleased to see he was starting to look uncomfortable.

"I did some poking around while we still had internet. You were the lead investigator in the murder of the vicar in Toot Hansell last year. Then you ended up being involved in the arrest of those kidnappers at Christmas, even though you weren't officially on the case. And the Toot Hansell Women's Institute – *this* Women's Institute – was involved every time."

DI Adams *had* been joking about the terrible things that should happen to journalists. Now she wasn't so sure. "Your point being?"

"I think you know more than you're saying."

"That is rather the preferred way to handle speaking of any sort."

"You know what I mean."

The inspector was saved from answering by Adele arriving with her coffee. "There you go," she said. "Oh – do you need another cup, Mr Giles?"

"*No*," DI Adams said. "I'd rather not have indigestion."

The journalist gave Adele a dimpled smile, and she returned it, tucking loose hair behind one ear. "I'll leave the detective inspector to it," he said. "Thanks anyway, Adele. And call me Ervin."

"Alright," she said, still smiling as he left, and the DI turned her attention to the small French press loaded with a reassuringly large quantity of coffee. Honestly, give a young man a pair of dimples and people just fall all over themselves.

"Anything else?" Adele asked brightly.

"I'll start with this," the inspector said. "How's everyone doing? Coping alright?"

Adele sighed. "We're alright. It's a horrible shock, of course, but he hadn't been here long. We didn't know him that well."

"No? When did he start working with you?"

"About a month ago. Mum wanted Nita to have a proper sous-chef in the kitchen. Reid was going to do it, but he's hopeless. Nita banned him from even going in there and was doing it all herself."

"Wow," DI Adams said, pouring some coffee. "Reid must've been pretty upset."

"Yeah, he wasn't happy. He still kept trying to go in and manage them both, and Nita's taken to keeping potatoes in her pockets to throw at him."

"Oh." DI Adams took a sip of coffee and had to put the cup down until her eye stopped twitching. There was strong, then there was industrial-grade. "Did Keeley use the sauna a lot?"

"Sure." Adele peered out the window at the trees, which were restless in the steadily building wind. "He was a beauty technician, you know?"

"Was he? I thought you did the treatments."

"I do the yoga and massage, and some facials, but he was going to do the manicures and pedicures, and some of the other treatments."

"You didn't mind working with him?"

"Oh, no. Not really." She flushed slightly.

"A little bit, then?"

"No ... I just didn't like the bee venom thing, because it's cruel, and the Botox is so unnatural. Plus he was a meat-eater." She was twisting her fingers together, her cheeks pink.

"But otherwise you liked him."

"Well. I mean, not like *that*."

DI Adams bit down on a smile. "So he was the one doing Botox, then?"

"Yes." She leaned in confidentially. "He used it on himself *all* the time. Said he didn't want to end up looking like Gordon Ramsey."

DI Adams took another sip of coffee, finding her eye twitched a little less this time. So Botox wouldn't be an unusual thing to find in a lab report. But it must have taken a massive dose to be the cause of death. "Had he been administering Botox for long?"

"Only since he came here. He wanted to offer something extra, he said."

"Huh. And did he get on with everyone else?"

"Well, obviously not Reid. And Boyd kind of had a thing for him, but Keeley thought he was weird. And I mean, you've met my brother. He is weird." She frowned at the inspector. "But it was an accident, wasn't it?"

"Oh, yes. Definitely looked like it."

"So why are you asking all this?"

She shrugged. "Habit, I guess. Nothing to worry about."

"Right." Adele straightened up, and looked around the room uneasily. "Are you sure I can't get you some breakfast?"

DI Adams' stomach growled hopefully. The coffee seemed to have kicked in and she was starting to feel less like she'd been running a marathon all night. "Some eggs on toast would be great."

"Poached, boiled, scrambled—"

"Scrambled. Brown toast. Thank you."

Adele left, giving her one final doubtful look before she ducked through the door marked *Private*, presumably on some shortcut to the kitchen. The inspector topped her cup up. So neither of the brothers had been happy with him. And from what the W.I. were saying, Reid thought it was hunt or sell. So maybe this had been a way to sabotage his mother's plans and get rid of the sous-chef all at once?

And then there was Boyd. If he'd carried on with Keeley the way he had with her this morning, she didn't doubt the sous-chef would have been unreceptive. A scorned lover scenario, perhaps? She sighed, and took another mouthful of coffee. It was tasting quite pleasant now, which was worrying.

Holt grabbed the chair opposite her and sat himself down, leaning his heavy forearms on the table. She sighed. "How can I help you, Mr Miller?"

"How do you think? When're we going to get out of here? We've got no phone signal, and we don't want to stay in this dump a moment longer than we have to. Someone's stealing from the rooms!"

DI Adams put her cup down. "That's a very serious accusation, Mr Miller."

He huffed. "It *is* serious, but look – we don't even care. We just want gone, y'know?"

Don't we all, DI Adams thought, although she had to admit that wasn't quite true. Not now there was an actual investigation to be had. "You don't care but you're disturbing me before breakfast to tell me anyway?"

He leaned over the table, breathing black pudding in her face. "I told you I should have sorted that tree out! We'd be out of here by now!"

She leaned forward despite the stink and hissed, "Then why don't you head out there right now, Mr Miller? Get it all sorted out for us." They glared at each other, and there was a gratifyingly well-timed clap of thunder that set the windows rattling and the lights stuttering. He jerked back with an alarmed look on his face, and DI Adams smiled at him. "Off you go."

"I— well—" Rain splattered against the windows, and he got up, almost knocking his chair over. "I don't have to go out in that!"

"Welcome to Yorkshire, Mr Miller," she said, and emptied the last of the coffee into her cup as he stomped away.

Adele had just slid the eggs onto the table and gone to make more coffee (looking slightly alarmed by the inspector's response to her suggestion that a herbal tea might be better) when someone else sat down at the table.

"*What?*" she demanded, slapping her cutlery back on the table. "What is it now?" She looked up to see Edie regarding her rather disapprovingly, and Lottie hovering just behind her with an apologetic look on her face. "Sorry. Sorry." She looked at her eggs longingly. "What can I do for you?"

"We were hoping to find out when we might get out of here," Edie said. "But obviously breakfast is far more important than the needs of civilian guests."

DI Adams scowled at her. "I've been up most of the night. I've been attacked with Christmas dinner condiments. And I'm about to go out into what is apparently the end of the world." She pointed at the windows, but the thunder didn't cooperate this time. She could hear the wind howling outside though, which seemed to illustrate her point well enough. "I'm very sorry to inconvenience you, but, to be quite honest, *I don't care.*" She took a mouthful of egg and chewed, still glaring at them.

"Well, that's just the level of professionalism we'd expect from country police," Edie sniffed.

"Edie, dear, she *has* been up all night," Lottie said. "And look at this weather! Our little van would really struggle in this anyway. He'd probably get stuck before we even got to the bridge."

"That's beside the point," Edie said, and DI Adams buttered her toast in as pointed a manner as she could manage. After a few more sharp comments regarding the efficacy of the police from Edie, and more angry eating on the part of the inspector, the two women left. DI Adams put her cutlery down and listened to the thunder, rumbling softly from one side of the house to the other. She didn't know much about weather, but the instinctive part of her suggested that this was the sort of storm small creatures ran and hid from. Big ones, too. She looked up as Jasmine and Priya started across the room, and pointed her mug at them.

"No," she said. "Just no."

They looked at each other and retreated into the lounge.

BY THE TIME she had finished the second lot of coffee (her hands starting to shake just slightly), the rain had set in properly, falling hard enough to turn the lawns into ponds and to knock blossoms from the trees. The wind was sneaking about in gusts that scooped the rain up and flung it against the windows of the house, and made the trees mutter even over the hiss of the downpour. She squinted into the wet day from the foyer door, wishing she didn't have to go out in it. But she had to make some effort to clear the bloody road before DI Collins got here. There was a murder investigation to be had, and she couldn't sit here pretending she didn't know, and doing nothing to help matters. Of course, the flip side was that people would then be able to leave when they wanted, but they couldn't hold them here. Collins had taken all their details from Maddie, anyway.

She turned the collar of the borrowed workout jacket up and ran to her car, the rain soaking through Teresa's kitten leggings almost immediately. She beeped the car open and scrabbled in the boot for her waterproof police jacket, shrugging into it hurriedly. She sat in the car to kick off her trainers and pulled her wellies on, wishing she'd thought to bring them up to the house earlier. She also wished she'd thought to bring more clothes, because she rather felt that the cutesy leggings and tight pink top were undermining the authority of the jacket to a certain extent. She zipped it up to her chin and headed for the old green Land Rover parked with the other staff cars by the entrance to the kitchen, stopping on the way to stare at the somewhat obscene topiary bushes arranged by the kitchen door. She wasn't sure if Boyd had been aiming them at his brother or Keeley, but either way they were more easily interpretable than a lot of his other work. Not that that was necessarily a good thing.

The Land Rover was unlocked and the key still in the ignition, and she turned the heater on full blast as she started it up. It still smelt of cranberry and bread sauce, but she'd managed to wipe the worst of it out when they got back. She wouldn't be surprised if there was more this time around, so there hadn't been much point cleaning it properly. She was just glad she hadn't taken her own car earlier. She put the lights on and headed across the sodden gravel toward the drive.

She wasn't quite sure how she was going to convince the protesters to let her have another shot at the tree, but she had an idea they might not be feeling quite so militant now the rain had come in. She hummed as she guided the 4x4 down the partly flooded drive, tapping her fingers absently on the wheel and enjoying the quiet and the absence of people asking silly bloody questions, and above all the sense of *something happening*. Maybe she just wasn't made for relaxing weekends. Maybe this *was* her form of relaxation.

She burped coffee and scrambled eggs, wrinkling her nose and pressing the back of her hand to her mouth. It hadn't exactly been a tranquil meal.

"Seriously, *ew*," someone said, and she yelped, grabbing the wheel with both hands.

"What the *hell* – Thompson?"

"Hey," the cat said. He jumped through to the passenger seat from the back.

"Where did you come from?"

"Lounge. Saw you leaving. D'you how hard it is to shift into a moving vehicle?"

"Shift?"

"Yeah. It's what we do."

"What who does?" DI Adams had a feeling she was losing control of the conversation, if she'd ever had it. Cats were worse than dragons for that sort of thing.

"Cats. It's our thing. You know, turning up in strange places. Vanishing from locked rooms. Or boxes." He wrinkled his nose. "Bloody Schrödinger."

"I'm pretty sure that was just a thought experiment."

"Sure it was. Because humans are so considerate of their fellow species, right?"

DI Adams decided she didn't want to start debating either ethics or physics with a cat. "What do you want?"

"It's not what I want, it's what I can do for you."

"From the kindness of your heart?"

"You wound me." She shot him a sideways look and he huffed what seemed to be the feline equivalent of laugher. "Okay, okay. Look. I'm Watch. And I know you don't know exactly what that is, but call us the police of the Folk world for now. Our main task is to make sure the magical Folk and the humans stay clear of each other. No little demigod babies, no wood nymphs imprisoning humans in trees, no faeries pinching children. Keeps you safe, keeps us out of the path of a human exercise in mass extermination."

DI Adams considered saying that wouldn't happen, but didn't. The cat didn't seem to have a particularly sunny view of the human capacity for tolerance, and she had a sneaking suspicion that he wasn't far wrong.

"Now, we've got this situation with the dragons. And I'm looking the other way, because Beaufort and I go back three of my lives, and I can see when things are working. I can be cool. But just because it works for the Cloverlies doesn't mean it'll work for everyone, and we don't want too many Folk getting ideas. Plus there can be fallout, like the bauble situation last year."

"And so?"

"And so it's in *all* our interests to get this sorted out as quick as we can. No one wants the actual Watch getting a whiff of dragons having tea parties."

"Okay, I get your point, but what could cats really do to *dragons?*"

"That is not a question you want the answer to," Thompson said, and for once he sounded serious. "And trust me when I say that the clean-up would not be limited to dragons."

DI Adams frowned. "You mean the Watch deals with humans, too?"

"They deal with everyone. Have you not noticed yet that cats are everywhere?"

She sighed and rubbed the back of her neck, grimacing as she found a stray cranberry in her hair. "And a clean-up?"

"Is not something we're even talking about. We need to get this whole thing tidied up quick as we can, Adams."

She gave him a sideways look. He'd stopped sounding like a cut-rate comedian and was sounding uncomfortably like her DCI. "Well, Beaufort's not going to leave just because I ask him to. He's getting far too comfortable with people just not noticing him."

"So I've seen. Just solve the bloody thing so you can get them out of here already."

"You may not have noticed, but I'm a bit short-staffed for a murder investigation."

"Gods. Look, I'll help out. Tell me what you need."

"Not much, unless you can shift that tree."

"How about some snooping? Come in handy? Nail the murderer before Collins gets here?"

She snorted. "Are you my informant now?"

"I prefer operative. It's got a better ring to it."

"Get on it, then."

"Done," the cat said, and she heard the faintest whisper of motion, air rushing in to fill a void. She looked at the empty seat and wondered what could actually surprise her these days. Because in a world of dangerous cats and tea-drinking dragons, it was starting to feel like not a lot.

She pulled up a safe distance from the fallen tree, looking around warily for protesters wielding bread sauce. No one appeared, and after a moment she got out of the car, pulling her hood up against the rain.

"Hello?" she shouted. "Rainbow?"

No one answered, and she approached the tree carefully, ready to retreat if she was rushed. Still no one. She wondered if the weather had driven them away completely. That'd make life an awful lot easier. She started pacing along the tree, wondering if she could hook it to the tow bar and just drag the whole thing out of the way. She had just decided that it was worth a try and was digging in the back of the Land Rover, hoping for some chain or at least some decent rope, when she heard a shout through the rain. She turned warily, still keeping her distance from the tree, and spotted someone in a red coat running along the riverbank. She frowned. The rain and low light was making it hard to see clearly, but she could just make out a cluster of figures on the shore by the bridge, made dim by the weather. They were shouting and waving, although she couldn't hear what they were saying through the wind. But it sounded urgent. Everything about them said urgent – the way they were huddled together, the jerky movement, the running figure who had reached them and stopped, hands on their head. She hesitated, then ran for the tree, clambered over it and jogged toward them. They couldn't have endless supplies of cranberry sauce.

She reached the bridge in time to see the knucker fling herself out of the river in an exuberant bound, crashing back into the surface and releasing a wash of water that drenched the man dancing in the middle of the bridge. He was entirely naked except for a woolly hat on his head, and seemed entirely oblivious to the weather.

"What's going on?" she shouted at Rainbow as she arrived, and the woman gave a yelp of surprise.

"Oh! It's you!"

"Pig," Ronnie announced, but quietly, and DI Adams glared at him.

"What the hell's he playing at?" she asked, waving at the man on the bridge. It had to be Barry.

"He says he's playing with the river spirit. Every time anyone tries to go out there to get him, the water gets so rough we have to come back."

Of course. Of course it did. The knucker was lonely and bored, and she'd found a playmate. And Barry looked like he was having a wonderful time, other than the fact that he was going to get hypothermia any moment.

"Right," she said, and handed her keys to Harriet. "Start the Land Rover and get it as close to the tree as you can. Crank the heater and get some blankets in there, if you have any dry."

"What're you doing?" the young man with the hopeful beard asked.

"Getting the silly old sod back." She stepped onto the boards.

The narrow bridge with its ankle-high sides had felt rickety enough when she'd driven across it. It felt positively perilous now. The wooden boards were slick, and away from the shelter of the trees the wind was howling. It tugged at her clothes and made her stagger, and she almost thought she saw shapes in it, grasping laughing little critters that swung from her hair and scooped foam off the river. The storm must have started upstream a while ago, because the river was high under the boards, and she could feel the bridge shivering with the assault of the water and the debris that was being carried along with it.

"Move to Leeds," she muttered to herself, arms half-raised for balance as she hurried across the bridge, careful not to slip on the treacherous surface. "It'll be so relaxed. So much less stress. Much lower chance of life-threatening situations." At least she didn't think anything could be living under this bridge, the way the things had in London. And if they were, she could sic a dragon on them this time. Or a cat.

"*Barry!*" she bellowed into the wind. "*Barry, you need to come with me!*"

He ignored her entirely. The knucker was leaping from one side of the bridge to the other, performing flips and twists like a gymnast, and he waved and jumped up and down every time the creature passed overhead. Knucker aside, it wasn't a sight DI Adams enjoyed immediately after breakfast, or would have at any other time, to be honest. She should have brought a blanket with her to wrap him in.

"*Barry!*" He still ignored her, so she switched her attention. "*Oi! Knucker! Knucker!*"

Mid-leap, the creature gave a startled squawk and twisted with liquid, feline grace to stare at the inspector. DI Adams had one moment to appreciate how astonishingly beautiful the knucker's opalescent eyes were before the water dragon crashed into the bridge with an impact that shook the whole structure. Barry, caught mid-leap, landed badly. He slipped, caught himself, wobbled wildly, and staggered toward the edge, his bare feet sliding until they hit the ineffective kerb. The knucker sat up, shaking her wings out with a pained expression on her face, and she and the detective inspector watched Barry pirouette on the edge, shriek, "*I'm flying,*" then pitch into the rushing water with a yelp.

"Oops," the water dragon said.

DI Adams said something stronger and took three running steps that sent her off the bridge and into the unfriendly torrent below, hoping there was nothing of an impaling nature below the roaring surface.

13

MIRIAM

Miriam was helping Maddie straighten up the bedrooms, washing the mugs in the basins and replenishing the tea and the sugar sachets while her sister made the beds. Well, in the case of rooms used by the ladies of the Women's Institute, tugged at the covers a little, plumped a cushion or two, then just laid fresh towels out.

"Protesters!" Maddie said, for about the twentieth time. "On top of poor Keeley. I can't believe it. This weekend is going to ruin us."

Miriam made a sympathetic noise, concentrating on getting the tea stains out of a mug.

"You know who it is, don't you?"

"We don't *know*," Miriam said, scrubbing a little harder.

"We do! Of course we do! It's her! It's *always* her!"

"Mads, we don't know. It could be—"

"How did she know? How did she *know* that this was our relaunch weekend? And why is she so determined to *ruin* me?" Maddie thumped the rolled towels down on the bed, and they immediately fell to the floor. She snatched them up again. "She's like a, a *lingering infection!*"

Miriam sighed. She thought Maddie was probably right, that it was their older sister Rainbow (previously Judith) down at the bridge. Boyd had been even more incoherent than usual when he got back, and between wanting to get cleaned up and the arrival of Thompson, DI Adams had refused to discuss anything other than where she could get some coffee, so they couldn't be certain it was Rainbow. But Miriam couldn't imagine anyone else bothering to protest one struggling country house on what was proving to be a very miserable spring weekend.

"I'm sure the inspector will sort it all out," she said.

"She didn't look like she was sorting anything out," Maddie muttered. "She looked like she'd been having a pillow fight in a jam factory."

Miriam snorted laughter, then covered her mouth with one hand. Maddie would be furious if she thought Miriam wasn't taking her seriously. But Maddie gave a reluctant chuckle. "Better than tar, I guess."

"Much better," Miriam said. "Tastier, too."

Maddie laughed properly then, gave the bedspread a last poke, and said, "I wish all guests were so tidy. Those children have clothes *everywhere*, and the birdwatchers have so many cameras and things cluttering up their room that I'm scared to do much in case I knock something expensive over."

Miriam thought a little guiltily of the room she shared with Alice, and wondered if she could get there before Maddie and tidy her clothes away. There just never seemed to be much point putting them in a dresser when one was only going to put them back in the bag two days later.

She was just about to claim she needed to nip to the loo before they moved on when they heard running footsteps outside, then the sound of someone knocking rather urgently somewhere further along the hall while shouting, "Miriam!" The sisters looked at each other, then Miriam opened the door and popped her head. Jasmine was just turning away from the room next door, already breaking into a run again. She yelped when she saw Miriam, bounced off a sideboard, and grabbed a very dusty but rather expensive-looking vase before it could fall over.

"Ooh. You scared me!"

"What's going on?"

"Alice says you need to get your boots on and meet her downstairs right away!" Jasmine's nose was very pink and her voice had gone all high and squeaky.

"What's happening?" Maddie asked, joining Miriam at the door. "It's not more protesters, is it? Everyone's alright? Is someone hurt?" There was an edge of panic to her voice, and Jasmine made an uncertain noise that could have meant anything, her own eyes wide.

Miriam wanted to look around and see if there was someone older or at least more leadership-inclined to take charge, but there wasn't. So she swallowed her own fright, patted Maddie on the shoulder, said, "Leave our room. I can sort it out later," and shooed Jasmine away. "Tell Alice I'm on my way."

As it turned out, when Miriam reached her room Alice was sitting on the bed lacing her boots, a fleece zipped to her chin and waterproof trousers on. She smiled at Miriam, but it was perfunctory. "Get your boots on."

Miriam scrabbled them out of the bag, sitting on the floor to pull them on and feeling grateful she was already in her outdoor gear. How had Alice *known?* She supposed she hadn't, but expecting *something* was what made Alice, well, Alice. It seemed a slightly exhausting way to live. "Is it the murderer?" she asked.

"No." Alice put her jacket on and tucked her keys into the pocket. "I'll explain on the way. I'm going to get the car started." She didn't need to say *hurry up*. Miriam heard it anyway.

Miriam rushed out of the room only a few moments later, pulling her jacket on as she went. It was bright orange with blue flowers on it, and she wasn't entirely sure it was suited to an Investigation, but it'd have to do. Alice was still on the stairs, glaring at the American couple. Paula looked very uncomfortable, but Holt appeared to be blocking Alice's way down. Miriam didn't think that was wise, even if Alice didn't have her walking stick with her.

"Where are you going?" Holt was asking.

"I'm running outside for a moment."

"In this?"

"Yes." He was a couple of steps lower than Alice, so she was looking down at him to meet his eyes, his belly almost taking up all the space between them. He fidgeted, as if suddenly aware that he wasn't in the best position.

"Where's that detective? What's she doing about getting us out of here?"

"As much as she can," Alice said. "Now, I really need to go."

He didn't move. "We can't be kept here against our will."

"I'm sure the detective inspector will be very happy for you to go out and try convincing the protesters to move, then."

He scowled at her, and Paula said, "She's right, honey. We saw the road was blocked."

"We didn't see any *protesters*, though."

"So you think she's making it up?" Alice asked.

"We don't even know if she's a real detective! We haven't seen any ID!"

Alice raised her eyebrows and said, "I'm heading down to the protest right now. You're welcome to follow us down."

"I don't want to go out in this," Paula said.

"They could be keeping us here under false intenses!"

"Pretences," Alice said. "False pretences. Ah, there you are, Miriam. Ready?"

"Yes," Miriam said, putting her hands on her hips and joining Alice at the top of the stairs as Jasmine hurried down the hall. "Are you coming too, Jas?"

"You're leaving, aren't you?" Holt demanded. "Sneaking off and leaving us here!"

"Without our bags?"

"They're probably already in the car!"

"Oh, give it a rest," Paula said with a sigh, and turned to go back down the stairs. "I'm having a gin." Gert and Pearl were hovering at the lounge doors, and they came forward to meet Paula and usher her into the room with them, which Miriam thought was a bit odd. They hadn't seemed so enthusiastic about the Americans last night, especially Gert. Or maybe it was only Holt they were unenthusiastic about.

"Paula! *Paula!*"

Alice smiled at him. "Are you going to let us past, then?"

"I— Well, I'm not going to forget about this! We'll talk later!" He shook a finger in her face.

"Don't do that," she said. "It's rude, and someone's going to break it off one day."

He snatched his hand back to his chest as if she'd bitten him, and pounded off down the stairs hard enough to shake dust from the banister railings.

"What a horrible man," Jasmine said.

"Quite," Alice agreed, and padded rather more softly downstairs.

"Did you notice Paula stopped sounding American?" Miriam asked, trying to get her rain hat settled firmly over her curls.

Alice smiled. "You're quite right," she said, as they hurried across the tiles to the door. "This day's just full of surprises, isn't it?"

Miriam didn't think she sounded very surprised at all.

§◆

THE WIND GRABBED the door and tried to snatch it off Alice, then tried to push her back inside, and when it saw that wasn't going to work settled to attacking the three women as they struggled out into the day. It was barely 11 a.m., but the sky was low and dark and the sun was lost behind the clouds. Miriam hissed as the wind attacked her jacket, rattling in the hood and tearing the hat off her head. Jasmine squeaked behind her as she ran after it, half sure that she could see small creatures in the wind with fine, nebulous bodies, dancing and spinning as they threw her hat from one to the other. There was a flash of lightning somewhere over the distant fells, and a few seconds later a boom of thunder. The hat took a final spin over the fountain and toward the woods, and she gave up, hair already plastered to her head by the downpour.

"*Alice!*" someone bellowed behind them, and they turned to see Teresa struggling down the stairs with an armload of blankets. "In case you need them!"

Alice nodded her thanks and took the blankets, shouting, "Anything?"

"Not yet," Teresa said, and retreated hastily to the shelter of the foyer.

"Anything what?" Miriam shouted.

Alice shook her head and led the way, hurrying across the gravel to her little Fiat 4x4. The drive had become a shallow stream, small pebbles shifting underfoot and milky water washing over the toes of their boots. The trees were roaring to each other like misplaced ghosts, and in another flash of lightning the house stood stark and black against the sky. Miriam hauled at the door as Alice beeped the car open, and the three women bundled themselves inside.

"Anything what?" Miriam repeated as the wind slammed her door shut rather enthusiastically. She had an uneasy feeling in her belly that was nothing to do with the storm.

"Everyone in?" Alice asked.

"Yes. What were you asking Teresa about, Alice?"

Alice started the car and the lights came on, painting colour across the grey day. "The dragons have been doing their part to help out DI Adams. I rather thought we should do the same."

Miriam stared at her. "We're investigating again, aren't we?"

"Well, we can't walk in this weather, and we can't all have massages at once. Nothing wrong with asking a few questions."

Miriam twisted in her seat to look at Jasmine, who smiled a little awkwardly. "I was just the lookout," she said.

"You could have *told* me," Miriam said to Alice.

"Yes," Alice said. "I could. But it is your family, which makes things a little awkward, and I know you don't enjoy investigating, even though you're terribly good at it. Plus you were busy with Maddie, so I thought it best to just carry on." She pulled onto the drive and they rumbled into the raging day in a cocoon of quiet, the heater already pumping hot air.

Miriam thought of pointing out that it was more than awkward to have a family member suspected of murder, but the compliment (which she didn't agree with) had made her go all pink and flustered, so she just said, "You don't really suspect my family, do you?"

Alice tapped her fingers on the wheel. "We know Reid hated Keeley."

"Yes, but—"

"And we know Adele has, well, a temper. Remember the mushrooms?"

"Yes, but they were hallucinogenic, not deadly!" Miriam's heart was tight in her chest. "And it *could* have been a mistake!"

"*Hmm.* It seems a little unlikely, considering how well she knows her plants. Plus there was that couple there she'd gone to school with, wasn't there? An ex and an ex-friend, if I remember right."

"Yes, I know, but no one was hurt." Other than a few scrapes from the rose bushes and some badly bruised dignity when the footage mysteriously made its way onto Facebook.

Alice smiled at her. "No one can ever accuse you of not being loyal, Miriam."

Miriam had almost stopped blushing, but now it came rushing back. She tried to look serious. "I'd still like to have known you were investigating."

Alice looked at her finally and smiled. "I'm sorry, Miriam. I'll tell you next time."

"Thank you." Miriam settled back into her seat, tidying the hair back from her face. "I lost my rain hat."

"Most unfortunate."

"I liked that hat," Miriam insisted. "It was handmade."

"That *is* a shame."

"And waterproof."

"An admirable quality in a rain hat."

"I shan't be able to find the same one again," Miriam said, feeling that Alice was rather underappreciating her lost hat.

"Isn't that just the truth of everything?"

"I'm very sorry about your hat," Jasmine said, leaning forward between the seats. "But where are we going?"

"It seems the detective inspector is having a spot of bother," Alice said.

Miriam glanced at the blankets in the back. "Those aren't all for her."

"No. Apparently one of the protesters fell in the river, and DI Adams went in after him."

Miriam's breath caught in her throat, and Jasmine gave an alarmed little gasp. "We're going to need more than blankets," she said. "And how will we find her? We need to get hold of emergency services, or—"

"The dragons are searching the river," Alice said. "We just need to be ready to meet them. I'm sure they'll find her."

Miriam didn't think Alice sounded very sure at all. With all this rain the river would be a mess of rapids and white water, flowing fast and unforgiving and dragging absolutely anything it caught with it. *If* DI Adams had managed to reach the protester, and *if* she could keep both of them afloat, the chances of her getting them both out uninjured, or even at all, were horribly small. Miriam wasn't even sure dragons could be quick enough to spot them and pull them out. Her belly turned over threateningly, and she wiped her lips, suddenly feeling the chill of the day as something vindictive and angry, scraping at the car and whispering at the windows.

Her thoughts were broken by Jasmine giving a little shriek and flinging herself forward as if she were about to clamber through the seats to join them in the front.

"Jasmine! What is it?"

"I don't know! Oh, *ew!* It's all wet and slimy! It's—"

"It's *me*. Gods. You'd think you'd never seen a wet cat before." Thompson pushed past Jasmine and onto the centre console, and Alice glanced at Miriam, biting her lip. Miriam covered her mouth, fighting not to laugh despite the foreboding of a moment before. Few things are more ridiculous than a wet cat. "What?" Thompson demanded, glaring at them both. "I can't help it if I'm all floof!"

Miriam burst out laughing, and Alice scratched the cat's head. "You really are," she said.

"Got any snacks?" he asked, ignoring Jasmine giggling behind him.

"Probably in the glove compartment."

Miriam, grinning broadly, found a packet of cat treats in with the charger cables and windscreen scraper, and offered some to the cat. He sat on her lap to eat them, but she didn't complain. Her trousers were already wet and unlikely to get drier, and his weight was oddly comforting. His smoky tabby hair had been rendered dark by the rain, parted sharply along the knobbles of his spine and hanging low and dripping under his belly. His ears looked too big for his head and his tail was as skinny as a rat's, and the pupils of his green eyes were huge in the low light of the car. He finished the last biscuit and shook himself off, splattering the car generously with rain and river water.

"Less of that, thank you," Alice said.

"Well, no one brought me a towel."

"There's some blankets," Jasmine offered, but the cat didn't move, just stared through the windscreen, examining the wind-torn day.

"Where's DI Adams?" Miriam asked. "Is she okay?"

Thompson looked up at her, then at the other women. "The dragons are looking still."

"They can't find her?" Alice asked, and Miriam felt the day crush around the car again, as if they were a bathysphere descending into the depths of the ocean, everything outside their little bubble lightless and unfriendly.

"They're trying. But it's bad out there. And cold, even for dragons. They can't risk getting too cold."

"How far have they gone?" Alice asked. "Are there tracks? Can we get the car near the river and reach them that way?"

"I don't know. You can't get over the tree, but there's a track up here on the right that might take us to the river a bit further down. You won't be able to catch them, though. If the dragons can't find them we're just going to have to hope they can get themselves out. I'll be able to find the inspector once she's out of the water, but not while she's in."

There was silence as they considered that, then Miriam said, "What happens if dragons get too cold?"

Thompson sighed. "They won't. They won't let it get that bad."

"But what does happen?" Jasmine asked, leaning between the seats to peer at the cat.

He looked at her with flat green eyes, then said, "Dragons are driven by fire. They run hot. You must have noticed that, right?"

Miriam nodded, thinking of the way Mortimer radiated heat like a particularly efficient oil heater, much to his annoyance when he was trying to eat anything with cream on it.

"If that fire gets too low, it doesn't come back easy. Sometimes not at all."

There was silence in the car, just the sound of the revs climbing as Alice pushed the car a little faster.

"They won't let it happen, though," Thompson said. "They're not that silly."

Miriam thought that they might not be that silly, but they might be that stubborn, which was quite often very much the same thing.

⁊

"PULL IN HERE."

Alice stomped on the brakes, bringing the car to a skidding halt that sent the cat crashing off Miriam's lap into the dashboard.

"*Hey!*"

"Well, some warning would have been nice," she told him, and peered at the gap in the wall to their right. It was blocked with a sagging gate, and the ground beyond was thick with old leaves and new grass and mud.

"Where are we going? I'm not having you destroy my car again."

"Relax, it's all pretty flat. And this car looks a bit more decent than your last one. That was rubbish."

"Excuse *me*. I had a *very* decent car before, until I followed a cat's directions."

Thompson sniffed. "Not very decent if it falls apart on a little old farm track."

Miriam would have laughed at the offended look on Alice's face if she hadn't been trying to decide who to be most worried about, the inspector or the dragons. And also the fact that she'd just realised Alice had said *I'll tell you next time* in regards to investigating, which was horribly ominous.

"*A little old farm track* may be understating the matter somewhat," Alice said. The last time they'd followed the cat he'd led them up some sort of rubble-clogged trail that would have made an army truck think twice, let alone a Toyota Prius. The car had not been repairable.

"Well, what do you suggest, then? We just sit here with protesters on one end of the drive and guests on the other, any of whom could turn up just as the dragons arrive? Or go back to the house and wait around for the dragons to bring the DI and the naked guy straight into the lounge? I'm sure no one will notice, right?"

"That's a little extreme, Thompson," Miriam said.

"Um, naked guy?" Jasmine said from the back, sounding worried.

Alice gave the cat a look that would have made most people hide behind something, but he just glared back. "I merely suggest you don't get us stuck in the woods where we're no good to anyone," she said. "Where does the track go? Are we going to be able to get back once we have the DI and the protester?"

"Gods, you humans and your need for absolutes. *I don't know*. I don't know where the track goes. I also don't know where the DI is. But right now I *can* reach the dragons, although I might point out it's bloody dangerous being my size and out messing around in storms. Someone open the gate. Take the track. Try not to get stuck. I will find the dragons. Either they will have found the inspector, and I'll bring them all to you, somewhere *no one will see them*, or they won't have, and you'll just have to wait until the search ends, however it does. Either way, *can we just move?*"

There was a pause, then Jasmine said, "I'll get the gate." She struggled out of the four-wheel drive and ran to it, slipping in the mud and fighting to keep her balance against the wind. Miriam followed her, hair whipping her face almost painfully, and together they got the latch open and dragged the heavy gate open. Alice inched through, and Miriam grabbed Jasmine when she went to close it again.

"Leave it," she shouted against the wind. "We'll be back through in no time." She hoped.

Jasmine nodded, gripping her woolly hat with both hands as if afraid it'd blow off, and they ran to the idling car.

"Move it, move it," Thompson yelled as rain swirled into the car with them. "This isn't a Sunday picnic, ladies!"

"I didn't even like cats before you talked," Miriam said, pushing him out of the way and climbing in. "You're not exactly changing my mind here."

"Oh, listen to my heart breaking," the cat said. "I'm off. Stop if you find a handy clearing." Then he was gone, the car suddenly quiet and dark.

Alice shifted the Fiat into four-wheel drive and crawled forward through the trees, going as quick as she dared on the slippery ground. Miriam peered into the heavy shadows under the trees, rendered deep and strangely shaded by the rain, and hoped for dragons.

14

MORTIMER

It was getting darker by the minute, the clouds crowding in so low above Mortimer as he flew that he could barely breathe, and every gasp was more water than air anyway. The angry grey river tumbled and roiled below his feet, and the wind threatened over and over to flatten him into it, attacking him with gusts from unexpected directions and slapping his face with foam torn from the surface below. He risked a glance back at Beaufort, following a little higher and further back, the High Lord a silvery grey that made him seem part of the storm.

"*Beaufort,*" he bellowed, "*can you see them?*"

The High Lord shook his head, a ponderous gesture that made Mortimer suddenly aware of just how cold it was, then his gold eyes flicked away from the younger dragon. "There!" Beaufort called. "The knucker!"

Mortimer looked back just in time to take a mouthful of river as the knucker breached below him, setting off a waterspout that looked for a moment as if it'd become a tornado.

"Hi!" she yelled, running with happy flecks of pink and blue. "Hey! Have you come to play too?"

Mortimer spluttered, lurched into a sneeze, caught a wing in the water, cartwheeled across the surface with a yelp of fright, and belly-flopped into the shallows, where the river immediately began piling up behind him and conspiring to turn his wings inside out and push his hindquarters over his head. He was vaguely aware of the High Lord roaring something, but he had so much water in his ears he couldn't tell what he was saying, and when he went to take a breath he discovered his whole head was actually underwater. He snorted and threw himself backward with a little too much enthusiasm, overbalanced in the opposite direction (with a little help from the knucker, who had just hit him with her bow wave), flailed like an upturned beetle for a few moments, then discovered he could actually sit up and wasn't drowning. He sneezed three times and looked about blearily.

"Hi?" the knucker tried again, as Beaufort, curving toward them in a rather graceful and stately manner, was caught by a gust. It threw him backward, a startled look on his face, straight into the waiting branches of a willow that was probably a lovely tree at any other time, but right now was flinging its branches around like a particularly enthusiastic sea anemone.

"*Beaufort!*" Mortimer yelled, ignoring the knucker, and galloped through the belly-deep water toward the tree as the High Lord vanished among the spring growth.

"Wait!" the knucker shouted. "There's a—"

Mortimer assumed she was about to say, *there's a ditch*, but by that stage the bottom had been whipped away from under him, and he was caught in a whirlpool that was spinning violently under the skirts of the willow's long branches, being buffeted by sticks and leaves and clumps of drowned foliage. He opened his mouth to shout something, took a gulp of water instead, tried to get his head up, was pushed further under by the water bubbling off the shallows into the vortex, bounced off something resoundingly hard, and suddenly couldn't tell which way was up. *Oh dear,* he thought. *This is it. I'm going to drown under a willow tree on a W.I. spa weekend.* It seemed both entirely impossible and completely apt, and he tucked his wings a little closer to his body to stop them being torn to pieces on the rocks he was bouncing off. He hoped Beaufort could manage both DI Adams and the naked man. His lungs were beginning to ache, and he supposed he should just take a breath and get it over with. He wasn't getting out of this one.

He let himself relax, the swirling roar of water in his ears oddly comforting, tipped his head back, and in the next moment was airborne.

He yelped, flung his wings wide, heard someone curse in a very non-dragonish manner, then was ploughing snout first into a mulch of mud and dead leaves beneath the willow tree. He pushed himself up on shaky legs, wheezing and coughing, and the next moment was being pounded so fiercely on the back that he couldn't breathe. His knees gave way, and he lay there spluttering while the back-thumping continued.

"Breathe, lad, breathe!" Beaufort bellowed, and Mortimer gave a helpless little squeak.

"Beaufort, stop!" someone else said. It was the voice that had been cursing, and it was very familiar. Mortimer managed to turn his head and squinted at DI Adams, who was still in the water up to her waist, shivering wildly in a filthy pink top. "Y-you're squishing him," she managed through chattering teeth, and clambered out of the river.

"Are you alive? Mortimer, speak to me!" The pounding had stopped, and Mortimer managed to flop onto his side and wheeze at the High Lord. "Do you need seepy-argh?" Beaufort demanded. "I saw that on Miriam's television. I'm quite sure I can replicate it." He sat back on his hind legs and rubbed his front paws together purposefully, and Mortimer rolled his eyes in panic at DI Adams.

"S-seepy what?" she asked, hugging her arms around herself.

"For when someone's dying. They give them seepy-argh to bring them back to life."

Mortimer made an urgent sound which he hoped communicated that he wasn't dying at this very moment, and would rather not have seepy-argh, whatever that might entail.

"Y-you mean CPR," she said "N-no, that's only i-if the heart's s-stopped."

"Yes, seepy-argh." Beaufort leaned over the smaller dragon and frowned at him. "Has your heart stopped, Mortimer?"

The High Lord sounded far too hopeful for Mortimer's comfort. He managed to shake his head and wave a paw at them feebly.

"Oh. Well, if you're sure." Beaufort straightened up again and gave DI Adams a toothy smile, although it didn't escape Mortimer's attention that the High Lord was as grey as he was. They needed to get warmed up, and soon. "I'm very glad to see you, Detective Inspector. We were very worried when Thompson said you'd gone into the river."

"S-something h-helped us," she managed. "I m-mean, the knucker t-tried, but sh-she just k-kept pushing us under. A-and I thought w-we were going to be w-washed to b-bloody Blackpool or something, b-but it was l-like the river j-just scooped us up and d-dumped us here."

"Ah," Beaufort said. "Thank you, Aggie."

There was no response from the river, and the inspector just looked at him blankly. She was shaking so much that Mortimer could see the water shivering off her curls, and Beaufort sat back on his hindquarters to open his wings in the shelter of the tree.

"You need to warm up. Come under a wing."

"Beaufort," Mortimer managed, pushing himself onto his elbows. "You're too cold."

"She's too cold, lad," the High Lord said.

"Let me," Mortimer said, dragging himself to his feet.

"W-we need to get out of h-here," DI Adams said, waving Beaufort away, and went to pull Barry to his feet. He was sitting by the riverbank with his feet still in the water, smiling happily at the knucker and wearing a very dirty jacket that said *Police*. "L-let's go, Barry."

"Aw, no," the knucker said. "Do you have to?"

"We have to," Beaufort said firmly. "No more playing with humans and especially no more knocking them in the water, understand?"

"I suppose," she said, somewhat sulkily, then brightened as Mortimer wobbled his way toward the bank. "Can you come play again?"

"*No*," he said, with rather more emphasis than he intended, then sighed at her hurt look. "Not now, I mean. Maybe later."

The knucker brightened. "Okay. See you!" She ducked beneath the surface, then went plunging across the river like a row of white horses, all flying foam and leaping waves.

"Aw," Barry said. "I liked her."

Beaufort patted his shoulder as gently as he could. "We all do. Just doesn't know her own strength."

"Let's get back," Mortimer said. He was shivering, his scales clattering together with the soft hiss of sea on sand.

"Yes," DI Adams said. "Um – how?"

MORTIMER DIDN'T THINK FLYING with a human was comfortable for anyone involved. DI Adams was lying on his back with her legs around his belly and her arms locked around his neck so tightly that he was having trouble breathing again. Dragons, much like cats, occupy a curious pocket in the world of physics. They fly while being entirely unsuitable for flying (unless you were Gilbert, who didn't fly unless in an emergency, and then it was probably better defined as a series of dubiously controlled crashes), and he wasn't entirely sure that having a human with him might not make physics take a closer look at who was meddling with the rules. But there was nothing for it. It was too wet to make a fire, and too far to walk back to the manor with the barefoot, shivering humans (DI Adams had lost her boots in the river), and Mortimer wasn't at all sure how much longer he could last out in the assault of the rain and the wind before he got too cold. Never mind how the High Lord must be coping. Mortimer was already feeling sleepy, and it was taking all his concentration to keep them flying as steadily as possible while radiating enough heat to keep the inspector warm.

"How much further?" she shouted now. "The Land Rover's at the bridge."

"I'm not sure," he called back. "It felt like it took a terribly long time to find you."

She started to say something else, then gave a yelp of surprise, her arms tightening enough to make him gag.

"Don't roll!" a feline voice yelled. "Come left ten degrees. There's a clearing a bit downstream of the bridge. On it?"

Mortimer made a strangled noise, and the inspector eased her grip. "Sorry!"

"'S okay." He altered course, fighting against the wind, too tired to even ask the cat who was waiting for them. He just wanted to be curled up in front of a fire with a fluffy blanket, a large tin of assorted cakes, and a whole pot of tea.

THERE WERE lights in the clearing, twin beams cutting watery swathes through the rain. Mortimer came in as gently as he could, but he was starting to suspect that physics really had sat up and started paying attention. He landed too fast and hard, flinging his wings wide to brake, and skidded across the wet grass toward the waiting car. Three figures scattered out of the way with a chorus of shouted warnings, and both he and the DI gave matching yelps of horror. He dug his hind legs in, tail dragging on the ground, and they came to a shaky stop staring at the grill of Alice's little 4x4 from a rather close-up perspective. Mortimer was panting, and DI Adams' feet were digging into his belly painfully.

She was the first to move, disentangling herself with a shaky, "Nice job."

He squeaked, and belly-flopped onto the ground as soon as she was clear. At least the adrenaline had warmed him up. He heard the snap of Beaufort's wings, and sat up in time to see the High Lord land rather more gracefully than they had. He supposed, a little sourly, that physics must take longer to catch up on that many centuries. Barry slid off Beaufort's back and collapsed in a wet and smiling heap on the ground, the DI's jacket undone and ridden up to his shoulders.

"Oh, my God. He really is naked," Jasmine said, and threw a blanket in his general direction. It hit the inspector on the side of the head instead.

"Well, th-that's helpful," she said, her voice still shaky with cold but her teeth not chattering quite as much as they had been. She picked the blanket up and draped it around the man's shoulders. He blinked at her, then broke into a wide grin.

"Spirits! Earth spirits! Water spirits! *Wind* spirits!"

"If you like." The inspector pulled the blanket tight around the man and accepted another from Miriam. "We really need to get everyone warmed up."

"Are you alright?" Miriam asked her.

"I'll be fine as soon as I get out of this bloody rain," she said. "The dragons, too."

"We're fine," Beaufort said, and the four women frowned at him. "Well, a little damp, I guess." They kept frowning, the rain whipping about them and soaking the blankets. "And quite cold," he added. "And I think I have some twigs stuck in my scales, and possibly a frog in my ear."

"That sounds rather unpleasant," Alice said. "You two get straight back to the house. I've told the ladies to watch for you. DI Adams, let's get you in the car. There's a little whisky in there, too, if you need it."

"Not going to say no." The inspector hobbled toward the car, and Miriam put a hand on Mortimer's shoulder as Jasmine swaddled Barry in three more blankets before leading him away.

"Are you sure you're alright?" she asked the dragon.

"Mortimer was magnificent," Beaufort said, as the younger dragon hesitated. "Glorious. Not a thought for his own safety, and he flew like a Hayling dragon."

"Is that good?" Miriam asked.

"Better than good," the High Lord said, and Mortimer started to blush pale orange, remembering his cartwheel and the fact that the High Lord and the detective inspector had had to pull him out of a whirlpool. "Wonderful."

"Well." Miriam patted the smaller dragon. "We always knew you were wonderful."

Mortimer gave an embarrassed little squeak and flushed entirely orange, starting to steam gently in the shadows.

"Miriam," Alice called. "You're going to need to come drive the Land Rover back."

"Alright," she called, then looked back at the dragons. "Get yourself back to the house. I'll find you a bath somewhere, and I've been keeping a coconut cake back."

"Coconut cake?" Mortimer asked, suddenly feeling distinctly less miserable.

"With cream cheese icing," she said, and ran to the car.

MORTIMER'S happy orange blush rapidly gave way to grey as he and Beaufort hurried back to the house, flying low for as far as they dared then splashing to the drenched ground in the trees beyond the terrace. They ran up the stairs shoulder to shoulder, not even trying to blend into the background. They were too cold to be any colour but stony grey. At the orangery, they sat up on their back legs and put their snouts against the wall, peeking cautiously through windows that were misted with condensation from the plants and heat. There was no one inside, and for a moment Mortimer thought he was going to cry. He was so cold, and so tired, and had been worried for so long, and he just didn't think he could keep going any longer. Everyone had limits. He sniffed, and a wave of shivering strong enough to shake three scales free passed over him. He sank back onto his hindquarters to collect them with wobbly paws, trying not to whimper.

"Lad?" Beaufort said softly, one chilly paw on his shoulder. "It'll be alright."

He nodded, concentrating on picking up the scales, not wanting Beaufort to see the hot tears that were threatening to spill, and the High Lord settled down next to him, picking up a scale he couldn't get a shivering claw under.

"Do you know," Beaufort said, "I never liked water much myself. Damn treacherous. And it gets in everywhere." He patted one ear, as if checking for the frog.

"I almost drowned," Mortimer mumbled. "And now I just want to crawl under a blanket and hide forever."

"Forever sounds like quite a long time," the High Lord said. "Maybe just a week or so. I'll leave cake by the west corner of the blanket."

Mortimer eyed him, not sure if he was being made fun of or not, but Beaufort looked entirely serious. Then the High Lord looked over the younger dragon's shoulder and said, "Ah, here we go."

Mortimer turned to see Priya running down the terrace in a dark green rain jacket that was far too big for her. She stopped when she saw them looking and beckoned urgently, then turned and ran back the way she had come. The dragons ran after her, Mortimer hobbling with his pawful of scales. She led them off the terrace and around the side of the house, then pulled open a heavy door that let out a gust of warmth and scent.

"Come in, come in," she said, and they pattered onto the hard floor, splattering mud everywhere.

"Um," Mortimer said, looking at his filthy feet, and she gave him a dismissive little wave, pulling the door shut and locking it. The big room was dimly lit by the grey light from the windows, and two lanterns that shone off the stainless counters and were reflected in the extraction hoods over the stove.

"I'll clean it." She pointed at the gas stove, on which twelve burners were roaring in full flame. "It's not a barbecue, but will it do?"

"That is *wonderful*," Beaufort said. "Mortimer, can we get one of these?"

"Where's the chef?" Mortimer asked. While no one here might be particularly perceptive, he could still foresee some difficulty explaining half-seen dragons cooking on the stove top.

"She's setting up some buffet thing. Apparently when the weather's bad they sometimes open all the windows in the orangery and do barbecues. Maddie's calling it a spring storm party."

"So the chef's definitely not coming back?" The burners looked terribly tempting. Mortimer could feel the heat baking his face.

"Well, it's good enough for me." Beaufort scrambled up onto the stove, wobbling on the edge of balance for a moment. Mortimer had the horrified thought that the High Lord might actually *fall*, like some old and decrepit dragon with his strength withered to nothing. But he recovered himself and curled like a cat over half the burners. "Come on, lad. We'll get warmed up then go see what we can do."

Mortimer didn't like that *see what we can do* too much. They'd already done quite a lot, and it had involved getting very wet and cold and half-drowned. Surely there was nothing else they could do, was there? Especially now the DI was back. She'd put a stop to any sort of investigating. He hoped.

But he did like the bit about getting warmed up. He climbed up next to the High Lord and snuggled down, careful not to smother the burners, the heat spreading across his scales and beginning to bake through to his bones.

"That's better," Beaufort sighed, and Mortimer mumbled agreement.

"The door to the dining room's locked, and I'll make sure no one comes in the other way," Priya said. "And I'll put the kettle on once you're up."

"Thank you." Mortimer yawned hard enough to make his jaw creak. The warmth was making him sleepy. Beaufort was already snoring softly.

"It's okay."

He shifted slightly. He wouldn't fall asleep. He hadn't got *that* cold. Well, maybe he had, a bit, but the stove was warming them up nicely, and while the temptation was to conserve energy while one warmed up, they were in a strange *kitchen* of all things, and even with the doors locked they might need to move quickly, and there was tea to think about, and ...

HE OPENED his eyes to four pairs of human ones, all regarding him somewhat anxiously. For one moment he wondered what they were doing in his cavern, then he realised that the room was much bigger and higher than his cavern, and that he was almost uncomfortably warm.

"Ooh, he's awake," Priya said, letting her breath out and straightening up. She'd been crouched down to his eye level.

Mortimer wiped his mouth on his foreleg, horrified to discover he'd been drooling. "Just resting my eyes for a moment."

"That's alright, Mortimer," Alice said. "You deserved a little rest."

"I'm awake." He looked down, puzzled for a moment by the stove, then the day pounced on him and he pushed himself up to sitting with a groan. His scales were still steaming slightly. "Beaufort?" he said. The High Lord was curled next to him, his scales dull grey and his breathing so slow that it was almost imperceptible. "Beaufort? Beaufort!"

15

DI ADAMS

In the car, DI Adams sat in the front with her hands flat against the heater vents while Barry kept trying to grab Thompson.

"Kitty," he cooed. "Pretty kitty!"

"Don't touch the kitty," Alice said. "He's not a nice kitty."

"Hey!" Thompson said.

"Shh," Alice told him.

"He's just been knocked into the water by a cavorting river dragon, and rescued by flying ones. A talking cat is the least of his problems."

"Being naked is kind of a problem, too," Jasmine said. She was almost sitting in Miriam's lap trying to stay well away from Barry.

"Humans are such prudes," the cat said.

Alice glanced in the rear-view mirror as they crept along the barely-there track. "He's well wrapped up, Jasmine."

"Pretty kitty?" Barry offered, making an ineffectual grab for Thompson. DI Adams took a swig from Alice's flask and wondered if clothes were overrated when it came to keeping warm in a storm. Barry didn't even have goosebumps.

"What do we do about him seeing dragons?" she asked.

"I'll handle it," the cat said.

She frowned at him. "Handle it how?" She hadn't liked the sound of clean-ups.

"He'll be fine, Adams," the cat said. "And seriously, he's off his rocker. No one's going to believe him about any of it even if I do nothing."

"It does rather explain the nakedness," Miriam said, reaching over Jasmine to tuck Barry's blankets in a little more securely.

"So do you really need to do anything to him?" the inspector asked the cat. "As you say, no one'll believe him anyway."

Thompson regarded her coolly. "It's a matter of controlling information. Too many humans start talking about strange things, people start asking questions. Like that journalist."

"He's clueless."

"Maybe. But he's not stupid. And I don't know where he is. Haven't seen him since breakfast."

DI Adams pressed her lips together, feeling the chill of them, and nodded. "Alright," she said. "You have a point."

"Bloody right I do. Because you lot are getting careless. And you know what comes after humans asking questions? The Watch asking questions."

"Got it," DI Adams said.

"You don't want that."

"Yes, I've kind of gathered that," she said, and they glared at each other.

"Puss, puss?" Barry offered.

"Naff off," the cat said.

There was silence for a while, just the purr of the engine and the clatter of rain on the roof. Finally, Miriam said almost reluctantly, "I don't suppose one of the protesters is called Rainbow?"

"Yes," DI Adams said. "Your sister, I believe?"

"My sister." Miriam covered her face with her hands and sighed.

"Oh dear," Jasmine said.

"Pretty kitty?" Barry tried again, *puss puss* having had no effect.

"That bad?" DI Adams asked.

"Sometimes worse," Alice said.

"Pretty kitty!"

"No, weird man," Thompson said.

"I did think protesting her own sister was a bit harsh."

"I'm getting the gate," Miriam said as the car eased to a stop beyond it, and clambered out into the rain. Jasmine scrambled out after her, and together they pulled the gate to and latched it again, both of them staggering in the wind.

"How much worse?" DI Adams asked Alice as they watched the two women in the rear-view mirrors.

"Not murder worse," Alice said. "I don't think, anyway. But she does hate Maddie having this place. Thinks she's sold out to the elite, and is desperate for her to have to get rid of it. Silly, really, as anyone she sells it to will probably tear it up and destroy half the woods and history. But Rainbow doesn't tend to look that far ahead."

DI Adams nodded, and thought she'd heard of murders happening over less.

🐾

THEY DROVE the short distance to the fallen tree in near silence, punctuated by Barry's wheedling calls to Thompson and the cat's increasingly impatient replies.

"I think you should just head back to the house," DI Adams told him finally.

"On my own? It's chucking it down!"

"Just do that shifting thing."

He gave her a ferocious look. "Does that look easy? It's not easy.

And you do too much at once and things start watching you from the other side."

"The other side of what?" Alice asked.

"Of here. From the Inbetween. We step into it from where we are, and step out where we want to be."

"Like a wormhole?" DI Adams asked.

"I don't know. I'm not a physicist."

Sure. Schrödinger he could discuss, but not wormholes.

"Look," Miriam said. "The Land Rover's already running."

It was, the lights on and the windows steaming, and someone was running back toward them from the bridge with a torch bouncing in one hand. Alice pulled up next to the 4x4 and DI Adams got out, still swathed in blankets. Harriet tumbled out of the Land Rover as the other doors started opening rather more reluctantly.

"Barry! Barry, is he okay? Is he—"

"He's in there," DI Adams said as Miriam got out. "We'll take him back to the house and warm him up."

"How'd you get him?" Ronnie demanded. "Where from? You went all to hell downstream!"

"I dragged him out at a shallow patch and was able to get hold of Alice on my radio," the inspector said, then added, "Um, water-proof radio."

"This seems weird," Ronnie said. "I don't like it. Smells like conspiracy. Smells like *bacon*."

"Yeah, bacon," the bearded young man echoed.

Jemima bounced up and down next to him, her eyes wild. "Bacon!"

"Shut up, you two," Harriet said, then addressed DI Adams. "Thank you."

"Glad to help," she said. "And in the interests of public safety, you can't stay here. You all need to come back to the house."

"Well, that's very kind, but—"

"Fight the power!" Jemima shouted. "We're *occupying* this river!" Her teeth were chattering so much DI Adams could barely understand what she was saying.

"This river is going to occupy your campsite if the rain keeps up," she said.

"It's a trick!" Ronnie waved a finger at DI Adams. "A sneaky, piggy trick!"

"I think you can see the problem," Harriet said, her tone almost apologetic.

"And we're not going anywhere with that traitor," Rainbow said. She'd been the figure with the torch by the river, and now as she arrived at the tree she trained the light on Miriam, who raised a hand to protect her eyes. "Probably set it all up, didn't you?"

"What, I threw Barry in the river?"

Rainbow hesitated. "Alright, not that bit. But this, trying to kidnap him and drive us all up to that hideous monument to class warfare? I bet that's all you."

"He's just about got hypothermia! We're trying to *help!*"

"Sure you are. Cosying up to the police, aren't you? Collaborator!"

Miriam pinched the bridge of her nose. "Jud—"

"That's not my name!"

"Miriam, get in the car." Alice's voice was sharp as she climbed out of the Fiat. "I'll drive the Land Rover." She walked around the car and held her hand out to Harriet. "Keys."

Miriam hesitated. "Alice, you don't have to—"

"And you don't have to stand here and take this nonsense just because you're related to the silly woman."

"Don't call me a silly woman," Rainbow snapped. "Always had a stick up your—"

"*Stop,*" DI Adams said sharply. "It's bloody freezing and we're all going to get washed to bloody Lancashire at this rate, and I'm being *really very nice* but I'm getting *really bloody sick* of the lot of you." She pointed at Harriet. "You. Give Alice the keys. Rainbow, I don't care how principled you are, you are *risking lives* right now. So get in that Land Rover and shut the hell up. Beardy—"

"Tom," he mumbled, but she ignored him.

"Get in this car. The rest of you into the Land Rover, and the next person that argues with me is going to end up arrested and locked in the bloody cellar until we can get this damn road open. *Are we clear?*"

There was a ringing silence after her words, as if even the wind was too scared to argue with her, then Harriet held the keys out to Alice.

Alice took them with a nod at DI Adams, and climbed into the driver's seat. Rainbow and the inspector stared at each other, then the older woman switched her torch off and said, "Only because the weather's so bad."

"Of course." DI Adams stayed where she was, her blankets getting wetter and wetter, until the Land Rover was fully loaded and had set off up the drive.

"Um, Inspector?" Miriam said. She'd climbed into the driver's seat but still had her door open. "You should get in. You'll freeze."

"I am freezing," she agreed, but didn't move. She didn't want to get in the car with all these people, as well as the chatty damn cat. The best thing about cats, she had always thought, was that they *didn't* talk, only now it turned out that they did. And they were rude, although that bit was hardly surprising. She sighed, feeling the rain running down her back. At least all the cranberry sauce would be gone.

"Please?" Miriam suggested, and the inspector nodded.

"Yes. Alright." She turned to the little SUV, then hesitated. "Miriam, do you ever feel that your life has taken a really strange turn, and it's not just that you're not sure where you are on the map, you're not quite sure there even is a map anymore?"

Miriam wiped rain off her face. "All the time, Inspector. I gave up looking for the map years ago."

"Oh." DI Adams got into the car, and leaned back in the seat as Miriam backed carefully away from the tree, peering into the rain-sodden day.

Thompson looked up at her and said in a low voice, "Maybe there never was a map."

"Shut up," she said, and closed her eyes.

They rumbled comfortably up the drive, Jasmine wedged between Barry and Tom in the back and looking worried. Barry seemed to have forgotten all about Thompson, who climbed onto the inspector's lap and peered out the windscreen. The presence of Tom had silenced him, at least.

"Whose cat is that?" the young man asked after a couple of minutes.

"Alice's," DI Adams said, and that was the end of the conversation. She kept her eyes closed, already picturing a deep bath and a large glass of something very strong.

Her daydream had progressed to the point of considering what sort of bubble bath she might be able to chase up (she was hoping for Radox muscle soak, as she'd knocked a knee and an elbow in the tumble down the river, and everything was aching from the effort of holding onto a wet and slippery dragon), when Jasmine shrieked and Miriam stomped on the brakes hard enough to throw the inspector against the seatbelt. She groaned, and the cat surfaced from the footwell where he'd fallen.

"Nice driving," he hissed at Miriam, before DI Adams flicked his ear to shut him up.

"What was it, Miriam?" she asked.

"I don't know! It just raced across the road—"

"It was *huge!*" Jasmine exclaimed.

"A deer?" DI Adams suggested, which was about as far as her local wildlife knowledge went.

218 | KIM M. WATT

"No, it was the wrong shape," Miriam began, then gave a squawk of horror as someone banged on her window. She all but fell into DI Adams' lap, and the inspector leaned over her to see the journalist grinning through the window. He waved. DI Adams and Thompson exchanged almost identical expressions of suspicion, then Miriam straightened up and wound the window down a crack.

"Hi," he said, and looked at the three passengers wedged in the back seat. "Oh, wow. Full car."

"What are you doing out here?" DI Adams asked.

"Walking."

"In this?"

"There's no such thing as bad weather, just bad gear. Although —" he tipped his face up so water ran down his face "—perhaps the good gear here would be SCUBA gear."

"What do you want, Mr Giles?" DI Adams asked, leaning over Miriam. "We've just pulled this man out of the river, we're cold and we're wet."

"What on earth was he doing in the river?"

"Ballet."

Ervin grinned. "Of course. And you? You look a bit damp, too."

"His unwilling dance partner. What do you want?"

"A lift?"

Miriam looked at DI Adams, who sighed and nodded. She clicked the unlock button. "You can get in the boot."

"Thanks." He gave them one final grin, and nodded at the cat. "Still carting him around, I see."

Thompson hissed, and Miriam wound her window up. "Should I drive away before he gets in?"

"That would be mean," Jasmine said.

"I'm not against the idea," the inspector said, but the journalist was already folding himself into the back of the car.

"This is the world's smallest SUV," he said, trying to wedge his skinny frame into the space behind the back seats.

"I'm sorry it's not to your liking," Miriam said, and started off while he still had the door open, making him yelp and grab Tom over the top of the seats. Tom squawked and pushed him away, and DI Adams swallowed a snort of laughter. It was becoming more and more clear to her that the Toot Hansell W.I were not at all as nice as they seemed.

The house was dark as they rumbled back up the drive, rendered stark and forbidding by the rapidly darkening afternoon and the building clouds. It seemed taller than it had in the sun of the previous day, and it leaned over the cowering car as if it would reach out and swat them at any moment.

"Goth-*ic*," Thompson murmured, and DI Adams gave him a poke in the side to shush him. He gave her a look that indicated she was being paranoid thinking anyone would overhear, especially given the din of the rain on the roof, but she didn't care. She'd decided to give up entirely on being day-off Adams, and to just stick to DI Adams. Day-off Adams didn't seem to be working out, and besides, she'd only have to use her first name if she kept up this sort of friendly relationship thing. (It was Jeanette, which was not a bad name, but DI Adams didn't use it. It wasn't that she didn't like it, exactly, but it didn't feel like it belonged to her. And why did anyone need an extra name anyway? Adams worked just fine.)

Miriam pulled the car to a stop in front of the steps, and said, "You may as well all get out here, then I'll go park up."

"Just leave it here," DI Adams said, struggling to collect her blanket while the cat wandered across her lap. "Get off!"

"I don't know if Alice'd like that," Miriam said, while the cat gave the inspector a disapproving look.

"I'm sure you'll be fine. Ah – Tom?" She had a twinge of embarrassment over calling him Beardy earlier. Very unprofessional.

"Um, yeah?"

"Help me get Barry out." She pushed the door open, holding it firm against the wind, and Thompson leaped off her lap and streaked up the stairs to the front door with his ears flat to his head. DI Adams started around the car to grab Barry, and someone took her arm.

"Get yourself inside," Teresa said. She was swathed in some sort of high-tech outdoor gear and had her grey-streaked hair bundled into a wrap. "There's a hot bath waiting for you, and you may as well get it now. Power's out, so no hot water later."

"You shouldn't be out here. There's no point in you getting all wet and cold too."

The older woman gave her a broad grin that suggested there was nothing she liked doing better in her twilight years than trekking about the place in a spring storm, dragging naked men out of cars. Not for the first time, DI Adams wondered what was in the water in Toot Hansell. "I'm not the one who's been playing about in rivers. Get yourself inside."

She blocked DI Adams' path around the car quite effectively, and Miriam and Jasmine were already fishing Barry out of the back seat, while Tom stood next to them looking confused and occasionally rearranging the other man's blanket. Yes, she should keep to DI Adams, not off-duty Adams. This was what happened when she had days off. Got bossed around by septuagenarians and had to borrow their clothes.

On the other hand, they did seem to have things under control, her boots were somewhere in the depths of the river, and she was fairly sure she was never going to feel her toes again. She picked her way up the stairs and was ushered inside by Rose and Pearl. Rose poked her somewhere around the midriff.

"Ow! What?"

"Are you hurt?"

"I don't know, I can't feel anything."

"You're fine then. Go take a bath." Rose turned away again, and DI Adams felt an almost irresistible urge to stick her tongue out at the little woman's back. Instead she padded across the tiles, her socks leaving sodden footprints behind her, and started fantasising about warm clothes.

"Ah, DI Adams. Detective Inspector!"

She groaned inwardly, and turned to face Reid. He let himself out of the office door and hurried up to her.

"Yes?"

He lowered his voice to almost a whisper. "These protesters can't stay here, you know."

"Oh? You want me to put them back out in the rain?"

"Well, it's just – it's not good for the other guests. It looks bad."

"It'll look worse if they all die of exposure out there."

"Right, but can't you just send them home or something?"

"No," the inspector said. "I don't know if the bridge is even safe to cross. Their camp is probably flooded, and a least one of them is on the verge of hypothermia. So I think a little hospitality is in order."

"Well, now—"

"Reid, honestly," Maddie said, pushing through the door behind him with a collection of small hurricane lanterns. "Why are you bothering the inspector? What's wrong with you?"

"I was trying to sort out the protester situation!"

"Oh, do go make yourself useful and help Nita or something. For the bathroom," Maddie said, giving DI Adams a lantern. "And ignore him. The power's out, which happens a lot with storms here, but Boyd and Adele are lighting fires in all the rooms. If you go take your bath now the water'll still be warm, and your room should be all cosy by the time you get done. Do you need more clothes?"

DI Adams wondered if country lady attire was any better than ageing track star attire, and supposed it wasn't. "That'd be wonderful."

"I'll give some to Miriam to bring up."

"And the protesters …?"

Maddie made a strange face. "We're settling them in."

"We *would* be settling them in," Pearl said, wandering over with a torch in hand. "Only Rainbow's declared she's occupying the dining room, and they've barricaded the doors."

"Oh, good," DI Adams said faintly, wondering if she was ever going to make it to the bath.

"Leave her," Rose said, pausing at the foot of the stairs. Thompson was walking next to her, and Barry was following on behind, cooing at the cat. "We've got cake enough in our rooms. We won't starve, even if we can't get to the kitchen."

"We can get to the kitchen from outside," Maddie said. "And you brought cake? Didn't you think I'd feed you?"

"To be fair," Teresa said, following Barry with a spare blanket, "last time we were here Reid was doing the cooking."

"Right." Maddie gathered herself with an obvious effort. "Anyway. Nita's got it all in hand. We're going to have a spring storm party. So you won't need your cake."

The inspector adjusted her blanket, aware there was a puddle spreading around her feet. "Well, if it's alright for now, I'll go get dried off—"

"Tom!"

DI Adams groaned, and turned to see Rainbow standing on the threshold of the dining room glaring at them all.

"Get in here," she ordered the young man, who looked longingly up the stairs.

"They said there were baths—"

"Is that all it takes to destroy your principles? A *bath?* I always knew you weren't committed! You only joined for Jemima!"

Tom sighed and shuffled across the floor, and Miriam said hesitantly, "If he doesn't want to—"

"You shut up, traitor!" Rainbow shouted at her, and pushed Tom into the candlelit room behind her. "Barry, you come too."

"There's a kitty," Barry said, already halfway up the stairs.

"He's staying here," DI Adams said. "He needs to warm up properly. You all do. You're drenched, it's cold—"

"They nicked all the blankets we were keeping for you," Rose said. "They're fine."

"Reallocation of wealth," Rainbow announced, and Maddie snorted.

"Oh, yes, we're so wealthy. That's why this place is falling down around our ears!"

"Bourgeois landowners—"

"Oh, *stop it!*" Miriam exclaimed. "Just stop it, Rainbow."

"You're the worst! You pretend you're spiritual, but you're just—"

"Enough," DI Adams said. "Go in and occupy the bloody room if you want. Just make sure everyone stays warm. We're not getting any help out here tonight." Rainbow started to say something, and she added, "I *will* arrest you and leave you in the cellar. In fact, I'll be very happy to."

Rainbow muttered something about pigs and the yoke of oppression, then slammed the dining room door. DI Adams turned and stomped up the stairs, glaring so furiously at the journalist that he didn't even try following her. She was going to have a bath. And after that she'd find where all these stashes of cake were. And after *that* she'd see what she could do about the murderer.

❧

THE CLAW-FOOTED TUB was deep and full, and she dropped her muddy clothes in the sink and clambered in, squeaking as the hot

water closed over her toes. They were wrinkled and unhappy looking, but she didn't think they were frostbitten. They only felt like it.
She sank to her knees, then lowered herself slowly all the way in,
smelling some lavender-y scent that might not be Radox, but which
seemed very in keeping with certain aspects of the Toot Hansell
Women's Institute. Not all of them, mind. She took a breath and
dipped below the surface, scrubbing her fingers though her hair to
get rid of the muddy river water, toes and fingers all but screaming
with the heat. She stayed under as long as she could manage, then
slid slowly up to lean against the curved wall of the big tub, draping
her arms along the edges and feeling like a movie star, albeit a very
cold and still slightly muddy one. She let her head tip back and rest
on the rim of the bath, savouring a little quiet, a little silence, only
the sound of the rain on the roof to disturb her. This was what she
needed. Quiet, not people. She took a deep breath, and frowned.

Something wasn't right.

She kept her eyes closed. *No*, she thought. *No, I'm having a bath.*

Something definitely wasn't right.

She'd locked the door. It was a shared bathroom, and she'd *definitely* locked the door.

It was this place. These *people*. They were getting in her head.

She wasn't going to look. She was going to lie right here and
enjoy this bath.

"Five minutes," she said to the room. "Just five minutes. That's
all. I'm not asking for a lot here."

No one answered.

She lifted her head and opened her eyes.

The dog, the great dreadlocked dog that looked more like a
carpet than any animal had a right to, had its heavy head resting
on the edge of the bath by her hand. It huffed at her when she
looked at it, and she felt its hot breath on her skin. She looked
behind it, and the door was still firmly shut. She couldn't tell from
here if it was locked or not. It couldn't be, obviously, because there

was a bloody great dog on the bathmat and no other way into the room. She stared at it, and assumed it was staring back at her from behind all that hair. Then she put her head back and closed her eyes again, and the room was silent.

16

ALICE

With the detective inspector safely ensconced in her bath, Alice returned to her own investigations, although the arrival of the protesters had sent everything rather into disarray. Gert could only report that Holt was a terrible poker player and that she and Rosemary had relieved him of most of his cash, which was unhelpful. Pearl had spent most of the time wedged into a sofa with Paula, and almost ran out the door to help organise the damp protesters. She was now trying to avoid going back into the lounge, and all she could tell Alice was that the American woman was very fond of small dogs and gin. And that she was almost certain none of them were actually American.

Which was definitely suspicious, if not necessarily in a murderous sort of way. Priya was looking after the dragons, and Nita had already thrown Carlotta out of the orangery for trying to tell her how to use the barbecue properly, then locked the door behind her. Which brought things rather to a standstill, at least until the family stopped running around sorting out the fires in the rooms and so on.

Alice sighed and sat down on the edge of her bed. She needed more time than just however long it took the inspector to have a bath.

"Are you alright?" Miriam asked. She was trying to get the knots out of her hair. It looked to Alice that she might be better with scissors than a brush.

"We need motives," she said, and Miriam regarded her doubtfully.

"We do?"

"For murder. Who wanted Keeley dead?"

Miriam wrinkled her nose. "Shouldn't we leave this to the detective inspector?" Alice just looked at her until Miriam groaned and sat down. "If it looked like an accident, that means there was no struggle, doesn't it?"

"Yes," Alice said, smiling slightly.

"So that means it was someone he was expecting to see in the sauna in the middle of the night, and didn't mind being close to. So I don't think it could be a guest, unless he was, um, friendly with one of them." Miriam blushed, and Thompson, who had been cleaning himself in front of the grumbling fire, looked up.

"Not bad," he said, then went back to grooming.

"You see?" Alice said. "You *are* good at this."

"But how does it help?" Miriam asked, going even pinker.

"I think it makes it unlikely it was Reid." Alice didn't say anything else, and Miriam went back to brushing her hair, the blush fading.

"Adele wouldn't," the younger woman said finally, her voice almost a whisper. "Those mushrooms were an *accident*."

Alice didn't reply, and the cat watched them both for a moment with his flat green eyes reflecting the light of the fire, then got up and vanished.

THE STORM KEPT up its steady assault outside, and Alice turned on the torch Maddie had given her to make sure the batteries were good. One never knew if people were conscientious about such things. But the light seemed strong enough, so she checked the hall for Americans, antique hunters, or, worst of all, journalists, then let herself out and walked to the door of the shared bathroom.

"DI Adams?" she said, and knocked lightly.

There was a splash, a pause, then the inspector said, "Is the door locked?"

Alice tried the handle. "It is."

The inspector muttered something Alice couldn't quite hear, then there was more splashing, and the sound of the key in the lock.

"You didn't have to get out," Alice said, as the inspector peered past her down the hall.

"Have you seen a dog?"

"A dog?"

"Yes. Big. Looks like a walking carpet. Smelly."

"No," Alice said, wondering just how cold the inspector had got.

"Of course not." DI Adams sighed. "What's up?"

"Miriam and I are just going down to the kitchen to see the dragons. Would you like to join us?"

"*Yes.* Yes, I would. Wait for me." DI Adams dived back into the bathroom, and there was the sound of the plug being pulled, then she rushed back into the hall and to her room. Alice stayed where she was, listening to the wind plucking at the house and the sound of furniture being dragged around in the dining room downstairs. After a moment a door further down the hall opened, and a man put his head around it. He blinked at her.

"Hello," she said pleasantly.

"Hi," he said, and sidled out the door, pulling it shut behind him. "What're you doing?"

"Waiting for my friends."

"Me too," he said, and fiddled with one of the many pockets in his jacket.

"How's the birdwatching going?" she asked him.

"Oh, good. Yeah. Very good."

"Even with this weather?"

"Um, right. No. Not so good with the weather." He blinked at her, then reached behind him and turned the door handle. "Forgot something," he said, and vanished. She waited, and in a lull in the wind heard anxious chatter behind the door. The door eased open just enough to create a gap big enough to peek through, then shut quietly again. Alice clasped her hands and thought that if they were basing this investigation on strange behaviour, she'd have even more suspects to deal with. Then DI Adams hurried out of her room, pulling on a black fleece that looked a couple of sizes too big. Her hair was still wet, and had been tidied unevenly into a wrap.

"Did you have enough clothes?" Alice asked her.

"Yes, they're fine." She pulled up the fleece to show Alice a pair of men's walking trousers that came up almost to her ribcage. "Can't say much about the fashion, but they fit, and they're dry."

"Very good." Alice smiled at Miriam as she hurried out of their room, kitted up in workout gear and trainers. She was evidently taking no chances when it came to being prepared for action. "Shall we go?"

MIRIAM LED them past the stairs and down a stretch of hall to a door marked *Private*, nestled unobtrusively between two of the rooms. Alice had known it was there, but had never had cause to use it, and now she and DI Adams followed Miriam onto a landing, one end lined with shelving stacked with sheets and towels and cleaning supplies, a vacuum cleaner lurking below them. A narrow spiral staircase led both up and down, the carpet here even more worn than in the main part of the house, and she supposed that up would take them to what had once been servants' quarters in the attic, and was now staff rooms. Miriam switched her torch on and took the stairs down, DI Adams following her, and Alice paused for a moment. There were scratching noises in the walls, and she wondered if it really was mice. Mice didn't normally fill her with such a certainty that she was being watched.

The bottom of the stairs ended in another landing, lit only by their torches. Miriam opened the door a crack and peered out, then led them into a narrow hall. A hurricane lantern perched precariously on a three-legged, drunkenly leaning side table gave off a mellow glow. The hall itself was cluttered with boxes of old newspapers, tins of paint, a couple of broken sunloungers, a set of rusting golf clubs, a manual lawnmower, and something that looked a lot like the stripy poles used for horse jumping. She wouldn't have liked to get through here carrying too much.

"You should see the library," Miriam whispered. "That's why they closed it up. This is all the stuff they can't get in there."

Alice frowned, remembering dust-speckled sunlight rolling through high windows to wash over straining shelves and jumbled books, everything from first editions in cracked leather bindings to penny dreadfuls with torn, lurid covers. "What happened to the books?" she asked, keeping her voice low as well. It wasn't that Maddie would mind them being in here, but explaining that they were sneaking to the kitchen to see about two defrosting dragons would be a little tricky.

"I think they're still in there," Miriam said. "It was only meant to be temporary, when the roof to the last of the outbuildings started getting too leaky. But they haven't had the money to fix it."

DI Adams tripped over a life-ring and mumbled, "People have too much stuff."

Miriam wound her way through the mess and opened a door that let straight onto the path that ran around the house, and the three women hunched their shoulders against the weather and ran for the kitchen.

§

"WE CAN MAKE some tea if you get down," Priya said to Mortimer. "The inspector would like some."

"And cake," DI Adams muttered. Her arms were crossed over her chest and she looked unhappy. "I also want cake."

"I brought cake," Miriam said, waving a tin at them.

Mortimer shook Beaufort again, but the old dragon's breathing didn't even hitch. "*Beaufort*," he insisted, and Alice clasped her hands together, worrying the fingers over each other.

"Maybe he needs a little longer?" she suggested, without much hope. Mortimer's scales were glowing with heat, the rich blues and purples lit on the edges with hot gold. Beaufort could have been carved from stone, some misplaced garden ornament, and her chest felt tight and sore.

"What's wrong?" DI Adams asked. "Why's he not responding?"

"I think he got too cold," Mortimer whispered. "I think he's hibernating."

Alice thought of the cat saying, *If that fire gets too low, it doesn't come back easy. Sometimes not at all.* She shivered.

"He's *what?*" the inspector demanded. "How? Why just like that?"

"Hibernation takes months," Miriam said. "He can't sleep on the stove for months!"

"He can't sleep on the stove at all," Priya said. "Nita's going to have to come back in here at some point."

"I'm sorry," Mortimer said, and his voice was shaky. "But I don't think he meant to. He's just ... gone."

"He's not *gone*. He's only fallen asleep," Miriam said. "Can't we wake him up?"

"No," Mortimer said quietly. "If dragons get too cold, they can go into hibernation. Old dragons are particularly susceptible. It's why I wanted everyone to have barbecues, so they'd always be warm."

"How long does it last, Mortimer?" Alice asked, her voice gentle. The young dragon pressed his face to Beaufort's, trying to pass his heat to him, but the High Lord was still grey and unmoving.

He took a deep breath. "Sometimes they wake up in a day or so, or a month, or a decade. Sometimes they … don't. They're just stone." He looked at his paws. "Beaufort's never hibernated. Not in my life, certainly. But I don't think ever. He always had too much to do."

There was a long silence, in which they could hear the hiss of the gas and the wind pawing at the windows, then Alice said, "Well. We just have to hope it's a short hibernation. We can keep Nita out of here for tonight, at least. We'll just tell her we'll take care of the clean-up, that she needs to rest up after yesterday."

"She doesn't seem like the sort of person that needs to rest up," Priya said.

"We'll have to move him," the inspector said. "Carry him out. We can do it with a few of us."

"Move him where?" Miriam asked. Her voice was almost as shaky as Mortimer's.

"Bring a car up to the door. He can stay in there."

"It'll be too cold," Mortimer said. "He'll go deeper."

"We'll run it."

"All night?" Priya said.

"If we have to. Take petrol from the other cars."

"No," Alice said, forcing her worrying fingers to relax. "We'll keep him inside. We'll find a way to do it. Let's just keep Nita out of here for at least the next hour or so. We'll think it through."

"*How?*" Miriam almost wailed. "How do we carry him around the house? How do we even *lift* him?"

"She's right," Mortimer said, staring at Alice with wide eyes. "I don't think even I can lift him."

"And how am I going to keep Nita out?" Priya asked. "I can't exactly ban her from her own kitchen! She didn't even want me to help her set up! And she's already furious with Carlotta."

Alice looked at DI Adams, who lifted one shoulder in a small shrug. They were right. That was the worst of it. "Tea," she said. "We shall start with tea, and we shall make a plan. One thing at a time." She turned to Mortimer. "Are you warm enough to come down?"

He nodded, and slid off the stove wordlessly, leaving sooty footprints on the floor. Well, that would have to come later, too.

"Priya, put the kettle on, please. Miriam, let's have that cake." She clapped her hands together lightly. "Everything will make more sense after tea."

She hoped she sounded more convinced than she felt.

"Dumbwaiter," DI Adams said suddenly, around a piece of Rose's shortbread.

"Eh?" Mortimer said.

Alice looked up from her cup and smiled. "Dumbwaiter," she agreed. "It should be big enough."

Miriam put down the cake tin and stared around. "You're right! There must be one!"

"Um," Mortimer said, taking another couple of pieces of shortbread. "Isn't that a bit rude?"

"We'll find it," Priya swivelled on her heel, surveying the room from where they stood clustered around a bench. "Do you think it's boarded up?"

"We'll soon find out," DI Adams said, running her hands over the wall next to the dining room.

Alice abandoned her tea and went to help them, and Mortimer said behind them, "Is that a common thing? Boarding them up? Only I think I read a story where someone was *bricked* up."

"Here!" Miriam exclaimed. She was peering behind a set of open shelving that was piled with plates and bowls. "There's something back here!"

"They've put them behind a shelf?" Mortimer asked.

"They don't get used anymore," Alice said, and started lifting the plates off. There were an awful lot of them in an astonishing variety of sizes, all plain white and oversized and expensive-looking.

"Priya," DI Adams said, joining Alice, "can you just nip out and make sure Nita isn't going to suddenly pop back? Maybe even stay there with her so you can get anything she needs."

"Of course." Priya pulled the hood of her jacket over her sleek dark hair, unlocked the door and slipped out into the rain. Miriam had joined Alice and the DI, shifting the stacked plates from the shelves to the counters while Mortimer hovered about looking like he wanted to help but didn't quite trust himself. Alice thought that was wise. Paws weren't made for handling pricey crockery.

The shelves were slim metal sheets on a metal frame, and once they were clear Alice reached between them to try lifting the white-painted hatch open. "It's a bit stiff," she said, straightening up. "I can't get it to budge from this angle."

"It might be painted shut," Miriam suggested, bringing a lantern over for a closer look. "We'll have to cut it open."

DI Adams tried to move the shelves away from the wall, but they didn't budge. "Sh-sugar," she said, with a sideways glance at Alice. "They're bolted."

"I've got it." Mortimer scampered around the counter, short-bread crumbs on his snout. "I'm surprised they're not shouting for help."

"Sorry?" Alice said, but the word was nearly lost in the screech of crumbling stone as Mortimer grabbed the shelves and pulled. The whole structure swayed wildly, swinging open like a door as the bolts on Mortimer's end pulled straight out of the wall. The ones at the far end bent at an unusable angle, and Alice wasn't quite sure how they were going to get the shelves back in place, but at least they could reach the hatch.

"We're in!" Mortimer exclaimed, and hooked his claws under the hatch as the women exchanged puzzled glances. He tugged hard, and after a moment's resistance the paint cracked and it slid up into the wall, revealing an empty wooden box. Mortimer stared at it, his eyebrow ridges pulled down in puzzlement. "But where's the waiter?"

Alice blinked, then covered her mouth to hide a smile. "It's just a name, Mortimer."

"Oh." He scratched an ear as DI Adams chuckled and inspected the interior. "I thought you were being quite unpleasant about someone, really."

"I can see how you'd think that," Miriam said, smiling.

"It's a silly name," Mortimer said, his snout starting to flush an embarrassed lilac. "Why not wall box?"

"That would make much more sense," Alice said gravely.

"It would." Mortimer dusted his paws off, not looking at them. "Anyway – what's the use of a box? We can't leave Beaufort in it."

"It moves," Miriam said. "We can put him in it, then use it to lift him upstairs."

"Not that we know where it comes out," DI Adams pointed out.

Alice glanced around the kitchen, trying to get a sense of the layout. "The hall, I think. Or an unused room. They wouldn't have it going into a guest room."

Mortimer nodded. "Okay. So we get him upstairs and into one of the bedrooms?" His voice was wobbly, and he'd stopped dusting his paws, clenching them together instead.

"He'll be alright," Alice said. Her stomach had an unfamiliar sick feel to it, but she put as much conviction in her voice as she could. "We'll get him upstairs and in front of the fire, and he'll be okay."

"Of course he will." Mortimer didn't quite look at her.

"How're we going to get him in?" DI Adams asked, crossing her arms and staring at the dumbwaiter. "It's not exactly roomy."

The three women and the dragon looked from the High Lord, still motionless on the hissing burners, to the dumbwaiter, clearly designed for taking trays of tea and plates of biscuits to the ladies' drawing room in earlier times. It did not look designed for dragons.

"Will it hold him?" Miriam said. "What if it falls all the way to the cellar?"

"And he's going to be hot," Mortimer said. "He's been on the stove for – well, for as long as I was asleep, I guess."

They all looked at Alice, and she allowed herself the luxury of a moment's speculation on why it was that even detective inspectors seemed to defer to her on matters of dragons, then said, "Oven mitts. There must be some around here somewhere. Tea towels. And we're just going to have to try, aren't we? No use standing around here playing guessing games. The doing's the thing." She strode briskly to the counters that lined the walls and started opening drawers, looking for anything that might be useful for lifting a piping hot dragon.

A THOROUGH BUT rapid search of the kitchen failed to yield any oven mitts, which Alice thought was rather symptomatic of the chefs she had known. Presumably they just burned themselves regularly and wore the scars as badges of honour. The three women had, however, rounded up an impressive array of tea towels, and now they gathered around the stove. Mortimer had left them to the hunt, curling up with Beaufort instead, his face hidden from them.

They looked at each other, then DI Adams said in a quiet voice, "Mortimer?"

Mortimer heaved an unhappy sigh and got up, sliding off the stove and leaving a trail of soot over the counter and onto the floor. "Alright," he said. "If you lift him onto my back, I'll walk him over to the dumbwaiter."

"Excellent plan," Alice said, and patted the younger dragon on the shoulder with a folded tea towel. Heat was baking off him with enough intensity to flush her face. "Are we ready, ladies?"

"Ooh. He is hot," Miriam said, snatching up another couple of tea towels so she could double up. Beaufort was still the dull grey of cold stone, but the heat of the stove was conducting across his scales with the efficiency of any metal pot. "I don't know how to hold him!"

"Well, just— his spines, I guess?" DI Adams grabbed Beaufort's shoulders, yelped, and let go. "Definitely more tea towels."

Alice positioned herself by the big dragon's hindquarters and took hold of his hips. His tail was still curled around him like a snoozing cat's. "Alright," she said. She could already feel her hands starting to smart. "Ready?"

"Ready," DI Adams said.

"Um," Miriam said, but nodded.

Mortimer just sighed again, but Alice took that as an affirmative.

"Lift!"

They heaved, and Alice heard something give a warning twang

in her back. Miriam squeaked, and DI Adams said, "Holy cow. He's been eating too many scones."

Mortimer looked up at them. "It's not *scones*. It's scales. Dragons are heavier than they look."

Alice thought they looked heavy to begin with, so this seemed to be a bad sign. "We're going to have to slide him off onto Mortimer."

"But we'll never lift him into the dumbwaiter," DI Adams pointed out. "And God knows if it'll hold him even if we get him in. I didn't think he'd be *this* heavy."

"Stairs, then," Alice said. "Mortimer, if we steady him, can you carry him?"

The younger dragon looked dubious, but nodded. "Sure. I think."

"Excellent. Good job." She looked at the others. "Ready? Slide on three. One. Two. Th—" She was interrupted by the clatter of a key in the lock, and Priya's voice from outside, too loud.

"I just thought, you know, lock it, in case anyone's wandering around, and—"

They were already pushing, had started on three, and the High Lord was moving. Alice threw herself against him, trying to stop his fall, then jumped back with a hiss as his leg touched her belly, burning through her clothes. Miriam gave a squeak as she did the same, and DI Adams let loose with some language that made even the chef hesitate as she came through the door. Not for long, though.

"What the hell are you doing?" she demanded as Beaufort, despite their best efforts, rolled gracelessly off the stove and landed with a very solid-sounding thump on top of Mortimer, who squawked, wobbled, then collapsed on the floor as his legs gave way. "What was that? Did you hear something?"

"No?" Alice offered.

"No?" Nita demanded. "*No?* You didn't hear a great bloody bang like *someone* is moving things about in my fridge or my pantry?"

"Definitely not that," Alice said.

"It might have been the door," DI Adams said. "It's still open."

"It wasn't the door—"

"It's that peacock!" Miriam exclaimed. "Look!"

Even Nita turned to look as, with an alarmed *bu-kurk!* the peacock, who had been peering in the door, bolted across the kitchen as if something had nipped its tail.

"Get out!" she yelled at it. "Stupid bloody bird!"

"Oh, not you again," DI Adams said, glaring at the empty doorway, and Alice wondered if there was something outside that she couldn't see.

"Help me!" Nita shouted, chasing the peacock as it raced around a counter and headed for the back of the kitchen. Miriam and Priya ran after her, neither of them looking very sure what they were doing.

"Get out," DI Adams said to a spot just inside the kitchen door.

"DI Adams?" Alice said, and followed her as she marched to the door. "What is it?"

"Can't you see it?"

"*Bu-KURK! Ke-ow! Ke-ow-ow-ow!*"

"I'm going to make a bloody pie out of you!" Nita bellowed, waving to Priya and Miriam. "Cut him off by the sink!"

"See what?" Alice asked politely, staring at the tiles. She was quite used to seeing dragons, and had had no trouble seeing goblins, but all she could see here was a damp mark on the floor. She wondered if the DI had actually warmed up enough after her dip in the river.

"Got him!" Priya shrieked behind them, and there was an explosion of panicked *eow-eow-eow*s, like a particularly piercing and colourful car alarm. "*No!*"

"Alice!" Miriam shouted. "He's coming your way!"

Alice and DI Adams turned around to see the peacock racing toward them with his head down and neck extended, tail flying. Then Alice thought she heard something like a growl somewhere on the edge of hearing, and the peacock tried to stop, legs flailing on the tiles. It fell over, slid toward them with an oddly human wail, then changed direction, almost as though something had flicked it away.

"Godammit," DI Adams said. "Bad dog!" Then she ran after the peacock. Alice stayed where she was for a moment longer, considering the possibilities of invisible dogs, then shook out a tea towel and walked to the edge of one of the counters. She waited without moving as the peacock led its pursuers from one side of the kitchen to the other, all of them shouting and bumping into walls and each other, then eventually streaked past her, still screaming. She dropped the tea towel neatly over its head.

"*Bu-kurk?*" it said, puzzled, and slowed to a walk as the four younger women came to a panting halt behind it.

"Seriously?" DI Adams said. "A tea towel?"

Miriam huffed and wiped hair off her face. "I should have remembered that."

"*Bu-kurk,*" the peacock said, and sat down. Priya picked it up and tucked it under one arm, keeping its head covered.

"We'll put him back, um, somewhere," she said.

Nita raised one finger as if she had a lot to say on the subject, then lowered it again. "Get out of my kitchen," she said. "All of you."

"We can clean up," Miriam offered. "We were going to anyway."

"Out."

"But," Priya began, and Alice spoke over her.

"Of course. We're terribly sorry, Nita. It was very rude of us."

Nita glared at her. "Rude doesn't cover it. We're having a party in the orangery starting from three. I don't care how hungry you are – that's the next time I want to see you. The *only* time, got it?"

"Understood," Alice said.

"Well," DI Adams said, and Alice raised her eyebrows at her, then looked at the floor in front of the stove. The *empty* floor. The inspector stared at it, then said, "Yes. Understood. Sorry again. Entirely my fault. I wanted a cuppa after the river thing."

Nita looked around the kitchen, at the smears of mud and soot on the floor, at the half-dismantled shelves and abandoned mugs, and fresh deposits left by the panicking peacock. "Get. Out." She wasn't shouting, but she looked as though she might start throwing things at any moment, and there were plenty of pans to hand. Alice turned and walked out into the wind and rain, trailed by Miriam, Priya carrying the peacock, and DI Adams and her invisible dog.

17

MIRIAM

A s they trooped out into the rain there was the firm and unmistakable sound of the door locking behind them. Miriam shivered in her fleece, wishing she'd thought to bring her waterproof jacket, and the little group paused in the questionable shelter of the eaves. It really was questionable, too – Miriam felt as if the roof were collecting rain just in order to be able to throw it at them in bigger handfuls.

"*Well,*" Priya said. "That's a bit rude."

"We did make rather a mess of her kitchen," DI Adams pointed out.

"Where are the dragons?" Miriam asked, trying to keep her voice level. "What happened?"

"I guess Mortimer managed to get out when the peacock had us all distracted," Alice said. She was looking at DI Adams curiously. "Very lucky, that."

"Yeah," DI Adams said, and glared at the ground. "Lucky."

Alice nodded, and said, "We'd best go find them."

"What about the peacock?" Priya asked. "We can't just let him go out here. It's pouring down!"

"*Buk*," the peacock said comfortably. Priya had tucked him under her jacket, his tail hanging to the ground like a particularly large and beautiful scarf.

"He must have come from outside somewhere," Miriam said doubtfully. She didn't fancy going out and getting wet again.

"We'd best check the outbuildings," DI Adams said. "The bird can get some shelter there, and we can see if the dragons went that way. They can't have just vanished."

"You need to go in," Alice told her. "You've already been cold enough for one day."

The inspector shrugged. "I'm starting to accept being wet as the normal state of things." She made a funny gesture with one hand, as if pushing something away from her. "You and Priya go check inside. Miriam and I will do out here."

Miriam gave an involuntary squeak of alarm as Priya offered her the peacock, and it *keow*-ed sleepily, tea towel still over its eyes.

"Detective Inspector, I really think you need to get warmed up," Alice said.

DI Adams stopped pushing her invisible dog away and petted the air instead. "No," she said flatly. "This is how we're doing it."

Miriam looked at Alice, trying to make her expression convey just how much she didn't want to be out here alone with the detective inspector, but Alice just nodded. "Alright," she said. "Take the peacock, Miriam."

"Aw," Priya said, as Miriam accepted the bird reluctantly. "Look after him."

"I will," Miriam mumbled, and Alice patted her on the shoulder then headed for the hall door, Priya pattering after her, and Miriam was left alone with DI Adams.

※

MIRIAM TRAILED after the detective inspector with one hand raised to protect her eyes from the rain as they splashed across the flooded lawn. The ground was littered with torn leaves and broken branches, and the trees roared like the sea. The wind funnelled around them with eager hunger, and Miriam clutched the peacock a little closer, wondering why the inspector wanted *her* out here. It didn't make much sense. Alice was far better at, well, *everything* than she was. But she didn't ask, just trudged on, her trainers already wet, and thought with some satisfaction that Alice would have no cause to tease her about bringing too many clothes after this.

The first outbuilding was a cavernous shell, the holes in the roof forming waterfalls that fell through the splintered boards of the attic flooring and formed mini-lakes on the floor beneath. Miriam could remember that when Maddie first started dating Denis this had already been nothing but a graveyard for old tractor tyres and ancient rusting farm implements. DI Adams switched on her torch and played it around the interior, but there was no safe pen for a peacock, just the accumulated debris of a big property. They moved on to the next building, where Miriam remembered them keeping pigs at some stage, but it now had no roof at all. Which left the third, biggest one, which used to have staff rooms upstairs and had been the storage area for all the might-come-in-handy-one-day objects that now cluttered up the hall and the library.

DI Adams dragged the wooden door, faded and unpainted but still solid, open and shone the torch across the floor. Stone flags were still visible through the dirt, and there were more dry patches than wet patches. "This looks more promising," she said.

"They were still using it up until last year, I think," Miriam said. "At least for storage."

"Let's take a look." DI Adams stepped inside, Miriam following with the peacock and trying not to step on its feathers.

Light seeped in through the small panes of the remaining windows, dull but enough to show stone pens that had once been stables built around the walls, the rest of the floor open but for a few stone support pillars. The wind and rain were muted by the heavy walls and the floor above, and DI Adams shone her torch into the first few stalls to reveal neat stacks of firewood.

"*Buk*," the peacock observed, and Miriam thought she heard a whisper of response. The shadows were strange in here, especially around the inspector, and she hugged the peacock a little tighter.

"*Keow*," he admonished her, and this time she was sure she heard a response.

"There's something in here," she whispered to DI Adams.

"Let's take a look," she said, and now Miriam thought one of the inspector's shadows seemed to be running ahead of her. The younger woman started after it toward the back of the room and Miriam trailed behind her, unsettled by the whispers she could barely hear over the rain.

"*Hey!*" someone bellowed from the door. "What're you *doing?*"

Miriam squeaked, and tripped over the peacock's tail feathers as she tried to spin around. The bird squawked in outrage, clawing at her wildly, and as she put out a hand to stop herself falling she lost her grip on it. It bolted for the door, *bu-kurk*-ing in outrage, and DI Adams grabbed her arm, steadying her, then turned the light on the newcomer.

"Reid!" Miriam exclaimed, still trying to get her balance. "You scared me!"

"What are you *doing* in here? This is private!"

"We're—" she couldn't exactly say *looking for dragons*, even though it was the first thing that came to mind. "Putting the peacock back."

"He runs around everywhere," Reid said dismissively. "Stupid bloody thing."

"The weather's terrible, though. He could get blown away!"

"So?"

Miriam crossed her arms, glaring at her nephew. *Honestly!* Well, he never had been her favourite. She immediately felt guilty for even thinking that, but it was true. He was the sort of boy who pulled butterflies' wings off, just because he could. She'd sent him back to his mother with no dinner when he'd done it at her house once, and she was inclined to do the same again.

"And what are you doing out here, Reid?" DI Adams asked.

He scowled at her. "It's my place. I can be where I want."

"So why do you want to be in here right now, in the middle of a storm? Evidently not for the peacock."

"I don't have to explain myself to you," Reid said, which Miriam thought was probably not a good response.

The inspector pointed at Reid. "You seem to be at the heart of every problem I've come across since I've been here. Fighting with your mother, fighting with Keeley, fighting with everyone."

He puffed his chest out, and Miriam thought that the peacock did it better. "So? Someone's got to take charge if this place is to have any chance."

"And you do that by making your mother's life harder?" she snapped.

"She's dreaming if she thinks she can make this place work with a couple of tourists and the Women's bloody Institute," he shot back.

"So what do you think you can do?"

"I know people! My school friends—"

Miriam flapped her hand at him. "Spoilt little rich boys, all of them."

"They're my *friends!*"

"They used to think pinching your sister's bottom was the height of hilarity."

"Oh, *those* sort of schoolboys," DI Adams muttered.

"Yeah, well, *they* can save this house! I just need—" he stopped, as if suddenly aware of who he was talking to. "Anyway. What she's doing isn't working."

"She's doing everything she can," Miriam said. "You've done nothing but make it hard for her!" DI Adams placed a hand on her shoulder, and Miriam took a shaky breath, willing her hands to relax. They seemed to be squeezing the life out of her forearms.

"You really didn't like Keeley," DI Adams said to Reid.

"He was a glorified kitchen hand who thought he knew *everything*."

"His food seemed pretty good to me."

"That's Nita. Keeley wasn't so great."

"Just how much did you dislike him, Reid?" The inspector's voice was soft. "Did you get in another fight with him last night, after dinner? Is that what happened?"

"Is what—? No! *No!*" For the first time worry crept into Reid's voice. "It was an *accident!* You *said* it was an accident!"

"Was it, though? You didn't like him. Hated him, even. And you want things to run differently around here. You don't *want* your mum's way to work."

"I do! And I wouldn't—" He seemed to be growing smaller, huddling down into a boy again. "I *couldn't!*"

"Maybe it *was* an accident, Reid. Maybe you never meant it to go that far, but it just *happened*."

"No. No, it didn't. I didn't see him after dinner at all, I swear!"

Miriam wanted to interrupt, to say she knew Reid wasn't the most pleasant man, but he wasn't a *murderer*, but she didn't think the DI would appreciate it very much. Plus she wasn't sure she actually felt like defending him right now.

"You can ask Nita," Reid added. "I was with her all night."

"*Nita?*" DI Adams and Miriam said together. "I got the impression she thought you were a bit ridiculous," the inspector said.

"I think she does," he said, looking at his feet. "But in a good way, you know?"

Miriam wasn't sure there was a good way for someone you love to think you're ridiculous, but she supposed there were many more varieties of relationships than she was aware of.

DI Adams watched Reid for a little longer, then shook her head. "I'll be checking with her."

"Sure." He shuffled a little, lifted his chin, tried to make himself taller again. "Are we done?"

"For now," DI Adams said.

"But you can't …" he started, waving at the building, and DI Adams smiled at him.

"Can't I?"

Reid gave her a worried look and retreated into the rain with his shoulders hunched. The two women watched him shuffle to the kitchen, try the door, and knock. There was a pause, Nita opened the door, shouted something, and slammed it shut. Reid sat down on the doorstep and waited. A moment or so later the door opened again and he got up and went in.

"Someone for everyone, I suppose," Miriam said.

"She's probably got him scrubbing the floor," DI Adams said dismissively. They were silent for a moment, and Miriam wondered if they were going to have to do more Investigating in the whispering damp of the outbuildings, then the inspector said, "Miriam, you're … sensitive, right?"

Miriam scratched her cheek. "I guess you don't mean in the sense of am I allergic to fabric softener?"

"No."

"Well, yes."

"So can you see a dog there?" DI Adams pointed at the doorstep between them, and Miriam pulled back a little. There was nothing there, just wet earth and boot prints.

"Um."

"Well, dammit." The inspector shoved her hands in her pockets and stared at the low, angry sky. "Is there something in the water around here?"

"Only if you're drinking Adele's tea," Miriam said. "You do seem to have a funny shadow, though."

"A funny shadow."

Miriam thought she sounded very sceptical for someone who had just been asking about invisible dogs. "Yes. An extra one that doesn't entirely stay attached to you."

"*Hmm.* I guess that's something."

Miriam wasn't sure if she'd be happy to have a funny shadow, but it seemed to have satisfied the inspector at least a little. "Are we going to keep looking for the dragons?"

"We are." The inspector gave her a small smile. "Not something that was in the job description."

Miriam laughed, a little nervously, then pointed across the lawn. "And should we tell them not to go out?"

DI Adams squinted at the birdwatchers as they struggled across the grass into a headwind, their enormous green poncho-style rain slickers rattling around them and threatening to sweep them off their feet. She sighed. "No. They'll work it out soon enough."

As they watched, Marv was blown back into Saul, and they stumbled into Keith together. He managed to steady them all, and they plodded on.

"I really need some cake," the DI said, and stepped out into the storm.

§♣

THEY LET themselves in the side door of the house and squelched their way down the hallway to the stairs, leaving soggy footprints behind them. The staircase felt terribly steep to Miriam, and she knew she was breathing far harder than she should be. But she was tired, and worried about her family and inquisitive journalists and murderers, and above all, the dragons. That was enough to weigh anyone down. Plus, now that DI Adams had mentioned it, the inspector's shadow really was starting to look a little like a dog. Sometimes it towered next to her, as tall as her shoulder, and other times it scampered around her heels like a spaniel, and Miriam didn't know exactly what it could be or what it meant.

"Are you alright, Miriam?" DI Adams asked as they reached the landing and Miriam paused with her hand on the door.

"I'm scared," she said simply. "Scared Beaufort's not going to wake up, and scared my sister's going to lose her house, and scared Reid's going to get arrested. Or Adele."

The inspector nodded, thought for a moment, then said, "I'm scared for Beaufort, too. And I'm scared I might be seeing things. Again. Which makes me wonder how much of what I thought was real actually is."

Miriam looked at DI Adams, the light of their torches giving her a Halloween mask, and patted the younger woman's arm. The inspector looked at her, surprised, and Miriam said, "It's like the map. The less tightly you hold on to having to be sure of exactly where you are, the more likely you are to find where you're going."

There was a pause, then the inspector said, "And that's relevant to invisible dogs how?"

"I don't know," Miriam admitted. "It sounded better in my head."

The inspector snorted laughter and reached for the door, then paused. "Adele?" she said.

Miriam squeaked. "Botox?" she offered.

"And?" DI Adams asked. "Tell me, Miriam. I'm not going to rush out there and arrest her."

Miriam wasn't certain. DI Adams was very fond of arresting people. But she swallowed and said, "The mushrooms. It *might* have been an accident, but she's actually very good at plant identification. And she, um, didn't entirely like all the guests."

"Huh," the inspector said, her hand still on the door.

"But they were only hallucinogenic. I mean, if she'd really wanted to—"

DI Adams held her hand up. "Enough. Enough for now." She opened the door onto a hallway full of the Women's Institute, hurrying in and out of rooms and muttering to each other urgently. "Oh, what *now?*" she groaned.

"Have you found them?" Rose asked, hurrying up to Miriam and the inspector.

"Us?" Miriam asked, suddenly finding it hard to breathe. "You haven't?"

"No," Rose said.

"We've checked all the rooms," Pearl said.

"We've had to be very sneaky about it," Rose added. "Carlotta and Rosemary are keeping an eye on the stairs. If anyone looks like they're coming upstairs they're going to start shouting at each other."

"Oh, well, you've got about two minutes then," DI Adams said.

Rose tapped the side of her nose. "You see? No one would ever suspect it was a signal!"

"But how can we not have found the dragons?" Miriam asked. She could feel her voice going squeaky on the edges and swallowed hard. "They're *dragons!* We can't *lose* them!"

"We won't," Alice said, emerging from someone else's room. She was wearing a pretty grey jumper and black trousers, and looked ready to chair a meeting at any moment. "Are we done, ladies? Nothing up here?"

"Nothing," came the answers from all around.

"Alright." Miriam almost thought she saw a flicker of uncertainty on Alice's face, but it was gone too soon to be sure. "I assume they weren't in the outbuildings?"

"No," DI Adams said.

"That leaves staff rooms upstairs and downstairs. Rose, you and Pearl go upstairs. You can little old lady your way out of anything."

"Thank you," they said together, and grinned at each other.

"Everyone else, as you were." There was some muttering, then the ladies scattered, chattering brightly as they went. Rose and Pearl vanished through the door to the staff staircase, and a moment later the hall was empty but for Miriam, Alice, and the detective inspector.

"Excuse me?" DI Adams said. "What was that? You can *little old lady* your way out of anything?"

Alice smiled. "One must work with what one has, Detective Inspector."

"They've *gone?*" Miriam asked, trying to keep her voice level. "They were right there in the kitchen! How far could they have gone?"

"I know," Alice said. "I don't understand it either."

DI Adams looked at her extra shadow, which was huddled next to her heel. "What do you know about this?"

Alice gave Miriam a puzzled look, and she shrugged.

"I don't think he knows," the DI said, looking up. "He's not very chatty."

"I really think we should get you into some dry clothes," Alice said. "And I'll find you some tea."

"Cake?" DI Adams asked hopefully.

"Of course." Alice examined the inspector, then headed for the room with her back straight and her head up.

Miriam looked at DI Adams. "I wouldn't talk to your invisible dog in public."

"I shouldn't think you lot would be bothered by anything," DI Adams muttered, and padded down the hall, her trainers squeaking damply as she went.

MIRIAM CHANGED into some baggy tie-dyed trousers and a bobbly green jumper in the bathroom, thinking that she was running low on practical clothing. Not that she was the only one – the bathroom was festooned with clothes in various degrees of dryness and muddiness, and there were three and a half pairs of socks lined up on the edge of the bath. She dried her hair in a towel, frowning at them, then padded back to the bedroom barefoot.

Rose and Pearl were perched on her bed, and Alice was making tea.

"Any luck upstairs?" Miriam asked them.

"None," Rose said. "Just a lot of buckets for the leaks and a suit of armour that scared Pearl silly."

"Did not."

Miriam tried to smile at them, her stomach rolling over as she thought of Beaufort, cold and still and lost. Alice handed her a cup of tea and said, "Thank you, ladies. Anything to report elsewhere?"

Rose shook her head. "Maddie has Boyd and Adele running all over the place for this spring storm party, and I don't know where Reid is. Paula banned Holt from playing poker, so he's sulking and they're both just drinking and arguing with each other."

"Charming," Alice said.

"Edie and Lottie are in the lounge," Pearl offered. "I think Priya and Teresa are chatting to them."

"Anyone seen the journalist?"

"No," Rose said. "And not the birdwatchers either."

"We saw them," Miriam said quietly. "And Reid."

Alice looked at her for a moment, then clapped her hands gently. "Well. The priority is the dragons. We need to be sure they're safe."

"What do you want us to do?" Pearl asked. "Check the staff areas downstairs?"

Alice glanced at Miriam, and she shrugged slightly. She supposed she could volunteer to do it, as she'd have the best excuse for being there, but she was cold and tired and she didn't think she could face it. Face empty rooms and lost dragons and talking to family members that were now suspects. It felt a little too much right now. Maybe it always would be.

"Yes, please," Alice said. "Pop back if you find anything, otherwise see if things have quieted down for Adele and Boyd."

Rose broke into an enormous grin. "I think this could be a second career for me," she said. "Investigating."

"Don't let the detective inspector hear you say that," Alice said.

Pearl tucked her arm through Rose's. "I'll keep her in check." They headed for the door, opening it just as DI Adams appeared on the other side.

"What was that about investigating?" she asked, and Rose gave her a little wave and hurried Pearl along, both of them giggling.

"I told them you wouldn't like it," Alice said. "Tea?"

"*Ooh*, please," DI Adams said, then looked faintly horrified with herself.

"BUT WHERE COULD THEY HAVE *GONE?*" Miriam asked again, nibbling anxiously on a Jammie Dodger. "They couldn't just vanish!"

"We're trying to find out," Alice said. "They're not in any of the rooms, or upstairs."

DI Adams, clad in the latest variation of borrowed clothes (which looked to be Teresa's leggings, judging by the unicorns, and a green fleece that had seen better days), took a biscuit. "What about the locked rooms? Maybe there was some of that shifting thing involved."

"Not in them either."

The inspector looked thoughtful, then shook her head. "No. I don't want to know."

Miriam put her biscuit down and clutched her tea with both hands. "Oh, this is just awful! Where *are* they?"

DI Adams looked around the room and said, "Well, both the dog and that bloody cat have gone, so fat lot of help they're proving to be."

"About this dog," Alice began, before being interrupted by a sharp voice.

"Bloody cat indeed. It's all poor dragons this, poor dragons that. Who's out in the rain coordinating rescues? Who's in and out of the Inbetween so much he's likely got leviathans on his tail, never mind the wraiths? Who's snooping for murder suspects? Who's now needed, *again?* This bloody cat." He glared at them as he padded to the rug in front of the hearth. "And does anyone ask if I'm alright? Do they heck."

"Are you alright, Thompson?" Alice asked, her eyebrows raised.

"I'm still wet," he said, his coat standing out at odd angles. It had acquired a generous coating of mud and dust, changing him from tabby to the dull brown of old leaves. "I haven't had time to finish grooming, and I'm cold and hungry."

"Would you like a biscuit?" Miriam suggested, and the cat sniffed.

"I'm a *cat.* I do not live on Jammie Dodgers."

"Milk?" DI Adams offered, eyeing the jug on the tray.

"I'm lactose intolerant."

"Tosh," Alice said, digging in her handbag. "You ate half my custard tarts while they were cooling last week."

"And I paid dearly for it."

Alice fished out a packet of cat biscuits and poured some into a saucer. "Stop your complaining," she said, putting the plate on the bed next to her.

Thompson jumped up and started crunching the biscuits down, purring loudly. "So, what's the drama now?" he asked, spraying crumbs on the bedspread.

"*Honestly*," Alice said, wiping them away. He ignored her.

"The dragons are gone," DI Adams said.

"What?" the cat stopped eating and swallowed a half-chewed biscuit. "As in, gone home?"

"No. As in they were in the kitchen with us, then they weren't. Could it be the Watch?"

The cat licked his chops, not answering straight away, then said, "Unlikely. I should know if they got wind of things, for a start. I mean, not definitely, particularly if they think I've been covering stuff up, but I've got my own contacts. I'd have heard rumours, at least. And if you're thinking they were shifted, that's unlikely. It takes about a dozen cats just to move a human. The amount of cats it'd take to move a dragon, even you'd have seen them."

"But they were right there," Miriam said. "The chef came in, then the peacock, and then by the time we caught the peacock they were gone."

"What the hell was the peacock doing?" Thompson asked.

"I think the dog chased him in," DI Adams said, then looked like she wished she hadn't.

"What dog?"

"It's nothing," the inspector said. "I'm probably imagining it."

"You aren't," Miriam said. "There's *something*, I just can't quite see it."

"So it's an invisible dog." Thompson sounded unimpressed. "Why do you need an invisible dog? Am I not enough for you?"

"I don't *want* an invisible dog. I also don't want a bloody cat giving me cheek." They glared at each other, and Thompson sniffed.

"There you go with the bloody cat again. I don't know why I help you. Ungrateful bloody humans—" His muttering was cut off as he stepped sideways into nothing, leaving the bed scattered with half-eaten biscuits and crumbs.

DI Adams rubbed her hands over her face. "*Why* is it always like this?"

"I don't know," Alice admitted. "Things were a lot calmer before. You know, pre-dragon."

"And nothing like as interesting," Miriam said fiercely. "I wouldn't change a *second* of it!"

Alice smiled at her. "Me either. I didn't mean it like that."

"I should hope not," Miriam said, and snatched another biscuit from the tin. "So how do we find them?"

"Well—" Alice stopped as a sudden commotion rose from downstairs. DI Adams was already off the bed and pulling the door open, hurrying to the stairs, and now the shouting was clear and furious.

"Murderer! *Murderer!*"

"Oh no," Miriam whispered. "Oh, what's *happened?*"

"I imagine we shall find out," Alice said, getting up and brushing cat hair off her trousers as she marched to the door. Miriam followed, wishing she had a cricket bat. Just in case.

18
MORTIMER

Mortimer, his chin grinding into the stone floor of the kitchen and his wings pinned rather painfully to his sides by the weight of the High Lord, listened to the women shouting at the peacock and wondered if they'd manage to catch it while he could still breathe. It felt like Beaufort was getting heavier with every exhale, and he couldn't get his lungs to fill up again afterwards. He tried to push off the floor, but no matter how hard he strained, he couldn't even lift himself enough to make room for his tummy. The ladies were chasing the peacock now, although it didn't sound like they were having a lot of success, and it all seemed very far away. He closed his eyes. He really was tired. Horribly so. He could just rest here for a moment. He wasn't cold, at least, so it was safe to snooze. Snooze. What a funny word that was. Snoooooooze—

His thoughts were interrupted as the High Lord was heaved unceremoniously off his back, and his lungs reinflated with a gasp that would have echoed around the room if there hadn't been so much shouting and *bu-kurk*-ing going on to drown it out. He groaned, black dots still swimming in his vision, and three very small and very scrawny somethings stared down at him. They were covered in long, silky fur, and their heads were ringed with little horns, like a built-in crown, that seemed to have tinsel wound around them. He wheezed.

"Yah," one said. "Is alive. Come, small dragon."

Mortimer considered pointing out that they barely came up to his shoulder, or would do when he stood up, so he was hardly *small*, but decided to concentrate on getting his legs to cooperate instead. He wobbled to his feet as he heard the peacock chase come to an end, and followed his furry rescuers to the back of the kitchen. Beaufort was being carried ahead of him, swept along by invisible porters, so he looked to be levitating just above the floor. He slept peacefully, still and grey, and Mortimer stumbled as he followed.

"Easy, small dragon," one of the creatures said. "Big dragon nearly squishes you!"

"Yah," another said. "Is bad idea. Sleeping dragons is heavier than waking dragons."

Mortimer wondered if that was true, and why he hadn't known it. And he also wondered where they were going, but he was having enough trouble making his feet work. He wasn't going to risk talking at the same time.

They hurried to the back wall, next to the big metal doors of the refrigerator and freezer, and the three creatures scrambled up the exposed brick, clinging to it with clawed fingers and toes, their fringed tails swinging for balance.

"One," the highest said.

"Twos," said the next one down.

"*Trois*," the lowest said.

"Ah, you is pain, Jacques," the first said. "Stop reading them foreign books."

"*You* is pain," Jacques said. "You needs to educate yourselfs."

"Opens," the second creature said wearily, as if it had heard this argument too often. They jumped free together, pushing the bricks they'd been clinging to into the wall as they went. There was a whisper of well-oiled movement, not even enough for the conversation behind them to hesitate. Beaufort was ferried through the gap, and Mortimer scurried after him, the door swinging shut again almost quickly enough to catch his tail. They were plunged into a momentary darkness, then there was the scratch of a match and a whiff of sulphur.

The tiny light of the match lit a narrow passageway, stone walls pressing in on both sides. The ceiling was as high above them as a normal room, and he supposed they were walking between the walls of the kitchen and the room next to it, whatever that might be.

"Where are we going?" he asked.

"We rescues you," one of the creatures said.

"Yes! Yes, thank you. Sorry." He still wasn't thinking straight. These weren't pixies or gnomes, or any Folk he knew, and he really wanted to ask what they were, but that seemed rather rude. He'd be insulted if someone asked what he was. He watched Beaufort gliding ahead of him, then said, "Isn't he heavy?"

"Not for bollies. Bollies is strong," the creature that had spoken before said. It was walking next to him, and put its arms up in a strongman pose. "Sees?"

"I see," Mortimer said, wondering if bollies were some sort of brownie. He'd never heard of them before.

"We helps dragons," the bolly said as the little procession came to a halt at a dead end. "Then dragons helps us, yes?"

"Um, yes," Mortimer said, because it wasn't like he had much choice. They had the High Lord, and he was trapped in the walls of the manor house like the dumbwaiter would have been if it hadn't been a silly wall box.

"Good." The creature that had been talking to him ran forward as the bolly carrying the match yelped. The light went out with a whiff of singed fur, and Mortimer stood in the dark, waiting, not even his dragon eyes finding the faintest glimmer of illumination.

Then there was the scrape of stone on stone, and a square of very dim light appeared, a bolly silhouetted against it.

"Is good," it said, and three of them ducked though the gap. Another pause, then the wall swung open with that same noiseless ease, and Beaufort was carried into the hall beyond. Mortimer supposed it must be the staff hallway, because it was cluttered with old boxes and bags of used clothes, broken lamps and chipped paintings leaning against the wall. The bollies hurried to the wall directly opposite, scrambled up it and dived behind a painting as Mortimer stood there feeling more and more exposed. There were voices coming from somewhere, and he couldn't tell if they were getting closer or not. He let his breath out in an anxious gust, and a voice from under Beaufort said, "Easy. You sets fire to things."

"Sorry."

There was some quick scrabbling behind the painting, then the wall swung back and the bollies carried Beaufort through. Mortimer dived after them, and emerged into a room lined on one side with tall, arched windows, their bottom halves covered with curtains. Shelves lined the walls from floor to ceiling, books crammed onto them in any sort of order, some spines out, some not, some upside down, others wedged on the top of other volumes. Piles of them were stacked on the floor and teetered on an abundance of side tables, more than one having collapsed due to the strain, and bowing shelves ventured out into the room from the wall on the far side. There were chairs and sofas in cracked leather jumbled about the place, and the bollies had arranged tattered quilts and throws into cosy nests on them. There was a rocking horse in one corner (with enough space around it that Mortimer thought it probably saw some use), a half-bald, taxidermied bear, two kayaks stacked in front of the door, and a child's wagon full of lawn bowls and croquet bats. Most of the spare floor area was taken up with boxes and bags, some spilling clothes or ancient plastic containers, others still closed, and the bollies laid Beaufort down in a circle of clear floor in the middle of the jumble.

"Wow," he said, unable to think of anything else.

"Yah," a bolly agreed. "Is bad. They tries to throw all this stuffs out!"

"We saves," another said cheerfully.

"Yah, we has to rescue things from fire and all," said a third, dusting its hands off after emerging from under the High Lord.

"And sometimes from the peoples," another added.

"Yah, is like rent. One sock, one night, yah?" They laughed uproariously.

"Is that— is that what bollies do?" Mortimer asked. "Saves – *save* – things?"

"Yah," they said, and looked at each other proudly. It had only taken six of them to carry Beaufort. Mortimer supposed you had to be strong to rescue this amount of stuff.

"Don't they come in here and see it?"

"No, we blocks the door."

"They thinks is shelf falling." The bollies looked at each other and burst out laughing again. "Silly humans!"

"Right," Mortimer said, wondering why no one had tried to climb in a window or anything. "So, I don't meant to be rude, but you said you could help us? Do you mean you can help *him?*"

"Helps dragon, yah." The bollies nodded agreeably. They were all terribly similar, Mortimer thought. One might be a tiny bit shorter, another have a tiny bit longer tail, but it was so hard to tell. He couldn't really be sure who he was talking to.

"That's wonderful." He glanced at Beaufort, still motionless on the floor, his scales festooned with cobwebs they'd collected in the passage. Mortimer's heart squeezed painfully tight. "How?" he managed, but his voice seemed to be coming from a very long way away.

"With magic stuff," the bolly closest to him said, and waved to one of the others. It rushed off, and a moment later the spout of a watering can appeared above the debris on the floor. It bobbed its way toward them, revealing the puffing bolly balancing it on its back. It set it down and grinned broadly.

"A magic watering can?" Mortimer asked, trying not to sound too sceptical.

"No, silly dragon. The magic is *in* the can."

He started forward, but the bolly put a paw on his.

"Waits. You is nice dragon, yes?"

"Yes," Mortimer said, trying to see into the watering can from where he stood.

"So. You has problem with being stuck in kitchen, and with sleeping dragon. We has two problems, too. We wakes sleeping dragon, you fixes our problems?"

Mortimer wanted to say *yes, yes, anything*, but a lingering thread of caution made him say, "What are your problems?"

"We has gnomes in the cellar."

"Boo, gnomes! They drinks all the wine," another bolly said, and the rest muttered agreement.

"And we don'ts likes them eating frogs. Is gross," another added.

"Not frogs. Frogs is nice."

"Yah, but eating frogs is gross."

"Oh. Yah."

"The French eats frogs. Is called *cuisses de grenouilles*."

The other bollies groaned. "Shuts up, Jacques!"

"Okay," Mortimer said hurriedly. "I'll deal with the gnomes. What's the other?"

"There's a dandy abouts."

"Brr, dandy," the other bollies echoed.

"A dandy?" Mortimer assumed they didn't mean a very smartly dressed gentleman, but he wasn't at all sure what they *did* mean.

"Yah, dandy. Brr!"

"Brr!"

"Okay." Maybe they meant Reid, but Mortimer wouldn't have called him that fashionable. He didn't wear a frock coat or anything.

"It steals the foods," a bolly said. "We always gets the foods, but it's quick! It steals them!"

"Yah, and is scary. Brr."

"Brr!"

Mortimer gave up. It didn't matter. He'd figure it out. The bollies could wake Beaufort. That was the only thing that did matter. "Okay," he said. "Wake him."

"Ah," a bolly said, raising one small claw. "No."

"No? But you just said—"

"One problem for yous, one for us. We gets you out of kitchens, you gets rid of gnomes. After, we wakes big dragon, and you gets rid of dandy, yah?"

Mortimer wondered just how strong bollies would be in the face of dragon fire, then had to admit to himself that he'd never be able to do it. Besides, this room seemed terribly flammable. And he knew gnomes. He could do this.

Hopefully.

§&.

MORTIMER WATCHED through a crack in the wall as Rose and Pearl left the cellar, wishing he could call out to them and tell them he was alright, and that Beaufort was going to be alright, too. But he couldn't, not with the bollies all around him, and the whiff of gnomes in the dampness of the room beyond. So he stayed quiet, and only when the door at the top of the stairs shut did the bollies push the wall open. He stepped out, and the brick immediately resealed behind him. He looked back, startled.

"Hey!"

"We waits," a small, muffled voice said, and he sighed, then padded up the small slope of the cellar, toward where he could see cobweb-encrusted wine racks, barely discernible even with his dragon eyes in the dark. There were what looked to be some very old bottles in one corner, and he thought it was a shame they hadn't been drunk. They'd probably all be bad by now. Closer to the stairs were newer racks with less dust on them, and bottles with crisp white labels that looked rather nice. There were also crates of beer and water and soft drinks, and Mortimer cleared his throat pointedly.

"Steve?"

There was a pause, then a small grizzled head popped up from behind the beer bottles. "Morts? What're you doing here?"

"Mortimer. Look, I need a bit of help."

"Sure thing." Steve climbed onto the edge of a step and regarded him critically. "You look like you're having a rough time of it."

"I feel like it," Mortimer said with a sigh, and more small heads, some wearing flat caps, others bare, began to emerge. Little flickering lights came on, phosphorescent lichen in bowls and glow worms caught in jars. One of the gnomes popped a cork out of a bottle and tipped it over so that a trickle ran out for the others to fill small wooden bowls from, filling the air with a rich tanniny scent.

"Good year, that," Steve said approvingly. "Want some?"

"No, thanks," Mortimer said. "About that help ..."

"Sure." Steve took a large swig of his wine. "Ask away. Anything for a friend of Beaufort's."

"Well, it is for Beaufort, really. See, he's not well—"

"He's not? What happened?"

"Well, he got too cold. Anyway—"

"He's *hibernating?* Oh, gods, that is not good at all."

"I know," Mortimer said, a little more sharply than he intended. "Look, the bollies say they can help, but they'll only do it if you leave the cellar. Will you do that? Please? You know you're woodland gnomes. It's not like you need to live in a cellar."

Steve took another gulp of wine, wiped his mouth on his sleeve, and said, "Well, since you ask so nicely ... No."

A roar of gnome laughter went up around the cellar, and one of them fell over, splashing wine in his face, which made the rest of them laugh even harder.

"No? But you said anything for Beaufort!"

"Sure, but you're asking us to give up our home. That's kind of a big ask."

"He's *hibernating!* He could *die!*"

"Aw, I'm sure it won't come to that, lad. Here." Steve patted the stair next to him. "Come have a little tipple and we'll talk about it."

"There's nothing to talk about! You need to leave!"

"Yeah, no." Steve shrugged. "We don't want to."

"'S good here," a gnome in a wine-stained tunic said. "Provisions on hand, like."

Mortimer stared at Steve. "Really? It stinks of rotting mushrooms and alcohol and it's dark and damp and *horrible,* and you won't even leave to help Beaufort?"

"We like it," Steve said, taking another swig of wine.

"'S right," one of the gnomes said, adjusting her tunic. "'S good here. Woods is bloody cold n' boring."

"And, and everyone's like, woodland creatures, yay! And they kind of stink, and are rude 'n' all." A gnome with his flat cap sliding over one ear blinked owlishly at his empty cup, then held it out unsteadily. "Time for a refill!"

"Yeah, I mean, have you ever *smelt* a rabbit burrow? And we're meant to live in those?"

"But you don't have to," Mortimer said. "You can build your own burrows or tree houses or anything you want."

"Yeah," a gnome agreed, sliding to the ground and resting his cup on his belly. "But why bother, with all this here?"

"The wine's the thing," Steve said. "You should have some, Morts. It'll make all your worries go away. It's like, like ..."

"Like *lightening*," a gnome said, and burped.

"*En*lightening! That's it!"

Mortimer looked at his paws, his eyebrow ridges pulled down tight, feeling his scales heating up. "You're drunk," he said.

"Yeah, it's a good way to deal with the inherent futility of life," Steve said, and sighed. Then he grinned and stood up, almost tumbling off the step. "Let's open a bottle to the futility of life! Drink with us, Morts!"

"*Mortimer*," the dragon insisted. His scales felt like they must be glowing, the heat that was pulsing through him. He was trembling. How could they? How could they be so selfish and thoughtless and *unpleasant*? Beaufort might never wake up if the bollies didn't help him. And all he was asking was this one thing. This *one small thing*. His breath rasped in his throat as he said, "And I don't want a *drink*. I want to save the High Lord of the Cloverly dragons. I want to save my *friend*." He looked up from his paws, and the whole cellar had, at some point, become flooded with purple and red light that seemed to pulse in time with his breathing. He ignored it, concentrating instead on Steve. "Do you really think I'm going to let you stop me?" And this time he meant it. He could *feel* he meant it, that a bunch of bored woodland gnomes who had decided to turn wine into religion were not going to stand between him and saving Beaufort. "*Do you?*"

The purple light flared, and Steve, who had been staring at Mortimer with a shocked look on his face, dropped his cup and shouted, "Out! Get out! He's going to blow!"

The gnomes shrieked, scrambling to their feet and bouncing

off each other, falling over and scuttling on all fours to the back wall of the cellar, abandoning their cups as they fled. Mortimer watched them go, then bellowed, "And *stay* out!" There was an explosion of purple and red, then it was gone, the cellar lit again by the feeble lights of the moss and glow worms. The very old wine rack swayed sadly then fell over with a reluctant *smash*, filling the air with so many alcohol fumes that Mortimer sneezed. Well, at least it wasn't the new stuff.

He trotted back to the wall the bollies had opened for him, and it whispered ajar, revealing a bolly holding a match and staring at him while the others clustered behind it.

"Morty is powerful dragon," it said.

"Mortimer, really."

"Morty go boom," another bolly said. "Is wow."

"No, whoa," another said.

"Is spectacular. Like *fête des lumières*," said another, who Mortimer assumed was Jacques. For once the others didn't shush him, and the first bolly tugged his paw. "Come. We wakes cold dragon now."

Mortimer followed them inside, feeling oddly tired and hot, as the wall eased shut and the floor sloped up, wondering what on earth they were talking about. He felt about as far from powerful as it was possible to be.

§.

MORTIMER WATCHED ANXIOUSLY as the bollies clustered around Beaufort. They'd managed to force his mouth open slightly, and now they held the watering can over his lower lip. They seemed to be having some trouble controlling it, and had already splashed one bolly, who had shrieked and fled. It was currently bouncing from one bookshelf to another, singing disjointedly. Mortimer still had doubts, though. He'd sniffed their magic brew, and it didn't have the cold sting of deep magic to him. And he'd never heard of any substance that could wake a dragon who didn't want to be woken.

"Easy, easy," a bolly said. "We mustn't drowns him."

"Yah, is bad," another agreed, which Mortimer supposed was good. The jug tipped, and a trickle appeared from the spout, drizzling onto Beaufort's lower lip and seeping into his mouth. Mortimer held his breath, waiting for, well, magic. Waiting for green to wash across the dragon's scales, for his wings to uncurl and his tail to twitch, but there was nothing.

After a moment the bollies poured a little more. It spilled out of the corner of Beaufort's mouth, and Mortimer swallowed a sob. The heat of the cellar was gone, and he felt colder than he had in the river. He closed his eyes, wings drooping to the ground around him, and wondered if he could just stay here. Sleep in the rubble of the bollies' lair until the world ended or the High Lord awoke, whichever came first.

Two small paws touched his, and someone whispered, *"Is working."*

Mortimer opened his eyes, staring at the grey form of the old dragon through a soft haze of tears. He blinked them away and watched a shiver of green chase down Beaufort's spines, like a ripple on the water. Another followed it, broader, and, more quickly, a third. There was a pause, then a shudder passed over the High Lord. His scales picked up the colours, stuttering between grey and green. His tail twitched. Colour flooded his wings, richest green shot through with gold, and they trembled, not quite opening. The scales on his snout turned green and stayed that way, then the green spread, running down his body like a flood, and when it reached the tip of his tail he opened his eyes, old gold and cracked with age, and said, "I say. I'm sure I didn't fall asleep *here*."

19

DI ADAMS

Shouts were boiling up from the foyer as DI Adams ran down the stairs.

"They're *bacon butties*, Judith!" Maddie screamed, holding a plate in each hand. They were stacked high with neatly cut sandwiches, some in brown bread, some in white, and the inspector's stomach growled. A couple of biscuits had not exactly refuelled her after the plunge into the river.

"You murdering bourgeois cow!" Rainbow bellowed, and a weak chorus of agreement went up from behind her. She was holding the dining room door open, her arm braced across the opening, the other protesters gathered behind her and eyeing the sandwiches somewhat longingly.

"These are bloody well egg!" Maddie shouted, shaking a plate at her. "And those—" nodding at Adele, who was holding two more plates and looking distinctly worried "—are vegan. And gluten-free. So stop being so ridiculous and *take* them!"

Rainbow hesitated, then shouted, "Keep your mass-produced offal and products of corporate greed!"

"For God's sake, Judith," Maddie complained. "This is all local, you know!"

"No! You're just trying to get us to open the door so you can haul us out!"

"And do what? Have you seen this storm?"

"We're occupying this territory! Squatters rights!"

"It's my *dining room!*"

"Only the dissolute rich have dining rooms!"

"I think she's been at the thesaurus," Alice observed as she and Miriam joined the inspector in the foyer.

"I'm just about *destitute,* never mind dissolute!" Maddie screamed.

"Okay," DI Adams said. "Let's take it all down a notch." The foyer was getting crowded as people emerged from the lounge, the ladies of the Women's Institute looking on with interest. Lottie was hiding behind Edie, and Ervin was leaning against the wall, grinning.

"Pig!" Ronnie bellowed from behind Rainbow. DI Adams ignored him.

"I was trying to *help,*" Maddie said.

"We can look after ourselves!" Rainbow shouted. "We don't need your charity!"

Maddie made a rude noise. "Yeah, you're doing just *great.* If it wasn't for DI Adams you'd have lost Barry, and you'd all have bloody hypothermia if not for *my* house!"

"This should be a house for the people! This *land* should be for the people, not the rich elite—"

"Oh, shut up!" Reid shouted, stomping out of the office. "You hate it that much, just go back outside!"

"Murderer!" Jemima screamed. "Hunter!"

"Hunts are for—" Ronnie started.

"Quiet!" the DI snapped, and he whispered the last word. She looked at Maddie. "Just put the plates down on the sideboard or something."

"What? Why?"

"We don't want your stinking murder food—"

"Rainbow, *shut up*," Miriam said. "Aren't you hungry?"

"I'll take nothing from you, traitor!"

"Pigs!" Jemima yelled, waving a well-manicured fist.

"One more of those and I'm locking the lot of you in the cellar," DI Adams said, her voice sharp and carrying. The foyer fell quiet.

"Yeah?" Ronnie said after a moment, and licked his lips nervously. "You and whose army?"

The inspector wondered if she really should just throw everyone in the cellar. It was becoming a more and more attractive option. Before she could decide, however, something hit her softly on the head. "Hey," she said. A pretty apricot rose tumbled to the floor at her feet. Another one hit her chest, and she looked up to see Boyd posed on the stairs in leather trousers and a black velvet jacket. "Oh, you've got to be kidding me."

He gave a dramatic gesture. "*Oh love that rages and fights like the storm—*"

"*Shut up*," she bellowed at him, then turned back to the protesters. "You really want to try it?" she asked Ronnie.

The bald man opened his mouth, hesitated, then just muttered, "Oppressor." Harriet patted his shoulder reassuringly, and another rose hit the inspector on the shoulder. She ignored it, and said to Maddie, "Just leave the plates."

"We don't want them!" Rainbow yelled.

"Well, actually, I'm pretty hungry," Tom said behind her, and she rounded on him furiously.

Miriam tried to take the plates from her sister. "Let go, Mads."

"I don't want to give them to her now," she said. "Let them starve!"

"You don't mean that," Miriam said.

"I do! Serves them right!"

"Roses bend before the wind of my passion—"

DI Adams rubbed her forehead, considering just retreating to the cellar herself.

"Adele, put the plates by the door," Alice said, and Adele did, putting them on the floor then scuttling backward as if she expected someone might grab her and drag her into the room.

"Do you expect us to eat off the floor like *pigs?*" Rainbow roared at her niece, and she squeaked, ducking behind Ervin, who had taken his phone out and was watching the scene with a look of wonder on his face.

DI Adams scowled at him. "You better not be videoing this."

"Audio," he said. "That's all. I'll never remember all this otherwise. And it's *way* too good to miss a word."

She shook her head and turned to Maddie. "Give Miriam the plates."

"No! They don't deserve such nice sandwiches!"

DI Adams took a deep breath, trying to ignore Boyd still spouting rubbish on the stairs. There was a generous collection of roses building up on the floor around her. "Maddie," she began, but Alice reached past her to put a hand on the woman's shoulder.

"Anger is easy," Alice said. "Being calm in the face of aggravation takes strength. Be stronger, Maddie."

Maddie looked at the sandwiches dubiously, then sighed and let Alice take them.

"Meet rudeness with grace and insults with calm," Alice told her, handing the plates to Miriam. "It frustrates people, makes them furious, and then they make mistakes. And you always want the enemy to make mistakes."

"Um. Right?" Maddie said, a little uncertainly. Alice patted her back and smiled at the inspector.

"The Theory of Alice?" DI Adams said to her.

"Something like that." They watched Miriam hand the plates to Harriet, who smiled her thanks.

"Do you need any water?" Miriam asked.

"No, we're catching it from the windows," Harriet began, then Jemima snatched the plates off her. "Hey!"

"*Death to the collaborators!*" she screamed, and hurled the plates at Miriam.

"Miriam!" DI Adams shouted, lunging forward. The plates were old and heavy, and if they hit Miriam at this range they were going to do some damage. She grabbed the older woman and rolled to the floor, smacking her knee on the tiles painfully, and the plates flew harmlessly overhead as Jemima screamed in delight. She looked up to see Ervin duck, raising an arm to protect himself, and the plate bounced off his hand with a painful sounding clunk. Sandwiches sailed away in all directions, scattering the tiles with bacon and tomatoes and splatters of egg mayo and hummus, and the plates hit the floor hard. Shards exploded, spinning off to every corner of the foyer, and the inspector ducked, covering her face. Teresa yelped and grabbed her shin, her hand coming away bloody where a piece of plate had sliced through her leggings, then there was silence but for the last pieces of porcelain coming to rest and the snarl of the wind outside.

"Is everyone alright?" DI Adams asked, sitting up.

Miriam gave an anxious squeak, but she didn't look hurt.

The inspector climbed to her feet, knee smarting, and pointed at the protesters. "Take your damn sandwiches and close that door."

"Down with the pigs?" Jemima offered, then Rainbow slammed the door and there was the sound of tables and chairs being dragged in front of it again.

"Are *you* alright?" Boyd asked, appearing at her shoulder, and she just managed to swallow a yelp of alarm. "You were heroic! Spectacular! Astonishing—"

"Boyd, I will lock you in the linen cupboard unless you back off."

He looked confused, but fell silent.

"We don't really have a linen closet," Adele said, and someone shushed her.

Ervin gave a strangled snort that sounded an awful lot like laughter, and DI Adams straightened her fleece, wishing she had anything rather than unicorn leggings on. "We're done here," she said, but no one moved.

Alice clapped her hands sharply. "Everyone back to what you were doing, unless you want to help clean up."

There was a pause, then Rosemary said, "Where's the bucket?"

"Oh, as if you can do it in this light, with your eyesight," Carlotta said.

DI Adams pinched her nose, revisited the idea of retreating to the cellar, and said, "I'm going to finish my cup of tea."

DI ADAMS STOMPED up the stairs, aware that everyone was likely watching her, and not caring. She'd been here one night, *one night*, and had been covered in stolen lamb, invisible dog slobber, coffee, cranberry sauce, bread sauce, river water, mud, and more rain that she cared to think about. She still had no idea who the murderer was, and the whole bloody house was acting suspicious as far as she was concerned. Plus they now had missing dragons. And that last bit made her heart do strange things in her chest.

She wanted to arrest someone. Actually, she wanted to arrest *everyone*. She wondered if there was a dungeon of some sort around. That'd be good. She rather fancied the idea of a dungeon.

These less than positive thoughts were interrupted by someone saying, "You! Policewoman – or officer, whatever – I want to speak to you!"

She found she was grinding her teeth as she turned to see Holt stomping toward her. "What?"

"What's going on down there?"

"Nothing that concerns you."

"Well, you know what does concern me? *You*"—and he poked his finger at her—"hanging about the place having cups of tea with your lady friends, and no one's doing anything about the road, or the power, or, or *anything!*" The finger was perilously close to touching her chest. "You're the authorities!"

"I am. And this authority has been in the river once already today, and is not going out again to chop up trees until the storm stops."

"But you have to *do* something! We're going to miss our flight!"

"Holt," Paula said from behind him. "Just leave it."

DI Adams glanced at her, peering around the door of their room, and said, "You're travel agents, aren't you? I'm sure you can rearrange."

"We need to *leave*. Now!"

"No one's going anywhere today. Even once the tree's cleared, I don't know how safe the bridge is, and won't until I can see it in daylight. So I suggest you just sit back and enjoy the atmosphere. That's what you came here for, right?"

"*Holt*," Paula pleaded.

He gaped at the inspector as if he couldn't quite understand what she'd said. "I – you – this would never happen back home!"

And that was enough. It was *all* enough. Time to get at least one bit of truth in this house. "Back home? Where's that? Hampstead bloody Heath?"

He spluttered. "Don't be ridiculous!"

"Why are you lying about being American? What else are you lying about?"

"I'm not lying!"

"Holt, please!" Paula exclaimed, hurrying out of the room and tugging his arm. He shoved her away, hard enough that she bounced into the wall, and DI Adams glared at him.

"Push your wife often, do you? Get upset easily?"

"I don't know what you're talking about," he insisted, his accent jumping from Texas to New York and back again.

DI Adams took a step forward, glaring up at the man. What was *wrong* with people? Why couldn't they just give her a straight answer? *"For God's sake, stop pretending to be American! You're not bloody American, are you?"* she bellowed at him, and he stumbled into the wall.

There was a pause, then he said, "I am too."

DI Adams resisted the urge to throw her hands up in exasperation. The shouting was bad enough, but if she started using her mother's hand gestures as well she'd be a moment away from threatening to send everyone to bed without supper. She looked away from Holt's sweating, anxious face and spotted the ladies of the Women's Institute crowding up the stairs looking alarmingly determined. Ervin was already on the landing, leaning against the banister. She startled herself by hoping it broke, then turned back to Holt. "You're not. And I want to know what your argument with the sous-chef was."

"I didn't have one," Holt said.

"No? So I won't find your prints in the treatment room?"

"Of course not!" He was still holding on to his accent, but it was veering about more and more wildly.

"You need to start being honest with me."

"I am!"

"You are *not* American, so let's start with that."

"We *are*," he insisted.

"What were you doing in the lounge last night?" she demanded, and Paula burst into tears.

Holt turned on her. "Go back to the room!"

"We never hurt anyone!" she wailed. "We do it all the time, and we've never hurt anyone!"

"Paula, shut up!"

"*Stop calling me by that stupid name!*"

DI Adams stared from one to the other. They do it all the time? Kill off sous-chefs? What were they, a family of foodie assassins? "You do what all the time?"

"*This!*"

"Paula, honey—"

"*My name is Pat stop calling me Paula goddammit!*"

"Pat—"

"*It's over!* Can't you hear what she's asking you? Talk to her before she charges us both with murder!" Paula/Pat was almost screaming, her hands clenched into fists at her sides.

"What?" Holt asked, looking bewildered, and DI Adams watched the realisation dawning on his face. She was harbouring serious doubts that he'd be smart enough to set up a murder to look like an accident so perfectly. "The sous-chef. Oh, crap." The accent had fallen away entirely, and he covered his face with his hands. "Fine. Fine, ask me anything."

"Finally," DI Adams said. "Right. Pat and …?"

"God's sake," the daughter said, peering out of her room. "This was always going to happen." She had a strong London accent.

"Oh, shut up, Amber," Holt said, and looked at the inspector. "Rob. I'm Rob."

"That's a start." She looked behind her at the crowded stairwell, and sighed. This was no place to stage an interview. "I'm going to need to talk to you both privately. Just wait in your room for now." She watched as Pat hurried her husband and daughter away, then turned to the audience on the stairs.

"What are you doing?" she asked them, and there was a general shuffling. Teresa brandished a taxidermied fox at her.

"Backup."

DI Adams wrinkled her nose at the fox, then looked at Ervin, who grinned. "Can I help, Detective Inspector? Any observations you'd like me to share with you?"

"You've been making observations, have you, Mr Giles?"

"It is what I do."

"Well. Do tell."

"It wasn't an accident."

"Considering you just overheard my conversation with Holt, that's hardly a brilliant deduction."

He chuckled, dimples surfacing. "That was merely confirmation."

"Do share your insights, then."

He glanced at the crowded stairwell and said, "Shouldn't we talk somewhere more private?"

She stared at him, then said, "That's a nice bruise on your face. Forget to cover it up?"

He touched it, his smile fading. "It's fresh. You can see that."

"Yep. Less than a day, I'd say." It was quite red. She supposed one might expect it to be going blue by now, but that wasn't certain.

"No, I mean *fresh*, Inspector. It just happened."

"In the sauna, perhaps?"

"No!"

"Who've you been scrapping with, then, Mr Giles? And why were you out wandering around in the storm? Looking for a way out?"

"*No.* Looking for you. I figured you were up to something, and I didn't want to miss out." DI Adams glared at him, and he returned her gaze steadily. "I'm just here for the story. That's it. And I'm happy to help you if I can."

He sounded worried but genuine, and she stepped away from him. She caught Alice's eye, and inclined her head just slightly. Alice walked down the landing while Ervin watched her apprehensively. She examined him without speaking, then looked at DI Adams and gave a very small shrug. She didn't know either.

The inspector looked back at the journalist. "Who hit you?"

He licked his lips and said, "I'd really prefer to do all this in private."

"Why?"

"I don't want to get anyone in trouble."

"I'm sure you deserved it," DI Adams said, and he looked at his feet.

There was a moment's silence, then a small but firm voice from the stairs said, "He did deserve it."

"*Adele!*" Maddie exclaimed. "You haven't been hitting guests?"

"He deserved it," she said again, and the general mutter that greeted that remark seemed to indicate that everyone else thought so too, even if they didn't know the exact details.

"I probably did," Ervin agreed. "Although using a china shepherdess was a bit harsh."

"What did you do?" Alice asked, in a tone that suggested she'd asked many young men such questions, and expected very little of them as a consequence.

"Well, I was talking to Adele, and she was crying about Keeley and the possibility of having to sell the hall. I just felt awful for her. So I tried to give her a hug, to comfort her, and she screamed that I was messing up her chakras and hit me in the face with a china shepherdess." He shook his head. "I was just trying to be nice." There was a murmur of disapproval from behind him, and he looked at the ladies, alarmed. "I didn't mean anything by it!"

DI Adams didn't bother covering her grin. "You're lucky all you got was a china shepherdess to the face."

He gave her a half smile and said, "Yeah, I can see that now."

She looked at Alice. "You believe he's just a bit of a silly man, rather than a murderer?"

Alice looked at Ervin for a long time. He met her gaze at first, his eyes dark and steady, but eventually looked down. "I said I was sorry," he mumbled.

"I believe him," she said to DI Adams.

"So do I, which is unfortunate, because I was really looking forward to locking him in the cellar until we can get road access again."

"We could do that anyway."

"It's tempting."

"Hey!" He clutched the banister as if afraid they were about to drag him off. "You can't do that!"

"I can," DI Adams said. "I *probably* won't, though. But keep your hands to yourself, Mr Giles, otherwise I may not be able to resist the temptation."

There was a pause while DI Adams wondered if wilfully misidentifying mushrooms and hitting guests constituted a pattern that could extend to murder by Botox. It seemed tenuous. Finally she said, "Well, show's over," and made a shooing motion at the little crowd.

"Are you sure you don't need backup?" Teresa asked, still clutching the fox. "When you speak to the fake Americans, for instance?"

"I'm sure I'll be fine," DI Adams said.

"I'll stay," Alice said. It wasn't a question, and the inspector looked at her thoughtfully. It couldn't hurt.

"Alright," she said.

"I can take notes," Ervin offered, and DI Adams scowled at him.

"You can go to your room and wait."

"You are no fun, Detective Inspector. No fun at all."

"I'm not meant to be fun."

"You could be." He flashed dimples at her, which quickly changed to an alarmed expression. "Sorry. Don't arrest me. That was inappropriate, right?"

"Hugely."

"I will go and sit in my room like a good boy until you're ready for me."

"Do that."

He retreated down the hall as the stairs slowly emptied, and DI Adams said, "Shall we go see what they have to say for themselves?"

"I shall follow your lead, Inspector," Alice said, adjusting her cuffs. DI Adams thought she looked at least a little pleased with herself.

જ

DI ADAMS KNOCKED SHARPLY on the door, a let's-have-no-nonsense-open-the-door-if-you-know-what's-good-for-you knock, and it was opened almost immediately by Paula. Or Pat.

"Come in," she said, stepping back into a room lit by the fireplace and grey light from the windows. "That chair in the corner's okay." She retreated to the bed, and DI Adams looked at the two little suitcases sitting on the floor next to each other. There was nothing out except for a bottle of whisky that was missing quite a lot of its contents.

"Still hoping to leave tonight?" she asked.

"We were," Holt – no, Rob – said, taking a sip from a mug. Judging from the smell in the room, that was where the rest of the whisky bottle had gone.

Alice sat down in the chair and crossed her legs, and DI Adams leaned against the wall. "Your kids in the room next door?"

"Yes," Pat said. "I'd rather they didn't have to watch this."

"That's fine. Tell me, then."

Rob looked at his mug unhappily. "I was in the lounge last night, but I didn't know anything until the screaming started. Didn't even know anyone else was still up."

DI Adams frowned. "You didn't see Lottie go past you?"

"No."

Lottie had said she'd seen him. And they'd have to have seen each other. The only other way into the treatment room was by the staff hall. "Are you sure? You looked to have had a few."

"I had, but I wasn't blacked out or anything. She didn't come past me."

What had Alice said to Rose and Pearl? *You can little old lady your way out of anything.* DI Adams pressed her lips together. "Alright. So you know nothing about it." She injected a healthy dose of scepticism into her words.

"Nothing. Nothing at all. We're not— we didn't come here to hurt anyone."

"Definitely not," Pat said, her hand creeping into Rob's. "We'd never do that."

"So why the American accents? Why the whole story about being travel agents?"

The couple exchanged embarrassed looks, and Pat said in a small voice, "It's a scam. We could never afford even little weekends like this if we had to pay full price for them."

"So you deceive hardworking people like Maddie, who're barely making ends meet?" Alice said, her voice sharp. "That's unacceptable."

"I know, I know." Pat wiped her eyes. "It started by accident. We were being silly with the kids at this little restaurant, putting on American accents and just playing around. The owner came over and asked if we were the travel agent family that was doing a write-up on the town." She glanced at her husband. "We said yes, just for fun, and they gave us the whole lunch for free. Even brought out desserts and stuff that we hadn't asked for."

"And then we started thinking about it, and realised it'd be easy," Rob said. "Make a little website, practise the accents. It doesn't *hurt* anyone."

"Tell Maddie that," Alice said, and the DI gave her a sideways glance. She returned it coldly, but didn't say anything more.

"So you're frauds but not murderers," DI Adams said.

"Yes. And, I mean, I *know* it's terrible, what we've done—"

"It's illegal."

"Well, it's kind of a grey area," Rob began, and DI Adams raised her eyebrows. He subsided.

"Shall we lock them in the cellar?" the inspector asked Alice.

"You really want to lock someone in the cellar, don't you?" Alice said.

"I wanted to lock *everyone* in the cellar half an hour ago."

"Oh. Well, I suppose that indicates an improvement."

DI Adams turned back to the couple, who were looking distinctly worried, and was about to tell them to keep to their rooms and out of the way, when there was a knock on the door.

"DI Adams? Detective Inspector?" Ervin said, muffled by the door.

"Honestly," Alice said. "The man won't quit."

DI Adams opened the door. "What? Didn't I send you to your room?"

"Yes, but there's something odd going on next door. Lots of noise."

"Who's next door to you?"

"The antique hunters."

DI ADAMS all but shouldered Ervin out of the way, sprinting down the landing as he ran after her.

"I'd normally just look myself, but what with being hit by china shepherdesses and things ..."

"This one?" she asked, pointing at the door.

"Yeah, that's it."

She could hear a struggle going on beyond the door. Something hit the wall with a thump and there was what sounded very much like a snarl, and possibly tearing curtains. "Bollocks," she said, and picked up a large vase from the side table.

"Pass me that lamp, young man," Alice said.

"No way," he replied, picking it up himself. "I might be an accidental creep, but I'm not standing here watching you two deal with whatever's in there."

"I think you should do just that, Mr Giles," DI Adams said. There was another snarl from the room, and something crashed to floor and shattered.

"No," he said, sticking his chin out in what he probably thought was a stubborn manner, but just made him look like a dog wanting its neck scratched.

She sighed, grabbed the handle, and threw the door open.

"About bloody time!" the cat shrieked from the top of the wardrobe as the dog rampaged below. It had hold of a pillow and was shaking it furiously, scattering feathers everywhere. There appeared to have been a pitched battle fought on the bed, and a broken vase was lying on the floor. "Is this the dog you were talking about? Do you know what this thing *is?*"

"Thompson!" DI Adams shouted. "Shut up!"

"*You* shut up!" The cat's tail was the size of a feather duster, his ears flat against his head.

Ervin made a curious noise behind her, and Alice removed the lamp from his hands. "Before you drop it," she said.

"That cat," he said, pointing at it.

"Now what?" DI Adams demanded of Thompson. "Now what're you going to do?"

"Just tell me if this is your invisible bloody dog!" the cat screeched.

"No is dog," a small voice said conversationally from next to DI Adams' ear, and she ducked away from it, diving into the room. "Is dandy."

"Who the hell are you?" she demanded, as Ervin peered around the door with wide eyes.

"Daz," the little creature said. It was sitting on a picture frame.

"Baz," the one next to it said.

"Gaz," the next said.

"Jacques," the fourth said, and the others sighed.

"Is Jaz," the first creature said confidentially. "But has silly ideas. Too many books."

"You lot!" Thompson shouted. "You've got the library sealed. I couldn't get in!"

"Yah, is sealed. No nosy cats."

The dog – or dandy – had abandoned the pillow and was standing on its hind legs, pawing at the cupboard. Thompson hissed at it, then looked back at the creatures. "Have you bloody bollies been stealing dragons?"

"Bollies is not thieves!" one of them said, shaking a small fist at the cat. "We is collectors!"

"Stealing dragons?" Alice asked, sounding mildly interested. "How on earth would one do that?"

"Dragons?" Ervin asked. He couldn't seem to decide if the bollies or the cat were more interesting.

"Dragons say they gets rid of dandy," Daz said. Or possibly Baz. They were all identical and DI Adams couldn't remember what order they'd named themselves in.

"Dragons?" she demanded. "More than one?"

"Yah, green one and blue one. We just has to find dandy. And now we does."

"There we go," Alice said, smiling. "Can't keep a good dragon down."

Ervin pointed at the creatures on the picture frame. "Am I hallucinating?"

"Thompson? What do we do about this?" DI Adams demanded.

"I'll fix it! Just get the bloody dandy away from me!"

DI Adams clapped her hands. "Er, here, pup?"

"Is no pup," Gaz said. "Is scary."

DI Adams supposed that if you were as small as the little creatures were, the dog would be terrifying. It was ignoring her, still on its hind legs and sniffing the wardrobe with its grey dreadlocks flopping everywhere. She sighed, steeled herself against the smell, and walked over to it. "Hey," she said, grabbing it by the scruff of the neck and tugging gently. "Enough."

It looked at her, its head almost level with hers, and she thought she saw a glint of redness among the hair, like LED lights. Then it dropped to all fours and looked up at her, tail wagging gently.

"There we go," she said to Thompson. "Happy?"

"Not hugely. Dandies are not good news."

"All I'm hearing is I'm a cat, and I don't like dogs."

"Is not dog," Daz insisted. "Is dandy. Brr!"

"Brr!" the other bollies agreed, kicking their legs gently.

"Where's the dog?" Ervin asked, and DI Adams made an impatient gesture at Thompson.

"Do something, would you?"

"I'm trying to recover my shattered dignity."

"We tells dragons we find the dandy?" Gaz asked.

"Maybe no need," Daz said, then looked at DI Adams. "Is your dandy?"

"Well, not really—"

"It no stay here. You takes it?"

DI Adams sighed. "Sure. Why not." She could drop it at the RSPCA. Even if she wanted a dog, her apartment block didn't allow them.

"Wow. You is powerful witch," Gaz said admiringly.

"What?" she yelled at them, but they were gone again.

"And now you have a dandy," Thompson said. "Well done, you."

"Can anyone tell me what the dandy looks like?" Alice said.

"A great, filthy dog," Thompson said.

"You can't see him?" DI Adams asked. "Even now?"

"They only reveal themselves to humans they choose," Thompson said. "And it's a him now. Fantastic. Just fantastic." He jumped from the wardrobe to the bed. The dandy growled, and DI Adams pulled him against her leg.

"Hush, you." The dandy subsided, then took her hand in his teeth. "Hey!"

"You horrible monster!" Thompson exclaimed, as the dandy tugged the inspector to the dresser and pulled her into a crouch. "I found that!" The dandy glanced at him, then back at DI Adams.

"What is it?" Alice asked as the inspector looked down the side of the dresser at a little bag that had fallen between it and the wall.

"I don't know." She fished it out, wrinkling her nose as the dandy panted all over her, and showed Alice a soft, zippered case of the kind airlines give out on long flights. She opened it, and shook a little collection of jewellery out onto the dresser. It was old, but not in a tatty way. Old in a family heirloom way. She picked up a locket and opened it. A man and a woman she didn't recognise stared back at her in the light of Alice's torch.

"Holy hell," Ervin said from over the DI's shoulder. "Those two are in portraits in the lounge."

DI Adams looked at him, then back at the locket. "Two lovely ladies," she said. "Antique evaluations, removal, and sales." She snapped it shut.

There was a moment of quiet, then Ervin said, "Can someone tell me what I just saw?"

"Thompson?" DI Adams said.

"Nothing, kid," the cat said. "You saw nothing, got it? There was a dog and a cat having a fight in the room."

"Right," Erwin said. "Only—"

"Meow. Meow meow meow."

"Oh, very convincing," DI Adams said.

"What is?" Ervin asked.

Alice and DI Adams looked at each other, and the cat inspected a paw, purring. The only other sound was the dandy's panting, and for a moment the inspector allowed herself to think she might be able to just go arrest the two lovely ladies and be done with it.

Then a door slammed open downstairs, and someone screamed, *"Fire!"*

She closed her eyes, shook her head, then shoved Ervin out of the way and ran.

20

ALICE

"Fire! *Fire!*"

Alice hurried after DI Adams as the inspector ran for the stairs, the journalist right behind her. He seemed to have forgotten all about the cat and the invisible dog, but Alice found herself hoping she wasn't going to trip over either of them on the stairs.

"*Fire!*"

Alice leaned over the banister and stared down at the tiled floor of the foyer, now clean of sandwiches, and found Boyd turning in a circle in the centre of it, arms wide. He spotted DI Adams coming down the stairs and waved wildly.

"Fire!"

"Where? Where's the fire?" Maddie ran out of the office, her torch bobbing about wildly, even though the grey light was enough to see Boyd by. More people were arriving, more torch beams pinning the man in place.

"Fire!" he shrieked, rather over-dramatically to Alice's mind. She started down the stairs.

"Where?" DI Adams demanded. "Where was it, Boyd?"

He waved again, took a breath, and said, *"Flames in the night, the way my thoughts of you break wind—* wait, no—"

"Boyd," Alice snapped, before the inspector started throwing things or arresting people. "Is there a fire or not?"

"Boyd!" Maddie shouted at him. *"Speak,* dammit!"

He lifted his arms dramatically, water running off his sleeves, and there was the sound of furniture being dragged across the floor in the dining room. "What's going on?" Rainbow shouted from beyond the doors. "Did someone say fire?"

"What have you done, you idiot?" Reid snarled, striding across the foyer to confront his brother. "Is this one of your stupid performance pieces, like when you knocked down the folly?"

"That was *art*, you philistine!"

Miriam grabbed Boyd before DI Adams could, which Alice thought was probably rather fortunate, and shook him briskly. "Focus!"

"Fire! It's fire!"

More furniture screeched and tumbled in the dining room. *"Where?"* Rainbow bellowed.

"Where is the *fire?"* DI Adams asked, leaning over Miriam's shoulder. "Straight answer, please, Boyd."

He took a deep, shaky breath as the dining room doors flew open, revealing Rainbow bundled in blankets with flames flickering happily in the grate behind her. The other protesters crowded around her, peering over her shoulders. "What's going on?" she demanded.

"Outside," Boyd managed. "The fire's outside."

"Right," the inspector said. "Everyone stay put, please." She marched to the door, and Alice followed her without a second thought. She had never considered that "everyone" applied to her very much.

Apparently no one else did either, because there was a general rush for the door. Miriam was right behind Alice, and they paused in the doorway to stare into the night.

"We're not coming out!" Rainbow shouted. "You're just trying to get us to abandon our stations!"

"Ha!" Maddie yelled back. "You probably *set* it, you horrible cow!"

"I'd never do that! Imagine the damage to the habitat!"

"How about the damage to *my* habitat! Wait— *what are you burning in there?*"

Alice looked at Miriam as Rainbow shouted, "You tried to freeze us out! We're burning your mass-produced, slave-labour-supporting dining furniture!"

"I hate you!" Maddie shrieked, sounding close to tears. "My home is *burning!*"

"Serves you right! Tool of the elite! Perpetrator of class war—"

"*Mum!*" Adele screamed as Rainbow stopped shouting with a yelp.

"Maddie! Judith! Stop that right this instant!" Miriam bellowed, turning to push her way back into the foyer. "What is *wrong* with you?" Everyone scuffled out of her way, trying to keep an eye on both the fight in the hall and on what was happening outside, and Alice sighed, then followed her. DI Adams would have the situation under control, and Miriam got far too emotional in these circumstances. The fact that they were her sisters was no excuse for being so soft with them both. She bumped into Barry, who was wearing fluffy pink socks and cycling shorts, and he plucked at her arm.

"Is the kitty here?" he asked hopefully.

"I imagine," Alice said, slipping around him to see Maddie and Rainbow wrestling in the doorway to the dining room. Maddie had her older sister in a headlock, and Rainbow was flailing and bucking like a fish desperate to make it back to the water. Ronnie was cheering, bellowing things like *stick it to the man*, which Alice thought was a bit ill-suited to the situation, and Harriet was hovering about making rather ineffectual comments to the effect that everyone just needed to calm down. Miriam jogged across the foyer, shouting as she went, "Stop it! Both of you just *stop it!* What are you, kids again?"

They ignored her entirely, and the two youngest protesters took the opportunity to sneak out of the dining room.

"*Mum!*" Adele wailed, bouncing from foot to foot anxiously.

"What are you doing?" Boyd shouted. "We should all be outside in case the inspector needs us! Join me as we defend—" Boyd gasped to a halt as his sister punched him, not particularly gently.

"The fun never stops," Ervin observed, looking on with interest.

Alice opened her mouth to tell them all to calm down right now and stop disgracing themselves, but before she could Miriam snatched a vase of daffodils off a side table and upended it over the two women rolling on the floor. Alice shut her mouth. Attacking goblins with cricket bats really had been very good for Miriam.

Maddie and Rainbow gave remarkably similar squalls of distress, and looked up at their sister in astonishment. "I'm so sick of both of you!" she shouted. "Just act like adults for five minutes, can't you?"

"You—" Rainbow began, and Miriam shook the vase rather threateningly.

"No! Maddie is *not* the enemy! And neither am I!"

"Ha," Maddie said, then flinched as Miriam glared at her.

"And you stop being so lady-of-the-manor, like we didn't all grow up in a bloody semi in Leeds."

They gaped up at her, and she slammed the vase down on the table and stalked toward Alice. "What's on fire, then?"

"You," Ervin said. "That was awesome."

"Shut up," Alice and Miriam said together, and headed for the main door with the journalist trailing after them.

"The dragons are okay," Alice whispered as they went out onto the stairs. Miriam pressed a hand to her chest, and in the low light Alice could see tears standing in her eyes.

"Really? Where are they?"

"I'm not sure. But they'll be here."

Miriam was still smiling as they walked out the door and saw the fire.

❧

THE FIRST OF the three outbuildings was burning, the one closest to the house. It hadn't looked like much more than a shell to Alice, but apparently there was still plenty to burn inside, because the fire was growling and chortling hungrily. She could imagine it devouring the old beams and scraps of frames, the desiccated floorboards and the plants that grew through the walls, the forgotten tins of paint and old fuel drums that boomed like firecrackers. The wind snarled through the flames, flinging handfuls of sparks across the storm-dark sky, spiralling the smoke wildly in every direction. It didn't look like it would spread to the house, and it was beautiful and awful all at once. She walked down the steps with Miriam to join the inspector, who gave them an irritated look.

"Didn't I tell everyone to stay put?"

"Yes," Alice said, raising a hand against the wind and rain.

"Well. I'm glad that worked so well." DI Adams turned back to the small crowd drifting out from the house, drawn unthinkingly by the sight of the flames. "Everyone back inside," she called. "Nothing we can do. Rain'll get it anyway."

Then several things happened at once.

A rafter or a supporting beam collapsed in the outbuilding, and a shard of wood spun up and out, cartwheeling through the air and eliciting an *oooh* from the onlookers. Then, neatly and without ceremony, it speared through a window of the old stables with a clamour of shattering glass.

On the steps, Reid shouted, "My pheasants!" and bolted toward the stables.

"Oh, no," Miriam said.

Rainbow, standing dripping with daffodil water by the door, bellowed, "He's got pheasants! I knew they were doing secret shoots! Get him!" She ran after Reid, Ronnie whooping and giving chase behind her.

"You leave my son alone!" Maddie screamed, shoved Harriet out of the way, and plunged after Rainbow.

In the parking circle, the Nissan Micra roared into life and gunned toward the little crowd at the foot of the stairs, hiccoughing and almost stalling a couple of times, spitting gravel from under the wheels.

"Oh, for God's sake," DI Adams said. "Really?"

Adele screamed, "*That's my little brother! You get away from him!*" and pelted after Ronnie.

Pat and Rob broke through the main doors and sprinted for the car, knocking Priya into Rosemary, who fell onto Teresa and Rose and started a domino wave of W.I. ladies staggering down the steps, all struggling for balance.

DI Adams abandoned her everything-is-under-control voice for the second time that night and roared, "*Everyone stop right where you are!*"

There was a moment (although it was admittedly very brief) when Alice thought it might actually work. Reid stumbled and almost fell. Ronnie slid to a stop. The car stalled. But Rainbow kept running. She threw herself at Reid, tackling him with both arms around his waist, and they went tumbling across the gravel.

"Murderer!" she shrieked.

"*Stop!*" DI Adams sprinted toward them just as Maddie threw herself after her sister, and hit the inspector instead. DI Adams gave a startled *oof* as she crashed to the ground, sliding in the gravel. Not far behind her mother, Adele tackled Ronnie, and the W.I. turned their attention to the escaping tourists.

"*Hold it right there!*" Gert bellowed at Pat and Rob, and Pat gave an apologetic little wave as she jerked the car door open. The engine roared back into life, gears grinding as an inexpert driver tried to find reverse, and Alice started toward them as DI Adams rolled to her feet. She hauled Maddie up with her and shoved her at Alice.

"Keep hold of her," she snapped, and grabbed Adele by the back of her jacket, dragging her off Ronnie.

"*Reid!*" Maddie yelled, struggling against Alice, who pushed her toward Miriam.

"Grab her," she ordered, aware that her hip was twinging in the cold and that she really didn't want to fall in the gravel out here.

"I've got her!" Miriam threw her arms around her sister, but Maddie elbowed her in the belly and stomped on her foot, then tore herself free and flung herself at Rainbow. Miriam squeaked, sounding more surprised than pained, and grabbed Rainbow's leg as being the handiest thing. Alice sighed and looked at the sky. Honestly, did no one learn even the basics these days?

"Traitors!" Rainbow squawked, trying to shake both sisters off.

"Am not," Miriam panted, as she and Maddie dragged Rainbow off Reid. He scrambled to his feet and raced toward the stables.

DI Adams was holding a fuming Ronnie and a still-shouting Adele by their collars, looking like she was about to bang their heads together. Alice had a sneaking suspicion that she was fighting the urge to do just that. The inspector had blood on her knuckles and a graze on her cheek, but she looked more disgruntled than hurt.

"Why does this happen?" she asked no one in particular. "Why does no one listen?"

"Poor training," Alice said, trying to see what was happening over by the steps. Alice, Gert and Priya were running after the Micra as it bunny-hopped backward toward the fountain, and there was an awful lot of shouting going on as Rob and Pat tried to get in the car while it was still moving. "Should you stop him?" she added, nodding at Reid as he ran toward the fire.

"I don't think that one'll get himself hurt over some pheasants," DI Adams said, looking at Ronnie and Adele as if not sure what to do with them.

"Very true," Alice said.

"Can we get up now?" Miriam asked, and Rainbow answered by thrashing around wildly. Miriam squeaked and renewed her grip.

"Why does Reid have pheasants?" Maddie asked, and Alice thought that was a very good question, but one with a very obvious answer. She looked at DI Adams, but the inspector wasn't paying attention. Alice followed her gaze up to the low clouds and spotted two shapes, barely visible between the rain and the churn of the sky.

"Oh," she said, and smiled as they took on familiar dimensions and plunged toward the burning stables.

A bellow drew their attention back to the not-Americans, still trying to escape the rather determined clutches of the W.I. Dell-Marie, or whatever the daughter was actually called, was hunched over the wheel, and her brother was trying to help pull their mum into the back seat. Priya was berating them as being unfit parents, and Gert was threatening actual bodily harm unless they stopped *right this instant*. Everyone was crowding around the car, putting themselves between it and the drive, and Alice didn't like the look of the situation at all.

"Leave it!" she shouted as the car jumped forward and Gert took up a wrestler's stance, looking very much like she was going to throw herself on the bonnet. "They can't get far!"

"I'm not letting them get away!" Gert bellowed.

"Murderers!" Jasmine shouted, and kicked one of the car's tyres.

"Oh dear," Alice said, glancing at DI Adams. She'd rather forgotten that not everyone was quite up to speed.

"Everyone *away from the car!*" the DI bellowed.

Priya glanced at them, looked at Harriet still hovering on the steps, then pointed at the car and yelled, "They're the shooters! It was for them! A tourist attraction!"

"*What?*" Rainbow roared, and thrashed about so enthusiastically that Miriam and Maddie had to let go.

"*Treachery!*" Ronnie ripped his jacket off, pelting across the drive in his T-shirt while DI Adams scowled after him, still holding the coat. Rainbow was ahead of him, and Miriam and Maddie looked at the stables as Reid gave a howl that was half-fury, half-surprise.

"Oh dear," Miriam said, and giggled. Alice followed her gaze as DI Adams let go of Adele.

There was no sign that the fire had caught in the stables, but Reid was sprinting away from them again, being chased by a furiously *keow-eow-eow*-ing peacock, while pheasants poured out of the wooden doors, scattering in every direction. Behind them, the dragons kept to the shadows as they slipped away, the light of the fire from the other, still-burning outbuilding gilding their wings and running liquid on the edge of their spines. The inspector was just starting to smile when there was a crash from the drive.

"Aw, no," she said, and ran for the parking lot, shouting, "*Stop! Enough!*"

The car had crashed into the fountain, and Dell-Marie was desperately trying to start it again as the protesters raced toward her, pushing some rather indignant W.I. members out of the way. Tom had apparently decided to redeem himself and exploded out of the foyer doors with a bag over his shoulder, Jemima in hot pursuit. They already had balloons in their hands, and they threw in unison, red and white blossoming across the bonnet of the Micra and invoking shrieks from inside.

"Victory!" Harriet screamed, although Alice hadn't seen her do anything more productive than hide behind the doors so far. Rose swatted her with a small branch, which did very little except make her splutter in surprise. The car roared into life and lurched forward again.

"Hold it right there!" DI Adams shouted, heading for the driver's door. "Out! Now!" The car swerved away from her. "*Oi!*"

"I've got it!" Teresa shouted, and grabbed Jemima's bag as she went past, pulling her to a spluttering halt and almost knocking her off her feet while she shrieked about oppression. Teresa ignored her, grabbed two water balloons, eyed the car as it stuttered away from the fountain, and pelted them at the windscreen in quick succession. DI Adams leaped back as there were two defiant pops, the windscreen vanished in a soup of cranberry and bread sauces, and the ladies of the Women's Institute rushed it.

"Everyone calm down!" the inspector yelled, which didn't have the desired effect. Priya pushed past her and hauled the girl out from behind the wheel, while Pearl pulled the passenger side door open and took the boy by the scruff of the neck in a grip that looked rather uncomfortable. Jasmine was trying to talk Pat out of the back of the car on one side, while on the other Gert was looking distinctly threatening and Teresa was bouncing water balloons in both hands and grinning at a cowering Rob. Rosemary and Carlotta were standing on the steps shouting at each other, and Rose and Harriet were peering at the palm leaf as if they'd discovered a new species.

It was most disorganised. And also rather ineffective, as the not-Americans weren't getting past the tree or down any tracks in their Micra. The W.I. would be better off spending their time looking for the antique hunters. Alice hadn't seen them since the sandwich incident in the foyer. She headed for the commotion, already deciding how to arrange the search, Miriam and Maddie following.

She'd just reached the edge of the crowd when there was a shriek from the parking area. Three hooded figures in dark clothes broke from the cover of the trees and ran for the house with the two young protesters yodelling in pursuit.

Maddie screamed and clutched her sister. "Oh my God! Is it a cult? Not a cult! What do I do with a cult?"

Alice did wonder where people got these ideas at times. Too much television maybe. She glanced at Miriam, who looked alarmed but not panicked, and one of the sinister figures screamed, "Birdwatchers! We're *birdwatchers!*"

"Likely story!" Ronnie roared. "More killers!" He charged toward them while Rainbow hesitated, torn between assaulting the not-Americans' car some more or joining the chase. The bird-watchers turned to run back into the shelter of the trees, and Tom and Jemima started to pelt them with balloons. Maddie let go of Miriam and ran for the protesters, screaming at everyone to just stop, right now, please, which made Rainbow's decision for her. She threw a balloon at her sister, catching Maddie in the side of the face and sending her reeling. The W.I. turned to watch, and the fake Americans seized their chance. Dell-Marie shoved Priya away hard enough to knock her to the ground, and leaped back into the car. The back doors slammed, and the engine roared into life as the boy head-butted Pearl and dived into the front seat.

"Brat!" she shrieked at him, and the car lurched forward. The W.I. scattered, and at the corner of the house another engine screamed. Headlights cut across the gravel, flooding the late afternoon with light, and the old green Land Rover bounded out of the staff parking area and barrelled toward the drive.

"*Run!*" Miriam yelled.

The W.I. broke for the steps. Alice took hold of Miriam before she could dash straight across the path of the oncoming Land

Rover and pulled them behind a sturdy-looking topiary, where they watched both cars race to where the broad sweep of the turning circle became the single-lane drive.

"Oh, I can't look," Miriam wailed, and apparently DI Adams wasn't feeling much different. She had both hands clamped to the top of her head as she watched the Land Rover pass, and Alice thought she was quite likely shouting, but she couldn't hear over the wildly over-revving motors. There was a chance, the smallest chance, that the charging Land Rover might overtake the smaller car, but Dell-Marie gunned the engine, and the vehicles bore down on the drive like a matched set, coming closer and closer together as they did so.

A flash of bright yellow caught Alice's eye, and she whispered, "Oh, no."

Miriam gave a strangled little half-scream. Caught in the oncoming headlights was a man on a mountain bike. He was wearing a police jacket, and as they watched he tried to throw the bike down and run, but the lights had blinded him and he tripped, his trousers caught in the chain. He sprawled to all fours and looked up as the cars, both braking hard, skidded on the water-logged drive and slid toward him and each other. The Land Rover spun sideways, clipped the Micra, then bore down on him, and he raised an arm to protect himself, closing his eyes.

"*No*," Miriam wailed, both hands over her eyes, and Alice waited for the scream, for the crunch of metal, for the awful sickening sound of a vehicle hitting a fragile body, sick to her stomach but utterly unable to look away. There was no shouting coming from the steps anymore, and even the protesters had stopped, all eyes on the spinning cars. The storm held its breath.

The cars kept going.

MORTIMER

"Mortimer," Beaufort bellowed above the wind. "It's Collins! Grab him!"

So Mortimer went.

He dived, his eyes narrowed against the rain and the speed of his own passage, his eight-chambered heart thundering in his ears. He wasn't sure that Beaufort couldn't have done this just as well as he could, or better, especially given the fact the bollies' magical elixir had him turning somersaults in the downpour above the woods, and he'd just about exploded out of the library when they'd opened a gap in the outside wall. But there was no time to argue, no time to even think if he could do this, if he was fast enough or good enough. They'd been sweeping on the edge of the cloud cover, watching the chaos below, and had seen both cars break for the drive. And from that vantage point they'd seen Collins, too, sprawling to the ground as the cars charged toward him like enraged beasts.

He arrowed for the man on the ground with his wings tight to his back, trying to ignore the people on the drive and in the cars, because that didn't matter right now. Only one thing mattered: there was no way those vehicles could stop in time, and no way that DI Collins could escape their path. Secrecy had never felt less important.

Beaufort was tumbling out of the sky behind him, barrelling down on the vehicles as if he were rabbit-hunting, and Mortimer heard the thud and crunch of dragon talons cutting into metal, saw out of the corner of his eye the smaller car slew sideways as the High Lord tried to slow it down, but not enough. It was still going to hit Collins. The Land Rover was moving with a hungry inexorability, and the vehicles came together with a scream that was like something living. Mortimer ignored them, too low to see them anymore, although he could feel them coming up on his tail like monsters at his back.

Collins had an arm raised to protect himself, eyes fixed on the oncoming cars, a look of horror on his face. He looked up suddenly, as if feeling the dragon's approach, and Mortimer saw his expression flicker from fright to hope. He snapped his wings open, stopping his fall hard enough to force a grunt from his chest, and grabbed the man's upraised arm, wrapping his claws around it as tightly as he dared. DI Collins clutched Mortimer's legs with both hands and the dragon brought his wings down in one savage beat, spine arching and tail snapping, feeling one of the cars nudge the tip of it as he launched himself up. Collins whooped, kicking his legs high like a child on a swing, and they swept over the Land Rover low enough for the man's boots to clatter on the roof, then they were clear.

"Let go," Mortimer said, loudly as he dared, hearing the shake in his own voice. He flashed past Beaufort as the High Lord scrambled to his feet and galloped for the cover of the trees, leaving behind deep grooves in the drive where he'd dug his hind legs in and forced the vehicles to slow. Collins didn't answer, but

Mortimer felt his grip slip away. He let go as well, and heard a thud as the man landed on the gravel below. Mortimer banked hard and low for the woods, glimpsing Collins with both hands pressed to his belly as if to make sure everything was still where it should be, then clipped a tree with a wingtip and crashed more noisily than he would have liked into some holly.

৯৯

MORTIMER STAYED in the prickly grip of the bush, panting with fright and adrenaline and promising himself that this would be his last spa weekend ever. If he had any scales left at all by the end of it he'd count himself lucky. He almost screamed when a large face appeared next to his, the High Lord grinning happily.

"Well done, lad!"

"Is he hurt?"

Beaufort peered out at the drive. "Not a scratch. Excellent flying, Mortimer."

Mortimer extricated himself from the holly, still too horrified to feel particularly pleased with himself. It had all been *much* too close. They had been so busy rescuing pheasants that they'd almost missed DI Collins' arrival, and as much as the big inspector made Mortimer feel somewhat grey and nervous, the thought that he might have been crushed by the two vehicles made his vision go a little funny.

He joined Beaufort, watching the house from the shelter of the tree line. The W.I. were clustered on the steps to the house, Alice and Miriam stepping out from behind some of Boyd's more tasteful topiary, and DI Collins still stood in the drive, rubbing the back of his head as DI Adams jogged toward him. He looked more pale than Mortimer remembered him being, which gave him a little pang of sympathy.

"Oh, I say," Beaufort said. "They don't know when the game's up, do they?"

"I guess not," Mortimer said with a sigh. There had been a single, lovely moment of calm, as if everyone was making sure that nothing too terrible had happened, but it hadn't lasted long. The Land Rover doors had popped open and Edie and Lottie scrambled out, sprinting for the woods. They dived into the bushes not far from the dragons, and Beaufort watched them go with interest. Back on the drive, the family of not-Americans piled out of the Micra and headed for the woods on the opposite side, and DI Collins shouted, "Oi! Stop right there!"

"Not much chance of that," Beaufort said, sounding far too cheerful for Mortimer's liking.

Everyone kept running, and DI Adams said, "Yeah, that never works around here."

"They won't get far," Maddie called from the steps, just audible over the wind. "Not if they don't know the trails."

DI Collins cleared his throat and put his hands on his hips, looking somewhat more like himself. "So," he said. "Who wants to start?"

"Pig!" Rainbow shouted at him.

He raised a hand in acknowledgement. "Hi, Mum."

"Wonderful," Beaufort said. He looked every bit as intrigued as he did when he was watching Miriam's television, and Mortimer wondered if they could go home. He was starting to shake, and he didn't think it was the cold. He kept hearing the crunch and shriek of metal on metal, and feeling the fragility of DI Collins' arms in his claws.

"Down with the pigs!" Ronnie yelled, and threw a balloon. It hit a startled DI Collins on the chest and exploded, sending cranberry sauce dripping down his jacket.

"Aw, c'mon," he said, and Jemima threw another, which he

ducked, but not the one Tom threw at the same time. It hit the side of his face, adding bread sauce to the mix.

"Stop that," DI Adams said, taking a step away from Collins and not sounding very convincing.

He gave her a sour look, and Beaufort chuckled. "Come on, lad," he said.

"Come on what?"

"Let's round these silly humans up. You take the family, I'll get the ladies."

"Beaufort, no! We can't let them see us!"

"Of course not. But they'll be out here till all hours, getting cold and wet, and our poor inspectors have had more than enough of that. We'll just shake some branches and growl a bit. No one will see us."

Mortimer groaned. "What, we're going to be invisible monsters?"

"Quite right, lad. Just pretend you're a bear."

"A *bear*? In the *Yorkshire Dales*?" But Beaufort was already gone. Mortimer took a hitching, uneven breath, and plodded sadly through the edge of the trees, wishing once again that he was at home. But there was no help for it.

He wished that the bollies' elixir had been maybe slightly less *energising*.

IT WASN'T hard to find the family thrashing about in the undergrowth. The parents were screaming at each other loud enough to drown out Mortimer's rather half-hearted growls, and the daughter was shouting at her brother for treading on her shoes. Mortimer wasn't sure why, as there was enough mud out here that he rather doubted it had made any difference whatsoever to their cleanliness. He sighed, and stomped as loudly as he could on some branches.

"What was that?" the woman asked sharply.

"What? What are you on about now, Pat?"

"I *heard* something. Like breaking branches."

"We're in the woods. What the hell do you expect?"

"*Grr*," Mortimer said, and sighed. What did a bear sound like? And why on earth was he trying to sound like a bear? It was entirely unbelievable, and he should be trying to sound like an enraged badger or something instead. Not that he was sure what they sounded like, either. Most badgers he'd met were taciturn but calm.

"*There!*"

"There's nothing there, Pat." The man sounded angry and dismissive, and Mortimer snapped a few more sticks hopefully.

A scream went up from the other side of the drive.

"What's that? Are you telling me *that's* nothing?"

"*Mum!*" It was the daughter, and she was making so much noise crashing toward her parents that Mortimer gave up on his twigs. "Mum, there's something out here!"

"I know! I know there is!"

"Now, nobody panic—"

The man was cut off by a growl that Mortimer felt in his bones, and he almost screamed himself. The family let loose with a chorus of terrified wails, followed by an enormous amount of thrashing and tripping and sobbing as they fought their way back to the drive. He sat where he was, looking around a little nervously, and a moment later a large, dreadlocked dog slipped between the tree trunks after the humans, soft feet soundless on the wet ground. It glanced at him as it went past, or at least turned its head his way, eyes invisible behind the mass of hair. Mortimer couldn't see the creature's eyes, but he had the distinct feeling that the creature saw him, and it wasn't impressed with what it saw. He wondered what the bollies would do if he couldn't hold up his end of the bargain. There was no doubt in his mind that he had just encountered the dandy, and while he still wasn't quite sure what that *was*, there was something very alarming about it. He wondered if it might be a problem best dealt with by a newly invigorated High Lord.

❧

AS SOON AS the dandy was gone, Mortimer ran for some clear ground and took flight, winging his way back to the house. He settled himself on the roof above the door to one side of Godfrey, who was still in his daytime stone form. Beaufort crouched on the other side of the gargoyle, seemingly having trouble staying a nice unobtrusive grey, or staying still for that matter.

"Did you have any problems, lad?" the High Lord asked.

"I don't think I make a very good bear," Mortimer said. Unlike Beaufort, he was finding it very easy to be grey.

"Well, it was very effective," Beaufort said, and nodded at the drive.

"Save us!" Lottie shrieked, running toward the house and waving wildly. "It's a monster!"

"An awful beast!" Edie exclaimed, and Mortimer saw the two inspectors exchange glances. There was crashing in the woods to the other side of the drive, then the young girl and her brother appeared, parents right behind them. The woman was whimpering and cradling her hands as if she'd run into some nettles, and the man was plastered head to toe with mud.

"It's a werewolf!" the girl screamed.

"A troll!" her brother said.

"What?" DI Adams asked.

"What sort of wildlife are you keeping in these woods?" the man gasped. "Should be locked up! All those teeth!"

DI Adams scratched her cheek and said, "I think you best all come with us."

As the two inspectors herded the would-be escapees toward the house, all but running in their anxiety to get away from the monstrous woods, a cranberry-encrusted birdwatcher standing by the steps asked, "Do you think there's more than one panther?"

"*Shh!*" one of the other birdwatchers said, then added, "We found it, though, if anyone asks."

"Found what?" Alice asked, her voice floating clearly up to the dragons.

"The Yorkshire panther. Got it on camera and everything."

"Just a shame it was so dark," another said. "It's kind of fuzzy."

"Yeah. Weird that it took the biscuits, too."

Beaufort gave an amused snort and grinned at Mortimer. "You see, lad? All is in hand."

Mortimer wished Beaufort would stop moving and talking, considering all the people below them that were quite prepared to see monsters now.

"Everyone inside," DI Adams said. She had hold of Edie's arm, less in a helpful gesture and more in a you're-not-going-anywhere gesture.

"You're alright! You survived the storm! And you caught every-one! You are *spectacular!*" Boyd rushed out of the foyer, where he'd apparently decided to remain safely out of the reach of car chases and cranberry missiles, and for one dangerous moment looked like he might try to hug the inspector.

"I have not given up the idea of locking someone in the cellar," she told him, holding a hand up.

"Admirer, Adams?" DI Collins said, grinning hugely.

"Plenty of room in there," she muttered, and Nita appeared at the top of the stairs, wiping her hands on a tea towel.

She stared at the bedraggled guests and staff, then threw her tea towel onto her shoulder and shouted, "What the hell is going on? You said barbecue ready at three, and it's bloody well half-past! The lamb's going to be overcooked!"

"Lamb?" Beaufort said hopefully, and Alice looked up. Beaufort gave her an enormous grin and she smiled back. It lit her entire face, and for a moment Mortimer forgot just how traumatic the whole weekend had been.

Then Godfrey said, "Evenin'," and Mortimer swallowed a yelp of fright, almost losing his grip on the roof.

"Evening," Beaufort said. "You're up early."

"With that storm it's just about dark already." Godfrey peered down at the bedraggled people slowly filtering into the house below, and across the drive to the crashed cars, then looked at the outbuilding, where the fire was running out of things to burn. The roof was gone, fallen in or burned out or both, and the tornadoes of smoke were becoming wisps dampened down by the persistent rain. The peacock stalked proudly across the lawn, every now and then preening and shaking his tail at a confused pheasant. The wind was too strong, and every time he opened his glorious tail feathers he pitched forward into his beak or was blown over backward. It didn't seem to dampen his enthusiasm. Godfrey scratched an ear. "What did you do?"

"Caught a murderer and released the captive birds," Beaufort said. "Possibly murderers."

"Oh." Godfrey thought about it. "And how did the yoghurt go?"

Mortimer looked reflexively at his tail, hanging off the edge of the roof and dripping rain everywhere. He'd lost at least ten scales at last count, and that wasn't including the ones that had been knocked off while he was pretending to be a bear.

"We didn't do as much as we'd have liked, but I think the whole weekend has been very refreshing, wouldn't you say, Mortimer?" Beaufort asked brightly.

"That's one way to put it," Mortimer said, and tucked his tail under his paws so no one could see how patchy it was getting.

Godfrey yawned. "Right, then. I'm going to grab a couple of those pheasants. Antigone might even be tempted by one of them." He shook out his wings, clipping Mortimer around the ear with one of the hard edges, then took flight, a scrap of grey against the early night.

"Ow," Mortimer observed.

They watched him go, then Beaufort looked at the younger dragon. "Wonderful work, Mortimer. With everything."

"Someone must've seen when I grabbed the inspector," Mortimer said. "Or at least they'll wonder how he escaped."

Beaufort lifted his snout to the rain. "Humans have an amazing capacity for stories," he said. "It's how they bring magic into the world, and how they take it out, too. They'll already be telling each other the inspector jumped onto the bonnet of the Land Rover and ran over the car like a superhero. That's what happens in the stories on the television, so that's what makes sense here. More than dragons, anyway."

"I suppose so," Mortimer said, and tried to stop worrying his tail. "Um, I think I saw the dandy."

"Did you now?" Beaufort nodded thoughtfully. "Interesting creatures."

"I promised the bollies we'd get rid of it."

"I don't think we need to," Beaufort said. "I think it's going to leave of its own accord when we do."

"It's following us?" Mortimer wished he didn't sound quite so squeaky, but that *look* it had given him ...

"Not us, lad. Dandies are for humans, not dragons."

Mortimer thought for a moment. "DI Adams? The dog she kept seeing?"

"DI Adams."

"But why? Why her?"

"You'd have to ask the dandy."

They were quiet for a while, Mortimer watching steam rising from the High Lord's wings. He considered suggesting they go back inside so no one got too cold, but he didn't think Beaufort was going to be hibernating any time soon. Gold danced across his scales like electricity, and had been since he'd woken up. He was as restless as a hatchling.

"Interesting place for a chat," a rough voice said. "Can't have it on a nice dry hearth, like civilised Folk?"

"Thompson!" Beaufort shouted with delight.

"Oh, you're feeling yourself then," the cat said. "Nice for some, these mid-crisis naps. Leave the rest of us doing the work." But the purr in the tom's voice and the perk of his ears despite the rain gave away his relief. Mortimer felt a grudging kinship with the cat. He hadn't been the only one worried.

"Up and fighting fit," Beaufort declared.

"Well, stay that way," Thompson said, and sat with them for a moment, staring out at the rain. Eventually he shook drops off his whiskers and said, "I'll leave you silly sods to it. I'm off to see if there are any kippers to be had."

They watched him pad off along the roof line as the last piece of rafter in the outbuilding collapsed to soggy ash, and Beaufort said, "Well done with the gnomes, too, lad."

"I got a bit grumpy," Mortimer said. "I think I might have burned a few things. And scared them. It wasn't right."

"They shouldn't have been in there. Woodland gnomes don't live in wine cellars."

"Dragons don't stay in hotels," Mortimer countered, and Beaufort made a surprised noise.

They watched the rain for a little longer, then Beaufort said, "I rather fancy going to see if we can get some of that lamb."

"And maybe some more fat rascals?"

"You never know, lad," Beaufort said. "But you've certainly earned them."

They got up and followed the cat's path along the roof line in single file, their wings folded against the wind and their scales steaming softly as the dark drew down and the storm rumbled from one side of the sky to the other, over dragons and dandies alike.

22

MIRIAM

It was almost two weeks since the events at the manor house, and the weather had taken a change, slipping from chill winds that still tasted of winter to a promise of summer. It was certainly warm enough for sitting out in Miriam's gently disorganised garden, with the wobbly wooden table laden with plates and cups and a rapidly cooling teapot, despite the cosy she'd put on it. She watched Mortimer put his snout around the corner of the garden table and meet DI Collins' gaze. The big inspector gave the dragon an encouraging smile, and Mortimer grinned back, grabbed a piece of lemon drizzle cake, and retreated behind Miriam's chair again. He still seemed to be feeling a little sensitive about his tail.

"So this is the reporter's story, then," Collins said to DI Adams, tapping the stack of printed paper that was sitting on the table. "I can't believe he sent it to you first. He must like you."

DI Adams snorted. "I think it was the threat of being locked in the cellar that did it."

"Huh," Thompson said. "Sure, don't mention the cat that cleaned all bollies and dragons and talking animals out of his head, and maybe, just *maybe*, made some suggestions about future behaviour at the same time."

"That worries me," Alice said. "You shouldn't meddle in people's minds like that."

"So ungrateful," the cat said, hooking a kipper off a plate onto the table. "That'd be an exposé piece on half the Folk in Yorkshire if not for me, and you wouldn't even have a copy."

"Well, I think he wrote it all up rather well," Miriam said, slicing some more apple cake for the dragons. "It makes for very exciting reading."

It did, even without dragons and bollies. Ervin had written a surprisingly sympathetic piece about the house, and concentrated on the rescue of the protesters, the flight of the suspects, and the mystery of the dead man rather more than the IKEA tableware.

"He made you all sound very heroic," Beaufort said, closing his eyes in the sun. "Which is entirely true, and very well-deserved."

"Don't be silly, Beaufort," Alice said. "No one was heroic but Detective Inspector Adams, you, and Mortimer, all going into that river."

"I think you were heroic," Beaufort said. "I think you're always heroic, all of you. People always think heroism is single big thing. Often the small things are much more heroic, in the end."

Alice patted him on the shoulder. "You are lovely."

The scrapes on DI Adams' face from her tussle on the drive were mostly gone, although she claimed she could still smell cranberry sauce in her sleep. And she still seemed to have an invisible companion. The shadows under her chair were odd, not lying right and deeper than they should have been in the bright morning sun. As Miriam watched, the younger woman passed a scrap of cake to the shadows, and it just *vanished*. Which really didn't seem right.

Alice poured a little more tea and said, "So. The not-Americans, then?"

"Were actually from Hollyfield, near London," DI Adams said. "It was just like they said. They both worked, but couldn't make the extra money for holidays. So they fell into this thing of pretending to own an American travel agency, and got freebies everywhere. Did it all up and down the country, at least once a month for the last five years."

"That's a terrible amount," Miriam said. She didn't know how they could have kept up the subterfuge. What an awful stress!

"It is. I don't think it's going to go to trial, though, because no one seems angry enough to press charges. They might have to make restitution, but to be honest, the story's getting such a lot of coverage already that I hear rumours they might turn the website into a real review site." She shook her head. "Social media to the rescue."

"I don't understand it," Alice said. "It's still stealing. It shouldn't be okay just because it's amusing."

"No," DI Adams agreed. "But that's just how it works sometimes."

Alice pursed her lips and took a sip of tea.

"Well," Miriam said. "The whole thing's worked out rather well for Maddie in the end."

"She's not going to have to sell?" DI Adams asked.

"Hopefully not," Miriam said. "It's actually given her some rather good publicity. It seems the birdwatchers are really crypto-zoologists—"

"Crypto-what?" DI Collins asked, frowning.

"Cryptozoologists," Miriam said, hoping she was saying it right.

"What on earth are they?" Beaufort asked. "Do they study animals that live in mausoleums and so forth?"

"Um, no. They hunt for mythical creatures."

Mortimer put his head around her chair and announced, "See? I knew it. I *knew* they were the ones talking about dragons."

"Well, apparently not," Miriam said. "They were looking for the Yorkshire panther."

Thompson made a rude noise around his kipper, and DI Adams said, "The what?"

"The Yorkshire panther. It's a big black panther that people claim to have seen all over Yorkshire," DI Collins said. "Oddly enough, it's usually spotted at around pub closing time."

"Oh. That sort of panther." She gave the shadows under her chair another scrap of cake, and Miriam stared until Alice said, "And?"

"Oh! Oh, yes. So, the cryptozoologists have a really big following on their blog, and now all these people are calling up Maddie wanting to come and try to spot the panther. Plus they also wrote something about the manor being haunted, because of the bollies taking things. And it seems lots of people want to stay in a haunted house. Some group even wants to do murder mystery weekends, and Maddie's got half a dozen bookings for next month already."

"That's wonderful," Alice said.

"They're going to murder people?" Beaufort said. "That can't be legal."

DI Adams snorted into her tea, and Miriam said, "Not really murder them. It's like acting."

"Oh," Beaufort didn't say anything else, but he looked alarmingly *interested*. Then he added, "We should go steal some more biscuits, Mortimer. Give them something to look at."

"No," Mortimer said.

Thompson shook his head. "Humans. Oh, someone's died in the house. Let's turn it into a tourist attraction! Oh, dragons don't exist, so obviously I saw a panther. And there can't be brownies in the house, they don't exist either. It must be ghosts!"

"They were bollies," Mortimer said. "They hoard rather than clean, which is just sort of unhelpful."

"Well, they were very helpful to me," Beaufort said. "That coffee is wonderful stuff!" He looked hopefully at his mug, and Alice topped it off.

"Tea," she said. "One should keep coffee for when one really needs it."

DI Adams looked like she didn't agree, but Mortimer gave a relieved sigh, and Miriam patted his shoulder gently. It seemed that the bollies' magic elixir had been exceptionally strong coffee, liberated from the lounge coffee machine and stored in jars in the library, quietly fermenting until needed. The High Lord had been so energised that he hadn't started sleeping again until yesterday. And he was, to put it politely, unbearable. He was rushing around the caverns getting involved in absolutely *everything*. He'd tried his paws at making baubles, and played with hatchlings, and gone swimming with Gilbert, and was doing dawn yoga sessions at the lake for anyone who wanted.

Which, after an enthusiastic start, had dwindled to Lord Walter and Mortimer, and Mortimer thought it was actually contributing to his scale loss. The High Lord had also been talking about travelling to other clans and spreading the word that coexistence was possible, and had spent a couple of days trying to persuade Miriam and Alice to come with him as representatives of humans. He had become so enthusiastic, in fact, that Mortimer had made him meet with Thompson. It had taken both of them to talk sense into him, and then only when Thompson had become very graphic about what the Watch did to Folk who forgot to stay secret. Miriam knew all this because Mortimer had told her in great detail, while spending at least a couple of hours a day shedding scales all over her kitchen floor and stress-eating scones.

"You did scare us," Miriam said to the High Lord now. "That whole hibernation thing was terrible."

"I'm sorry," Beaufort said. "I was just a silly old dragon who got a bit too cold."

"Nothing silly about you," she replied. "You were very brave to go out when you knew what could happen."

"You were," DI Adams agreed. "So what happened to the protesters?"

"Maddie gave them some land," Miriam said.

"Really?"

"Yes. She decided she couldn't be doing with Rainbow trying to sabotage her every time she turned around, so gave her a nice bit of land downriver that they can turn into a self-sufficient commune. Apparently they're going to make soap and stuff for the manor, and trade it for supplies."

Mortimer wrinkled his snout. "Isn't that commerce with the elite?"

"I try not to think about it too much."

"And the antique hunters," Beaufort said. "The murderers! Are they in jail?"

"Ye-es," DI Adams said, and Collins snorted.

"What?" Mortimer asked.

"Well, they're being charged with theft. They've been at it for about forty years. They do legitimately trade as antique dealers, and are very successful, but they're also thieves. They stay at these manor houses while they're on buying trips, and go off in the day doing business. Then at night they sneak around and steal all these little, unnoticed things from where they're staying, figurines and ornaments and jewellery and the like."

"Terrible," Beaufort said gravely, and licked cream off his nose.

"It's pretty awful. What they take from these old homes is irreplaceable, but it's always things the owners won't notice for months. By then they have no way of knowing who did it."

"So the sous-chef surprised them, then, and they did away with him?" Beaufort asked, his eyes bright with interest. "But they never counted on the Toot Hansell Women's Institute!"

"I don't think anyone ever counts on that," DI Collins mumbled, and the cat huffed laughter.

"Well," DI Adams said. "Not exactly."

"You caught a family of con artists *and* two elderly thieves," Collins said. "That's a good weekend's work, that is."

"Excellent work, I'd say," Beaufort said, cupping his soup mug of tea in both paws. "How did they know to use the Botox? Did they come prepared? Or was it luck?"

DI Adams rubbed her face and groaned. "It wasn't murder," she muttered, barely loud enough to hear.

"*What?*" Alice, Miriam, Beaufort and Mortimer stared at the inspector, and DI Collins burst out laughing. DI Adams glared at him, and he covered his mouth with one hand.

"Sorry, sorry," he mumbled. "Carry on."

Thompson got up and stretched, prowling toward the petunias.

"You can stay right there," DI Adams told him. "This is all your fault."

"Hey, I just told you what my buddy heard."

"Yeah, well, you need to check your sources next time."

"I'm a cat. The exact details of a toxicology report are entirely within our understanding, but we very rarely care."

"You should care when it's so important!"

"To be fair," DI Collins said, "You did take the word of a talking cat that it was murder."

"He said he had a contact at the lab!"

"I do!"

"A *decent* contact."

"What constitutes a decent contact to a cat, I wonder," DI Collins asked, leaning back in his chair and making it creak warningly. "Good kippers?"

DI Adams put her cup back on the table carefully. "Yes, okay. I should have waited for confirmation. But we were cut off!"

DI Collins tutted. He looked like he was enjoying himself.

"So what did happen to the sous-chef?" Mortimer asked.

"Just like we thought originally," DI Adams said with a sigh. "Too many drinks, too long in the sauna, and a heart defect he didn't know about. There was Botox in his system, and empty syringes in the rubbish, but he was using it on himself. It wasn't suspicious. Lottie really did just find him. The only reason they wanted to get out the next day was because they didn't want to be anywhere around a police investigation just in case someone got suspicious enough to look into them properly. They never killed anyone."

"I feel a little better about that," Miriam said. "I quite liked them."

"They're still criminals," Alice pointed out.

"Yes, but it's degrees, isn't it?" Miriam said.

"*Hmm.*" Alice poured more tea. She was wearing a floral green headband that was very in keeping with the spring day. "So, Colin. What made you decide to come up to the house right then?"

"And the cat saves the day again," Thompson said.

"You mean you were cleaning up your mess?" DI Adams said.

"I was assisting with the investigation."

"By almost getting my nephew killed," Miriam pointed out, patting Collins' arm.

"Ah, it wasn't that close," DI Collins said. "Mortimer was on it. And I got to fly!"

DI Adams stirred her tea in a pointed manner. "*I* flew. You ... hopped."

The inspector looked at Mortimer. "Why does she get to fly and I only hopped?"

"Um," Mortimer said, turning grey. "I wasn't— I mean—"

"Sorry. Joking. You were amazing."

"He is amazing," Beaufort agreed, and Mortimer flushed orange so quickly Miriam could feel the heat baking off him.

"Yeah, yeah. Amazing bloody dragons," the cat said, and put his paw in the cream.

"Stop that," Alice snapped. "We were all eating that, you know. Just ask if you want something. You can, after all."

"Can. Don't want to."

DI Adams flicked his ear, and Thompson glared at her as DI Collins said, "So. How did I get there. Chatty here turns up in the car—"

"Big man here was having a sneaky kebab."

"And that helps how?"

"Details matter."

"Right. I was having a kebab—"

"I thought you were watching your cholesterol," Miriam said, then went pink when the big inspector gave her an exasperated look.

"It was a Saturday, Auntie Miriam. It was a *treat*. Anyhow, Chatty turns up and says, what was it—"

"You don't have to have it word for word," the cat said.

"I thought you said details matter? Chatty says, and I quote, *the geriatric army has gone all vigilante after this murderer. It's pearls and golf clubs at dawn up there, and no one can get out.*"

"Geriatric army?" Alice asked, frowning at Thompson.

"It's a term of affection."

"Are you still liking talking cats?" Beaufort asked.

"I never liked them to start with," Miriam sniffed. "And I've never worn pearls, *or* played golf."

"Figure of speech," the cat said.

DI Collins took two custard creams, passing one to Mortimer with a wink. Mortimer took the biscuit happily. "I tried calling," the inspector said, dunking his biscuit in his tea, "but of course you had no mobile reception and the tree took the phone lines down. So I threw my bike in the back in case the road really was blocked and came up to see what was going on." He took a bite of biscuit, chewed thoughtfully, then added, "I might have left it a bit if I'd known I was going to get marinated."

"They must have been buying sauces in bulk," DI Adams said.

"I doubt there was any buying going on," Miriam muttered. "Rainbow probably liberated it from somewhere."

"Did we hear that?" DI Collins asked DI Adams, and Miriam went pink.

"We hear very little around here," DI Adams said, and passed a custard cream under her chair.

"I can't believe you're still keeping that dog around, Adams," Thompson said, peering into the shadows under the inspector's chair. Miriam thought she heard a small sound against the bird song, a growl on the edge of hearing.

"What dog?" DI Collins asked.

"The invisible devil one," the cat said.

"Hang about," DI Collins said. "An invisible devil dog? This is news to me."

"It's nothing," DI Adams said, dropping one hand to her side, where it rested on something. Thompson spat.

"It's not *nothing*. It's a dandy devil dog. And that is not a good thing to have haunting you."

DI Adams scowled at the cat. "It showed me who the real culprits were."

"Hey, *I* found the evidence first. And okay, look. Dogs suck. Dandy devil dogs suck *magically*."

"That's hardly an explanation," DI Adams said.

"Did you miss the devil bit in there?"

"Now," Beaufort said. "Dogs always have masters or mistresses. Even dandies. And dogs are only as bad as the person who commands them."

"I'm not its mistress," DI Adams said. "It just turned up!"

"Yeah, but you said you'd take it," Thompson said. "That's what you told the bollies."

"I was trying to get them to calm down and go find the dragons!"

"You *claimed* it. Words have power, Adams. You need to remember that, especially if you're hanging out with dandies."

"Well, I'm sure you'll look after it perfectly well," Alice said. "It may even come in handy."

"I can't have a dog in my apartment," DI Adams said. "There are rules."

"Even for invisible dogs?" Collins asked.

DI Adams made an annoyed sound.

"Well," Miriam said, and got up. "I've made mint lemonade. Would anyone like to try some?"

DI Adams shot a nervous glance in the direction of Miriam's herb garden, which seemed a little rude. The inspector still hadn't quite got over the fact that Miriam grew belladonna as well as other, friendlier plants. But she said yes anyway, and Miriam pottered off to the kitchen.

The jug was in the fridge, the glasses already on the table, and as Miriam started back along the garden path with the lemonade cradled in both hands she stopped, framing the tableau in her memory, something precious not to be lost or forgotten.

The garden washed green and half-wild around her, full of the rumble of bees and the frantic springtime rush of small things to live and love and thrive. The sun washed over her head and shoulders, the breeze lifting her hair from her neck, and even from here she could smell the soft smoky scent of the dragons. DI Collins leaned back in his chair with his hands laced comfortably over his belly, while Alice appeared to be both remonstrating with Thompson and scratching him between the ears. Beaufort took another slice of lemon drizzle cake and dipped it in his tea. It broke off, vanishing under the surface, and he shrugged, then drank the whole thing. DI Adams, worried by her invisible dog or not, had her eyes closed and her face lifted to the sun, and for a moment Miriam couldn't breathe. It was all so desperately fragile, and precious, and beautiful.

Then Mortimer rose to his feet and trotted to her through the overgrown grass, and looked up at her with amber eyes. "Do you need help?" he asked, and she smiled, not sure why she felt like crying. She leaned down to rest a hand on his back, the scales smooth and warm beneath her fingers, and thought that, just like people, life was terribly complicated and confusing, and never quite what one expected, or even what one believed it to be. And it could be sharp and painful and raw, but it was also wonderful and beautiful and full of astonishing things, so maybe that was alright. Maybe that was exactly as it should be.

All one could do was remember the sun and the breeze and the cake, and hold on to the formidable magic of friendship, and know that it was there, even when things were darker than anyone should be asked to bear.

"Lemonade?" Miriam asked the dragon, and he grinned at her.

"Please."

And that was magic enough for her.

A BEAUFORT SCALES MYSTERY

THANK YOU

Thank you so much for taking the time to read *A Manor of Life & Death*, lovely person!

As always, I hope so much that you enjoyed reading Beaufort's latest adventure, and I'd appreciate it immensely if you could take the time to pop a quick review up on the website of your choice.

Reviews help to spread the word about sleuthing dragons, and ensure everyone appreciates the joys of cake and a well-made cuppa. Which can only be a good thing, right?

Plus, reviews are rather like cake themselves. Exceptionally tasty and vital to the writing process.

And if you'd like to send me a copy of your review, chat about dragons and baked goods, or anything else, drop me a message at kim@kmwatt.com. I'd love to hear from you!

Until next time,

Read on!

PS - want to know what happens next? Head over the page for the next adventure, and to claim your free, W.I.-approved recipe collection!

BRIBERY. CORRUPTION. MURDER. ALARMING POTATO SALAD.

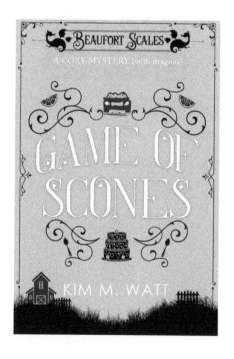

Who *ever* said local politics were boring?

Suspicious deaths on the Skipton city council don't sound as though they should have anything at all to do with the Toot

Hansell Women's Institute or dragons, and DI Adams would rather like to keep it that way.

She should know better, though ...

Murder, mayhem, and old secrets come to light in the Yorkshire Dales - with dragons, of course.

Grab Game of Scones today and join Beaufort and Alice as they get a little *too* involved in the world of Yorkshire politics - and in DI Adams' investigations. *Again.*

Scan above or head to books2read.com/GameofScones to discover the difficulties of Toot Hansell politics today!

INVESTIGATIVE RECIPES INSIDE!

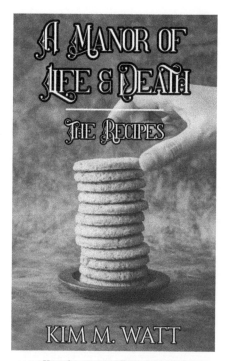

Your free recipe collection awaits!

Arm yourself with some tasty treats ...

Lovely person, I hope you're not as exhausted as DI Adams by the aftermath of a Toot Hansell spa weekend (I mean, it was never going to end well, was it?).

And should you need to provision for your own spa weekend / dragonish investigation, you can now get baking with some tried and tested recipes!

Plus, if this is your first visit to Toot Hansell and my newsletter, I'm also going to send you some story collections - including one about how that whole barbecue thing started …

Your free recipe collection is waiting - grab it now!

Happy baking!

Scan above or head to https://readerlinks.com/l/2369424/mldpbr
to claim your recipes

ABOUT THE AUTHOR

Hello lovely person. I'm Kim, and in addition to the Beaufort Scales stories I write other funny, magical books that offer a little escape from the serious stuff in the world and hopefully leave you a wee bit happier than you were when you started. Because happiness, like friendship, matters.

I write about baking-obsessed reapers setting up baby ghoul petting cafes, and ladies of a certain age joining the Apocalypse on their Vespas. I write about friendship, and loyalty, and lifting each other up, and the importance of tea and cake.

But mostly I write about how wonderful people (of all species) can really be.

If you'd like to find out the latest on new books in *The Beaufort Scales* series, as well as discover other books and series, giveaways, extra reading, and more, jump on over to www.kmwatt.com and check everything out there.

Read on!

amazon.com/Kim-M-Watt/e/B07JMHRBMC
bookbub.com/authors/kim-m-watt
facebook.com/KimMWatt
instagram.com/kimmwatt
twitter.com/kimmwatt

ACKNOWLEDGMENTS

To you, lovely reader. For reading, for commenting, for reviewing, for believing in tea and dragons and friendship. In magic, in other words. You are all entirely wonderful.

To Lynda Dietz at Easy Reader Editing, who has once again proved herself to be the best editing companion possible. I will never dread the editing process when it comes with humour, tact, fantastic suggestions, and such wonderful support. And one day I will actually remember all the things you're teaching me. Maybe.

To my utterly fantastic beta readers, Anna, Alison, Jon, Tina, and Debbie, who dole out support, suggestions, and the best sort of constructive criticism. You are all *amazing,* and I don't know what I'd do without you. Write really bad books, I suspect.

And (always) to the SO, the Little Furry Muse, and all my real-life friends and family who ensure I have actual human contact on a reasonably regular basis and don't exist entirely on tea and cake.

Although I'm sure it wouldn't be *that* bad if I did. And besides, it's research ...

ALSO BY KIM M. WATT

The Beaufort Scales Series (cozy mysteries with dragons)

"The addition of covert dragons to a cozy mystery is perfect...and
the dragons are as quirky and entertaining as the rest of the
slightly eccentric residents of Toot Hansell."

– Goodreads reviewer

The Gobbelino London, PI series

"This series is a wonderful combination of humor and suspense
that won't let you stop until you've finished the book. Fair
warning, don't plan on doing anything else until you're done ..."

- Goodreads reviewer

Short Story Collections

Oddly Enough: Tales of the Unordinary, Volume One

"The stories are quirky, charming, hilarious, and some are all of
the above without a dud amongst the bunch ..."

- Goodreads reviewer

The Tales of Beaufort Scales

A collection of dragonish tales from the world of Toot Hansell, as a welcome gift for joining the newsletter! Just mind the abominable snow porcupine ... (you can head to www.kmwatt.com to find a link to join)

The Cat Did It

Of course the cat did it. Sneaky, snarky, and up to no good - that's the cats in this feline collection which you can grab free via the newsletter (it'll automatically arrive on soft little cat feet in your inbox not long after the *Tales* do). Just remember - if the cat winks, always wink back ...

Lightning Source UK Ltd.
Milton Keynes UK
UKHW010636180722
406010UK00001B/34

9 781916 078017